The Third Nanny

A Secrets of Redemption Novel

Other books by Michele Pariza Wacek

The Secret Diary of Helen Blackstone
(free novella available at MPWNovels.com)

It Began With a Lie (Book 1 in the "Secrets of Redemption" series)
This Happened to Jessica (Book 2 in the series)
The Evil That Was Done (Book 3 in the series)
The Summoning (Book 4 in the series)
The Reckoning (Book 5 in the series)

The Stolen Twin

Mirror Image

The Third Nanny

A Secrets of Redemption Novel

by Michele Pariza Wacek

.

For my family, for always believing in me.

Chapter 1

It all started with the letter.

It was waiting for me when I arrived home after my late-afternoon class, sitting patiently under a pile of other envelopes like a fat spider hiding in the shadows until its prey appears.

Of course, at the time, I had no idea how it would eventually destroy the life I had so carefully built, poisoning every aspect and draining it of its vitality and essence.

I should have smashed that spider when I had a chance.

"You got a weird letter," Bryn, my roommate, said as she stood by the stove stirring a pot of macaroni and cheese. She had tied a hot-pink bandana around her wild, sandy-colored hair, as if to contain the explosion of curls. It didn't seem to work, as tendrils spiraled out every which way.

I glanced at the pile. "They look normal to me."

"Not those. The one underneath. From the post office."

The post office? I shifted the envelopes aside until I found a plastic bag containing scraps of a handwritten letter. A note starting with "We Care." and ending with "Please accept our apologies." was attached to the front.

I tapped the bag. "Wow, what a mess."

"I know, right? It's really chewed up. Guess that's why they sent it to you like that. I didn't even realize they did such a thing."

"Yeah, it happens," I said as I squinted at the envelope with a return address I didn't recognize. "We got a couple of these when I worked in the mailroom that one summer. Sometimes, the letters get caught in the sorting machine. But I don't know why they would even bother sending this to me. It's got to be junk mail."

"That was my first thought, too, but look at the address," Bryn said. "It's from Redemption, Wisconsin. I've never gotten junk mail from that weird town. Have you? Ugh, just thinking about what goes on there gives me the creeps. Besides, it looks like a house address, not a business."

I eyed her. "How do you know the difference between a house and business address?"

Bryn rolled her eyes. "Marigold Lane? Come on, that hardly sounds like a business district."

She had a point, but it still didn't make any sense. "But I don't know anyone in Redemption," I said, shaking the plastic bag to get a better look at the letter inside it.

"Didn't you say you used to spend summers there?"

"A long time ago," I said. "I don't know who would be sending me anything now. Especially through the mail. Wouldn't someone I knew back then be more likely to message me on Insta?"

Bryn scooped up a couple of macaronis, blew on them for a moment, and popped them into her mouth. "Maybe it's a condolence note."

I jerked my hand back like I had been burned. My parents had died in a car crash just ten months before, and while I put on a brave face around Bryn, doing my best to pretend like I was getting my act together and successfully moving on with my life, inside I still felt lost and alone ... untethered from "normal" people and things. How could I focus on the day-to-day living when I was now an orphan—the last living member of my family?

Except that isn't completely true, a little voice deep inside me countered. *There is one more.*

I squashed it. I wasn't going to think about *her* and how *she* abandoned me.

As far as I was concerned, she might as well be dead.

Bryn glanced over, as if finally noticing I hadn't responded. Her expression softened. "Sorry. Didn't mean to blindside you. Do you want me to open it?"

"I'm okay," I said, gritting my teeth as I peeled back the tape and carefully dumped the contents onto the table. A few words and phrases immediately jumped out at me.

"Stalker." "Alone." "What have I done?"

"It's like a puzzle." Bryn had abandoned her meal on the stove to join me at the table. "You're going to have to piece it together to read it."

"Hopefully, there won't be too many missing pieces," I said, poking at the paper. Now that it was on the table, I could start to arrange the scraps. "See, right here, look how it's torn ..." I paused, sucking in my breath with a hiss.

Bryn glanced at me, her baby-blue eyes concerned. "Janey, what just happened?"

I couldn't answer. I shook my head violently and pointed at the signature.

Bryn followed my gaze, but I could tell by the way her eyebrows knit together that she wasn't getting it. "Kelly? Who's Kelly?"

My mouth was so dry, I didn't think I could force the words out. I tried to swallow, but it felt like sand in my throat.

Bryn was starting to look alarmed. "Janey, are you sure you're okay? Why don't you sit down?" She pulled the chair out for me and helped me into it, then hurried back to the kitchen sink to pour me a glass of water. "Here." She thrust the wet, dripping glass into my trembling hands. Water sloshed over the sides and onto my lap, soaking my jeans, but I managed to get some of it into my mouth.

Bryn pulled a second chair up close to me, her eyes never leaving me. She was so close, I could see the dusting of freckles on her button nose and the dimple in her cheek. Bryn was cursed with adorable little girl looks that never aged well. "Breathe," she said, and paused while I tried to catch my breath. She was going to school to be a nurse, which made perfect sense, she was forever taking care of everyone around her. Especially me.

I definitely needed a lot of taking care of.

After I calmed down and my hands stopped shaking so badly, Bryn put a steadying hand on my knee. "Okay, so can you tell me who this Kelly person is and why she upset you so much?"

I swallowed hard. I didn't want to say it, because the moment I did, it would become real. This odd little pile of torn paper would suddenly mean something. Something important.

If only I had kept my emotions in check, this wouldn't be an issue. I could have told her it was nothing … I had no idea who Kelly was. It was probably all a mistake, or a joke. Ugh. Mentally, I kicked myself. I was such an idiot sometimes.

But it was too late. I either needed to tell her the truth or make up something really good. Since my mind was a complete blank, I had no other option but the truth.

"She's my sister," I croaked out.

Bryn's eyes widened. "Your sister?" She ducked her head down to study the signature. "But it just says 'Kelly.' How can you be sure it's her?"

I swallowed. "It's … look at the signature. That's how she signed. With the flourish with the Y, almost like a heart?"

Bryn looked again. "I see it. But … didn't you tell me she was dead? How can this be her?"

I was silent for a moment. In my mind, I was back in that hot summer day in August, the humidity so thick, it was difficult to breathe. The sound of buzzing insects. Kelly lounging next to me in the boat, clad in a tiny blue bikini and dark sunglasses. Her long, bleached-blonde hair gleaming in the sun, lips coated with bright-red lipstick, the smell of suntan lotion mixed with Calvin Klein's Eternity—her 'signature' perfume. In fact, for a moment, I thought I caught a faint whiff of it. Was it coming from the letter?

"I don't actually know what happened to Kelly," I said. "No one does."

Bryn's eyes went wide again, but she stayed quiet, waiting for me to continue.

"She disappeared one afternoon about eight years ago now," I said. "We didn't even realize she was gone until almost a day later. She was almost eighteen, and my parents gave her a lot of leeway. When she still wasn't home the next morning, we started calling her friends, but no one had seen her. When we checked her room, we found that she had taken some things. Money. Clothes. Makeup. Her computer."

"So, she ran away."

"That was the official conclusion."

Bryn raised an eyebrow. "Official?"

I frowned, trying to figure out the best way to describe Kelly. "My sister ... I guess you would say she told a lot of stories."

"She lied?"

"More like exaggerated," I said. "It was always difficult to sort out what exactly was going on with her. In this case, around the time she ran away, she was telling people she had a secret boyfriend who was much older than her. She also claimed to have a stalker."

"A stalker?"

I sighed. "I know, right? The problem was, no one was really sure they ever saw the stalker. One of her friends thought she had seen some shady person following Kelly one night, but she didn't have much description to go on, other than 'a guy who seemed to be wearing black.' Another of her friends described a car following them one night as she drove Kelly home. But could it have been the secret boyfriend?"

"What do you think?"

Kelly standing in front of the mirror applying eye shadow. The sound of a car backfiring outside. Kelly jumping, smearing eye shadow across her face. "Now look what my stalker made me do." Laughing as she wiped a wet towel across her cheekbone, the tremble in her hand so faint, I wondered if I had imagined it.

"I don't know," I said. "With Kelly, I was just never sure what the truth was."

"So, what did the cops think happened to her?"

"That she ran away," I said firmly. "Although, to be fair, they did poke around a bit and ask a few questions. Especially about the stalker and the secret boyfriend. She was almost eighteen, and as the cops kept telling us, it wasn't against the law for an adult to disappear. I don't think they took it as seriously as if she had been younger. But, once we received the postcard, that closed the case."

Bryn's mouth dropped open. "A postcard? Seriously?"

"Yeah. It was postmarked in Chicago. Had a picture of the skyline." I paused, remembering how frantic my parents had been, wanting to drop everything and drive to Chicago to look for her, and how the police officer in charge of Kelly's case had convinced them to stay put and hire a private investigator, instead.

"So?" Bryn nudged me. "Don't leave me hanging. What did it say?"

I shrugged. "Not much. That was the problem. 'I'm fine. I'm happy. Don't worry about me. I'm living the dream. Xoxo. Kelly.'"

"Living the dream?"

"Yeah, another thing Kelly said. She wanted to be famous. Actress, singer, model. Something like that. She had been saying for years the moment she turned eighteen, she was moving to Hollywood."

"But she wasn't in Hollywood. She was in Chicago."

"I know, right? That was what my parents said. There was something wrong. If Kelly was going to run away, either with her secret boyfriend or on her own, she would have gone to California, not Chicago. But the cops didn't see it like that. As they said, she could be working her way up to Hollywood. Maybe she landed a couple of gigs in Chicago and decided to start there. Or maybe she was just passing through and dropped the postcard off on her way to Hollywood. There could be a million explanations that didn't involve her being abducted and forced to write it against her will.

"Anyway, that pretty much put a bow on it for the cops. They closed the case and my parents hired a private investigator. But that didn't pan out, either. I don't think my parents ever stopped looking for her, but it didn't matter. As far as I know, that was the last any of us ever heard from her."

Bryn sat back in her chair. "Wow. I mean … wow. What a story. Why didn't you tell me before? And why did you tell me Kelly was dead?"

I reached out and started worrying a corner of one of the envelopes, which appeared to be a credit card offer, trying to ignore the hurt accusation in her voice. "It's just … well, it's complicated," I said. "For a long time, I was so angry at Kelly. Why didn't she reach out to me? Why didn't she tell me she was going to run away? Why the radio silence? She always told me everything before, so why did she stop? So, I guess in a way, it was easier to think she was dead. Because if she wasn't, and she was ignoring me …" My voice trailed off.

Bryn squeezed my hand. I blinked a couple of times and tried to force a smile. "The other thing is, people treat you differently when they know you are a victim of a crime … or that your family is, in our case. I hated the way everyone would stop talking when they saw me, and how the teachers would hover. No one knew what to say. My friends were uncomfortable and awkward around me until eventually, it was just easier to stop being friends." I shook my head at the memory.

"Later, I found some new friends who either hadn't heard of Kelly or didn't realize I was her sister, and I saw how much easier it was if people never knew my history. If I just created a new version of Janey without this whole sordid past. So, when I went to college, that's exactly what I did. Just rewrote my history. Instead of a sister who just disappeared under strange circumstances, I had a sister who tragically died in a car wreck. Which was still a nightmare, of course, but it didn't take long for me to realize that people rarely asked questions about death. Death scares them, almost like they are afraid if they talk about it too much, someone in their family will die, too. But a missing sister? That's the stuff of true crime. Everyone loves to talk about that."

"But I wouldn't," Bryn started to say, but I held up my hand to interrupt her.

"I'm not saying you would. In fact, I know you wouldn't. But after we spent time together and got to know each other,

I didn't know how to bring it up, because I would have gotten questions like this. I realize now I should have, and I'm sorry."

Bryn's face cracked open. "Oh, Janey. You don't have to be sorry. I get it. I really do." She reached over to give me a hug.

I hugged her back, relieved by her acceptance of my explanation.

Not that it was a lie. What I told her was all true.

It just wasn't the *whole* truth.

Chapter 2

Even though I knew Bryn was dying to know what the letter said, I begged off, saying I needed a little time to process the fact that Kelly was apparently alive and well, and had been all these years. Bryn was disappointed, but said she understood. I left her to her macaroni and cheese and went into the bathroom to clean myself up.

But the truth was, I was furious.

How dare Kelly ignore me for eight long years only to reach out now?

How dare she not reach out after our parents died, when I really needed my sister?

How dare she only reach out when SHE was in trouble! Never mind me or what I need.

It's *always* about Kelly. No one else matters.

And I was tired of it.

I would read the letter if and when I felt like it. I was done jumping at Kelly's bidding.

Except ... my mind kept circling around the words I saw on the torn paper—"stalker," and "What have I done?"

No, I wasn't going to think about it. It wasn't my problem. Kelly ceased to be my problem long ago.

Yet no matter what I told myself, I couldn't stop the images of Kelly lounging in the boat from popping into my head. And every time I saw them in my mind's eye, my blood turned cold.

That day was the last I saw her alive.

Did Kelly get herself into something she couldn't handle and was looking for me to save her? Again? Why did I always have to be the "reasonable" one ... the one who had to swallow all the letdowns and times she disappointed me?

Why couldn't she do the right thing just once in her life?

I dug my fingers into my forehead, the sharp pain a welcome interruption to my swirling thoughts.

A good sister would put all that aside and piece that letter together immediately.

I wanted to be a good sister, but I was too furious.

My blood felt like it was oscillating from ice cold to boiling hot, and all I wanted to do was scream at something. Anything. Instead, I splashed cold water on my face. I was going to have to calm down. Getting overly emotional about the situation wasn't going to help anyone, especially me. Or Kelly. I had to be calm and rational. After all, she'd been gone for eight years. I should be more in control of my emotions after that much time. I also should be adult enough to go back into the kitchen and read what Kelly sent.

But I didn't. I stayed where I was, water dripping down my face and onto the sink, forcing myself to breathe deeply. *I can do this*, I told myself. *I can get myself under control.*

Finally, when I felt I could trust myself not to run out of the bathroom like a crazy person, probably giving Bryn a heart attack in the process, I reached for a towel to dry off. As usual, I avoided looking at myself in the mirror, just as I had been doing for years. But now, it was even more crucial. I could hear Kelly's voice in my head: *"You don't want to be a plain Jane, do you?"*

No, I didn't. But not everyone could be blessed with Kelly's golden looks.

The truth was, I had a complicated relationship with my sister. I loved her, but I was also envious of her. She had everything she wanted. She was the perfect child, the one who could do no wrong, while I was the black sheep, the disappointment. When she disappeared, I could almost hear my parent's despair.

Why couldn't it have been you instead of her?

Despite all of that, I still missed her dreadfully. Not a day had gone by when I hadn't felt the same yawning hole in my chest. It got even worse after our parents were killed. I wanted to talk to her so badly. Night after night, I would pace the tiny apartment, wishing and praying to hear from her, checking my phone incessantly for a Twitter or Instagram message, fruitlessly searching her name.

Of course, I knew it was stupid and irrational. The private detective couldn't find her; why on earth did I think my pathetic Internet searches would produce different results? Still, I couldn't stop myself.

I had to find her. I had to know I wasn't alone in the world.

Eventually, with the help of a compassionate therapist and some good medication, I stopped looking for Kelly. But not without an equally irrational surge of disappointment and anger.

She had to be dead. It was too painful for her not to be dead.

And now, I had to deal with all the emotions—the resentment, the despair, the rage, the guilt … all of it.

She was alive. All this time.

And she hadn't reached out to me.

Before I did anything, I had to come to terms with that.

***

It took two more days before I could sit down with the letter.

Bryn didn't say much, but I could see the concern in her eyes whenever she looked at me.

I had pushed the pieces of the letter into the corner, covering it with the "We Care" plastic bag and then anchoring it all in place with the salt and pepper shakers.

I knew I was being ridiculous. This was my long-lost sister. I should have pored over the contents of that letter without hesitation.

But every time I thought about it, I could feel the emotions rear up inside me. When everything happened, I couldn't deal with the onslaught of feelings. So, I had shoved it all down.

It was Bryn who pulled me out of my paralysis.

"Perfect timing," she said when I got home from my class. "The pizza I ordered should be here in ten minutes. And here." She thrust a glass of cheap red wine in my hand.

"What's this?"

"I'm celebrating." She grinned. "I just found out I got an A on my clinical rotations."

"Oh!" I clinked her glass with mine. "That is definitely worth celebrating." Bryn had been sweating her clinical study work all year, convinced her advisor didn't like her. I found that hard to believe. I couldn't imagine anyone not liking Bryn and kept telling her she had to be wrong.

"Yeah, it turns out you were right all along," Bryn said. "I guess she's always that prickly and critical with everyone, not just me."

"I'm so excited for you. Congrats!"

The doorbell rang. "Oh! Our pizza. I'll get it," Bryn said, wiping a trail of red wine from her chin.

"I should be the one treating," I protested, but Bryn waved me off as she hurried to the door with her wallet.

We talked about nothing and everything while we ate, enjoying our normal, free-flowing conversation. Bryn made sure to keep topping off my glass, even though I laughingly told her I still had a paper to finish.

I was picking at crust when she gave me a solemn look. "Are you ready to talk about why you haven't read Kelly's letter yet?"

It felt like my stomach dropped through the floor of our apartment. I tried to deflect. "What do you mean?"

She gave me a long, knowing look. "You know what I mean."

I didn't answer. Instead, I focused on breaking apart the piece of crust into little crumbs. The pizza sat inside me like a chunk of coal, causing me to question whether I should've eaten so much.

Bryn shifted to sit closer to me. "Janey," she said quietly, "I don't know what went on between you and your sister. But she reached out to you. After disappearing for, what was it, seven years?"

"Eight," I automatically corrected.

"That's a long time," she said. "Most people would be dying to know what she wrote."

I couldn't answer ... just kept pulling the crust apart into smaller and smaller pieces.

"There's no judgement," she said. "I'm sure it's complicated ..."

"We fought," I suddenly interrupted, feeling like the words were being torn from me.

Bryn's eyes widened, but she stayed silent.

"I didn't tell you everything," I said. "We had a huge fight the day she disappeared. We were on a boat and ..." I turned away, blinking back tears. In my mind, she was there again, stretched out, her red lips curving into a slow smile as she told me how "ridiculous" I was being.

According to her, I was *always* being ridiculous. Never mind all the stories, exaggerations, and even outright lies *she* told.

"You don't have to tell me if you're not ready," Bryn said.

"It's just ... that was the last time I saw her. And I know it was just a fight, and that sisters fight. And I know I said some awful things, and so did she, but still. Is that why she didn't tell me what she was planning? She had dragged her big backpack with her on the boat, which didn't make a lot of sense to me at the time, but, like I said, Kelly did a lot of things that never made a lot of sense. That was just ... Kelly. But, still. Maybe if we hadn't had that huge fight, she would have told me what she was planning, and I could have talked her out of it. Or maybe she would have even changed her mind and decided not to run away in the first place." My voice cracked. "I keep thinking, is this all somehow my fault? Why she didn't come home?"

"Oh, honey, no," Bryn said, throwing an arm around me. "You were just a child. And your sister made her own choices."

I was fourteen, I thought. *Old enough to know better.* But I didn't say it. "My head tells me you're right. I realize it's not logical to think that Kelly wouldn't have reached out or come home because we had a stupid fight. Especially since she had already packed up her things. But trauma doesn't necessarily breed logic."

"Don't beat yourself up," Bryn said. "What you went through would be horrible for anyone, let alone a kid. Have you ..." her voice trailed off, and she looked distinctly uncomfortable. "Have you thought about maybe going back to therapy? It seemed to help a lot."

"It did," I said drily. "Why do you think I'm studying to be a psychologist? I'm trying to heal myself."

She laughed. "Well, there is something to that. But you still have a few years to go. It might be beneficial to see someone a little sooner."

"You may be right," I said. It probably would be good for me to talk to someone again. I did miss seeing Dr. Nelson. I felt like she really understood me. Of course, I hardly had the time between classes and papers and studying and everything else. Maybe after the semester ended, I could give Dr. Nelson a call and see if she had room to see me.

"You know," Bryn said. "It's not too late to reconnect with your sister."

I sighed. "The letter."

Bryn gave me a sideways smile. "She did reach out. Yes, it was a long time coming, but she finally did. Maybe it's time to see what she has to say."

My stomach clenched at the thought of reading it, but Bryn was right. I couldn't very well keep feeling sorry for myself about Kelly never reaching out when I had evidence to the contrary right on my kitchen table.

Maybe this would be the first step toward healing for both of us.

"You're right," I said, standing up and brushing my hands off on my black leggings. "Let's go see what Kelly has to say."

Bryn's eyes sparkled. "I can come, too?"

"Of course," I said, even as my stomach twisted into more knots. Hopefully, Kelly hadn't written anything that would make me regret it.

I sat down at the kitchen table, pulling the pieces of paper toward me. Bryn set both our glasses of wine on the table and slid the second chair next to mine.

It took a while to assemble. There was a lot missing. But what *was* there was chilling.

I'm still being stalked. Leaving Riverview didn't help. How did he find me? I'm in Redemption, for God's sake ...

No one believed I had a stalker. No one. Not even Dr. C. Either they told me I was mistaken, if they were being kind, or that it was all in my head, if they weren't ... if that were the case, then how is it that he is still *following me? Why is he still here? What have I done? Why can't I get rid of him?*

I saw him again last night. Outside my window. He was hiding in the bushes, but I could tell he was there. I was so careful not to leave a trail. It must have been Lisa. She's always had a big mouth ...

I know I made mistakes. I know I screwed up. I'm sorry ...

I need help. I can't do this alone anymore. Clearly, I'm doing something wrong. I'm all alone here.

Help me. Please. Help me.

"Wow," Bryn said. She looked shaken. "She sounds terrified."

I swallowed. An image of Kelly standing in front of the mirror, purple eyeshadow smeared across her cheekbone, hand trembling.

Must be my stalker.

"She does," I said. I noticed my own hand shaking and quickly balled it into a fist before dropping it into my lap.

"The problem is," Bryn mused, scanning it again. "How can we help her? How do we even get in touch with her? There's nothing here."

"I wonder if her contact info was on one of the pieces that was lost," I said.

"Yeah, that really sucks that it got so trashed," Bryn said. "We also don't even know when she sent it. There's no date, and the postmark is illegible. For all we know, she could have sent this months ago."

Months ago? My whole body began to shake. Now my idiotic decision to leave the letter sitting on the table for two days felt even more awful and childish. What was wrong with me? Kelly had reached out, clearly in trouble, and my reaction was to shove the pieces of her plea under the salt and pepper shakers.

I was a terrible person.

"Hey," Bryn said, grabbing my shoulders and turning me to face her. "We can do this. We can find her and help her. There ARE clues here. We just have to do a little research. We can't panic. If we stay focused, we can do this."

"I didn't look right away," I said. "We lost two days."

Bryn tightened her grip. "Don't think about that right now. There's a lot we don't know. And you can't beat yourself up. You had no idea. Plus, you had a lot of unresolved issues come up that you had to deal with. You have to take care of yourself first. Then, you can worry about the rest. It's like what they tell you when you fly—put your own oxygen mask on first, before you help anyone else."

I wasn't at all sure she was right. It felt like I should be blaming myself more, not less. There was a lot about the situation that felt like my fault.

On the other hand, it was true that I couldn't waste more time beating myself up. There would be plenty of time later for that. What I needed to focus on was finding Kelly, so I could help her.

"Okay," I said. "How should we get started?"

Chapter 3

"Well, we have this return address in Redemption," Bryn said. "I say we start there."

I nodded. "I'll go get my computer."

I got up to fetch my laptop and phone. When I returned, Bryn was hunched over the letter scribbling notes in a notebook. "Before she was in Redemption, she was here in Riverview. Pretty wild, wouldn't you say? You guys both in the same city."

"I know," I said, feeling the familiar knife twist inside me. She was so close, yet she still didn't reach out.

Bryn looked up and saw my face. "Riverview is a pretty big place," she offered. "Even without the university. She may not have known you were here."

That was true. It could have just been coincidence.

That still didn't make it feel any better.

Bryn moved the pieced-together letter over, so I could set up my laptop on the table. I put the address in the search bar and got a link to Zillow.

"Think the house is for sale?" Bryn asked, peering over my shoulder.

"I don't think a house has to be for sale to be on Zillow," I said, clicking the link.

I read the description. It wasn't for sale, but it *was* huge. Especially for Redemption. Almost 4,000 square feet.

"Looks like whoever owns it now just bought it two years ago," Bryn said, pointing to the date. "Do you think it could have been Kelly?"

I gulped when I saw the purchase price. "For that much? How would she have gotten that kind of money? Also, in reading the letter, it doesn't seem like she moved to Redemption that long ago."

"There's no dates, so we don't know that for sure," Bryn said. "But yeah, what we have does sort of read like she just arrived a few months ago."

Zillow didn't include a photo of the house, which was a disappointment. All we had was the satellite shot of the neighborhood.

"Wait a minute," I said, squinting to get a closer look. "I think I know where that is."

"You do?"

"Yeah." I traced Marigold Lane. "I think this street backs up to this wilderness area. There's a big lake surrounded by woods."

"Not developed?"

I shook my head. "There are cottages and summer homes around there, but a lot of it isn't developed. Eventually, it backs into a big state park, which is what attracts tourism to Redemption. People come to hike or swim or camp or whatever."

Bryn made a face. "Yeah, along with all the ghost hunting and unsolved crime tours. Redemption has something for everyone, doesn't it? But anyway, do you remember the house at all?"

I screwed up my face, trying to think back. "Not really. I just sort of remember the neighborhood because we used to drive through it."

Bryn tapped her finger on her pad of paper. "Go back to the search results for that address and see if you can find a name."

After a little more searching and messing around, I finally had what we were looking for.

"The Johnsons," I said. "Julia and Max."

"Are those names familiar?" Bryn asked.

I shook my head. "Not in the least." They sounded like normal, all-American names. Why would they possibly know anything about my hot-mess family?

"You think they had something to do with Kelly's disappearance?"

I stared at the names. "I have no idea. Your guess is as good as mine."

"Hmmm." Bryn went back to tapping on her notebook. "Let's see if we can find them on social."

"With a name like 'Julia Johnson'? This might take a while."

It took a little time and digging, but I managed to find Julia's very active Instagram account. Based on her profile description, it appeared she was self-employed as a consultant as well as a wife and mom. Her profile was filled with fun, happy, carefully composed pictures of her beautiful house, her loving husband, and her three adorable children.

I already didn't like her.

"Now that you see her, does she look familiar at all?" Bryn asked.

I clicked on one of her selfies to enlarge it, but I suspected it wouldn't change my answer. She appeared to be in her mid-to-late thirties, with wide, sparkling, brown eyes and a friendly smile. Her brown hair was cut stylishly in a chin-length bob with blonde highlights, and her carefully applied makeup didn't quite cover the fine lines around her eyes.

"I've never seen her before," I said.

"That's so weird," Bryn mused. "Why would Kelly send you a letter from her house? Do you think they were friends or somehow knew each other?"

"I suppose anything is possible," I said, scrolling through images of Julia's charming, perfect life while trying not to think about how pathetic and lonely my own was.

"Kelly must have met the Johnsons at some point. Although why she would use their address on her letter is beyond me."

"Maybe ..." I had to swallow hard before I continued. "Maybe Kelly didn't think it was safe to use her real address."

"So, she used a friend's instead?" Bryn mulled it. "That's possible, I suppose. But why would it matter what return address she had on the envelope? It's not like the post office won't mail it if you don't put a return address on it."

"Maybe she wanted to make sure there was a way the letter would be returned if I didn't get it, without revealing her real location," I said.

"Maybe." Bryn sounded doubtful. "Sounds a little far-fetched."

Julia's next post caught my eye, and I stopped scrolling. "Julia had a nanny," I said.

"A nanny?"

"Yeah." I held up the phone so Bryn could see. Julia had typed: *Thank God my new nanny started today. Now we can finally all get back to a regular schedule again.*

"Was Kelly the nanny?" Bryn asked excitedly. "Is that the connection?"

"I don't know," I said, scrolling through the pics and searching frantically for something, anything. "I don't see a name or picture anywhere."

"Go back," Bryn said. "Maybe she posted something earlier or mentioned a name after she hired her."

I started scrolling back through the feed.

"Wait," Bryn said, pointing. "Maybe that's her."

The main focus of the picture Bryn was pointing to was the two children. The girl had her mother's large, soulful brown eyes, but lacked the sparkle. Instead, she stared solemnly at the camera. Her younger brother, who was missing his two front teeth, wore a mischievous grin. There was also a baby who smiled broadly at the camera, one tiny fist clutching the hair of the younger woman who was holding her.

I leaned closer to the monitor to get a better look. Her face was cut off, but from what I could see, she had jet-black hair and pale skin, a misshapen nose, and a pointed chin. She didn't look anything like Kelly.

"It's not her," I said, sitting back dejectedly.

"Are you sure? Maybe she dyed her hair or changed ..."

"Her skin is too pale," I said, thinking of Kelly's peaches-and-cream complexion. "And her bone structure is off."

"Oh." Bryn sat back, disappointed. She drummed her fingers against her notebook, looking down at her notes.

I found myself studying the face of the young girl. She didn't look much older than ten. Such a serious, sad-looking little girl. Why would someone so young who lived in such a beautiful house be so sad?

"Wait a minute," Bryn said. "Didn't Julia say a *new* nanny? What about her last nanny?"

"That's true," I said, starting to scroll back.

"That would make more sense with the timing," Bryn said. "If she was the nanny a few months ago, then it would make sense for her to mail the letter from her house, so ... oh my God."

The picture was of an open door with just a glimpse of an out-of-focus empty bedroom. Underneath, Julia had typed in all caps.

SHE'S GONE.

Below that was a little more.

Our nanny just up and left. Without a word. How could she do this to us after all we did for her?

"Gone?" Bryn breathed next to me. "Her nanny just *left?*"

My hand was frozen on my phone. I couldn't breathe. I couldn't think. In that moment, I was back in the kitchen of the cabin we had rented for the summer, a bowl of cereal in front of me, my mother's voice calling from the back of the house. "Kelly, time to get up. Kelly? Adam, have you seen Kelly? Her bed wasn't slept in last night. Janey? Do you know where she is?"

Bryn's warm hand covered mine. "Breathe," she said, her voice low. "Look at the date. It was two months ago."

I tried to focus on what Bryn was showing me, but my brain refused to cooperate. All I could think about was how I had lost two full days because of my childish stupidity.

No one believed I had a stalker.

"Janey, I don't think it would have made a difference," Bryn said, clearly reading my mind. "What's important is that we're researching now. Okay?"

My body was frozen, awash with guilt and despair. I really was a terrible person.

"It's going to be okay," Bryn said, her voice still soft and gentle. "Listen, we don't know if Kelly was her nanny yet. Why don't we look at the comments and see what they say?"

My fingers didn't seem to want to properly move, but after a few tries, I was finally able to touch the link to show more comments.

Most of them were about how inconsiderate some people were and how difficult it was to find good help. But one thread caught my attention.

Did you call the cops? What if something happened to her?

Her car is gone and so are some of her things, Julia replied. *We thought she was just going ice skating for the day, but she never came home.*

Wait. Some of her things?

Yeah, I don't know why she didn't pack everything. She's not responding to any messages or calls, so I guess she doesn't want the rest.

I think you should call the cops. Maybe something did happen to her.

Julia didn't respond to that last comment, but she did provide an update a little further down.

Update: We did end up calling the cops, who investigated. I don't want to share much more, but it appears our nanny was troubled. Pray for her.

"Well, that's ominous," Bryn said. "I wonder what it means."

No one believed I had a stalker.

"I don't know," I said, scrolling down again. Maybe I could find a picture of the nanny… or better yet, a name, so I could check her out.

Further down the page, I struck gold.

The picture was of the little boy sitting at the kitchen table, reaching for a cereal box, his hair every which way and his face screwed up in deep concentration. A woman was standing behind him, reaching over to help him. Her blonde hair fell like a curtain across her face, so I couldn't get a good look, but an uneasy feeling seemed to uncoil itself like a snake inside me as I studied it.

OMG, @ashleysorrel568 is the BEST NANNY IN THE WORLD. Last minute, we found out one of my dear clients was going to be in town and wanted to meet Isabelle. I was trying to figure out take-out options when Ashley not only offered to cook an amazing meal, but to do it WHILE watching the kids! AND she kept the kiddos occupied while we ate!

I couldn't tear my eyes off the name.

Ashley Sorrel.

Bryn squinted at the screen. "I'm assuming that's Ashley. Does she look like Kelly? I know it's hard to tell with her hair in her face."

My mouth didn't seem to work properly, so I gave my head a little shake.

"Hmm, yeah too much to ask. It's a cute pic, especially of her son, but you'd think she could have asked Ashley to move her hair out of her face. Oh well. At least Julia thought to tag Ashley, so we can find her account and see if it's your sister or not," Bryn said. "It's possible she changed her name. Especially if she thought she had a stalker."

I didn't move the mouse. Sorrel. The name was still ping-ponging in my head.

"Janey?" Bryn eyed me. "What is it?"

"It's ..." I licked my dry lips. "'Sorrel.' That name sounds so familiar. I think ... I'm sure ... one of her friends in high school had that last name."

Bryn's eyes widened. "Wow, that's some ... coincidence."

I nodded, still staring at the name on the screen.

"Do you ... should we see if it's her, or not?"

My hand seemed to be moving on its own, like it wasn't a part of me at all. I couldn't even feel my fingertips as they hovered over Ashley's name. It felt like I wasn't in control at all—that my hand had a life of its own and was doing whatever it wanted. All I could do was helplessly sit there and watch. My eyes followed my finger, as it moved across the screen and then, if by magic, clicked on the link.

Ashley's profile popped up on my phone, her picture front and center.

I stopped breathing.

I was staring at my sister.

Chapter 4

I opened my eyes to find myself peering up at a very worried Bryn.

"Janey! Thank God. Can you hear me?"

I couldn't figure out where I was. I seemed to be lying on something cold and hard. Strange, exotic shapes loomed above me. "What ... what happened?"

"You fainted," she said. "Just slid out of your chair and onto the floor before I could catch you. Are you okay? Does your head hurt?"

I raised my hand to gingerly touch the back of my head, wincing at the lump I found. "Yes."

Bryn frowned. "Let me get you some ice. I'm not surprised. You banged it pretty good." She disappeared, and I heard the rattling sounds of her preparing an ice pack.

Cautiously, I pulled myself up, so I could sit cross-legged and examine myself for any other injuries. It appeared my head was the only casualty.

"Here," Bryn said, kneeling down next to me and pressing a towel full of ice onto my head. "You're probably going to have a pretty big bump there. Let me see your pupils to check for a concussion."

She studied my eyes for a moment. "You should be fine. I'll look again before you go to bed."

"Thanks, doc."

She smiled slightly, but her eyes kept searching my face. "Do you remember what happened?"

I thought about it. "We were sitting at the table, right? Looking at my phone and ..." my voice trailed off as my memories pieced themselves back together. "I saw my sister."

Bryn's mouth dropped. "So, Ashley *is* your sister."

I nodded. "And now she's missing. Again. And maybe I had a chance to save her, and I didn't." My voice was starting to rise, and I could feel myself getting hysterical.

"Janey, stop. Hush. Remember, you got the letter two days ago. Two DAYS ago! That post from Julia was two MONTHS ago. Even if you had read it immediately, Ashley still would have been gone for two months already. If anything, it's the post office's fault for chewing it up in the machine."

"I can't believe that happened," I moaned. "Of all the terrible luck."

"I know. It's awful. But we can't focus on that now. We just have to do the best we can now that we know."

Bryn was putting a pretty good spin on it, but I still couldn't get my head around what was happening. Was Kelly cursed? Was I? Or maybe it was like that one horror movie, where the passengers were supposed to die in a plane crash, but they didn't get on the plane. So then, they started dying in all sorts of weird and disgusting ways.

Had Kelly been abducted all those years ago after all? And had she somehow survived, even though she shouldn't have … and now fate was forcing what should have happened, but didn't?

That would certainly explain the current mess.

"Do you want to continue this tomorrow?" Bryn asked. "At this point, I don't think a day is going to make any difference, and you've had quite a shock. Plus, your head is probably really hurting! It might be better for you to rest."

"I'm okay," I said, grimacing as I pulled myself back into the kitchen chair with Bryn's help. "I realize it's been two months already, but I'd rather keep going. We've lost enough time."

"Okay," Bryn said, sitting down next to me. "If you're sure. Let's see what we can discover."

I took a deep breath, steeled myself, picked up my phone, and met the eyes of my sister.

She was older, of course, and her hair was cut in a different style—more of a shaggy bob. She also looked a little rough around the edges. I wondered how difficult life had been for her the past few years. Her dark-blue eyes framed with thick, black lashes looked directly into the camera, but they didn't sparkle like they did when we were kids. They were haunted, as if the ghosts of what she had seen and experienced had taken their toll.

I clicked on the first picture, the last one posted, dated end of December.

So excited for the new year. I'm finally feeling like all my problems are over! Yay! Here's to new beginnings. And no more being controlled by fear!

She included a selfie taken in the snow in front of what I assumed was Julia's house. There was a silhouette of a Christmas tree in one of the windows.

Her cheeks were hollowed, as if she had lost weight, and her eyes still had that hint of some emotion—was it sadness? Fear? Post-traumatic stress? Something else?—buried in their depths.

Next were a few generic holiday pictures and messages, wishing people a happy Thanksgiving and such. From there, the pictures jumped to summer.

"This is a little, well, disturbing," Bryn said as we scrolled down her feed. "She was posting regularly at the beginning of last year. A couple, maybe three posts a week. And then all of that just stops on August 3 until Thanksgiving."

No one believed I had a stalker.

"Do you think that's when her stalker appeared?" I could hear the tinge of guilt and fear in my voice.

"Your guess is as good as mine, but it sure seems that way," Bryn answered.

I paused my scrolling on a picture of her in a bar with three other women. *Best group of friends in the world!* Ashley was holding a glass of wine, toasting the camera and smiling. Her eyes were bright and sparkling. So very different from the one she'd posted last.

Did her stalker do that to her? Or did something else happen?

"Wait. Scroll back up to that first picture. I want to see something," Bryn said.

I obeyed.

Bryn leaned forward. "That's what I thought. Click on the comments."

I did. There were quite a few—nearly two dozen. Initially, they were responses to Ashley's picture, wishing her a happy new year and congratulating her on her life.

You go girl! one said. *Glad to finally see your beautiful face again.*

Yes, it's time. Ashley replied. *I'm ready to take my life back!*

But gradually, there was a notable shift. While the thread started out benign, it quickly became more anxious.

Still liking the new job? Inquiring minds want to know!

What's new? Haven't heard from you in a while.

Hey Ash! I hope this radio silence doesn't mean you've replaced us. Let us know what's happening!

Hey, haven't seen a pic from you in a while. How are things?

Hey, girl. Haven't heard from you in weeks. Call or text me.

Is everything okay? I haven't seen anything from you in too long.

I just sent you a dm. Can you respond?

Did anything happen to your phone?

Have you been getting my texts? Call me. I'm getting worried.

The last one was posted just a couple of weeks before:

This isn't funny anymore, Ashley. Why aren't you responding? I'm really worried about you.

"See, most of those comments are from the girls tagged in that picture," Bryn said, pointing to them. "It sounds like they haven't heard from her, either."

I scrolled back and forth, matching up the names. Crystal commented the most, including the last one. But there were also a couple from Lisa and Brianna.

Bryn was scribbling their names in the notebook. "Kelly mentions a Lisa having a big mouth. I wonder if it's that Lisa?"

"Could be," I said, scrolling around. "I'm not seeing anyone else by that name."

"Hmm," Bryn said, putting a big star next to Lisa's name. "Do you think we should reach out? See what they have to say?"

"Do you honestly think they would talk to us?" I asked, rubbing the back of my neck where it was starting to crick. "I mean, if someone I didn't know called me out of the blue wanting to know about a friend of mine who was missing, I wouldn't talk to her."

"Good point," Bryn said, frowning.

"Especially a friend who had a stalker," I continued. "Can you imagine? Your friend says she has a stalker. She disappears, and then someone else you don't know calls you out of the blue asking about her? That screams stalker behavior."

Bryn laughed. "Okay, okay."

"Besides, it probably wouldn't do any good. It's not like they seem to know anything more than we do right now," I mused. "Really, there's one place to start. We have to talk to Julia."

"Don't you think you'll run into the same problem as with Ashley's friends?"

I sat back, biting my lip. "Maybe. Probably. Maybe the thing to do is drive to Redemption and see what I can learn."

Bryn gave me a worried look. "Do you think that's safe?"

I shrugged. "I don't really know what else to do right now."

Bryn tapped the pen against her notepad. "Didn't Julia say she contacted the police? Maybe start there. See if you can talk to whoever was in charge of her disappearance. See what they found out."

"That's a good idea," I said, although I was already planning the trip to Redemption in my head. I wanted to stand in Kelly's, or Ashley's, last known location. I wanted to breathe the air she breathed, feel the things she touched. My sister was alive.

Alive! At least, as of a few months ago. If I could just trace her last steps, something would happen. Some spark, some psychic connection. I just knew it.

It made no logical sense. I knew that, too. But I couldn't stop the longing in my heart.

"You could even call the cops tomorrow," Bryn continued. "I agree, you'll probably need to drive down there eventually, but we're in the final few weeks of class. Do you even have the time to go back and forth?"

"I can't lose any more time," I said, my voice rising in frustration. "I've already lost two days because of my own stupidity, and at least two months because of the post office's ineptness."

"I know," Bryn said. "I get it. But you can't just toss out everything you worked so hard for this semester, either. You have no idea if you'll even be able to get a lead on where she is."

"I have to at least try. She's my sister."

"I know," Bryn said again, her voice gentle. "That's why we'll start by calling the cops tomorrow. I'm not saying you can't make a trip to Redemption as well before the end of the school year, but at least be as prepared as possible, so you can be efficient with your time."

A part of me wanted to howl from exasperation and disappointment. I needed to go now! I couldn't afford to wait any longer.

But, at the same time, I was also suddenly and keenly aware of how exhausted I was and how much my head hurt. Bryn was right. I needed to at least get some sleep. Tomorrow would be another day. Hopefully, after a good night's rest, I would be able to think a lot more clearly.

I sighed, scrubbing my face with my hands. "You're probably right. I should go to bed."

"Good idea," Bryn said. "Do you need any help?"

"No, I'm okay," I said, slowly getting to my feet. I knew, of course, that Bryn would ignore me and insist on walking me to my room, checking my eyes one more time and fetching some pain medicine for me. "It will help you sleep," she said.

I took the pills without complaint as I could already feel my headache getting worse. Hopefully, it would take the edge off, so I could fall asleep.

"Come get me if you have any problems," she instructed firmly. "I'll be up a few more hours studying. But even if I'm asleep, wake me. Okay?"

"Okay, doc," I said as she closed the door.

I stared up at the ceiling, sure the turmoil in my head would keep me up for hours. But within minutes, my eyelids fluttered closed, and I was sound asleep.

Chapter 5

I dreamed of Kelly.

We were in the boat on the lake. I was struggling with the oars.

"Janey, just use the motor," Kelly said lazily, face turned up to the sun. "Why do you always have to make things more difficult?"

"I want the workout," I said. "Besides, I thought this was supposed to be a relaxing day on the lake."

"It would be more relaxing if I knew I could count on you."

I froze, one oar in the water, one out. "You *can* count on me."

Kelly glanced at me, pulling her sunglasses down her nose so she could look at me over the lenses. "Really? Then why don't you know where I am?"

I cringed, trying to avoid her eyes so I didn't have to see the accusations glaring back at me. "That's not my fault," I said. "I didn't get your letter."

Kelly continued to stare at me. Her eyes were dark blue, the color of a smooth, deep lake. "That's just so like you to blame everyone but yourself. Why don't you take some responsibility?"

"I do take responsibility," I ground out. "But I can't take responsibility for what the post office does or doesn't do. How can that possibly be my fault?"

Kelly shook her head, pushing her glasses back up her forehead. "I need to be with people I trust. I can't trust you."

"You CAN trust me," I said, feeling desperate. "What do I need to do to prove it?"

Kelly straightened up, her head slowly turning to face me. "Find me." Her voice was no longer light and playful, but dark and ominous.

I dropped the oars, hearing the splash as they hit the water. My skin prickled from the cold drops. "How?"

"Find me," she said again.

"But where?" I begged. "Where do I start? What do I do?"

The light grew dark, as if the sun went behind the clouds. Kelly turned her face away from me. "Follow the yellow brick road until you get to Oz," she said as she started to laugh.

It was a cold, hollow, sound ... without humor, without soul.

I woke with a start, gasping for breath, my heart pounding.

How could I have forgotten?

The light in the bedroom was already turning grey with the dawn. I pulled the sweaty sheets away from my skin and got up. *It was just a dream,* I told myself. *Just a nightmare. It's not real. He isn't a threat anymore. I just had a bad dream, brought on by the shock of the letter from Kelly and hitting my head. That's all.*

But it didn't matter. Now that fear had been introduced, it burrowed inside my brain like a worm, and I knew I would get no rest until I checked.

I went over to my desk, opening the bottom drawer and pawing through the various files and papers until I located the well-worn, dog-eared business card. Clutching it, I made my way to the kitchen.

It was way too early to call, so I made coffee and took more pain medicine for my head, which still ached. My stomach was tied up in too many knots to tolerate any sort of breakfast, so I pulled out my notes and tried to focus on the paper I had meant to work on the night before. But I couldn't concentrate. My eyes kept straying to the clock above the stove, watching the hands slowly tick their way to a more reasonable calling time.

I made it to seven, which was still too early. But I knew she was an early riser.

She answered before the second ring. "Hello?" Her voice was like a coiled spring, waiting for bad news to drop.

Guilt shot through me. I shouldn't have called so early. "It's me, Janey."

"Oh, Janey," her voice relaxed before coiling up again. "Are you okay? What happened?"

"Nothing, I mean ..." My voice trailed off as I realized I hadn't thought what I was doing through. While I had planned to tell the now-retired detective who was in charge of my sister's disappearance that I received a letter from her, was I to start with that? Or would that throw off the entire conversation? I decided I couldn't wait to hear the update on Oz, so I forged ahead with that topic.

"It's just my regular check-in on Oz," I said. "I know I usually do it sooner, but this year has been particularly crazy with school and ... and everything."

There was silence on the other end of the phone.

"Hello? Are you still there?" I wondered if we were cut off.

"Janey," Karen said, her voice gentle. "Didn't you get my letter?"

Letter? My eyes darted to the pile of scraps on the table, and I fought the urge to dig at it to see if Karen's name was on it somewhere that I had missed. "Letter? What ... what are you talking about?" I stuttered.

She sighed. "Janey, Oz was paroled."

My throat tightened, and I suddenly found it painful to breathe. *"Paroled?* What? When?"

"Almost a year ago. Late June, I think. Maybe early July."

I closed my eyes. That was right after my parents died, when I was still deep in the throes of grief. There was a lot I didn't remember from that time. There were black, patchy holes in my memory caused by either my inability to sleep for days on end or the drugs Dr. Nelson finally prescribed me. If Karen had sent me a letter during that time, it was no wonder I didn't remember.

"My parents were killed in a car accident then," I said. I could hear Karen suck in her breath. "I ... well, there's a lot that's a blur from that time."

"Janey, I'm so sorry," Karen said. "That is just so ... terrible. After everything you've been through. Truly. I'm so very sorry."

"Thank you," I said, hoping to change the subject. "So, if you sent a letter, I just missed it."

"Yeah, I was going to call, but I had my own family emergency, although nothing like what you went through. It was just easier to write the letter and mail it, but now I'm wishing I had phoned."

Writing a letter doesn't feel easier, I thought. *You had to write it out, put it in an envelope, locate an address, and stick a stamp on it. Wasn't calling easier?*

Unless, of course, what she was really saying was that it was emotionally easier to write a letter. That way, she didn't have to deal with me. My stomach twisted in a familiar knot. Story of my life. Everyone thought it was easier to not deal with me.

Although in the moment, none of that mattered.

Oz was a free man.

That was all that mattered. That was the real issue.

I'm still being stalked.

"It's fine," I said, even though it wasn't, and it never would be.

We talked for a few minutes more despite my desperation to get off the phone. Karen kept trying to reassure me about Oz's parole. "He has to register as a sex offender for the rest of his life, so he's always going to be on the police's radar," she said.

"I understand."

"Try not to lose any sleep over it, okay? And you can call me anytime, if there's anything that seems off."

I glanced down at the pieces of the letter still strewn over the table. I suspected she would consider receiving it as "something off." I was just too agitated to try and explain it all to her at that moment, so I let her know I'd of course stay in touch before hanging up.

What was happening? Was Oz behind Kelly's disappearance after all? Karen had assured me they had fully investigated him at the time, and he had an alibi. But now, I wasn't so sure.

I had never trusted in coincidences, and I sure wasn't going to start now.

Kelly's voice echoed in my head. *You always did miss the obvious, Janey.*

What does that even mean? I argued back. *Are you saying Oz was stalking you after all?* For an answer, the Kelly in my head just laughed. I pushed her aside. Kelly always did know how to make me second-guess myself, and in that moment, it was the last thing I needed.

I wasn't sure how long I sat there, my brain whirling while trying to make sense of all the pieces, before Bryn found me.

"You're up early," she yawned, shuffling toward the coffee pot. "How are you feeling?"

I rubbed my face with my hands. "I need to tell you something."

Bryn glanced at me as she held the coffee pot, her face full of questions. "Okayyy," she said, drawing out the word.

"Kelly had a boyfriend, well, an ex-boyfriend. His name was Oz. He was older by a few years. He wasn't a good guy. Actually, he was a real ass. Anyway, they broke up before we left for the lake that summer, which made me happy, because I didn't have to worry about him hanging around the cottage. But then …" I sighed. "I told you Kelly and I fought the day she disappeared, but I didn't tell you what we fought about."

Bryn brought her coffee to the table and sat down across from me. "You fought about Oz."

I nodded. "I guess he wanted to talk … to try and get back together. So she was going to meet him. We were out together in the boat. I was going to drop her off closer to where he was. We only had the one car, and our parents were gone for the afternoon, so Kelly thought it was better to meet him somewhere rather than have him come to the house. I, of course, was totally against all of it. I didn't think it was safe and didn't want any part of it. We got into a big fight, and she insisted I move the boat closer to the shore so she could get out. We weren't anywhere near where she wanted to be dropped off, but that's what I did. She jumped out, waded to shore, and kept walking. That was the last I saw of her."

"Oh, Janey," Bryn put a hand on her mouth. "No wonder why you've blamed yourself. So, was Oz there?"

"That's the thing. I told the detectives about Oz, and I guess he and Kelly had been in touch, but he wasn't anywhere near the lake that day. He had an alibi. But, despite all of that, I never could shake the feeling that he had something to do with her disappearance.

"A couple of years later, he ended up going to jail for sexually assaulting a minor."

Bryn spilled her coffee. "*What?*"

"Yeah, I know. I told you the guy was a real piece of work. I've been keeping tabs on him, making sure he was still safely in jail, but I just called Karen, the detective on the case, and she told me he was paroled last summer."

Bryn's eyes went very wide. "Are you kidding me? He's out?"

I nodded. "I know I should have told you all of this yesterday, but quite honestly, I had kind of put him out of my mind. I thought he was still in jail! So, I really didn't think it mattered."

Bryn put her hand on mine. "Janey, it's fine. I get why you don't want to talk or even think about this. It's just awful. So, what did the detective say about you getting the letter?"

I ran my hand through my hair, avoiding Bryn's gaze. "I didn't tell her yet. I was so shocked that Oz was out, I just wanted to get off the phone and process what I heard."

"I can understand that," she said getting up and heading for the kitchen. "Have you eaten?" she called over her shoulder. "Maybe we should get some breakfast. Want some toast?"

"Sure," I said, even though the last thing I wanted was anything to eat. My stomach was still twisted up. "The other issue with Karen is that she's retired now. So I don't know how much she can help."

"Hmm," Bryn said, pulling out a couple pieces of bread and sticking them into the toaster oven. "That's a good point. Maybe we should do what we talked about yesterday and start with the Redemption police department. See what we can get from their investigation. Then, you can bring all of that to Karen and see what she thinks."

"That makes sense," I said. "I'd like to know why they think Kelly, or Ashley, was 'troubled.'"

Bryn pulled out butter and plates. "Especially since it sounds like they ended their investigation. That would be good info to know, right?"

As Bryn buttered the toast, I went in search for the phone number to call.

The dispatcher who answered knew exactly what I was talking about. "Oh, Ashley. Yes, that was a sad case. Are you a relative?"

"I might be," I said. "If it's the Ashley I think it is, then yes."

"Let me connect you," she chirped, clicking away. I put the phone on speaker so Bryn could hear, too.

"This is Officer Hicks," a deep male voice said.

I glanced nervously at Bryn, who gave me an encouraging look. "My name is Janey Moore, and I'm wondering if you can share some information about Ashley Sorrel?"

"You're related to her?"

"Maybe," I said. "I had a sister who disappeared eight years ago, and I think she might be Ashley."

"Oh." His voice perked up. "Why do you think that?"

"Well, Ashley's social media pictures sure look like her," I said. "And she sent me a letter."

"A letter?"

"Yeah, it was delayed by the post office, so I'm not sure when she actually mailed it."

"Ashley disappeared two months ago," Officer Hicks said. "When did you get this letter?"

"Three days ago."

"And it was mailed from where?"

I read him the address.

I heard papers rustling. "Yes, that's the Johnsons' residence. That's really strange, that you got the letter now."

"Yeah, it was ... 'eaten' by the post office."

"Eaten?"

"It's in pieces," I explained. "They sent it to me in a bag."

"Really?"

"So, it's not clear when she sent it, either. It could have been two months ago."

"What does it say?"

"It's mostly talking about her having a stalker."

Officer Hicks sighed heavily. "Yeah, I was afraid of that."

I jerked my head up and met Bryn's eyes, who looked just as shocked as me. "You knew she had a stalker?"

"I knew she thought she had one. And maybe she did. But we were never able to verify it one way or another. There were no witnesses or any other proof. And, when we checked with some of her friends, it wasn't a one-off thing. Unfortunately, Ashley has a history of mental issues, and was on medication, but it's unclear if she was still taking it. It's all very unfortunate."

"So, you don't think there really was a stalker?" I wasn't sure if I should feel relieved or worried.

"We never found evidence of one."

"What do you think happened?"

"I don't know, but my guess is she left on her own," he said. "Apparently, Ashley also has a history of disappearing for short periods of time. I suspect she'll eventually resurface at some point. Whether or not you can find her is another story. Did you say your sister disappeared eight years ago?"

"Yes."

"And she never reached out?"

"Not until this letter."

"And her name is Ashley?"

"No, it was Kelly, actually."

"How did Kelly disappear?"

"She didn't come home one day," I said. "No one knows what happened to her, but at the time, she talked about having a stalker, as well."

"Did they find any evidence of a stalker?"

"Not really. And then a week later, we got a postcard from her, basically telling us not to worry ... that she was pursuing her dreams. That was the last we heard."

"Did she have any history of mental illness?"

Images of Kelly's laughing face filled my mind, her dark-blue eyes sparkling as she tossed her golden hair over her shoulder. "I don't think so. At least, she was never diagnosed with anything."

"How old was she when she disappeared?"

"She was seventeen. Almost eighteen."

"So, you think she changed her name and was living a different life?"

I studied the sad pieces of the letter. "Maybe."

"Unfortunately, that behavior isn't inconsistent with what we learned about her," he said with another sigh. "Including her mental illness. It's common for symptoms to manifest in teenagers and young adults, like in the early twenties. It's possible this was the start of a pattern."

"You think my sister left because she was having some sort of mental breakdown?"

"I don't know," he said. "I'm not a doctor, and I've never met either your sister or Ashley. But what you're describing seems to fit Ashley's pattern. Including her sending you a letter. It's just like the postcard she sent when she first disappeared."

"I ... suppose you could be right," I said.

"I wish I could help more," he said. "But there's really nothing we can do."

"What do you mean? She's still missing."

"Yes, but it's not against the law for an adult to go off on her own and not tell anyone. If there's no evidence of a crime, there's nothing to investigate."

"Even though she thought she was being stalked?"

"There's no *evidence* of that, I'm afraid. Nor is there any evidence that she didn't leave on her own free will. I'm sorry about your loss. I hope Ashley, or Kelly, reaches out again, so you can find her and get her the help she needs."

Clearly, there was nothing more to say. I thanked him and hung up.

Bryn looked stunned. "I can't believe this. He doesn't sound like he's taking the stalker possibility seriously."

"You heard him. There's no evidence," I said.

"But we do have evidence! Oz. You need to tell him."

"We don't know if Oz was stalking her," I said. "Hell, according to Karen, there's no proof Oz had anything to do with her disappearance when she was seventeen. They looked into it then. At this point, the cops would just say it's all speculation."

"Yeah, but you should tell Officer Hicks, anyway."

"Maybe," I said doubtfully. "He sounded pretty much done with it. With her. He didn't even ask to see the letter."

"I know! We need to do something to light a fire under him. Maybe we need to get Karen involved. What if Kelly changed her name to Ashley to escape an actual stalker, but he found her anyway?"

The thought made my blood run cold. "Okay, I'll call her." I picked up my phone, then saw the time and balked. "I'll have to do it later. I'm late for class."

"What time is it?" Bryn squinted at the clock and then shot to her feet. "Oh no. I am, too."

"Yes," I said as I hurried into my room, but my mind was already elsewhere. After my phone call with Officer Hicks, I was already suspecting Karen wouldn't be able to help. If Officer Hicks didn't think what happened to Ashley was a crime, this new information wasn't going to change anything. I couldn't prove Oz was the stalker. Kelly hadn't even mentioned Oz in what remained of the letter. And, if Kelly and Ashley were the same, then what happened eight years ago wasn't a crime, either. Kelly left on her own, just as the postcard said.

Still, just because the police wouldn't help didn't mean I wasn't going to get to the bottom of what happened to her.

I would just have to find a different way.

Chapter 6

The "different way" I chose to investigate my sister's disappearance was to go straight to the source—to Julia Johnson. But before I could make contact with her, I needed a better understanding of precisely what I was dealing with.

What was Julia like? How did she treat her nanny? What were the kids like? The husband?

Maybe there was something going on in that house that made Kelly/Ashley feel unsafe. Maybe the rest of the family was completely unobservant, and that's why no one had noticed a lurking stalker.

The only way I was going to get the information I needed was if I did my research—in this case, that meant watching the family for a few days. It wasn't an ideal scenario, of course, but I couldn't afford to make a mistake. I would only have one chance to make a good first impression, and Kelly was counting on me to succeed.

To start, I needed to locate Julia's house. Which wasn't difficult at all, as it turned out.

And it was just as lovely in real life as it was on social media. A two-story Craftsman-style home with dark-grey siding, white trim, a red door, and a huge backyard that blended right into woods.

It also didn't take long to find the perfect hiding place in the trees that provided a clear view into the kitchen, part of the family room, the nanny's room, and the baby's room. A second hiding place to the right allowed me to see right into Julia's downstairs office.

Julia appeared to work at home. Her home office was on the first floor, and she seemed to spend a large portion of her day on a headset while talking to the computer screen. If she wasn't in a virtual meeting, she was typing away.

Max, on the other hand, left each morning for work. He carried a briefcase and wore business clothes, which made me think he worked in an office. He also left early and came home late, so he was likely commuting to wherever his company was, which clearly wasn't in Redemption.

The nanny's job was to watch the kids, keeping them out of Julia's hair while she worked, and to cook dinner for the family. Watching her, I wasn't terribly impressed. She was a thin, scrawny, unpleasant-looking thing. Her unnaturally black hair was cut in an asymmetrical, spiky style, and she had several ear piercings as well as a nose ring. Her lips were always pulled down in a frown, even when playing with the kids. The only time she seemed to be even somewhat happy was when she was on her phone.

Julia must have been quite desperate to hire her.

It didn't take me long to figure out the family's routine. During the week, the nanny was up first, changing and feeding the baby before herding the other kids downstairs for breakfast. Max was also an early riser, showering and dressing before heading down to the kitchen. After pouring coffee and cream into a to-go mug and toasting some bread, he would stand next to the counter, munching toast and checking his phone or going through some paperwork as the nanny worked around him, fetching the older kids' breakfast. They would exchange a few words, and sometimes, they would smile at each other, her pale cheeks flushing.

Okay, so maybe being on the phone wasn't the *only* time she was happy.

Julia always got up last. She would appear in the kitchen, looking exhausted and grumpy, her hair sticking up all over the place and a ratty robe thrown over a T-shirt and pair of shorts. She would immediately head to the coffee pot to guzzle a cup before interacting with her children.

Clearly not a morning person.

After she swallowed enough caffeine, she would wake up enough to sit at the table with her kids as they ate breakfast.

The nanny would hover by the counter as she ate, usually staring at her phone.

After the children finished breakfast, everyone would scatter, eventually returning downstairs fully dressed. Then, they would leave at the same time, the kids and nanny going one way and Julia another.

Where was Julia going? I wondered. The house was empty, albeit not for long. Around twenty minutes or so later, the nanny would re-appear with the baby in the stroller. Julia, however, wouldn't return for another hour, at which point she would hole up in her office.

Was Julia going to a morning exercise class? She wasn't wearing workout clothes, which didn't mean she wasn't changing into something there. Still, it was odd.

The day would pass with the nanny tending to the baby, maybe running some errands, and picking up the children from school while Julia worked. Pick-up took a lot longer than drop-off, close to an hour, so I wondered if they stopped at a park on the way home.

Once they arrived, Julia would typically take a break for a quick hug and exchange a few words before heading back into the office while the nanny handled snacks, playtime, and dinner preparations. For the most part, the nanny was the only adult moving around the house. That is, except for Wednesdays, when a cleaning lady would come by.

Max would arrive late in the day, as the sun was starting to set. After greeting the kids, he would pour a drink and sit on the back porch. Most evenings, Julia would join him. Then it was time for dinner, family time, and bed. The nanny, again, appeared to do most of the work.

Maybe the reason the nanny wasn't happy was because Julia didn't seem all that excited to spend a lot of time with her kids.

It was late at night when things got interesting again. Once the kids were safely tucked away and the parents were otherwise occupied, sometimes watching television, sometimes working (Max especially tended to work a few hours after the kids were in bed), the nanny would crawl out onto the roof, pull out a hidden ashtray, light up some sort of cigarette, and smoke for a bit.

Why would she smoke on the roof? I understood why she was smoking outside—neither Max nor Julia smoked, so they of course wouldn't want it in their home. But sneaking through the window and sitting on the roof implied a forbidden habit. You would think if smoking outside was acceptable, she would simply go out the back door and sit on the porch.

I filed that juicy little nugget away.

Weekends were a little different, but not as much as I would have thought. Both parents worked Saturday morning, at least I assumed. Julia headed off to her mysterious errand before locking herself back in her office for at least a few hours. Max left as well in the morning, returning early afternoon, or sometimes, even later. The kids watched some television, Saturday morning cartoons probably, if that was still a thing, before heading out for a walk or visit to the park. It was only after the parents wrapped up whatever it was they were doing that the nanny got a break. She didn't cook Saturday nights; apparently, Saturday was pizza night. And Sunday was her day off.

I could always tell when the nanny had some time off, because she would leave the house. I wondered if that was because she didn't want to be called back to duty during her limited off hours. Especially Sunday nights, when Julia appeared to be lost in the kitchen as she tried to prepare some sort of meal. Max kept the kids out of her hair; actually, Max appeared to be in charge of the kids both Saturday and Sunday, but even that didn't seem to help Julia much. She still seemed overwhelmed and frustrated, even requiring wine to get started.

I wondered why Julia even had three children, considering raising them seemed to be such a source of stress for her.

When I started my surveillance, a part of me assumed I would end up getting most of my questions answered. Maybe not all of them, but enough so I'd at least be clear on whether or not

Julia and her family were to blame for Kelly/Ashley's abrupt disappearance.

Instead, the longer I watched, the more questions I had. Was it because Julia was strangely hands-off when it came to the rearing of her own children? The nanny seemed to be the real mother.

Had Ashley felt the pressure of all that responsibility? Or maybe something had happened, and Julia blamed Ashley? Maybe even blamed her unfairly?

Or maybe it was because Max had smiled and flirted with Ashley like he was doing with the current nanny. Comparing Ashley's looks with the odd-looking girl currently working for them, it was pretty much a given.

Had Max taken it further with Ashley?

Was that the real reason she left?

Or maybe there really was a stalker, and Julia and Max were blissfully unaware. Neither one of them struck me as terribly observant, as both seemed more focused on their work than their family or each other.

Really, the only one who seemed aware of her surroundings was the oldest girl. Again and again, I observed her sitting quietly in her home, studying the adults around her, taking in what they said and didn't say, and how they interacted with the world.

Sometimes, she'd even stare right out into the woods, seemingly directly at my hiding spot, and I'd find myself holding my breath, my heart beating frantically, sure she knew I was there, and I was about to be found out.

But, if she did see anything, she never gave any indication.

No question, that little girl definitely knew more than the adults around her.

I wondered if she knew what happened to Ashley.

And that's when I knew I had to do more than figure out how to talk to Julia. I had to find a way into that house. I had to experience what my sister experienced. I needed to find a way to get that little girl to trust me and open up to me, so she could tell me what she knew.

Because it was clear she was far wiser than her years.

What I needed to do was become the new nanny.

* * *

"You think this is a good idea?" Bryn asked doubtfully.

She was sitting on the faded, brown, plaid couch, and I was sprawled out on the floor, both of us with glasses of cheap red wine in hand.

I hadn't laid out my full plan to become the new nanny to Bryn—even I knew it sounded a little crazy. Instead, I told her I was going to try to become friends with Julia, eventually maybe offering to be a backup babysitter, or something.

I knew if I told Bryn I wanted be the new nanny, she would have questions. Plenty of them, and none of which I particularly wanted to answer. After all, the Johnsons already had a nanny, even if she wasn't all that great. So, before I could get myself hired, I was going to have to find some way to get the current nanny out … whether she quit or was fired didn't really concern me. I hadn't quite figured that part out yet.

I had no interest in hurting the nanny; I bore her no ill will. But, even after just a few days of observing them, it seemed pretty clear she wasn't terribly happy doing what she was doing. Quite honestly, it felt like I would be doing her, and the entire family, a favor by encouraging her to gracefully exit the situation.

"I want to find a way to meet Julia," I said. "I'm thinking if I can figure out where she hangs out, especially if it's somewhere conducive to having a friendly chat, I can get to know her and start asking questions about Ashley."

Bryn eyed me. "You don't think she'll be suspicious?"

I shrugged and took a sip of wine. "Why? It'd just be a friendly chat. I'm new to Redemption and looking for a friend."

Bryn sipped her wine. "I don't know, Janey. First off, don't you have classes to finish?"

"I got an extension," I said. "I explained I had a personal emergency come up, and I needed some time off."

Bryn sighed. "You're so close to finishing this semester, though."

"But this *is* an emergency," I insisted. "Kelly, or Ashley, is gone. She might be in trouble. The trail is already more than two months cold. I need to act now, and fast, if there is any hope of tracking her down."

Bryn opened her mouth like she wanted to argue, but then she closed it and gave me a sad smile. Her thoughts were written all over her face: waiting a few weeks for the semester to be over wouldn't make that much of a difference—that it would be better to finish the semester and spend the summer figuring out what happened to Kelly.

But Bryn wasn't alone in the world. Her parents and siblings were alive and well. She could reach out to them any time she wanted, and they would respond. She had no idea what it was like to be the only one left of your family … to have no parents and no idea where your only living relative was.

"How can I help?" she asked instead.

I gave her a grateful smile. "For now, just being a sounding board is perfect," I said. "I know you don't have a lot of time."

"I should have more in a few weeks, though," she said. "And I'd be happy to do whatever I can."

"I appreciate that," I said.

"So, how are we going to figure out where Julia hangs out?" she asked. "Do you want to check her profile again?"

I had gone over and over her profile already, and I still couldn't figure out where she went in the mornings. But I hadn't looked specifically for her hangouts, so I dutifully pulled out my phone.

"Here," Bryn pointed. "I've seen this park in a few pictures. She probably takes the kids there regularly. Maybe if you can hang out there, you'll find some way to naturally start a conversation."

"Good idea," I said, although based on my observations, I didn't think I would ever find Julia at the park. More likely than not, that was where the nanny took the kids after picking them up for school. She probably took those pictures as well, maybe so Julia could see how much fun the kids were having, and Julia posted them on her account.

Nevertheless, I made a note of it. Maybe finding that park and striking up a chat with the nanny actually made more sense.

We went through the profile a few more times, but weren't able to find anything else. We even tried to figure out who the new nanny was, but there weren't any links or names mentioned at all. The last thing we checked was Ashley's profile, to see if there had been anything new posted there, but it was still the same as before.

"I'd love to help more, but I still have studying to do," Bryn said.

I tossed my phone onto the coffee table. "Yeah, I'm actually beat myself. I think I'll turn in early and see how things look in the morning."

Of course, that wasn't the real reason I would be up early. My plan was to be at Julia's house when the sun came up, so I would be in a good position to follow her.

Chapter 7

As it turned out, Julia was spending her mornings at a coffee shop.

It was called The Brew House, and it looked like a Starbucks knockoff. Along with a variety of coffee drinks, they offered several baked goods.

From what I could make out, Julia bought herself a large coffee drink, something like a latte, and a bagel and cream cheese. Then, she would sit in the corner at a table scribbling in a notebook. Every now and then, she would remove an iPad out of her bag and switch between that and the notebook.

I was fascinated. Why was she sitting in a coffee shop when she had a lovely home she could work in? And what was she writing? Did she come here every day, or was this a one-off?

I knew I needed more data, which meant waiting another 24 hours until the next morning. So that afternoon, I decided to follow the nanny when she picked up the kids.

It was exactly as I had assumed. The little group walked over to the same park we saw on Instagram. It was grassy and spacious, and filled with trees, benches, and a pretty extensive playground. The two older children played on the equipment while the nanny sat on a park bench and played with her phone (no surprise there), her foot gently rocking the baby stroller. I circled the park once or twice before heading back to the house and my little backyard hiding place.

It didn't take long at all before my surveillance became a regular routine. I followed Julia to The Brew House every morning and waited for the nanny at the park every afternoon. I didn't think it was wise to keep following her to the school—too many people who might notice me. Plus, the school could have surveillance.

In between, I kept an eye on the house and watched for changing patterns. But there were none.

Julia always sat at the same table with the same drink and the same bagel in front of her. The nanny always sat at the same park bench.

After a few days, I decided it was time to make my move.

My plan was to befriend Julia. Or at least, strike up enough of a conversation to see how I might best get rid of the nanny. So, I started by arriving at the coffee shop ten minutes before Julia normally showed up. I bought the same thing I knew she would, a latte and bagel and cream cheese, and sat next to her normal table. I also bought a copy of the local paper, *The Redemption Times*, and had it opened to the Want Ads.

The first couple of days, Julia ignored me, but I forced myself to stay the course. I didn't want to rush things. It was important she didn't suspect anything.

Following the nanny became something I did just to break up my afternoons. I also didn't think it a bad idea to keep an eye on her. Who knew what else I would discover on my daily walk around the park? Maybe the nanny would end up doing something stupid that I could use to my advantage.

Even though I had no intention of striking up a conversation with the nanny, the opportunity presented itself.

It started as a normal afternoon—the kids on the playground, the nanny on the park bench, and the baby in the stroller. As I ambled around the park, I was mulling about Julia. She had progressed to nodding at me in greeting as she sat down with her bagel and coffee, which on one hand, was great. I was thrilled she was starting to acknowledge my presence. But I was also keenly aware that the process was taking too long. I could hear the ticking clock in my head—each day I wasted trying to work my way into Julia's house was another day Kelly drifted further and further away from me.

A sudden movement caught the corner of my eye, jerking me out of my thoughts. The nanny had jumped to her feet and was running across the park.

For a moment, I thought something had happened to one of the kids, so I immediately started searching for them, sure I was about to see one of them in some sort of danger or distress. But no. The girl was swinging on the tire swing, and the boy was clattering across the wooden bridge.

I looked back to find the nanny and saw she was already halfway across the park, heading toward a clump of woods.

Where was she going? What was going on?

I looked back to the park bench, and my jaw dropped.

She had left the baby alone!

The stroller was in the exact place it always was. Even from where I stood, I could see the baby inside, trying to get a set of big, plastic, colorful keys into its mouth.

The nanny's back had almost disappeared into the trees, leaving me standing there wildly trying to keep an eye on the two kids on the playground and the baby in the stroller at the same time.

What kind of nanny runs off into the woods and leaves her charges alone? At a park? Where any stranger could stroll by and snatch them, and no one would be the wiser?

It took me a split second to make a decision, and then, I was hurrying across the park. Someone had to be the grown up, and apparently, it had to be me.

Good thing I was there.

I slowed down as I got closer to the bench and stroller. If anyone was watching, I didn't want them to think I was planning on stealing anyone's children. I just wanted to be close enough so if anything were to happen, I could jump in and stop it.

The baby, a girl, it would seem, looked up at me as I approached, gurgling happily. She was wearing a pink shirt with purple elephants and had a pink ribbon in her sparse, blonde hair. Her eyes were round and blue as she gazed at me, kicking her legs and mouthing her plastic key ring.

I couldn't help but smile at her joy. "Well, hello there. What a cutie. Aren't you a happy girl? You are a girl, right? You're dressed like a little ..."

"What are you doing?" a voice shrieked at me.

I turned and saw the nanny running toward me. "Get away from her," she yelled. "I'll call the police." She waved her phone.

I squared my shoulders and faced her. "Go ahead and do that. I'll be happy to share how I saw you run off, leaving this baby alone. Maybe Social Services would like to have a conversation with you about that."

She stared at me, the blood draining from her already pale skin. Now that I was closer, I could see she had a silver stud in her nose and a silver skull dangling from one ear lobe. "It's not what you think," she said, her voice low.

I put my hands on my hips. "Then what is it? I came over here when I saw you dart off to God knows where. I figured someone should keep an eye on your baby."

She swallowed hard and leaned over the baby, who looked up at while her grinning wildly. "She's not my baby. I'm her nanny," she said.

"Oh, so that makes it better, then?"

She shook her head, her black hair falling into her face. "No, that's not what I meant. I'm trying to protect them."

Protect them? I glanced over to the clump of trees she had run toward. Was there someone there? I felt the hairs go up on the back of my neck as I studied the area, and for a moment, was sure I saw a shadow. "Protect them from what?"

She didn't answer right away. I could see her shoulders heaving beneath her black hoodie. "It's just ... I thought I saw someone."

"What do you mean, you 'thought you saw someone'?" My voice rose an octave. Was the stalker over there? Was it Oz?

"It's nothing. It's fine."

"So, no one was there?"

"No. Yes. Look, it's not a big deal. I took care of it."

"No big deal?" My voice went up an octave. "If there's a child predator hanging around the park, it *is* a big deal. We should call the police." I yanked my phone out, trying to remember the name of that detective. Maybe Bryn was right after all, and I needed to tell him about Oz. Maybe this would be the break they needed to finally find Kelly ... or Ashley ... or whatever her name was ...

"No. Wait." The nanny lunged forward, like she was going to knock the phone out of my hand. "Don't call."

I held the phone away from her. "Why not? Don't you think the police need to be involved?"

She was frantically biting her lip. "Look, it's not what you think, okay?"

"I don't understand ..."

"There was a nanny before me," she said in a rush. "She left, or disappeared, or something. Anyway, this guy ... he's looking for answers, and sometimes, he just shows up."

I stared at her aghast. "Has he been questioned by the police? Maybe he knows something."

"I think so. I don't know. Look, it's not a big deal. Honest. I can handle him. I have to get going." She grabbed the handles of the stroller and took off toward the playground yelling "Kids! We have to go. We're late. Come on." The stroller shook dangerously as she pushed it over the uneven ground. I heard groans as at least one of the kids protested leaving.

I watched her for a moment before realizing how exposed I was standing there. Slowly, I began melting backward toward the trees. The nanny threw a quick peek over her shoulder, as if to keep an eye on me, before focusing on corralling the two older children.

I started circling the park again, careful not to make it too obvious I was headed to where she had run. She would probably find my checking over the area weird—even weirder than what had already occurred between us. Hopefully, she would dismiss me as a nosy stranger, and that would be it.

Because the last thing I wanted was for her to be on guard. If she was, it might take me longer to set my plan into action.

And I couldn't afford any more wasted time. I had to get rid of her as quickly as possible.

The Third Nanny

Chapter 8

The next day, I decided I had to make my move with Julia.

As soon as the nanny had disappeared from view the day before, two reluctant kids in tow, I searched the park. Twice. I didn't find any strange men, but what I did find was a stubbed-out, half-smoked cigarette.

Was that from whoever the nanny had chased? Or had someone else left it?

It was impossible for me to know for sure, but even looking at it made my skin crawl.

Oz was a smoker. I could still remember the stink of the smoke on his clothes, his breath.

The whole situation had ratcheted my anxiety even higher than it already was, which is why I was even more determined to get the ball rolling with Julia.

As usual, I got to The Brew House early and positioned myself at the same table. I waited until Julia made herself comfortable in her usual spot before I made my move.

I stood up to head to the bathroom, and as I walked by Julia's table, I "accidentally" knocked over her coffee.

When I envisioned it in my head, I had seen the cup rolling around the table dribbling coffee. I would apologize profusely, fetch a rag to clean it up, offer to buy her another (which she would likely refuse, as not much had spilled) and in the lull, find a way to ask her if I could pick her brain about Redemption.

Needless to say, that wasn't what happened at all.

Instead, it was an utter disaster.

Unfortunately, either the lid wasn't on the cup tightly enough, or I used more force than I had intended, because when I knocked it over, the lid flew off, and all the contents spilled out at once, spreading across the table like a black tidal wave.

Julia jumped to her feet, but it was too late. Coffee spilled into her lap, soaking her grey leggings and staining her blue tunic. Worse, it also drenched part of her notebook.

"Oh my God," I said, horrified. "I am SO sorry. Here let me get ..."

I didn't even finish my sentence before one of the employees appeared with a rag and started wiping up the mess.

I grabbed a handful of napkins and hurried over to help Julia, who seemed torn between cleaning her clothes or her notebook. I kept apologizing as I pressed them into her hand.

"It's fine," she said shortly. "I'm going to the bathroom to clean up." She shook her notebook again, trying to shake as much liquid out as possible before disappearing into the bathroom.

"Of course," I said, shifting from one foot to the other. How was I going to fix such a colossal blunder?

"Do you know what she had?" I asked the young girl who was wiping up the table. Her black hair was streaked pink on one side; her nails were painted a bright purple; and she had a sparkling red stone piercing in her nose. She reminded me vaguely of an Easter egg. "I'll buy her another."

"You don't have to," she said. "We'll replace it on the house. It was an accident."

But it wasn't, I wanted to shout. *I really ought to pay for it, along with her cleaning bill and a new notebook*. But I held my tongue.

"Thanks," I said. She gave me a quick smile as she finished wiping the table.

I chewed on my thumbnail as I anxiously watched the bathroom door, waiting for Julia to come out. It seemed to be taking much longer than it should. Everything was tidied up and a replacement coffee on the table before she finally emerged, clothes dripping wet.

"I'm so sorry," I said again as she took her seat.

"It's fine," she said, waving me off. "I shouldn't have had my coffee so close to the end of the table."

"I can pay for your cleaning if you need it," I said. "Or a new notebook."

"Really, I'm fine," she said shortly, turning away. Her shoulders were tense as she surveyed the damage to her notebook, shaking her head as she pulled the wet pages apart.

Clearly, I was being dismissed.

Biting my lip, I stared at my folded newspaper, the various circled job opportunities and apartments for rent swimming before my eyes.

Janey, you really can't do anything right, Kelly said in my head, disgust in her voice. *I mean, come on. How difficult is it to knock over a cup of coffee? But, no ... you somehow manage to turn it into the Titanic of coffee spills.*

It's not my fault, I tried to argue. *How could I know the lid wasn't on?*

But it was no use. Kelly was right. How stupid could I be? What an idiot. Stupid, stupid, stupid.

I could feel the tears hovering behind my eyes, threatening to spill over. I blinked rapidly, trying to stop them. *I can't cry*, I told myself firmly. *No one is going to understand. All I did was accidentally spill someone's coffee. That's not something people cry about.*

But despite my best efforts, a couple of tears dripped down my nose and onto the newspaper. Absurd. I was just so frustrated. How did I manage to screw everything up so badly? Not only did I ruin my chances of having an informal chat with Julia, but she surely wouldn't be open to hiring me as her nanny after all this.

A couple napkins appeared in my vision. I looked up to see the Easter-egg girl. She gave me a sympathetic smile. "It's going to be okay," she said. "These things happen."

I forced myself to smile back, even though I could feel the entire situation quickly unraveling. Maybe the best thing to do was to just get out of there. Retreat, lick my wounds, and try again another time. Maybe I could make a joke about it the next day ...

"Hey."

Julia had turned toward me, her voice soft. "Really. I'm okay. I'm sorry if I was too abrupt. I know it wasn't anyone's fault."

I dabbed at my eyes and blew my nose, an idea blossoming in my mind. "You don't have to be sorry. I ruined your notebook and maybe even your clothes."

She glanced down at her wet tunic and leggings. "The clothes are going to be fine. I was able to rinse them off in time. As for my notebook," she shrugged and gave me a self-deprecating smile. "It's probably a sign that what I was doing wasn't all that important, anyhow." There was a bitterness to her voice that seemed disproportionate to my mistake.

"You should definitely not take my clumsiness as a sign of anything other than my having a bad day," I said, hoping that would be enough to defuse the strange tension in the air.

Her smile became more of a friendly grin. "I guess we're both having a day, then. Should we swap war stories?" She patted the chair next to her.

"Sure," I said, trying to tamp down the excitement in my voice. I was experiencing emotional whiplash—from the despair around my plan being in tatters to the giddiness of it working out exactly as I had originally envisioned. I gathered my coffee, bagel, and newspaper and sat next to her.

"I'm Julia, by the way," she said once I was settled.

It was on the tip of my tongue to say, "I know," but at the last moment, I managed to swallow the words. "Janey," I said.

"Nice to meet you, Janey. Did you just move here? I haven't seen you before the last few days."

I dropped my gaze to my bagel. "That's part of why I'm having a bad day," I said. "Well, actually, it's turning into a bad week. I'm trying to move here, but it's just not working out."

She gestured toward my folded newspaper. "Job hunting not going so well?"

"Or apartment hunting," I said with a sigh. "I just feel like I'm hitting one brick wall after another."

She nodded in sympathy. "What are you looking for?"

"Really, anything that will pay the bills. I'm not picky." I laughed, but it sounded a little forced. "I'm taking a break from things and was hoping I could live here for a little while until I sorted stuff out."

"God, I would love a break," she said, picking up her coffee. "I totally get that."

"What do you need a break from?"

"My life," she said with a forced laugh. "Sorry. It's really ... I should be grateful, I know. I'm so lucky in so many ways." Her tone didn't match her words. One of her hands crept over to the notebook to pick at the wet pages. "But, enough about me and my tale of woe. Let's finish with you. Why do you need a break?"

I sighed. "It's been ... well, it's a rough year. Last summer, my parents died in a car crash." Julia's eyes went wide. "As you can imagine, it's been hard. I tried to keep going, but it's just not working out, so I decided it was time for a break."

"I'm so sorry to hear this," she said.

"Thank you."

"That's just so terrible," she went on. "I can't even imagine. I have three kids, and the idea of leaving them without their mother or their father ... I can't even contemplate it."

"Yeah, it was tough," I said. "But, you know, there's nothing much you can do other than keep moving forward. So, that's what I'm trying to do."

"What are you taking a break from?" she asked. "Are you in school?"

I nodded.

"What are you studying?"

"Psychology. Specifically, child psychology." I actually had no desire to be a child psychologist, but Julia didn't need to know that, especially since I was betting she would love to hire a nanny who was in some sort of child-centric field. As I watched the eagerness flit across Julia's face, I could see I was right. "I love kids," I continued, trying to gush a little. "So eventually, I'm hoping to make a career out of helping them."

"That's incredible," she said, but then her face fell. "I wish we had had this conversation a month ago."

I arranged my face in a puzzled expression. "Really? What was happening a month ago?"

"That's when I hired my new nanny."

"You have a nanny?" I widened my eyes in surprise.

She nodded. "Live-in, actually. Oh, it would have been perfect for you. You wouldn't have had to worry about an apartment or a job. You could have just focused on doing something you loved."

"Oh, that does suck," I said with a sigh. "The story of my life. Bad timing, bad luck." I shook my head. "Well, enough of that. I'm sure the nanny you hired is working out, right?"

"Yeess," she said, drawing the word out slowly, her face unreadable. Then she gave herself a shake. "Yes, I think so. The kids seem to like her, and that's what's most important."

Ah! Now we were getting somewhere. I was so pumped up, I wanted to do a little dance to burn off some of my elation, but I forced myself to take deep breaths and move slow. The last thing I wanted to do was scare her off by pouncing on her opening.

Instead, I cocked my head and gave her a knowing look. "But do *you* like her?"

She let out another one of her forced laughs. "I actually don't know. No one has asked me that." She paused, pondering the question. "I guess it's not really about me liking her or not. It's more about trust."

"Trust?"

"Yeah. I'm not sure if she's being completely honest with me."

Ohhhh. This was so perfect. I couldn't believe my luck. I just had to make sure to contain my emotions and keep moving slow. "How so?"

"Well, it's kind of hard to explain. It's more like a feeling. So, for instance, cooking is part of the job duties. Not only making breakfast, lunch, and snacks for the kids, but also cooking dinner for the entire family. Heather told me when I hired her that she loved to cook."

I blinked. *Heather?* That awkward, goth-looking girl I met in the park was named "Heather"? I had imagined something a little more exotic and strange, like maybe "Drusilla" or "Zelda." "Heather" was the name of the quiet, plain girl who, after removing her glasses and shaking out her hair, was transformed into a beauty. The girl who kept nervously insisting everything was fine the day before seemed about as far away from a "Heather" as I could imagine.

Julia was still talking, so I forced my attention back to her. "... so excited, because making sure my family was eating healthy, homemade meals is a priority. I personally am a terrible cook, and I don't want my family eating takeout and frozen dinners all the time. But, her meals are ... lackluster, I guess. Just no real imagination or thought behind them. For instance, yesterday she made spaghetti, which of course the kids loved. But she just threw it together. Just the pasta and sauce, garlic bread, and a salad with only lettuce and tomatoes, no other vegetables. It probably took her ten minutes. And I swear the sauce tasted like it came from a jar. I even searched the trash," here, her face reddened, "but there was nothing there. Actually, there was nothing at all in there—no cans of tomato sauce or anything. So I casually asked her about it. Just like, 'Hey, that was pretty good. How did you make it?' And she was really vague. 'Oh, a little of this, a little of that. I never cook with a recipe ... it's just what comes to me.' And, before I could ask her more questions, she said she had to check on the kids and left the room. I just feel like she's lying to me. And if she lied to me about loving to cook, what else might she be lying about?

"And then there's the smoke."

My eyes widened. An image of Heather on the rooftop, the red glowing spark near her face, flashed through my mind. "Smoke?"

"I told her smoking was not allowed," Julia said, squishing up her face as if she could smell it. "I especially emphasized smoking pot was strictly prohibited. Nicotine is bad enough, even if she used an e-cigarette. I don't want the children exposed to that nasty habit. But pot, that's completely unacceptable. Not only is it illegal, but I can't have her taking care of my children when she's high. That's just not an option. Anyway, during the interview, she assured me she was a nonsmoker and didn't use pot. But there are times when I can smell it on her. I get a whiff of her clothes, and they smell like something—I think it's pot. But when I ask her, she keeps denying it. Says she doesn't smoke. I ask her why it smells like smoke, and she says she sometimes lights candles in her room, and I must be smelling the smoke from the candle. She's showed me the candles, and some of them are sweet, like pot, but I light candles, and I don't remember my clothes ever smelling like smoke. It makes no sense to me."

She stopped talking, frowning as she stared at her wet notebook. "Sorry," she said. "I didn't mean to go off like that. I guess I'm more frustrated that I thought. I really hate it when people lie to me, you know? And I just have this feeling ... well ..." She gave her head a quick shake. "I'm probably just being paranoid."

"It's okay," I said. "You did say you were having a bad day, as well."

She glanced up, her lips twisting in her attempt to smile. "Yeah, I did. But it's not about Heather. Well, not completely. It's just ..." she paused and gestured with her hands. "It's everything."

"Everything?"

"I know how it sounds," she said, biting her lip. "I have a beautiful home, a loving husband, three incredible children, and a live-in nanny. Everything I want. I should be happy, right? So why do I feel so ... empty? Like life is passing me by, and I'm just going through the motions. And then, sometimes I start to think I must be a bad person. Because if I were a good person, I wouldn't have these thoughts, right? So I try to shove them down. After all, I love my family. This *is* the life I want. I need to focus on what's in front of me.

"Then other times, I think to myself, what if it all were to disappear?" She snapped her fingers. "Poof. All gone. Just like that. And if that happened, would I be heartbroken? Or would I be ... *happier?*"

Julia paused, clamping her lips together as if she were afraid of what else would spill out if she wasn't careful. She gave her head a quick shake and let out a short, waspish laugh. "I know, I know. First-world problems, right?"

I tried to smile back, but it felt forced and brittle. "Right." Inside, I was seething. She DID have it all. A beautiful family and home—a place where she belonged. She wasn't an orphan. She didn't have a sister who wanted nothing to do with her. She had everything she could possibly want, that anyone could possibly want, and instead of enjoying it, she was sitting in a coffee shop alone feeling sorry for herself.

But I couldn't say any of that. Not if I wanted the one chance I had to find my sister and maybe not be so alone in the world. I had to suck it up and be as sweet and sympathetic as possible.

"So, why do you think you're so unhappy?" I asked. "Or is that what you're trying to figure out?" I nodded toward the notebook.

She studied the soggy pages. "No, not really. Well, sort of. It's just ... well, it's silly, really. It's just something I need."

Clearly, she was hiding something, but what? A part of me wanted to push and get it out of her, but my instinct told me to back off. If I went too far, I risked upsetting her, and she might decide not to hire me. Instead, I bit my tongue and smiled sympathetically at her.

She picked up her coffee, but her arm jerked to a halt on the way to her mouth. "Oh my God! Look at the time. I have to go. I'm late." She jumped to her feet, grabbing her purse and notebook before snatching the coffee from the table.

"Oh, okay. What about the bagel? Do you want me to get you a bag?" I was already turning to gesture to the Easter-egg girl, but Julia was shaking her head.

"No time. I have to go. But I'll see you here tomorrow, right?" I nodded, trying to keep my excitement from bubbling over. "Thanks, Janey. I really enjoyed talking to you."

"I enjoyed talking to you, too," I said, but she was already flying out the door, her purse flapping behind her.

I went back to my coffee and bagel, taking my time as I began sketching out my plan for the day. Even though it was Friday, I still had a lot of things to do, especially since I had decided that Monday would be the day Heather would leave her nanny position.

Tuesday would be the day Julia would offer it to me.

And, of course, I would accept.

Chapter 9

My plan was simple.

I was going to wait until Heather left to pick up the kids and take them to the park. Then, I'd climb onto the roof, find her ashtray, and drop it to the ground in front of the back door.

This way, when Max came home, he would see the mess. He'd then call Julia to come see, who would in turn call Heather to come out, and the whole thing would unravel.

It was like pulling at a piece of knitting and watching the stitches collapse into a single strand of yarn.

I couldn't wait.

In the meantime, I had two hurdles to overcome.

The first was getting onto the roof, which seemed fairly straightforward. The roof was slanted, and there was a white trellis covered by a dead vine that appeared sturdy enough to climb. I wished it were later in the summer. A thick, green, thriving vine would probably make it easier.

But, no matter. I would make do.

The second hurdle was Julia, of course. She would be home, so I'd have to make sure she didn't hear me. Hopefully, she would be on a meeting with her headset on, like she was most days. Plus, her office was on the first floor. She really shouldn't suspect a thing.

Still. The worry niggled at me.

I stayed in my hiding place until I saw Heather leave to collect the kids from school. I carefully shifted positions, so I could watch her until she disappeared around the corner.

I had roughly 45 minutes—it was a ten-minute walk to the school, a ten-minute walk home, and about thirty minutes of play.

Should be plenty of time.

But before I did anything, I needed to check on Julia. I found her sitting at her desk, staring at her computer. She wasn't talking, but that didn't mean she wasn't on a meeting.

I carefully emerged from my hiding space, glancing around to make sure no one saw me before crossing the backyard and approaching the back of the house. I was pretty sure neither of Julia's neighbors were home at that time of day, but I found myself holding my breath regardless, waiting for the moment someone would fling open a window and start screaming at me.

But despite my fears, nothing happened. Around me, everything was silent, even my footsteps in the thick, green grass. The birds didn't even chirp.

So far, so good.

I reached up to grasp one of the rungs of the trellis and immediately realized my miscalculation. The wood was flimsy and barely attached to the siding. There was no way it would hold my weight.

I stood there, hands on my hips, searching for something else I could grab onto and use to hoist myself up. But there was nothing.

Idiot, Kelly's voice in my head. I *told you this plan would never work. None of your plans ever work.*

I ground my teeth together. No, I wouldn't listen. This was too important. I *had* to get on that roof.

What I needed was a boost. Even better, a ladder. But of course, there was nothing like that lying around the backyard.

But maybe there was something in the garage? Assuming I could get in, of course.

It was worth a shot.

There was a side door I could try. It would likely be locked, but maybe it would be flimsy enough for me to break.

Right. You can pick a lock.

I didn't say 'pick,' I answered Kelly's voice in my head. *I said 'break.'*

I gave myself a shake. Was I really arguing with myself? Time was quickly ticking away. I had to get focused and moving.

I quickly moved to the side of the house toward the garage door and realized the second problem—I would have to pass by Julia's office to get there. I had spent enough time watching her profile in the window to know her desk was right on the other side.

I was going to have to be very careful. Even if she was on a meeting, she still could hear something or catch a glimpse of me walking by.

I bent over as low as I could and scuttled past the window, hardly daring to breathe, moving as quickly and silently as possible. I didn't stop until I reached the side door.

As soon as I got there, I realized I'd made a huge mistake. I was more exposed than I thought. Anyone walking or driving by would see me, not to mention the houses across the street. I had assumed they worked during the day, but what if I was wrong? What if there was someone home who I'd just missed?

I briefly considered other options, if I couldn't find something to get me on the roof. How else could I get Heather fired? I could try talking to Julia … convince her that Heather was all wrong. But that might take too long.

No, I had to do this now. Every moment I wasn't Julia's nanny was another moment that Kelly/Ashley's trail went cold. Not to mention the kids being at risk. Every time I thought about Heather's bizarre behavior at the park, I got chills. And if Oz was still around, I had to find him as quickly as possible.

I reached up and grasped the doorknob, sure it would be locked. To my utter astonishment, it turned easily in my hand.

Well, well.

I was about to slip into the garage when I heard the harsh, muted sound of a cell phone ring.

For a moment, I froze. Where was it coming from? Was it mine? Was there someone else home?

Then, I realized it was Julia's.

Before I really thought it through, I ducked into the garage and closed the door quietly behind me.

Inside was dim, but the dirt and cobweb-infested window brought in enough light to allow me to see. It looked like a normal garage, stuffed with a variety of tools, outdoor toys, and other odds and ends, and barely enough space for the two cars, one of which was gone. It smelled of gas, motor fluid, and old grass clippings.

I began searching for a ladder when I realized I could hear Julia's voice. I couldn't make out any specific words, but her tone seemed angry.

What was she so upset about?

I found myself drifting closer to the door to see if I could better make out her side of the conversation.

Her voice seemed to be bouncing around, like she was striding through the house, moving from room to room as she talked. But why? I never saw her walk around during the day. She always stayed in her office, usually with the door closed.

Unless ...

I ducked behind a plastic garbage can in the nick of time. The door between the garage and house flung open, and Julia marched out. "I'm leaving right now," she yelled into the phone while her other finger stabbed at a button and the garage door clattered open. "Yes, I'll be there in five minutes, maybe ten," she said, holding the phone between her shoulder and her chin while she dug around in her purse for her keys.

It was a good thing she was making such a commotion, or she might have noticed me huddled in the corner, holding my breath. My heart was pounding so loud, I was sure she would hear it, but logically, I knew better. What I was more worried about was my hiding place. It didn't disguise me very well, with the trash can only blocking half of me. But I was too afraid to move more behind it. If she looked in the right direction, I knew she'd see me. Luckily, all her attention was focused on getting into her car, starting it, and backing out of the driveway. I waited until she had disappeared and the garage door had firmly closed behind her before straightening up. I took a moment to check to see if I had knocked anything over or shifted anything out of place, but there was so much junk strewn about so haphazardly, I didn't think anyone would notice if I had.

My heart was still pounding, and my breathing was ragged. I stood for a minute, pressing my hand against my chest and willing myself to relax. I needed my wits about me if I was going to be able to quickly drag that ladder to the back of the house and get on the roof. I needed to move fast before Heather returned ...

Wait a minute.

The house was empty.

I didn't need to screw around with a ladder. I could just walk in the garage door, up the stairs, into Heather's room, and open the window and climb onto the roof.

I had watched her do it multiple times. No question that would be the easiest way.

Except ... I glanced at the closed garage door. Did I dare? What if Julia came home as quickly as she'd left? What if Heather came back early?

From inside the house, it would be much more difficult to get away if something went wrong. It would be a lot easier to sneak away if I were already outside.

But did I even have time anymore to screw around with a ladder? I was going to have to drag it to the backyard, climb on the roof, and then bring it back to the garage. I would be far more exposed outside. A neighbor who happened to be walking his dog would certainly notice me carrying a ladder in Julia's yard, whereas that same neighbor would have no idea if I were in the house.

It definitely made more sense to go through the house.

I still couldn't move.

You better do something, and do it quick, Kelly's voice said. *Otherwise, that garage door is going to open, and Julia is going to find you still standing here. Want to try and explain that?*

That broke me out of my paralysis. I carefully picked my way to the door to the house. A part of me wondered what that phone call was about and where Julia had gone. I hadn't seen her do anything even remotely like that the whole time I'd been watching her. Her daily patterns were always the same. She never did anything spontaneous, much less run out in the middle of a workday.

So, what could have possibly caused her to up and bolt?

I couldn't focus on that. I had an ashtray to break. Then, I could try to piece together the mystery of Julia's phone call.

The door opened easily, and I was about to step inside when I noticed a keypad for an alarm system. I froze, one foot still in the air. Was the alarm set? Was I about to be found out after all?

I took a closer look and realized it wasn't on. Julia must have been in too much of a hurry to set it. Or maybe she didn't think she would be gone long. Either way, it was time to move fast.

It was weird being in the house after spending so much time watching it, and it took me a bit to orient myself. Initially, I turned the wrong way on the second floor and almost walked into the master bedroom, but I quickly recovered and hurried to Heather's room.

Her door was closed, and for a moment, I was worried she had locked it. But the knob turned easily, and suddenly, I was inside.

The first thing I noticed was that Heather was a slob. Her dirty clothes were strewn on the floor, and her bed wasn't made. Plus, it stunk ... a revolting combination of stale sweat and overly sweet perfume. I wrinkled my nose in disgust.

For a moment, I fought the urge to rummage through her things. What else might I find if I went through her closet and drawers, or searched under her mattress? But no, I had a job to do, and time was ticking. I had completely lost track of it, though, and for all I knew, Heather was about to walk in the front door. Not to mention I had no clue when Julia would return home.

I went to the window, forced it open, and hoisted myself onto the roof. It was even easier than Heather had made it look. No wonder she went out there to smoke rather than sit inside next to the open window. It was flat and felt safe and secure. Like an outside porch.

I found the ashtray immediately. Heather hadn't even tried to hide it. All she did was push it up against the house. Now, in her defense, it likely would be difficult to spot if you were inside the house staring out a window, but once outside, it was obvious.

I picked it up. It was one of those big, heavy, old-fashioned ones made of thick glass. It was also full to the point of over-flowing with ash and stubbed out, half-smoked cigarettes. By the smell, they were definitely laced with pot.

Bullseye.

I walked over to the other side of the roof, right above the back door, and got ready to drop it. At the last minute, I re-moved a couple of the butts, in case I needed to position them in a more obvious place.

Then, I let go.

I heard the crack as it hit the cement. It bounced once, then tipped over on its side, spilling its contents. I leaned over to peer at it. As far as I could tell, it was still in one piece, although I could make out a crack down the middle. The ash had spilled in a heap next to it, darkening the white cement like a grey stain.

It couldn't have gone more perfectly.

It was time to get out of there. I hurried to the window, climbing through and shutting it firmly. Again, I paused; did I have time to dig through her things? No, I decided, feeling the pressure building in my chest.

Hurry. You're running out of time.

I was down the stairs and heading to the garage door when a movement caught my eye outside the living room window.

Heather. Pushing the stroller with the kids in tow. About to turn onto the front walkway.

I froze. Could I still make it to the garage? Maybe wait there until she got into the house, and then, creep out the side door?

The little boy left Heather's side to charge toward the front door. Was it locked? I didn't think Julia had checked anything before she left. I could hear the little footsteps pounding up the stairs. In another minute, he was going to fling open the door and see me standing there like an idiot.

Move! Kelly's voice shrieked in my head. *Don't just stand there. God, can't you do anything right?*

I took another step toward the door when I saw Heather pause, glancing to the side. The little footsteps also ceased.

That's when I heard the second noise.

The sound of the garage door opening.

My stomach hit the floor as fear flooded through me. I could even taste it—coppery, like my mouth was filled with old pennies.

The garage was out. I had to think fast.

"Mommy!" I heard the little voices shrieking outside the door and could see Heather still paused in the walkway, uncertain as to why Julia would be driving anywhere in the middle of the day when she otherwise never left the house.

I had precious few moments to act before I would be caught. I had to move. Immediately.

I dashed to the back of the house. The sliding glass door was locked, and also in full view of the front door. If Heather or one of the kids were to walk in …

My hands slipped as I tried turning the lock, either because they were sweating or shaking or both. I gritted my teeth as I struggled with it, the seconds pounding away in my head, and finally heard the satisfying "click" as it turned. I shoved open the door.

It was a deadbolt, so there was no way I would be able to lock it behind me, but I made sure to close it tightly.

Then, I ran like I had never run before, across the backyard and into the woods. There, I slid into my familiar hiding place, dirt and leaves showering into the air as I skidded to a stop and dropped flat on the earth, still trembling. My breathing was so loud, I was sure they could hear it at the front of the house.

I focused on the window, expecting to see them charge out after me, Julia's face round with shock. "Janey? What are you doing here?" she would yell.

But instead, I saw an empty house. A moment later, the little boy appeared, running to the kitchen, and then the girl, followed by Heather and Julia. Heather was holding the infant in her arms.

They must have joined Julia in the garage and walked into the house that way rather than using the front door. Clearly, no one had seen my attempt at sabotage, yet.

I pulled out the small, travel-sized binoculars I carried in my fanny pack, along with my keys and wallet, to get a better look. Julia appeared to be speaking to Heather in the hallway while the girl took a couple of juice boxes out of the fridge, handing one to her brother. Heather was bouncing the baby, her lips pressed into a thin line, her attention everywhere but on Julia, who was still talking to her.

Actually, the more I watched, the more I wondered if Julia was reprimanding Heather. Julia's face was flushed, and she seemed to be getting more and more agitated as Heather's mouth grew flatter and flatter.

What could Heather have done to get Julia so worked up? As far as I could tell, the day had proceeded normally.

Until Julia's call, that is.

Was Julia just taking her frustrations out on the nanny?

Impossible to tell.

Finally, Julia seemed finished. She stood there for a moment, hands on her hips, until Heather responded. Heather's chin was down, so I couldn't make out any words, but Julia seemed satisfied and walked past her en route to her office.

Heather moved into the kitchen, where the girl was helping her brother open the juice box. Her movements were jerky and abrupt. She yanked open the fridge and pulled out a bag of baby carrots and a container of some sort of dip. She dumped both items in the center of the table, said something, and then stalked out, still holding the baby.

I shook my head in disgust. Normally, Heather would make a little bit more effort with the kids' snack. At the very least, she could have put everything on a plate for them. I watched as the girl opened both items and helped her brother get some. That shouldn't be her job. Heather should be in the kitchen with them, maybe cutting up some celery, bell peppers, and an apple to go with the carrots. I could definitely see why Julia had issues with her.

On the second floor, a light snapped on in the baby's room, and I saw Heather lay the baby on the changing table. Well, maybe she had good reason for leaving the kids to fend for themselves with their snack, if she were tending to the baby. But she just stood there. The baby kicked her legs as Heather leaned against the table, head down, eyes closed. Her thin chest rose and fell deeply.

It appeared none of the kids were getting taken care of. I got that Julia probably upset her, but Heather likely deserved whatever dressing down she received. And, if she were a good nanny, she would set her own feelings aside to do her job. Maybe Julia wouldn't feel the need to reprimand her if she didn't do things like hide in the baby's room.

Honestly, I was doing them both a favor, here. Julia clearly needed a more caring nanny, and Heather would most certainly be happier in another job.

Back in the kitchen, the boy was happily munching on carrots and sipping his juice. The girl was on her knees, leaning across the table to dunk her carrot in the hummus when she suddenly paused, carrot in the air as a glop of hummus plopped back into the container, her gaze fixed on something outside.

I held my breath. Had she spotted the ashtray?

Still holding the carrot, which was now dripping humus down her arm and onto her yellow shirt (Heather really should have taken one more minute to at least give them plates), the girl clambered down off her chair and walked over to the back door. She peered through the window before reaching up to fumble with the door latch. It took her a minute—I wondered if she had inadvertently locked it. But eventually, she managed to slide it open.

She took a few steps outside toward the ashtray and peered down at it before squatting to take a closer look. I held my breath, hoping she wasn't going to try and clean it up.

"That's a dirty, icky habit," I muttered under my breath. "Don't touch anything. Go tell your mom."

She suddenly froze, cocking her head. My eyes widened as my heart leapt into my throat. She couldn't possibly have heard me.

But then her head swiveled around, and she gazed out toward the woods, right in my direction.

I bit my lip hard as I swore to myself. How could I be so utterly stupid? Did I just blow this whole thing? What was wrong with me? Everything was going so well, and then I just had to open my mouth.

I stayed as quiet as possible, not daring to move or breathe. Her gaze landed on my hiding place.

I started to panic. Did she see me after all? What was I going to do? Was there enough time for me to get out of there before she found me out?

I tensed my muscles, ready to bolt if she took as much as one step toward me. But then, the little boy saved me. I could hear him calling out to his sister as he scrambled off his chair and ran to the door. "Madison! What's going on? Why are you out there?"

"Don't come out here," she said, quickly standing up.

He stopped in the doorway. "What is it? What are you looking at?"

"I don't know," she said.

"It smells funny."

"I know. It looks like something was burned. See?" She pointed at one of the cigarettes.

"Why was something being burned?"

"I don't know. I think we have to get an adult."

"Should I get Heather?" he asked, bouncing from foot to foot.

No! I wanted to shout. *Go get your mom, not Heather!*

She thought for a bit. "We need to tell mom."

"But mom doesn't want us to bother her," he said. "Not unless this is an em-mer-gen-cie. Is this an em-mer-gen-cie, Madison?"

Madison looked down at the ashtray. "I ... maybe," she said. "Maybe we tell both of them."

The boy brightened. "Okay!" He turned and started running through the house, yelling for both his mother and Heather.

Madison took a bite of her carrot as she followed her brother into the house, shutting the door behind her. My breath let out in a whoosh. She had apparently forgotten about whatever had caught her attention in the woods.

Upstairs, I saw Heather press the heel of her hands against her face. I chuckled, even though I knew I shouldn't. Heather shouldn't be so quick to dismiss what her little charge had come to tell her. If she moved fast enough, she might be able to mitigate some of the damage.

Yet more proof of how she wasn't up to the job.

Julia was the first to emerge, striding down the hallway, looking just as frustrated and angry as she had earlier. The boy was trotting next to her, and I watched her lips move. "How many times have I told you not to bother me while I'm working?"

"But, mom," the boy wailed. "This might be an em-mer-gen-cie."

"Emergency? What emergency?"

The boy pointed. "Out there."

Julia followed her son's finger, and I watched as the red flush slowly drained from her face. The girl, Madison, was back in the kitchen. When she saw her mother, she started moving toward the door, but Julia waved her back.

She pulled the door open and took a few cautious steps forward, approaching the ashtray like it was a coiled snake waiting to strike. She stared at it for a few minutes, dumbfounded, before the red started creeping back up her neck and into her face.

She whipped her head toward the house. "Heather!" she bellowed at the top of her lungs. "Get down here!"

Upstairs, Heather dropped her hands and jerked her head up. Her face had gone pale, and I could see the fear and trepidation on her face.

The two older children were still in the kitchen, but they had backed up and were pressed against the island. They were holding hands, and the boy had his thumb in his mouth.

"Get down here," Julia yelled again. "Now!"

Scooping up the baby, still unchanged, she turned and disappeared from the room. A few moment later, she emerged in the kitchen. She glanced from Julia to the kids, her eyebrows going up in question. Then, Julia stamped her foot, and Heather's head snapped back around. At first, her expression was puzzled, but as she finally got a look at what Julia was standing over, her eyes grew round with horror.

"What is this?" Julia demanded.

"It's not ... it's not what you think," Heather said. Her voice was high, more like a squeak.

"This is an ashtray, right? And I see ash right here, right?" She nudged her toe on the grey smudge. "And what's this? Half-smoked cigarettes that happen to smell like P-O-T??"

"It's only on my days offs," Heather said. "And I don't smoke much. Just enough to take the edge off. You have a couple of glasses of wine at night ... it's the same thing."

"It's NOT the same thing," she snapped. "Drinking wine isn't illegal. And I'm paying YOU, not the other way around. I specifically asked you about smoking, and you said you didn't smoke at all! I told you smoking was NOT allowed in this house, and yet you were doing it anyway."

"But I wasn't," Heather said, her voice louder. She started pacing back and forth, trying to comfort the baby, whose face was starting to squish up and turn red.

"You're still lying to me," Julia shouted. "What's this?" She gestured to the ashtray.

"I never smoked in the house, only on the roof," Heather said.

"And you think that makes it okay?"

The baby started to cry. Heather was still pacing back and forth, bouncing her, when suddenly, she did an abrupt turn and barreled toward Julia, who was so surprised, she took a couple of steps backward. Heather thrust the baby into Julia's arms.

"I'll go pack," she snapped. "Sick of this place anyway." She turned as if to march back into the house.

"You'll clean this up first," Julia said.

Heather spun around. "Why?"

"Do you want a bad review?"

Heather's hands balled into fists. "Seriously?"

"Clean this up," Julia said, pushing past her and marching into the house. "There's a broom in the garage, although a hose might be better. I expect you out before dinner," she said before firmly shutting the door behind her.

Heather stood there on the porch, breathing deeply, her chest rising and falling. She stared at the door, and for a moment, I thought she was going to stomp back in without cleaning it up after all.

But then she looked back down at the ashtray, and her face twisted into an expression that resembled grief. She knelt down and poked at it, and it promptly came apart into two pieces. I guess it didn't survive the fall, after all. I wondered if it was a gift, or maybe it was owned by someone close to her … a beloved grandma or aunt.

Then, her expression shifted again, this time into something that looked more thoughtful. She glanced up at the roof, head cocked, and stood up.

I held my breath.

Slowly, she began circling, straining to see on top of the roof, and stopping in the approximate area where she had stored the ashtray.

She stared at the space for a long time.

Then, ever so slowly, she rotated around, her eyes carefully studying every inch of the properly.

I pressed into the ground even lower, praying I had hidden myself well enough to avoid being spotted.

I watched her eyes as she made her way closer and closer to me, my heart pounding so hard, I wondered if it would give me away.

Then, Julia saved me.

"Heather!" The back door was open, and she was leaning out. "What do you think you're doing? Why aren't you cleaning this up?"

Heather's head snapped around to Julia. Her mouth opened, and all the hair at the back of my neck stood on end.

She's going to tell her, Kelly hissed in my head. *She's going to tell her that there was no way that ashtray fell off that roof without someone climbing up there and dropping it.*

My mouth was dry as beads of sweat formed on my temples and the back of my neck. Heather was going to tell her, and then they would both search the property. Would I be able to escape in time? Would Julia still hire me?

Heather closed her mouth with a sharp click. "I'm going to get the broom and the garbage can," she said. "I'm assuming that's okay with you?"

"Fine," Julia said shortly. "I'll open the garage door for you."

Heather turned on her heel and strode across the yard, heading toward the front. I wondered if she would try the side door. If she did, she'd find it unlocked.

But I had a feeling, based on what I just saw, that Heather had no desire to help Julia anymore.

Clearly, I'd made the right choice. Both Julia and Heather would be happier moving on.

As Heather made her way to the front, I saw her cast one last, searching glance behind her. Her eyes were so cold and hard, it made me shiver.

Yes, I had unquestionably done Julia a huge favor.

Chapter 10

"And this is the kitchen," Julia said, waving her arm in a flourish. "We just had it remodeled. I hope it will work for you."

"It's beautiful," I said, admiring the white granite counter-tops, grey cabinets, and stainless-steel appliances. "I can't wait to get started."

That was a lie. I wasn't much of a cook at all, but I had started watching cooking videos on YouTube whenever I wasn't watching the house. With any luck, and regular video watching, I would hopefully be able to muddle through.

Julia was full of nervous energy as she gave me the grand tour, although the job wasn't officially mine yet. I still had to meet Max.

As I expected, Julia had found me at the coffee shop that morning, eager to tell me what happened and curious whether I was still interested in becoming their nanny. What I didn't expect, but in retrospect should have, was that she would be late.

For nearly twenty agonizing minutes, I sat there with my newspaper, worrying away at my bagel because I was too nervous to eat, wondering what was taking her so long. Did she not want to hire me after all? Did she already find someone else? Or had Heather somehow talked her way back into Julia's good graces?

Although the last option seemed least likely.

In reality, she no longer had a nanny to take the kids to school and had to bring the baby with her in the stroller, so she was of course later than normal. When she showed up, she was red-faced and out of breath, her hair falling out of her ponytail as sweat dripped down her neck. As soon as she saw me, a huge grin stretched across her face.

"Oh Janey," she said, dragging the stroller over to where I sat, the baby happily gurgling. "I was so afraid I would miss you. Can you stay?"

"Of course," I said. "In fact, I'm happy to watch the little one if you want to get your coffee."

She let out a sigh of relief and started digging in her bag for her wallet. "Oh, yes, thank you. Her name is Isabelle."

I was right. She was a little girl. "What a beautiful name."

She gave me a quick smile as a reply and headed over to get in line.

I leaned over to pull Isabelle's stroller closer to me. Her eyes followed me as she chewed on her plastic keychain. I made a funny face and she smiled, kicking her feet.

"Aren't you a happy baby?" I cooed, rocking the stroller back and forth. My hands were sweaty, but I didn't want to pause to wipe them on my jeans. I knew Julia would be watching me, and I wanted to make sure I made a good impression.

Isabelle, in her orange, flowered onesie, bounced up and down in delight. I noticed a yellow stain down the front of her clothes and that she wasn't wearing a ribbon in her white-blonde air. Both were abnormal.

Well, Julia clearly wasn't used to getting all three kids ready to leave in the morning. I would be there soon, and we would get everything straightened out.

I reached down to tickle Isabelle's tummy and she giggled. I wondered if I should pick her up—if that might impress Julia, seeing how much I adored children. But I also thought it might be creepy, to just pick her child up without permission, especially since she wasn't crying or making a fuss. I decided it would probably be smarter to leave her be and continued playing with her in her stroller.

"You're a lifesaver, Janey," Julia said, plunking down across from me, her usual coffee and bagel in hand. She took a long sip of her drink and sighed again. "It's been the craziest twenty-four hours."

I gave her a sympathetic look, trying to hide the jolt of anxiety that shot through me. I was so nervous, I wished I could fast forward to the part when she'd offer the nanny position to me already. "What happened?" I asked.

Julia pressed her lips together in a thin line, so tightly they turned white. "Heather was lying to me. Just like I thought she was." She then proceeded to tell me all about how the ashtray had fallen from the roof and ended up in her backyard. "I still can't even believe she did that. My kids found it! It makes me ill every time I think about what could have happened." She shivered, holding her coffee close.

"That's awful," I said. "So, she really was smoking pot."

"And who knows what else. I couldn't sleep last night. I kept running through everything she ever told me. Was it all a lie? I just hate liars. For all I know, she wasn't taking the kids to the park after school after all. She could have been doing God knows what with them, and I had no idea. No idea." Her fingers tightened on her cardboard cup, and I found myself staring at them, wondering what would happen if she squeezed too tightly. Would the cup collapse in her hand, spilling hot coffee all over?

"I'm sure she was taking them to the park," I said. "How old are your other children? Wouldn't they tell you?"

She dropped her gaze, hiding her eyes from me for a moment. "Levi is almost six and Madison is ten."

"So, both of them are old enough to know if they went to the park or not."

"You're right." She raised her head and flashed me a sideways smile, but I noticed her fingers were still clutching the cup a little too tightly. "I know I'm being ridiculous. That's what Max, my husband, says. He thought I blew this all out of proportion. 'So what if she's smoking a little weed late at night or on her days off? We've never seen her act high,'" she said, mimicking his voice.

I started to panic. Was that what was going on? Had Max convinced her not to fire Heather after all? "But that isn't the point. The point is, she lied," I reminded her.

"That's exactly what I said!" Julia sat up straight in her excitement, slamming her hand on the table. "That's what I said to Max. It's not even about whether she smoked pot or not. It's the lying. Just like I'm sure she lied about cooking, and maybe even about how much she loves kids. *That's* the problem."

"She never should have lied to you," I said. "Because you're right—how can you possibly trust her?"

"I know. I can't." Julia collapsed, slumping back against her seat.

"So, what did you do?" I asked, hardly daring to breathe and terrified my urgency was obvious to Julia. "Is Heather still working for you?"

Julia shook her head. "No. We're done."

I tried to keep the relief from showing on my face. "So, now what? Hire a new nanny? Try and do it yourself? Or ...?"

"No, we definitely need a new nanny," Julia said flatly. "I work out of the house, but I have clients and meetings and deadlines. And Max works full-time, as well. So we need someone to help out with the kids. Which is why, I was wondering," Julia paused, looking almost shy. "Have you found something? Or do you think you might be interested in working for me?"

I widened my eyes, trying to channel my exhilaration and relief into surprise. "Really? You want me to work for you?"

She laughed in delight. "Of course. Why wouldn't I? Although," her expression became more serious. "You will have to meet Max, first. And the kids. But I'm sure all of that will be a formality, and they'll be as excited to have you as I am! How soon can you come over to meet them?"

Her expression was eager as she waited for my answer, but my brain was whirling. Meet Max? The kids? I hadn't anticipated any sort of interview process. I just assumed Julia would immediately offer me the job.

What would Max ask me? Was I going to have to come up with a resume?

Julia's smile faltered. "Have you already accepted another job? Are you not interested?"

My mind raced. "It's not that. I would love to work for you," I said. "But ..." I paused, unsure of just how honest I should be. Knowing Max was going to ask me questions, though, I figured

I'd better come out with it. "I've never been a live-in nanny before," I said. "In high school, during the summer, I basically *was* a nanny, but the parents called me a 'full-time babysitter.' I took care of two kids every day during the week. But I didn't stay the night." This was a bit of an exaggeration, as a few of us had shared those babysitting duties.

She narrowed her eyes. "But you're okay being a live-in a nanny, right? You want to do this?"

"Of course," I quickly assured her. "Taking care of those kids was what made me decide I wanted to work with children."

Her face relaxed. "I'm sure it will be fine," she said. "It isn't like you're going to be alone, anyhow. I'm home during the day. But it's important I'm not disturbed."

"I'm sure I would love the job," I said. "I just wanted to be clear about my experience."

Julia leaned forward and squeezed my hand. "I appreciate that. But you know, maybe it's a good thing you don't have years of experience. My last two nannies both had experience as live-in nannies, glowing references, the works. And look how that's gone for me. I'm on my third nanny in six months." She shook her head. "Anyway, I'm sure Max will love you. Can you come over later this afternoon? I can introduce you when he gets home from work, and if everything goes well, you can hopefully start right away. *Can* you start right away?" Her expression looked a little desperate.

"Yes, I can definitely start right away," I assured her. Watching her close her eyes in relief, I was suddenly struck by inspiration. "What are you going to do today, though, for help?"

Julia let out a groan as she sat back. "I don't know. I'm going to have to cancel my meetings. I already cancelled my 9:00 so I could meet with you. I'll just have to cancel the rest."

"Well, what if we do this," I said impulsively. "What if I just watch the kids for you this afternoon? No strings attached."

Her eyes widened. "You would do that for me?"

I smiled. "Of course! We're friends, aren't we?"

She smiled back. "Yes, but still. That's so generous."

I waved my hand. "It's not a problem. Truly. I don't have an interview until tomorrow afternoon, so it's fine. I'm happy to help."

Julia's expression melted into panic, exactly as I'd hoped. If I played my cards right, everything would run smoothly that afternoon: the kids would love me; I'd be able to get a decent dinner on the table; and Julia would pressure Max to hire me before someone else could the next day.

She opened her mouth as if she were about to ask a bunch of questions about the mythical job interview, but I interrupted her. "Oh! I didn't realize the time. I have to go run a quick errand. Can I meet you at your house in say, 45 minutes?"

"Oh my God. You are such a lifesaver. Yes, yes, yes."

"Great," I said, gathering my things. I needed to call Bryn before she started her day. "I'll see you very soon."

"Aren't you forgetting something?"

I stared at her, feeling a chill run through me. Did I screw something up? My mind was a blank as I frantically flipped through everything I had said. "Ahh ..."

"My address," she said with a laugh. "How are you going to find me?"

"Oh!" I pressed my hand against my chest, suddenly terrified by what I had almost done. Show up at her house without her ever telling me where she lived? I could hear Kelly's sigh of disgust in my head. "Of course. I forgot I didn't have your cell phone. I was going to text you for your address."

"That's a great idea. We should exchange numbers," she said, picking up her phone and punching a few buttons. I recited my number to her, and she sent me a text with her address.

"Great," she said, placing her phone on the table. "We're officially connected. See you soon?"

"Yes," I said, rising out of my chair. I was going to have to hurry if I wanted to catch Bryn.

I hurried out the door, waving at Julia, and immediately punched in Bryn's number as soon as I was outside.

"Janey!" Bryn said, picking up almost immediately. "I was wondering when I was going to hear from you. What's going on?"

"A lot," I said, walking away from the coffee shop as quickly as possible. I glanced over my shoulder to make sure Julia wasn't outside yet, but the street behind me was deserted. Perfect. I would be safely in my car in five minutes, and then I definitely wouldn't be overheard.

"When are you going to be home? Are you going to be around tomorrow? Maybe we can grab some dinner, and you can fill me in."

I turned the corner where my car was parked on the street. Since I had started watching Julia and her family, I'd fallen into a bit of a routine. I would sleep in my car overnight, so I could watch late and get back to my hiding spot early morning. Then, during the day while the kids were at school, I'd drive home for a shower and a meal. Sometimes, I would even do a load of laundry.

With a near hour commute one way, it wasn't ideal, but I kept telling myself it was worth it. Luckily for me, it had been an unseasonably warm spring, so being outside wasn't that uncomfortable.

Unfortunately, that schedule kept me from seeing Bryn. She had texted me a few times, but I kept putting her off, telling her I would get back to her when I could.

"That's why I'm calling," I said, unlocking my car and sliding into the driver's seat. I wrinkled my nose at the smell—fast food and morning breath. I always made a point of stopping at a gas station to freshen up before I went to the coffee house in the morning, brushing my teeth, washing my face, and changing my clothes, but that didn't help the interior of my car any. "I think I'm going to be Julia's nanny."

"What?! How did that happen? I thought she had a nanny?"

"Well, she did," I said. "But it ended up not working out."

"Wait. What? I have so many questions, but I've got to get to the hospital." I heard a car door slam as Bryn got in her car.

"I promise I'll call you soon and fill you in, but right now, I need a favor."

"Well, of course. What do you need?"

I took a deep breath. "I may need you to give me a reference."

"Okay. I can do that." She sounded puzzled. "I'd be happy to."

"But, not as my roommate," I said in a rush. "As a former employer. Actually, more specifically, as someone I've babysat for."

"But Janey. That's not ..."

"I know," I cut her off. "I know I'm asking you to stretch the truth."

"*Stretch* the truth?"

"I know, I know. What I'm asking is big. And they may not call, but if they do, I just need you to tell them what a good job I did and how trustworthy I am."

"But I don't understand. Why can't you ask someone who you actually worked for to give you a reference?"

"Because it's been too long," I said. "I don't even know if I could track them down in time. This was back in high school. And time is essential. You know this. I can't afford to wait around while we try and find them, assuming I even do."

"I don't know, Janey," she said.

"I promise I'll keep paying my share of the rent ..."

"It's not about that," she cut in. "And you should know that. I can always find another roommate if I had to. I want you to find your sister. And I want to help. You know I do. This just doesn't feel right."

"Do you doubt I'll do a good job?"

"Of course not."

"Then, it's not really lying," I pressed. "You're just reassuring them that they're making the right decision. That's all. You know I'll be good with the kids."

"Maybe," Bryn said, her voice hesitant. "But still ..."

"Please," I begged, my voice cracking. "I know it's a lot, but every day that passes, Kelly is drifting further and further away from me."

I heard Bryn sigh. "Do you really think it's going to help? You becoming their nanny?"

I smiled in relief. Bryn was going to do it. "There's a lot of weird things going on here," I said. "I think there may be someone stalking the family ..."

"The family?"

"Something is going on," I said. "Because there still appears to be someone watching them."

"Oh my God."

"And Julia? She's hiding something. I've been spending some time with her, and there's something she's not sharing. The sooner I get in that house, the better."

"Okay, okay, you convinced me," she said. "I'll give them a reference. But I expect you to give me regular reports on what you discover."

"Deal! Thank you so much, Bryn."

"I have to go," she said. "But call me later. I want that update."

"I will," I promised. "It might not be today, but I will as soon as I can."

"You better," she grumbled. I could tell she was disappointed she had to wait, but I couldn't help that. I needed to focus on getting myself settled. Only then could I figure out a way to safely connect with her without anyone overhearing.

I checked the time, wishing I could drive to my apartment and pack my clothes. I was going to have to either delay my start or carve out a few hours when I could drive back and forth after they hired me.

With the time I had, I wanted to clean out my car, just in case Julia saw it. I didn't want her seeing the pigsty it had become.

I drove it to the self-service car wash so I could vacuum out the inside after I threw all the trash away. I also gathered up a collection of dirty clothes and shoved them inside a tote bag I'd been using. Maybe if I started right away, that night, I could wash my clothes at the house, and then I'd have enough to get me through a few days until I could get back to my apartment.

Once I finished with the car, I headed over to Julia's.

I had barely knocked before she was throwing open the door. "Janey! I'm so glad you're here." She was so grateful, I wondered if she had been questioning whether I was going to bail on her. "I can't even tell you how much I appreciate you doing this. I just had a text from my biggest client, and there's an emergency meeting I have to get on in an hour. But that gives me enough time to give you a quick tour and get you settled."

"Sounds good," I said, following her as she showed me around the clean and tastefully decorated house. The cleaning lady appeared to be doing her job.

"I'll have to pick the kids up from school today," she said, the words spilling out of her in a torrent as she led me upstairs. "I have to put you on the approved list for you to be able to, so it would just be easier if I did it today."

"I get it," I said. "I can watch Isabelle."

She shot me a grateful look. "Yes. That would be a huge help, not having to worry about the stroller. So, here are the kids' rooms." She opened the door. "Madison and Levi share, because I don't want the baby waking them up. Eventually, Madison and Isabelle will share this room, and Levi will be by himself." I poked my head in to see what looked like completely different bedrooms shoved into one room. One side was all pink and white, the bed neatly made with a white comforter trimmed with pink and white pillows. The lamp next to the bed had a pink base and white shade. The dresser, nightstand, bookshelf, and desk were all white and clean of clutter. A mirrored jewelry box sat on the dresser while the bookshelves were filled with a variety of young adult mystery books.

The other side was all blue and red, dinosaurs and Thomas the Train, and a complete mess. The bed wasn't made, and the floor was littered with toys and clothes.

"Levi needs a little help keeping things clean," Julia said, shaking her head. "Also, with laundry. There's always a lot of laundry."

"Of course."

She closed the door. "I don't expect you to do the heavy cleaning. Val comes in every Wednesday for that, although I think she told me she was coming in Thursday this week. But, no matter. You'll still be in charge of picking up after the kids, toys and whatnot, along with the laundry and keeping the kitchen clean."

I nodded.

"Plus the grocery shopping and other errands," Julia added. "Usually, a good routine is to drop the two older kids at school, then do the shopping or laundry before picking them up in the afternoon. Here's Isabelle's room."

She pushed open the door to a much smaller room with yellow walls and light-green bedding. Butterflies hung from a mobile over the crib. There was a dresser and a changing ta-ble—the one I had seen from the window.

Isabelle gurgled as we entered her room.

Julia made a face. "I think she needs to be changed, but let me quickly finish showing you around, and then, would you mind?"

"Not at all," I said, but inside, I rolled my eyes. I guessed I'd better get used to it.

"The kids share this bathroom," she opened another door, revealing an array of children's toothbrushes, soap dishes sport-ing the characters from *Frozen* and *Batman*, and towels and rugs covered with brightly colored, smiling fish. "Your bathroom is down here, next to your bedroom." She led me to the end of the hallway and opened the door.

I took a quick peek inside and hid my disappointment. The room was simple, plain, and clean. There was a four-poster double bed with a silver comforter and dark-grey pillows, a light-blue/grey carpet, a dresser, nightstand, and a desk made of light wood—pine, maybe. The walls were white and the curtains sheer.

The problem, of course, was how clean it was. I'm not sure what I expected—that Heather would leave in such a rush that half her things would be left strewn about? Obviously, Julia wasn't going to put me in a messy room. She must have been up late getting it ready for me.

Which meant Julia would have been in a hurry. Was it possible something could have been left behind? Maybe, if I was *really* lucky, I might even find something of Ashley's that had been overlooked. I could only hope.

I'd have to search.

Julia made a face as she sniffed the air. "There's that smell again," she said, striding around the room. "I thought it was all gone." She sniffed again and eyed me. "You don't smoke, right? I did ask you."

"No, I don't smoke," I assured her.

She shot me a smile that didn't quite reach her eyes, and I found myself wanting to sniff my clothes. I was still wearing the same jeans I had worn when I had dumped the ashtray off the roof. Could I have gotten ash on them accidentally?

And then it hit me. Oh no.

I had taken a couple of half-smoked cigarettes from the ashtray and thrust them into my pocket as a precaution, in case I needed them later.

And then promptly forgot about them.

Luckily, Julia was looking at her buzzing phone and not at me, which gave me a minute to compose my face. She groaned, and thrust Isabelle into my arms, still without looking at me. "I better go. I can finish the tour later. You're fine, right? Any questions, just wait until I'm off this meeting, and I can answer." She was hurrying down the stairs before I could respond. I leaned over the banister and watched her go into her office and shut the door.

I wondered how I was supposed to know if she was on a meeting with the door closed?

Well, no matter. I had things to do. I started by going into the bathroom and flushing the two cigarettes down the toilet. I made a mental note to wash the jeans the moment I could.

Next, I changed Isabelle, which took longer than it really should have as it had been a while since I'd changed a baby. After a couple of false starts and not-so-great attempts, I finally emerged victorious.

Luckily, Isabelle was a very happy, forgiving baby.

I wondered what I should feed her and decided to take her back downstairs to rustle around the fridge, where I found a huge supply of formula.

"I guess that answers that question," I said to Isabelle, who happily waved her hands at me.

I poked around some more, wanting to see the ingredients available to me while considering my limited cooking skills. Once I knew what I was working with, I could do some quick Internet searches for recipes and hopefully cobble something tasty together.

The fridge was stuffed with a ton of healthy food: cage-free chicken breasts, grass-fed ground beef, a variety of vegetables I assumed were organic, refrigerated pasta, eggs, a few different types of organic milk, and organic cheeses and yogurt. In the cupboards, I found organic cereals, brown rice, nut butters, and cans of organic beans, soup, and macaroni and cheese. There were also loaves of multi-grain bread and a very large selection of wine, vodka, and scotch.

Some sort of chicken and brown rice dish with the vegetables would probably work. I didn't know if that was "special" enough, but I also tried to be careful not to oversell my cooking abilities. I made a point of saying I had done very little cooking while in school because my apartment's kitchen was too small.

If Julia said anything, I would just tell her I was rusty and out of practice. She would believe that.

I hoped.

I prepared a bottle for Isabelle, fed her, put her down for a nap, and then searched the kids' bedroom and bathroom under the guise of "cleaning." Not that I expected to find anything in either place, but I had to start somewhere.

I also wanted to check if there were cameras anywhere. I didn't think so—my feeling was if Julia was the type of person to fill her home with nanny cameras to watch the nanny, she would have found some way to stick a camera in Heather's room to see if she was smoking, but I needed to be sure.

I really wanted to search Julia's office, or even the master bedroom, which was beckoning me from down the hall. With Julia holed up in her office and Isabelle asleep, it would be so easy to slip inside ... but no. I contained my curiosity. I couldn't afford any screwups. I wasn't even hired yet.

Once I was in, I could plan my investigation.

Still ... maybe I could sneak a quick peek when Julia left to get the kids.

Between entertaining Isabelle when she woke and searching/cleaning the upstairs rooms, before I knew it, Julia was calling for me.

"I'm leaving now," she said, standing at the foot of the steps. "I should be back in, oh, fifteen, twenty minutes? Heather usually took the kids to the park after she picked them up from school. It would be great if you could do the same once you start, as the kids really loved it. I'll go fetch them and bring them back so I can introduce you."

"Sounds good," I said.

She started to go, then turned back. "Oh! Did you find the formula for Isabelle? I'm assuming so, as I didn't hear her cry."

"Yes, she's been fed and changed, and she napped," I said.

Julia looked relieved. "Oh good. And did you get yourself something for lunch? We have all the fixings for sandwiches—turkey, ham, cheese. I forgot to tell you to feel free to help yourself to anything in the kitchen. Breakfast, lunch, dinner, midnight snacks. And if there's some favorite food or drink you want, let us know. We'll be happy to stock it for you."

"Thanks," I said, as my stomach rumbled. I was so absorbed, I had forgotten to make myself something to eat, but too late now. Maybe I could have a bite while giving the kids a snack.

As soon as I heard the front door close, I went downstairs and watched Julia walk down the sidewalk until she disappeared around the corner.

I had fifteen minutes. I needed to make the most of them.

Chapter 11

I pulled my phone out of my pocket to check the time. As much as I was itching to dig through everything, I had to be careful.

I still wanted the job, and if Julia found me in her office, I wasn't going to get it.

Before heading that way, I forced myself to check out the living room. I didn't think I'd find any cameras, as I hadn't found anything upstairs. Still, you could never be too careful.

I was right about the lack of cameras, even though I uncovered a couple really good hiding places for them, including in an overstuffed bookcase that wasn't getting much love or attention, if the amount of dust was any indication.

I filed that little detail away for later consideration.

Feeling as ready as I could be, I took a deep breath and walked over to Julia's office.

The door was locked.

Hmm. Julia was going to be gone less than twenty minutes, and she locked her office door.

I was definitely going to have to find a way in there.

Examining the lock, I suspected I could pick it, with a little time. If the Johnsons didn't have the tool, I was sure I could find it at my parents' house.

As my parents' only surviving heir, I had inherited everything—their house, my mother's car, which I was currently living out of, the bank accounts, and even a not-so-shabby life insurance policy. It wasn't enough to live on for the rest of my life, but it was a decent enough nest egg to get me through college without loans and enough left over to fall back on as I built my career.

I still owned the house. Eventually, I would probably sell it, as I couldn't see myself ever living there, but before I did that,

I needed to go through it. And I definitely wasn't ready to do that.

So, all my parents' belongings were still as they left them, including all the useful items my dad, who had dabbled as both a survivalist and prepper, had collected over the years.

In fact, he had built an extra garage to house all his stuff, including tools, guns, rifles, fishing tackle, and camping gear.

I could still remember hanging out with him in that garage, breathing in the scent of motor oil and cleaning supplies as he taught me everything from basic car repair to how to make my own bullets. "It's always good to be prepared, Janey," he would say. "You just never know."

Kelly wanted nothing to do with any of that, often rolling her eyes when my father came home with a new find.

But I cherished those moments with him. Learning how to cut my own wood made so much more sense to me than fiddling with makeup and hair.

My eyes welled up with tears. I missed him so much.

Isabelle patted me on the cheek, and I suddenly realized I was still standing in front of Julia's office door. I had no sense at how much time had passed. I quickly reached for my phone, fear lodged in my gut that Julia was just about to open the front door and find me frozen in front of her office.

I clicked on my phone and breathed a side of relief. I was fine. I still had about seven minutes.

Enough time to take a peek in the bedroom.

Unfortunately, there wasn't much to see. It was so neat and tidy, it was nearly sterile. Similar to my room, it was decorated in shades of silver, white, and black. A white comforter edged in black with white and black pillows, black lamps with white shades, a silvery grey rug, and long grey curtains decorated the room. I opened up the walk-in closet to see rows of carefully pressed clothes on either side, organized according to color.

Standing in the middle of the room, I felt more and more creeped out. It was so ... cold. Especially for a bedroom. Other than a pair of antique porcelain figurines positioned on either side of a silver jewelry box and an eBook reader on one of the nightstands, there was nothing personal. Not even any photos.

Now that I thought about it, I realized there were very few family photos anywhere in the house. The living room had three, one of each child, on the mantel, interspaced between three more antique porcelain figurines, and there were a couple of all three kids in the family room. That was it.

It was all very ... unsettling. Almost like Julia didn't really want a family after all.

And those antique figurines. There were a couple more in the kitchen and two in the family room. They looked French— the women with their porcelain hair in an updo and ruffles on their dresses and the men wearing pantaloons and wigs.

They didn't quite fit the rest of the house. I wondered what their story was.

I heard the sound of the front door opening and hurried out of the bedroom, making sure I closed the door behind me as I had found it.

"Janey," Julia called as she herded both kids inside.

"I'm here," I said, hurrying down the stairs. Isabelle started clapping her hands as soon as she saw her mom.

Julia smiled a thin smile at the baby before turning to her other two children. "Madison, Levi, I want you to meet Janey."

"Hi Janey," Levi yelled at the top of his lungs. "Mommy, I'm hungry."

"In a minute,' Julia said, impatiently.

Madison regarded me with her large brown eyes. "Are you our new nanny?"

"I hope so," I said. "It's nice to meet both of you."

"Will you take us to the park like Heather?" Levi asked.

"Absolutely," I said.

Madison continued to stare at me. "I remember you."

My heart skipped a beat.

Julia looked confused. "You met Janey?"

Madison shook her head. "No, we didn't meet. I saw her."

My heart seemed to stop all together.

There was a very long silence, during which Julia and I both stared at her daughter. In my mind's eye, I saw all the times Madison would stand there peering out into the trees, or after she discovered the ashtray on the ground, how she seemed to look right at my hiding space.

She couldn't have seen me.

Could she?

Kelly laughed harshly in my head. *Busted. By a ten-year-old. You're pathetic.*

Even though my face felt frozen, I forced my lips into something I hoped was a smile. "You saw me? Where?"

"At the park."

Julia gave me a sharp look. "You were at the park?"

My mind raced. Was it possible Madison saw me on my daily walks around the park? How could I possibly explain that?

"She was talking to Heather."

Julia's expression turned even more suspicious. "You knew Heather? How did you know Heather?"

My mind spun wildly as the pieces fell into place. She must have seen me the day Heather left Isabelle in the park. "Ah," I said, trying to make my mouth work properly. Would I be able to explain this in a way that Julia would accept?

But then, Madison saved me. "Heather ran off," she told her mother.

Julia blinked, her attention back on her daughter. "Heather. Ran. Off?"

Madison nodded. "Yes, she did that sometimes."

"She just ... left you?"

"Yeah. But she was never gone long."

Julia staggered back, her hands flying up and pressing against her face. "She would just take the stroller and leave you and Levi?"

" She usually took the stroller," Madison said. "But that day, she just left."

One of Julia's hands went to her throat as her knees buckled and she half-fell, half-sat on the couch.

Madison looked concerned. "Mommy, are you okay?"

Julia reached out and pulled Madison toward her, enveloping her in a big hug. She buried her face in Madison's hair.

"Mommy, you're suffocating me," Madison said.

"Sorry," Julia said, reluctantly releasing her. "So, what happened when you saw Janey?"

"Heather ran off and Janey appeared," Madison continued obediently. "She was standing a little ways from Isabelle, talking to her, and then Heather came running up screaming at her to leave Isabelle alone. She," Madison pointed at me, "told Heather she shouldn't leave the baby alone like that. They talked a little longer, but I couldn't hear anything else. Then Janey left, and Heather stayed."

Madison stopped talking, then looked between us, her head swiveling on her neck. Her eyes were so dark, so old. I never really understood the term "old soul" before, but every time Madison's penetrating gaze fell on me, I got it.

"I'm hungry," Levi said.

"In a minute," Julia said. She seemed as flummoxed as I was as to how to respond to any of it.

"You said that an hour ago," Levi fretted.

Julia squeezed her eyes shut as she massaged her temples, almost like she had a migraine. "I just need one more minute," she said, an edge to her voice. "I have to think."

"I ... I think I should feed Isabelle again," I said hesitantly, wondering if Julia would simply snatch her out of my arms and order me out of the house. "I can get a snack for Levi and Madison while I do that."

Julia's head jerked up, almost like she had forgotten I was there. Her eyes were round, and I couldn't read her expression.

I swallowed hard, cursing myself for not breaking into her office when I had the chance. *Idiot.*

"That's a good idea," she said, her voice strangled. "I need to go back to work anyway. You've got this?"

I forced myself to nod, afraid if I said anything, I would break the strange spell.

Julia nodded and slowly pulled herself to her feet. She started walking, but it seemed off ... rigid.

"Are you sure you're okay, mommy?"

"I'm fine, sweetie," she said, forcing a smile on her face. "Go on with Janey. She'll get you a snack."

"Snack! Snack!" Levi yelled from the kitchen, drumming his feet against the chair legs.

Madison didn't look so sure, and I was sure I didn't, either. Julia moved woodenly, her limbs twitching uncontrollably as if she were a short-circuiting robot. She paused when she passed Isabelle and me, smiling at her as she gently stroked her soft baby cheek. Isabelle squealed in delight. I wondered if I should offer the baby to her to hold, but before I could say anything, Julia started her strange, disjointed walk again.

She reached her office, tried the door, and realized it was locked. I then watched her fumble with a key that hung from a chain around her neck.

A detail I carefully noted.

Madison and I both waited until she had opened her office door before heading to the kitchen and an impatient Levi.

"So, what do we have for snacks?" I asked, opening the fridge while trying to interject a cheerful tone in my voice despite the knots in my stomach.

"Apples and peanut butter," Levi suggested with enthusiasm.

That made it easy. "Apples and peanut butter it is then," I said.

* * *

Time slowed to a crawl. I fixed the kids their snack, fed Isabelle, set Madison up at the kitchen table with her homework while Levi built a tower with Legos, and started dinner, all the while listening for the sound of an opening office door.

But Julia stayed stubbornly in her office even as the clock ticked straight past 5:00, which is when she would normally come out to chat with the kids and have a glass of wine.

I made a salad and cleaned up the kitchen, and was just starting to wonder if I should feed the kids when I heard the garage door open.

"Daddy's home," Levi shrieked, running in from the family room where he had shifted from the Legos to watching *Thomas and Friends*. Madison slid off her chair and followed her brother.

I wiped my hands nervously on a dish towel, wondering how I would introduce myself if Julia didn't come out of her office, when I heard the door between the garage and the house open.

"Hey there champ," a male voice boomed out. "How's my princess?"

I hesitantly moved from the kitchen to the hallway, not sure if it was better to stay discreetly hidden or to make my presence known.

Max was still in front of the garage, crouched down and hugging the kids. He looked up and saw me hovering in the corner.

"You must be Janey," he said.

I was startled, and my expression must have reflected it, because he smiled. "Julia called me."

"Oh, of course," I said. "It's nice to ..."

Julia's office door opened, and she stepped out. Max saw her and released the kids. "Go on," he said, standing up. "Mom and I have to chat for a minute."

"I was watching *Thomas the Train*," Levi said.

"That sounds fun," Max encouraged. "Maybe Madison can watch it with you."

Madison rolled her eyes. "That show's for babies."

"I'm not a baby!" Levi insisted.

"Hey, enough of that," Julia said. "Madison, it will just be a few minutes. Can you go watch with your brother?"

"Fine," Madison said with a big, put-upon sigh as she followed Levi into the family room.

"Let me grab a drink first," Max said to Julia.

"Pour one for me, as well."

Max smiled again as he walked past me and into the kitchen. "Sure smells good in here," he said.

"I made dinner," I explained. "It's nothing special, but I thought I should do something."

Max selected a bottle of red wine and began to open it. "I'm sure it's wonderful." I noticed when he smiled, his eyes crinkled at the corners.

"Janey," Julia said softly. I turned to her, meeting her red-rimmed eyes. Had she been crying in her office? She reached out and hugged me. I was so shocked, I wasn't sure what to do. I was so rarely touched by anyone other than Bryn, who occasionally put a hand on my arm or my shoulder, that I hadn't even realized how much my skin longed for human contact.

Julia's hair was soft against my cheek, and she smelled like lemon and mint. Cautiously, I hugged her back, half-afraid that, by touching her, I would somehow destroy the moment—that she would jump away, screaming at me to get out of her house and never come back.

But she didn't.

"Thank you," she whispered in my ear. "Even before you knew who Heather was, you were watching out for my kids. You're my guardian angel."

"I just did what anyone would do," I said.

"No!" I could feel her shaking her head against my shoulder. "You saw a wrong and decided to make it right. And you did it anonymously." She leaned back so she could look me in the eye. "Do you know how rare that is in this day and age? No social media selfie, no rant? You didn't even tell me, and I have no doubt you recognized Isabelle when you saw her."

"Well," I said, dropping my eyes. This had taken such an unexpected turn, making it difficult to keep up. "Heather was already gone, so there was really no point."

She gave me a gentle shake. "Exactly. That's what makes you so special." She let go of me and went to pick up the glass of wine Max had poured for her. "Do you mind keeping an eye on the kids for a few minutes? We won't be long. Then, you can have dinner with us. If you don't have plans."

I stared at her, the eager, naked, desperate energy in her eyes. I smiled. "I wouldn't dream of leaving."

She smiled back. "Excellent. Give us a moment." She winked at me and walked over to the back door. Max was already there, holding it open for her.

I watched them go, hoping it meant what I thought … that they were about to give me the nanny job.

Eying the open bottle of wine, I wondered if they would care if I poured a glass, but I pushed the thought away almost as quickly as I considered it. Now wasn't the time to show weakness. Now was the time to show them they were making the right choice.

I took the time to carefully set the table. This would be a night of celebration!

I was one step closer to finding Kelly.

Chapter 12

Dinner was amazing. The food tasted better than I expected, and everyone included me in the conversations as though I were a member of the family. Once the kids were in bed, Max and Julia asked me to join them in the living room for a glass of wine.

"Julia told me what you did," Max said. "I have to say, I'm impressed."

"You shouldn't be," I said. "Anyone would have done it."

Max cocked his head, studying me. "I think you're selling yourself short. You aren't our first nanny ..."

"Third," Julia said, gulping her wine. "In the last six months alone, you'll be our third."

"So," Max continued, giving his wife the side-eye. A second bottle of wine had been opened at some point, but I had barely touched my glass. "I think you can trust us when we say that's not necessarily true."

"I just don't know how it all went so wrong," Julia burst out. "First Ashley, then Heather. I just don't understand what happened. How could they lie to us like that after all we did for them?"

My eyes widened at Ashley's name, and I quickly ducked my head to hide it, pretending I was picking up my glass of wine. "Ashley?" I asked, trying to keep my voice nonchalant.

"The nanny before Heather," Max said. He paused, swirling the wine in his glass. "She disappeared."

"Disappeared?"

"I think she went off her meds," Julia said, reaching for the wine bottle. Max frowned at her.

"Meds?" I asked.

"We shouldn't be discussing this," Max interjected.

"Why?" Julia asked defiantly. "She left us in a lurch. Actually, it's worse than that. My biggest client was in the middle of a huge launch, and I needed help. I had to replace her asap, and I hired Heather without doing my due diligence. And look what almost happened." Her eyes shined with unshed tears.

Max reached out to stroke her arm. "WE hired her. We both made the decision."

Julia shook her head and dashed her hand across her face. "I should have been more careful."

"I don't think it's your fault," I said. "You're right, Kelly shouldn't have left you like that."

"Ashley," Julia corrected.

My face reddened. *Stupid, stupid, stupid.* "Of course, Ashley," I said. "I must have just remembered it wrong."

Julia kept talking like she didn't hear me, which was probably a good thing. "I don't know if I can ever forgive either of them. Or myself. I feel like such a fool."

"Which is why we're so glad you're here," Max said, giving his wife a stern look. I wanted to bring the conversation back to Ashley and ask more questions about how she disappeared, but clearly, Max was done talking about it. "Needless to say, we both feel like we owe you a huge debt of gratitude."

I shifted uncomfortably. "Really, it's not that big of a deal."

"It is to us," Max said firmly. "I know Julia talked to you about the nanny job. Are you still interested?"

I nodded. "Yes, I am."

Max asked me about my experience, and I tried to make it seem like I had more than I did as a high school babysitter.

He kept his expression blank, so I couldn't tell how he was feeling at all. When I got to the part about studying to become a child psychologist, he interrupted me. "So, what are you going to do about school? Are you planning to go back this fall? Next spring? Julia and I are really looking for someone who will be committed at least until Isabelle is in school. But it doesn't sound like that will be you."

I stared at him, feeling the edges of panic press against me. I hadn't planned for this question. I thought I could just skate on the "I'm-taking-time-off-because-my-parents-died" explanation, and that would be the end of it. Usually, the moment I mentioned my parents, all conversation ceased. People didn't know what to say, so they typically changed the subject.

"I ... well ..." I swallowed hard, wishing I had some water. My mouth felt so dry. "I'm taking at least a year off," I said, which wasn't exactly true. "And I'm open to extending that time, if it works out for all of us. Maybe we can see how it goes and revisit in a year?"

Julia opened her mouth, but Max interrupted. "I appreciate the offer, but I think this is something Julia and I are going to have to discuss. As you can imagine, this nanny situation has been very disruptive to our lives. The idea of you spending a year with us and becoming a member of the family only to leave and go back to school is, well, not something I'm sure I want to go through again."

Julia's eyes were round. "Max ..."

Max held up his hand. "I'm not saying 'no,' Julia. I'm saying we have to talk about it. Everything is in disarray right now anyway, so it might make more sense to take the time now and look for the right nanny who will definitely be here for the next four or five years at minimum."

I was having trouble breathing. Was this really happening? All my hard work, and he wasn't even going to hire me? And not even because of my experience or lack thereof, but because of my school status? My brain scrambled to figure out how I could salvage the situation. Could I tell them I changed my mind and would definitely commit to four or five years? Or would that seem desperate?

Julia's lips were pressed into a thin line. "I need help now," she said. "I can't take time off again like I did before. It's too soon ..."

"We'll figure it out," Max interrupted. "But we need to talk about it."

But Julia had given me an idea. "I could fill in temporarily."

Both of their heads snapped toward me, almost like they were surprised I was still sitting there. "I'm sorry?" Max asked.

"To give you time to find the right person," I said. "Look, my preference would be for you to hire me, because I truly need that break from my life. Plus, I wouldn't have to go looking for a job and a place to stay. But barring that, I'm happy to just fill in while you look for the right person. That way, you don't have to rush and risk hiring another Heather."

Max drew his eyebrows together. "Hmm, that's an interesting possibility." He turned to his wife, and they stared at each other for a moment. "Okay, let's do this," he said. "We do need to talk about it. Hiring you for the year isn't out of the question. And yes, we definitely need the help regardless, so let's plan to have you start tomorrow. We can figure the rest out later."

"Great," I said, rising to my feet as Julia mouthed "thank you" at me. "I'll get going then and see you in the morning."

"Do you have a place to stay in town?" Julia asked.

I didn't want to admit I would be sleeping in my car, but I also didn't want to tell her I was staying in a hotel when I wasn't. "I'm still living in Riverview," I said. "But it's no big deal ..."

"It *is* a big deal!" she exclaimed. "That's almost an hour trip. Why don't you just sleep here, and then tomorrow, after we go through the morning routine, you can run back for the rest of your things?"

"Oh, I couldn't," I started to protest, while inside, I jumped for joy. The sooner I moved in, the sooner I could start my investigating.

Especially since I was likely working on limited time.

"Nonsense," Julia said, getting to her feet. "The sheets are clean, and there are fresh towels in the closet. Let me get you something to sleep in."

"Oh no, you don't have to do that ..."

"Of course I do. Come on, I'll take you up." She wobbled as she took a step toward me.

But I stayed where I was, as if wavering in my decision. "Are you sure it's no trouble?"

"Positive," Max said. "No trouble at all. We'd love to have you stay."

"Okay, then. Thank you."

Julia smiled at me and tucked her hand inside my arm on our way out of the living room. "I'll talk to him," she whispered. "I want you to stay."

I squeezed her arm back, an unfamiliar warmth filling my belly. "I hope I can."

Chapter 13

"Janey, want me to do your makeup?"

Kelly stood by the mirror, all her various powders and potions carefully laid out on the vanity.

"Won't it be a waste? I'm not going anywhere," I said. My only plans that evening were to eat dinner and watch a movie with mom and dad.

She smiled, revealing her very white and straight teeth. "Come on. It will be fun. You don't want to be a plain Jane."

Half-excited, half-nervous, I sat down. I always secretly wished to be that girl in the movie who was plain in the beginning, but after taking off her glasses and getting her hair and makeup done, was transformed into an absolute beauty. And every time I took Kelly up on her offer to make me up, I always prayed for that transformation.

And every time, I was disappointed.

Kelly's smile widened as she turned me away from the mirror so she could get to work. "I could teach you some tips, you know," she said. "You don't have to settle."

My stomach twisted in a familiar knot. "I'm not 'settling.' I don't think I look that bad."

She sighed. "Janey, of course you're settling. You don't even try."

I dropped my gaze to my lap, unable to look at her perfectly made-up face and perfectly styled hair.

She sighed again before her fingers painfully jerked my face up. "None of that. I have to see."

I could feel the brush light as a butterfly against my skin. "Look, I know there's a lot here that isn't your fault. But that doesn't mean you can't make the best of a bad situation. I'm willing to help. Why don't you let me?"

My hands balled into fists, squeezing painfully. "I'll try harder," I whispered.

"Good." I could hear the smile in her voice. I sat in silence as she continued to slather on the makeup—all of it smelling like her, as if it were soaked in her perfume. It was like she was painting on a mask to hide my true self. With each brush stroke, my real self, my essence, began to disappear, piece by piece. When she was done, others would only see what she wanted them to.

Soon, there would be nothing left of me … not even my own scent.

"There," she said, her voice satisfied. She turned me to the mirror. "What do you think?"

I gasped. I couldn't believe the difference. My eyes, normally a dull blueish-grey, looked bright and huge. She had highlighted my cheekbones, minimized my large nose, and transformed my mouth into a perfect rosebud. Even my normally lank, dishwasher-blonde hair was somehow brighter and thicker in a stylish bob.

It happened. She had turned the ugly duckling into a swan.

"I love it," I squealed. "Thank you."

She laughed in delight. But then, she *kept* laughing … and it somehow turned darker, more sinister.

"I'm so glad you like it," she said. "Because Oz is coming."

My stomach hit the floor. I tried to swallow. "Oz is coming?"

Kelly had turned away. "Yeah, we're going to hang out together in the basement. Maybe you can hang with us." She glanced back at me, and a slow, disturbing smile spread across her face. "I think he's going to love the new you."

I awoke with a jerk. For a minute, I panicked. Where was I? The moon slanted across the carpet of the unfamiliar room, and I couldn't figure out how I had gotten there.

But then, it all came flooding back. I was in Julia's house, sleeping in the nanny's bedroom. Well, MY bedroom, now, if I had anything to do with it.

I glanced at the clock. It was two in the morning—too early to get up, but after that dream, I sure wasn't going back to sleep.

Along with images from that terrible dream, I also couldn't get the picture of Heather running off to confront someone at the outskirts of the park out of my head.

Who was she dealing with? Was it Oz? Was that what my dream was trying to tell me?

That thought alone was enough to inspire my frantic peeling of the sheets away from my sweaty, sticky body and jumping out of bed.

If Oz was lurking around, I was going to have to do everything I could to protect Julia and the kids.

There was no way I was going to allow him to tear apart another family.

I padded across the room to stare out the window. I studied the woods, trying to see if there was someone back there, watching. Waiting.

Someone in the same spot I had been in, surveilling the house.

You're being silly, I told myself. *There's no way someone is out there right now.*

I had been back there every day and night for weeks and had seen no sign of anyone else. It would be much too big a coincidence if, on the first night I wasn't there, someone had decided to take up where I'd left off.

Even though I knew it wasn't possible, I couldn't stop searching the area. Was I absolutely *sure* no one else had been back there with me? I had been so focused on the house, after all. Was it possible I just hadn't noticed?

Could someone else have even been watching me?

I shivered. No, that wasn't possible. I would have known. I would have seen or heard or smelled something. There was no way someone else could have hidden themselves from me for weeks on end.

It just wasn't possible.

I forced myself away from the window. This wasn't helping. I needed a real plan to not only figure out what happened to Ashley/Kelly, but also to find out if Oz was stalking her.

I briefly considered trying to break into Julia's office, but pushed that thought out of my head almost immediately. Now was certainly not the time for her to catch me snooping. As much as I was dying to get in there, I had to wait for a better time.

But I *could* search the room I was in.

Even if someone woke up and saw my light on, I could say I couldn't sleep and decided to read. Although I didn't have a book in the room. Maybe that was the first place to start. Get a book, maybe a glass of water, and while I was at it, see if anyone else was a night owl. Then, I could quietly start my search.

I carefully opened the door and peered out. As far as I could tell, everyone was asleep—even Isabelle, which was good. Hopefully, she was at the age where she slept through the night.

I crept down the hall and made my way downstairs. All was silent and still. If anyone was awake, they were in bed.

I selected a mystery from the bookshelf, poured myself a glass of water, drank most of it, and refilled it. I hadn't realized how thirsty I was. My throat was parched, my hair stuck to the back of my neck, and the T-shirt and shorts Julia lent me to sleep in were damp with sweat.

I made my way back up to my room, quietly closed the door behind me, and turned on the light. The brightness shocked me, and for a moment, I was sure I had woken the rest of the house. I told myself I was being foolish.

I also considered stuffing a blanket under my door to prevent anyone in the hallway from seeing the light on, but I dismissed that idea. If I were really reading in bed, I wouldn't worry about blocking the light from the door. That would be suspicious. It would be better to just leave it alone.

Although I did lower the shade in the window. Just in case.

Quietly and methodically, I began to move through the room, searching every corner. I started with the closet, feeling every inch of the top shelf and checking the floor before moving to the dresser, end tables, and bed. Other than a few dust bunnies, the place was clean. Even the trash can was empty.

Even though I knew it was a long shot that I would find anything useful, I couldn't stop the feelings of frustration and discouragement from piling up inside me, zapping my energy and depressing me.

Finally, I turned to the desk. My last hope. If there was nothing there, I would have no choice but to lean on Julia to tell me what happened when Ashley/Kelly disappeared. And, judging from Max's reaction, I was going to have to be very careful when I approached her.

At first, I thought the desk was going to be a dud, as well. The top drawer held a handful of pens, a box of paperclips, and a couple of notepads. The bottom drawer was empty.

Nothing.

I stared at the desk, the weight of despair crashing over me. This really was a wild goose chase. Even though my head had repeated that to me over and over, my heart had always believed I would find something. But now, faced with an empty, bare room, I had to accept the truth.

The chances of me somehow tracking down Ashley/Kelly were slim to none.

I collapsed, my head in my hands, blinking rapidly to keep the tears away. In that moment, all I wanted was to have a nice, big, loud cry. Bawl my head off. Just let it all out.

But I couldn't. I couldn't afford to wake the rest of the house. How could I possibly explain myself? I had to hold it all in.

I'm just exhausted, I told myself. *I haven't had a good night of sleep since that letter was delivered. What I really ought to do is turn out the light and climb back into bed to see if I can salvage a few more hours of sleep ...*

A scrap of white paper caught my eye. It was wedged between the wall and the corner of the desk, barely peeking out. I blinked a few times, wondering if I was just "seeing something" because of the tears in my eyes.

No, the paper was still there.

I bent down to pick it up. It appeared to be torn from a note-book, maybe from one of the ones in the drawer.

There was something written on it. I turned it over to read it.

889ABX

What on earth? Was it a code for something?

I turned the paper over again, but there was nothing else.

What did it mean?

It was written in a blocky handwriting, which I couldn't iden-tify. I had no idea if Ashley wrote it, or Heather, or someone else, like Julia or Max.

I got down on my hands and knees to see if there was any-thing else back there, but there was nothing but dust. The little scrap of paper was it.

As grateful as I was that Val, the cleaning lady, wasn't more meticulous in her job, I still found myself shaking my head. First, the dust missed on the mantles and bookshelves, and now this.

Julia really didn't know how to hire help.

Even though in the grand scheme of things, this was by no means a helpful clue, I found myself feeling hopeful. It was a sign. I was where I was supposed to be, and I would find the clues necessary to find Ashley/Kelly.

A sudden wave of peaceful exhaustion engulfed me, and I knew I'd be able to fall asleep. I opened the top desk drawer and hid the piece of paper underneath the notepads. It might not be the best hiding place, but until I brought some of my stuff from home, it would have to do. Then, I turned the light out and climbed back into a bed. My alarm was set, so I was sure I would wake up in time to get Isabelle up and ready, and I finally slid into a deep, dreamless sleep.

Chapter 14

My first day did not go well.

At all.

My nocturnal activities caused me to oversleep, right through my alarm *and* Isabelle's crying. By the time I was awake enough to realize what was going on, she had woken up the rest of the house.

I dragged myself out of bed and opened the door, only to see a half-dressed Max opening his door. He was wearing pants and a shirt, but the shirt wasn't buttoned at all, and his hair was dripping wet. He scowled when he saw me.

I winced. "Sorry," I said. "I'll get her."

"I have to get to work," he said. "I thought you could handle it."

"I can, I can," I said, starting to run into her room. "I just, I didn't sleep well. Had a terrible nightmare. It won't happen again."

He scowled again and disappeared back into the bedroom while I fetched the baby.

You really can't do anything right, Kelly's voice taunted me. *All you needed to do was wake up with your alarm, and you couldn't even do that.*

I pushed the voice away.

Isabelle's face was red and swollen as I scooped her up. She needed to be changed, and probably fed, as well. Her cries quieted some with my attention, but she was still pretty distraught.

"Mommy won't be happy."

I turned. Madison was standing in the doorway, her round, blue eyes owlish in the dim light.

"What do you mean?"

"Mommy hates mornings. She especially hates mornings when Isabelle wakes her."

I turned back to Isabelle, unzipping her soaked onesie and tossing it in the laundry. No wonder she was so upset. I apparently hadn't done a very good job with her last diaper. "I overslept," I said, even while wondering why I was explaining myself to a ten-year-old. "I didn't mean to. It won't happen again."

"Was it because of the nightmare?"

My hands faltered for a second, until I remembered that was the excuse I gave Max, and she must have overheard. "Yes."

"Nightmares are scary," she said. "I don't like them, either."

"Do you have them a lot?"

"Sometimes," she said. "It depends."

"On what?"

"On the others."

I eyed her. "What others?"

"The others who dream."

I finished cleaning up Isabelle and grabbed a fresh diaper and clean onesie. "I don't understand."

"No one does," she said seriously. "Mommy and daddy think I should go talk to child psychic."

"A psychic?"

"Yeah, because they think there's something wrong with my brain."

After thinking for a moment, I asked, "A psychic, or a psychologist?"

"A psy-chologist," she enunciated. "Mommy especially doesn't like it when I talk about my dreams." She dropped her voice to a whisper. "She gets really scared."

Now I was intrigued. An image of Julia's mad dash into her car the other day flashed across my mind. "Why does she get really scared?" I whispered back.

"Because her dreams are scary, too," she said, widening her eyes. "Just like yours."

The temperature of the room seemed to drop. It felt like someone had pressed icy cold fingers down my spine. "How do you know my dreams are scary?"

"Because I dreamed about it, too."

I frowned, shaking my head. "That's impossible. You dream your own dreams, not other people's."

She cocked her head. "I told you. No one believes me."

Levi chose that moment to come running in. "Janey, Janey! I'm awake!"

"That's great," I said. "Do you want to go to the bathroom, and I'll help you get dressed?"

"Okay," he said, and ran right back out of the room.

"You probably need to get dressed, too," I said to Madison. The conversation had gotten way too strange for me, especially since I hadn't had coffee yet.

"Okay," she said. She spun around in a little circle and started walking toward her room. Pausing after a couple of steps, she looked back over her shoulder at me, her face scrunched up as if she were studying me.

"I think you look fine without any makeup," she said.

I fumbled with the clean diaper, my fingers too wooden to work properly.

She nodded her head, as if agreeing with herself, and disappeared from view.

It was all I could do to keep breathing. It was as if an icy snake had wrapped itself around my chest and was slowly squeezing the life out of me.

There was no way Madison could know about my dream.

No way. It wasn't possible.

I must have said something in the middle of the night.

Yes, I must have been sleep talking.

Which actually wasn't as reassuring as I'd hoped when I thought about it.

I didn't like that I might be saying things in the middle of the night, when I was most vulnerable and least able to filter myself.

What else would I say?

Isabelle was still fussing and crying, her face red and blotchy, so I finished as quickly as I could. My ears strained over her cries, trying to hear if Julia was awake and moving around. I couldn't tell, which didn't mean anything.

Finally dressed in a clean onesie and wearing a fresh diaper, I scooped Isabelle up and headed downstairs for a bottle.

Max was already in the kitchen, standing by the coffee pot, a stern expression on his face. I faltered as he made eye contact, wondering if Isabelle could wait a little longer before I got her fed. But then again, if he was going to fire me, then he was going to fire me.

I was suddenly very conscious of the old tee shirt and shorts Julia had lent me to sleep in. Heather was always fully dressed around Max. I wondered if this would be yet another black mark. I wondered if I stunk; after all, I had sweat quite a bit during my nightmare. I cursed at myself, unable to believe I slept through my alarm. If I had just gotten up when I was supposed to, I would have had enough time to get properly dressed.

Cautiously, I approached the fridge as Max pointed to the stove, where a bottle of formula was already being heated in water. "I got it started for you," he said, his voice clipped.

I murmured a "thank you" as I reached for it, shaking it as I adjusted Isabelle to test it on my wrist.

He watched, his mouth a flat line. I felt clumsy and awkward, as I re-adjusted Isabelle, who let out a loud squawk while turning her head toward the bottle and opening and shutting her mouth eagerly. For a moment, I was worried I might drop her as she kept reaching for the bottle while I tried to test it, but eventually, I got enough on my wrist to decide the temperature was close enough. I popped it into her mouth, and she instantly quieted. I was looking for a way to adjust a chair so I could sit down when Max cleared his throat.

"I know this all happened very quickly, so I'm going to assume Julia hasn't had a chance to go through everything with you."

I bounced up and down as Isabelle fixed her big, blue eyes on me, wishing Max would pull a chair out for me and kicking myself for not being more on top of things. I had been watching Heather long enough, so unbeknownst to Max, I actually did know what was expected. "She said I needed to get the kids ready and walk them to school, but that was really it."

He nodded as if he had expected that answer. "The moment Isabelle starts to wake up, make sure you get her. She's a pretty easy baby, so if you can get her out of her crib and change her while she's still waking up, she should stay quiet enough to not wake the rest of the house. Once she's been fed, you can help the other kids." He continued on, running through the kids' morning routine, including what they ate for breakfast.

I nodded as he talked, wishing I could sit down, and that he would offer me a cup of coffee. My head was foggy, and I wasn't sure if I would remember everything he was telling me. It's not like I had been able to see *every* single thing Heather did in the morning.

From upstairs came the sound of running feet, and Max glanced up, sighing. "They'll be down in a moment. I'll get breakfast for them *today*," he clearly emphasized the word, "but you'll probably have to finish their morning routine after breakfast."

"Of course," I said as Levi ran into the kitchen to hug his father. I noticed he was still wearing his pajamas. "Madison tried to help me get ready, but I didn't want to wear her clothes."

Max shot me a disapproving look. "That's okay, champ. Let's get you some breakfast, and then Janey can help you."

"Okay," he said, running to the table and pulling a chair out as Madison appeared in the kitchen, dressed and ready.

I started nudging a chair out for myself, finally getting it into position so I could sit. It wasn't ideal, as there weren't any armrests, but I improvised by propping my arm against the table.

It worked. Mostly.

The kids were finishing up when Julia came downstairs looking exhausted and grumpy. She didn't say a word to anyone, just went straight to the coffee pot and poured herself a cup. Max leaned over and kissed her on the cheek. "I told Janey what we expect, so you don't have to worry about it," he said. "I gotta get going. Bye Levi. Bye Madison."

"Bye, bye," Levi shouted.

Isabelle had finished her bottle, so I adjusted her to burp her as Julia brought her coffee to the table, collapsing in a chair across from me. She buried her face in her hands.

"I'm so sorry," I said in a rush. "I overslept, which I never do. I had a bad night."

"Janey had a nightmare," Madison pipped in.

Julia squeezed her eyes shut. "Not now, Madison."

"I promise it won't happen again," I said.

Julia opened one eye and looked at me. "It's okay," she said. "You didn't know. I'm just ... mornings aren't good for me. It will be fine." She gave me a ghost of a smile, which seemed to shoot across the table and warm my insides. "If you can finish getting the kids ready, we'll walk to the school together, and then you can go get the rest of your things. That work?"

"Sounds like a plan," I said, as Isabelle let out a loud burp. Levi giggled. "Come on, kids. Let's get you ready for school."

Chapter 15

After dropping the kids off, I went back home to clean up the kitchen and get myself some breakfast before driving to my apartment. Julia went to the coffee shop. I was briefly tempted to take a peek in her office before I left, but I had no idea when she would be back. As much as I itched to get in there, my gut told me to wait.

Rather than mess around with the car seat, Julia told me to take her car, so I could bring Isabelle. That came as a surprise, as I had expected to leave Isabelle with Julia. But I swallowed my disappointment and thanked her.

Now, not only was I going to be a nervous wreck driving with a baby AND in a car that wasn't my own, but it would take me twice as long to pack while caring for Isabelle.

Despite all of that, I managed to get back to Julia's early enough to start a load of laundry before picking up the kids. I desperately needed clean underwear and shirts, but I also wanted to throw in a few items from the kids, to make up for my morning mistake.

Once I got Isabelle inside, I dumped off my bags in my room, intending to unpack later, and scooped up my dirty clothes. I wasn't sure where the laundry room was—I hadn't seen anything on the main floor, and Julia hadn't told me. Maybe I'd try the basement.

Julia was in the kitchen, making herself a sandwich and talking to Isabelle, who was still in her carrier. She grinned sheepishly when she saw me. "I know. Late lunch. Sometimes I forget to eat. I promise I'll still eat dinner though. I take it everything went smoothly?"

"It did," I said, inwardly smacking myself on the head. I had forgotten about my dinner duties. What was I going to make? I mentally added it to my growing to-do list. I definitely was going to need to get more productive, so I'd have time to get back to my sleuthing. "With all my job hunting and going back and forth, I haven't had time to do much laundry. I hope it's okay if I do a load?" I held up my arms full of clothes.

Julia immediately put down her knife. "Oh, yes. Of course. That's right, I forgot to finish our tour. Let me take you to the basement and show you around."

"Great," I said, following her. I glanced over at Isabelle, but she seemed happy in her carrier, chewing on her plastic key set.

Julia led me to the basement, which was finished and turned into a game/rec room. The walls were painted an off-white, and there was a light-beige carpet and black furniture. A huge flat-screen television hung on one wall across from the couch. On the side wall, there was a dartboard and a mini basketball hoop. There was also a foosball table, a ping-pong table, and a bar complete with a sink and mini fridge.

"Man cave," Julia said, with a strained smile.

"It's pretty nice," I said. "The kids must love it, too."

"Yeah, although they only get to come down here with dad. It's their special time." She had her face turned away so I couldn't see her expression, but there was a definite edge in her voice.

Why did Max's man cave bother her? It seemed to me she would love sending the kids down to play with dad. Yet another detail to file away.

Past the man cave was a short hallway that led to a bathroom, storage room, and laundry room. The door to the storage room was open, and I saw something covered in a sheet that took up most of the center of the floor. "What's that?" I asked, gesturing with my head.

She glanced in the room. "Oh, that's Ashley's stuff," she said dismissively.

I froze. "Ashley?" My voice sounded strangled in my throat, and I cleared it. Ashley had *stuff* here? I tried to contain my excitement. "I thought she left."

"She did," Julia said, pausing with her hand on the door to the laundry room.

"So, why did she leave her belongings here?"

Julia shook her head. "That's what was so frustrating about what happened. There was no warning. Nothing. She left the house on Sunday for the day as she usually does. But she just never came back. She just ... left."

"Did you call the police?"

She gave me a look. "Well, of course. And they checked out all the places she hung out—ice skating on the lake when the weather was nice, Aunt May's diner, the library ... even the Tipsy Cow, where she'd sometimes go for a drink. But no one had seen her that day."

I was so afraid that anything I said or did would cause her to stop talking, I could barely breathe. "Are you sure she left, and something didn't happen to her?"

Julia frowned, and my heart stopped, sure I had asked the wrong question. I waited for her to clam up, but then I realized she was thinking. "At first, that's exactly what we thought. She had packed a bag with some clothes, her makeup and toiletries, and her computer, which wasn't unusual. Heather used to do the same thing on her days off. Neither of them would return until very late Sunday night. I'm not sure what Heather was doing ... she was always more secretive about her time off, but Ashely told me she liked to change clothes if she ended up sweating a lot during ice skating. But, as you just saw, she certainly didn't pack everything, which if she wasn't planning on returning Sunday night, didn't make sense. On the other hand, the cops found no sign of either her or her car, which pointed to her leaving on her own. But the more we thought about it, we realized ..." Julia paused again and sighed, running her hands through her hair. "I know Max doesn't like to talk about it, but I do. It's all so weird, and I really haven't been able to process it properly."

"My lips are sealed," I said. "I completely understand. I need to process things out loud, as well."

She gave me a little smile. "You're just so easy to talk to. You're going to make a great psychologist someday." She rubbed her chin and glanced over my shoulder, almost as if she thought Max would suddenly materialize behind me and stop her from opening up. "Ashley had been acting, well, peculiar for a while before she disappeared."

"Peculiar how?"

"Just ... it's hard to explain. At first, she was perfect. She had worked as a nanny for a few years after high school and was working full-time at a daycare center right up until we found her. She was looking for a fresh start in a smaller town, like Redemption. Her references were impeccable. She clearly loved kids, and ours just adored her. But then it all started to change. She had only been working here for a few weeks when she became convinced someone was following her. Of course, we took it seriously. We went to the cops and talked to the neighbors, the kids' teachers, and the mothers at the school. But no one had ever seen anything. And we never saw anything, either. Eventually, she calmed down somewhat, and agreed that maybe she was mistaken or being overly protective.

"But then, the last week or so before she disappeared, it all flared up again. She was sure she was being followed. We looked again, but just couldn't find any evidence.

"But, this time, rather than agreeing that maybe she was just mistaken, she got defensive and angry. She stopped talking to us except when absolutely necessary. We were concerned, of course, and tried reaching out to her, but she wasn't interested in having a conversation about it. We were trying to figure out what to do next—I mean, the kids loved her, and everything was working so smoothly. She was still a wonderful nanny, except when she would have these paranoid flare ups.

"And then she seemed to come out of it on her own. The Saturday before she disappeared, she was fine. Back to her old self. She was back to talking to us, and when we asked her about the stalking, she said everything was fine and not to worry about it.

"So, we thought she had moved through it, like she had before. But of course, the next day, she was gone.

"And then ..." she sucked in a deep breath while biting down on her bottom lip. "Well, the police investigated, and one of the things they did was contact her old friends. They said this wasn't the first time Ashley thought she was being stalked. In fact, that was why she came here in the first place. She thought she was being stalked before, even though no one could find any evidence to prove it. So, she quit her job and moved here. We also found out she had some mental issues that she was supposed to be taking medication for. But when we went through the medicine cabinet in the bathroom, there was nearly a full bottle. So, clearly, she had stopped taking it."

She paused, making fists in her hair and yanking. "I'm just so angry about it all. I'm angry she didn't tell us the truth ... about her mental illness, about how she thought she had a stalker before. I mean, what if she really DID have a stalker, and that person followed her here? Our children could have been in danger! How could she have put us in that position? And I'm of course angry about her leaving the way she did. I mean, she knew how much we depended on her. For her to not tell us? To just leave? Why would she do that, after everything we'd done for her?"

Julia's voice was getting faster and louder, as if all the words had been piling up inside of her and were finally spewing out in a torrent. "Why didn't she tell us she was struggling so much? We could have helped her! Instead, she didn't say a word. Why not? Didn't she trust us? Why wouldn't she? We trusted her to live in our home, to take care of our children. It hurts that she didn't trust us as much as we clearly trusted her.

"And then I question myself. Should I have asked more questions? Should I have seen the warning signs? What does it say about me, that I missed all of that? Am I a terrible mother? I have to work, too, and my work is just as important as Max's. Just because he goes into an office and I'm at home doesn't mean I'm not working just as hard as he is. It shouldn't matter. But because I'm at home, and I'm the mother, I'm the one who gets blamed when things go wrong. And that isn't fair. There's no reason he shouldn't shoulder some of the house duties and child rearing instead of letting it all pile up on me while he gets to be the fun dad. I have enough responsibilities. I shouldn't have to take on the lion's share of the household duties, too."

She stopped talking, probably to take a breath, and in the silence, we heard a single cry from upstairs.

Julia started. "Oh! Isabelle! She's probably lonely up there without us. Can you ..." she blinked, as if just now realizing I was still standing there with my arms filled with dirty clothes. What was it with Julia and Max both not seeming to care if I had to listen to them with my arms full? Although at least the clothes were a lot lighter than Isabelle. "Oh! I never showed you the washer."

"That's okay, I can probably figure it out," I said as I walked toward the washing machine. "I'll be up as soon as I get this started."

She looked relieved. "Okay, perfect. I'll stay with her until you get there. I should probably finish making my sandwich, anyway. I definitely need to get back to the office asap."

"I'll be right there," I said, opening up the top cupboards to search for laundry detergent.

I heard her footsteps lightly running up the steps and took a second to just stand there and breathe. I needed a moment to process the avalanche of words Julia had left me with. I wished I had my notebook with me so I could take notes, but maybe once Julia was safely back in her office, I could dash upstairs to jot everything down. I could take Isabelle, under the guise of changing her.

But even more than my desire to take notes was the pull to search Ashley's belongings. Even if I could just take a peek under the sheet ...

Did I have time? No. I had to control myself. I had way too much to do right then, especially since I was going to have to leave to pick up the kids from school shortly. The right time would emerge. Eventually.

Just like it would for searching Julia's office.

I got the laundry started and headed up the stairs, knowing if I took too long, Julia would get impatient. And it was important for Julia not to get impatient. In fact, my most important duty was keeping her as happy as possible.

Chapter 16

"Want to go to the park?"

"Park! Park!" Levi shouted, running ahead.

"Hold on, Levi," I called out, pushing the stroller to try and catch up with him. I couldn't help but smile, even though I was completely stressed out on the inside. I desperately wanted to get back to the house to tackle my to-do list. I had to get dinner started, and I was sure my laundry was about done. Plus, the kids needed snacks, and then there would be homework ... ugh.

It's my first day, I reminded myself, pushing the stroller as quickly as possible. Surely Max and Julia would give me a break. Even with my terrible morning start.

Right?

A quick stop at the park would be good, I reasoned. The kids would tell their parents they went to the park, which would be good for me. And anyway, we didn't have to stay long. Fifteen, twenty minutes, and then back home. Just long enough to score some brownie points.

Madison hung back, pacing her speed to match the stroller as her brother ran ahead. Her head was down, her long brown hair in her face as she walked.

I asked her how school was, and she answered in monosyllables: "Fine," "Okay," "Good." Finally, I gave up trying to draw her out and just walked in silence, both of us listening to Isabelle coo in her stroller. At least she wasn't talking about my dreams. That was something to be thankful for.

She cheered up when we reached the park, running off with her brother and leaving her backpack on the bench where Heather always sat. My initial reaction was to scoop it up and move to a different one. My goal wasn't to be like Heather. Heather was awful. I was so much better than Heather.

But I quickly realized why Heather picked that particular bench. It had the best view of both the playground and the surrounding park. A capable, conscientious nanny would choose that bench.

With a sigh, I sat down.

At first, it was nice to just sit and not have to do anything. No baby to change or feed, no meals to cook, nothing to pick up. Just sit and relax.

A few more minutes later, I started to squirm. This must be why Heather was on her phone so much. All I could think about was my massive to-do list on top of all the investigating I wanted to do. I was antsy.

The last thing I wanted to do was sit still in the park.

But I had to do certain things to keep the job, and that was the most important thing.

Neither Max nor Julia had said anything to me about looking for another nanny, which probably meant I had a shot at becoming the permanent nanny. For a moment, I let myself fantasize about how that would feel. Being able to sit at the park and enjoy the silence as I watched the kids play, knowing dinner was already cooking on the stove, and then joining the family at the table to eat what I'd prepared while Julia gushed about how wonderful it tasted, and Max teased the kids while asking them what they did with "Aunt Janey" that day ...

I blinked.

What was I doing?

I couldn't be a part of this family! I was there to investigate what happened to Ashley, otherwise known as Kelly. I was there to find MY family, not try and worm my way into another one.

I couldn't afford to take my eye off the prize. After all, the moment I figured out where Ashley went, I would follow her. Which meant I would have to quit.

I would have to leave.

My insides seemed to hollow out at the words.

Leave Julia's house.

Even though I knew I didn't have a choice, my thoughts were filled with Julia hugging me, her scent of lemon and mint in my nostrils, how happy I was eating dinner with them, how much I felt like I belonged.

It had been so long since I had felt that. After Kelly disappeared, everything changed. Even though my parents were still alive, they were no longer connected to me. It was as if they were simply going through the motions of life.

Kelly was always the favorite. The one they truly loved. The golden child. I was always second place in their hearts.

And, after Kelly left, it was clear how much they wished it was me who had disappeared instead.

Still, at least they were family. At least I had someone, even if they thought of me as a poor substitution for who they truly wanted.

Now, I had no one. Not even the sorry excuse for a family I had then.

But dinner with the Johnsons had given me a taste of what it would feel like to be a part of a family once again. And that taste had cracked me open, making me realize how much I was missing ... and how desperate I was to have it.

But, no. I couldn't allow myself to get distracted. I had to focus on what was most important, which was finding my own family. I couldn't get emotionally involved with someone else's.

Julia will be fine, I assured myself. She would have no trouble finding another nanny, one who could stay until Isabelle was old enough to go to school.

I had a sister to find, college to get back to, and a life to build.

I had my whole life ahead of me, as they say.

So why did I feel so empty?

You're pathetic, Kelly's voice sneered. *That's why you want someone else's family. You're so pathetic, even your own family doesn't want you.*

That's not true, I argued back. *Mom and dad are dead. It has nothing to do with how they felt about me.*

Are you sure? Kelly taunted. *Maybe they were so sick of you, they crashed their car on purpose. Ever think of that?*

My whole body began to tremble, but I forced myself to push her voice away. *It's not real*, I said to myself. *You know how Kelly was. She had a cruel streak.*

My hearing her voice was nothing more than unprocessed trauma. Maybe Bryn was right, and I did need to make an appointment with Dr. Nelson again.

In the meantime, I had to get my head on straight. I had to focus on what was important, making sure I kept my job long enough to properly investigate. Which reminded me to call the kids and head for home. It had been long enough.

A movement caught the corner of my eye, and I jerked my head around. Was that a figure that darted behind the trees?

The same clump of trees Heather went running toward?

Was someone watching us? Watching *me?*

My skin was crawling so much, I thought it might leave my body. I could feel eyes on me, burning a hole into my skull.

I desperately wanted to run over there myself, but I couldn't leave the kids. Especially now. Julia was on high alert. She'd probably question the kids when we got home about what I did and didn't do at the park, and the last thing I needed was to have Madison tell her I went running off just like Heather had.

Instead, I jumped to my feet. "Madison! Levi! It's time to go."

"Five more minutes!" Levi yelled back from the sandbox where he was digging a hole. Madison was on the swings, but she started dragging her feet to stop.

"No, not five more minutes. We have to go now," I said.

Levi groaned. "But Janey. I'm still playing."

I pushed the stroller toward him, maneuvering it around the grass and rocks. I could still feel eyes on me, and it was hard not to scream with frustration. *What if Ashley was right all along, and there WAS a stalker? What if that stalker was still stalking this family ... including me right now?*

I felt so exposed and vulnerable. I had a baby, a five-year-old, and a ten-year-old to protect. How could I possibly do all that myself?

I had to get out of there. Immediately.

I approached Levi, concentrating on keeping my breathing and tone even. This wasn't the time to panic. Kids were experts at picking up energy. If he thought I was freaking out, he would start freaking out, and that would be a disaster. I had to stay as calm as possible.

Levi was making a point to not look at me. Instead, he focused on scooping the sand up, a grumpy look on his face.

"That's a really nice sandcastle," I said.

"It's not nice," he said. "It's not finished yet."

"You can finish it tomorrow."

"I want to finish it today." He furiously attacked the sand.

What I wanted to do was grab him by the scruff of his neck and haul him out of the park. But I restrained myself. Instead, I squatted down so I was at his level. "What if I make you a deal?" I asked.

He paused, intrigued. "What?"

"If you come with me now, I'll help you build an even better sandcastle tomorrow."

His head snapped up. "You will?"

"Scout's honor," I said. Inwardly, I hoped he would forget my promise, but even if he didn't, I could handle a little digging in the sand.

I wasn't sure what I was going to do if I saw the stalker again the next day, but I would worry about that then.

"Okay," he shouted, leaping to his feet. His eyes were bright, and he had a huge grin on his face. "Let's go."

"Great," I said, smiling back, but my smile felt stretched and fake. I straightened up as Levi grabbed my arm.

"You promise. Right? You promise you'll play with me tomorrow?" His voice was urgent.

"I promise," I said, trying not to sigh. The chances of him forgetting seemed to sink to zero.

He grinned at me again, and this time, my smile was more genuine. He really was an adorable child, with his big brown eyes and curly hair. He went running up to his sister. "Madison! Janey said she'd play with me tomorrow!"

I pushed my stroller behind them, watching them as they walked ahead. I was a little taken aback about how excited Levi was by my offer. In the moment, I had felt like it was pretty lame, and was just trying to buy some time as I tried to remember which desserts or treats were acceptable to offer him. Instead, it seemed I hit the jackpot.

Was he lonely? I thought about all the times at the park he begged his sister to play with him. Sometimes she did, but most of the time, she liked to be by herself. And then I realized that, in all the days I'd watched the family, I'd never seen any friends come over to play with either child. Isabelle was a little young for play dates, but Levi and Madison surely had friends.

Was it possible that even with friends at school, he was still lonely? It was true his family life left a lot to be desired. His mother virtually ignored him, and his father wasn't around a lot.

Maybe he needed a friend. Or a really big sister to play with him.

Growing up, I always wanted a brother. Every year on my birthday, for years, I wished for a baby brother. Someone to be on my side.

Maybe I was finally getting my wish.

I gave myself a quick shake. *Stop it. This isn't helpful. Remember why you're here. You have to find Ashley. Not be Levi's new sister.*

But still. I felt a yearning in my chest as I watched him, and I wondered how different my life might be now if I had gotten a brother all those years ago.

Chapter 17

I had just finished cleaning up the kitchen after dropping the kids at school when I heard the front door open.

Figuring it must be Julia returning from the coffee shop, I quickly dried my hands on the red hand towel and headed over to meet her. I was dying to talk to her alone.

Last night had gone ... okay. Well, maybe a little less than okay.

It started with dinner. I really didn't have enough time to do a lot. I was already running so late, and I still had my laundry to deal with. So, I pulled a Heather by throwing together a spaghetti dinner. I thought it would work as I did make the sauce from scratch, thanks to the ground beef in the fridge and cans of tomato sauce in the cupboard. I also made a salad and garlic bread.

But Julia didn't seem pleased. "Oh. Spaghetti," she said, her smile strained as she pulled out a bottle of wine from the wine rack.

"Spaghetti is my favorite," Levi announced.

"It was my favorite too when I was a kid," Julia said, digging in the drawer for a corkscrew. Her hair hung like a curtain in front of her face. "Comfort food."

The smile froze on my face, but I continued chopping the cucumber, my movements wooden. Was Julia unhappy with my choice? Did she always want me to make more complicated meals? I had thought she had liked my simple-yet-tasty dish the night before. Maybe I'd better step up my video watching, if I could figure out how to work it into my already overflowing schedule.

Maybe you shouldn't have lied about knowing how to cook, Kelly piped in. *You could have told her you didn't have much experience because you had to work your way through school. She would have accepted that. You could have even added how excited you are to learn how to cook. But no. You had to lie about it.*

A gentle "pop" interrupted my thoughts as Julia uncorked the wine. She caught my eye as she reached for a glass and smiled at me. A warm smile.

I felt something in my chest start to thaw. I was overreacting. It was fine. Everything was fine.

But the rest of the evening still felt off. Julia was distracted at dinner, the kids having to repeat what they said to her a few times. And Max wasn't nearly as friendly as he was before. He didn't say much to me at all, or Julia, for that matter, focusing most of his conversation on the kids.

The tension seemed to grow even more after dinner. By the time I had the kitchen clean and the kids in bed, I was a wreck. Kelly was constantly yapping in my head about how I was one step away from being fired. I was sure they were going to call me down and tell me they were looking for another nanny.

But nothing happened. I said "goodnight" and headed up to bed to watch a few cooking videos and set *two* alarms to make sure I woke up on time.

Which I did. And the morning went more smoothly, maybe because I was up early and able to get everything done without a lot of fuss. Max was more civil, but Julia was still off. Although she wasn't a morning person, I reminded myself.

As usual, she left for the coffee shop while I took the kids to school. Back home, I puttered around the kitchen waiting for her to come home so I could grab a moment with her.

Just a few minutes was all I needed. Just a moment to connect. To have her smile at me, so I knew all was well.

Then, once she was safely tucked away in her office, I could start going through Ashley's things.

Except it wasn't Julia who had opened the door. It was a woman I had never seen before.

She had short, dark hair streaked with grey, horn-rimmed glasses, and a no-nonsense manner. The skin on her face was weathered, reminding me of leather that had been in the sun too long. She wore an oversized grey T-shirt and stretched-out black yoga pants.

She started when she saw me, pressing her hand to her chest. "You scared me."

"Sorry," I said. "Who are you?"

Her eyes narrowed as she looked at me over her glasses. "I should be asking you that. Where's Heather?"

"Not here," I said. "I'm the new nanny."

She blinked. "But what happened to Heather?"

I shrugged. "You'll have to talk to Julia about that. So, who are you?"

She studied me, her expression unreadable. "I'm Val," she said finally. "I do the cleaning once a week. Usually, I'm here on Wednesdays, but I had to switch my schedule this week to today."

Of course. Val. How could I have forgotten? I could feel my stomach slowly sink to the floor. With Val there, there was no way I would be able to go through Ashley's stuff. I was going to have to wait.

"I'm Janey," I volunteered, but Val seemed to be done with me, shutting the door behind her and opening the basement door. She disappeared down the steps like she hadn't heard a word.

I stood there blinking and listening to Val's heavy steps on the stairs. How rude. Did she actually just do that to me? Man, not only was she a terrible housecleaner, but clearly, she was also a terrible person.

Although, maybe I was rushing to judgement. Was it possible she hadn't heard me? Or maybe she was running late and had to get started.

Or maybe she's got your number and knows you're no good, Kelly muttered into my ear.

She's just barely met me, I argued back. *How in the world would she know that?*

Some people are smarter than others.

I pushed Kelly's voice away. No, Val surely hadn't just up and decided she didn't like me. People don't do things like that.

I was still standing there when the front door opened again, and Julia walked through. "Looks like Val is here," she said briskly. "Did you two meet?"

I nodded. "Yeah, she just went into the basement." It was on the tip of my tongue to tell Julia what Val did and ask her if she was always that rude, but I could already hear Val's heavy steps coming up the stairs, so I knew it was definitely not the time.

Julia nodded. "That's where all the cleaning supplies are." She pulled her keys out of her purse and started to unlock her office door. "Would you mind doing a few errands for me today? I have a list."

"Not at all," I said, trying to sound competent and efficient but feeling like I was failing badly. Julia was professional and polite to me, but there was something missing. The warmth and camaraderie I had while sitting at the coffee shop with her, or even yesterday, had vanished.

Maybe that's how she treats the people who work for her, I told myself.

Or maybe she's just done with you, Kelly hissed.

"Great, give me a second," she said, opening her office door. I wanted to ask her why she kept it locked, but Val was starting with the kitchen, and I didn't want her to overhear.

She emerged with some cash and two typed sheets of paper. "It's probably best if you go now," she said. "Before Isabelle's nap." She handed me the paper and bills.

I took them, trying not to sigh. Heather always took the baby when she went on errands, but I hadn't realized how much of a production it was to take a baby anywhere. It would make things so much easier if I could run errands while Isabelle was sleeping.

But that clearly wasn't an option.

I swallowed and smiled. "I'll go get her."

* * *

I kept Isabelle in her car seat, balancing her on the front of the cart as I slowly made my way through the store. I didn't know where anything was, so it was taking me three times longer than it normally would, especially since Julia was quite explicit about brands.

She had also written a note on the list saying I was welcome to buy anything I wanted to eat or anything I needed for dinners over the next few days, and I started to feel a little panicked as I realized I hadn't decided on what I was making that night much less over the next few days. I was considering teriyaki chicken or maybe something Mexican, because who doesn't love Mexican food? But I realized I'd better make that decision while I was there, so I could get what I needed.

While Isabelle happily watched people walking by, I pulled out my phone to do a few quick searches.

Maybe I should plan for both meals, teriyaki chicken and Mexican, while I was still in the store ...

"I thought that was you. What are you doing with Isabelle?"

I glanced up from my phone at the same time Isabelle gurgled out a greeting.

It was Heather.

She was standing by the foot of the cart, a horrified expression on her face. One hand held a basket of groceries, and the other, a phone.

Crap. This could be a problem. On the other hand, Julia already knew I had seen her a few days ago at the park, so maybe it didn't matter after all.

"I'm shopping," I said airily, nodding toward her basket. "Same as you." I tucked my phone in my pocket, intending to push my cart past her.

She must have sensed what I was about to do, because she took a step to the side, blocking my path. "That doesn't explain why you're with Isabelle."

"Quite honestly, I don't see why that's any of your concern." I tried to nose my cart past her, but she took another step closer.

"It's a concern because a couple of days after I met you in the park, someone sabotaged my job."

"I don't know what you're talking about."

"I think you do," she said, her eyes narrowing. "How do you fit in? Are you friends with Julia? A family member?"

"It's none of your business who I am," I said, my voice growing sharper. "Now, if you'll excuse me, I have a lot of shopping to do."

She didn't move. "If you're not a friend or a family member, how did you even know I worked for Julia?"

"I didn't," I said, my voice a little too loud, a little too exasperated.

"Then how did you get my job?"

I wanted to end the conversation, but I didn't see how I could do it without picking up Isabelle and leaving the store altogether. And I really didn't want to do that—how would I explain the lack of groceries? "Julia and I are friends. She knew I was looking for a job. After she fired you, she offered it to me. That's it."

"But that still doesn't explain why you were in the park that day." Isabelle was waving her little hands toward her, so Heather held out the hand with her phone so she could grasp it.

"I wasn't in the park. I was walking by the park, and I saw you run off and leave the baby. I didn't put two and two together until after Julia hired me."

She shot me a look that clearly said she wasn't impressed. "Seems awfully coincidental."

"Well, sometimes coincidences happen. I don't know what you want me to say."

"Especially considering," she continued as if I hadn't said anything, "the way I was fired. It was awfully ... suspect."

I stared at her in disbelief. "You left a baby alone! How could you possibly consider being fired 'suspect'?"

"It was only one time, and I had good reason. But that's be-side the point, because why I was fired didn't have anything to do with what happened at the park."

My eyes widened. "How many things were you screwing up?"

"Why are you assuming I was screwing up anything?"

"Because you don't get fired unless you're doing something your employer doesn't want you to be doing."

She gave me a hard look. "Not necessarily. Especially when it smells like a setup."

I laughed, a hard, bitter laugh. "You actually think you were set up?"

Her eyes narrowed. "So you DO know what happened."

"Well, of course I do. Julia told me."

"How does she think the ashtray fell from the roof?"

"I have no idea. She didn't speculate."

Heather frowned, her eyes studying my face. Inside, I was squirming, but I didn't want her to see. Was it possible she could make trouble for me? I didn't think so. I was pretty sure Julia was done with her, but I couldn't be 100% sure. Especially since I didn't know if my job was all that secure.

That reminded me—I was wasting too much time. I needed to wrap it up with Heather.

"I don't know what your game is," she said finally. "But you're not as smart as you think you are."

Despite myself, I was intrigued. "What do you mean?"

"Let's just say that house isn't all it seems."

Now I was really curious. "What does that mean?"

She shrugged. "I don't know why I should help you. You got me fired."

"You got yourself fired," I corrected.

She gave me a thin smile. "Whatever. Although, quite hon-estly, you may have done me a favor. So, because of that, I'm just going to say this." She leaned closer to me, almost whispering in my ear. "Watch yourself. And whatever you do, don't let your guard down."

Her breath brushed against my neck like a cold winter wind. Goosebumps rose on my skin, and I shivered. "What am I guarding myself against?"

She stepped back, flashing that thin smile again. "You'll need to figure that out yourself."

Even though there was now more than enough room for me to leave, I didn't move. I wanted to ask, no, *demand,* that she explain herself. The words burned like acid at the back of my throat.

What was she trying to say? Does she think someone in that house had something to do with Ashley's disappearance?

No. I didn't believe it. Julia would never, could never, hurt anyone. Heather was just trying to cause trouble.

She continued to stand there, smiling at me, looking like the cat who ate the canary, and I knew she wouldn't answer my questions. Worse, it was clear she wanted me to ask, probably just to have the satisfaction of refusing.

Angrily, I shoved the cart forward. I had to finish shopping anyway.

She watched me go, the smile never leaving her face. I turned away and told myself not to turn around. It was good the conversation was over. Heather was just a dissatisfied ex-employee. I shouldn't listen to her anyway. She would probably like nothing better than to make Julia's life difficult, and what better way to do that than to turn me against her, so she loses her nanny again?

Well, it wasn't going to work.

When I reached the end of the aisle, I took a quick peek behind me. I wanted her to see how little I cared about her and what she said.

But she was gone.

Chapter 18

I was still fuming about Heather when I left to pick the kids up from school.

As I finished my shopping, I kept replaying the conversation over and over in my head. How dare Heather stop me and try to feed me such lies? Did she really think I'd be so easily persuaded? As I went through the conversation, I imagined myself answering differently, telling her what I really thought of her. Or, maybe I didn't stay and talk at all, just jammed the cart forward, and if she got hurt, well, it was her own fault.

I was so preoccupied with Heather that I forgot a few essential items (hello, ground beef for beef tacos) which I realized once I got home. I had no choice but to run back to the store a second time once I got Isabelle down for her nap. Val made a face when I asked her if she could keep an eye on her for just fifteen, twenty minutes while I dashed back to the store, but she begrudgingly agreed.

I didn't understand what Val's problem was. I hadn't done anything to her, so why was she so negative toward me? The more I thought about it, the worse my mood got.

Then, on the way back, I nearly sideswiped an old blue car, a Chevy, I thought, parked on the side of the road just up the street. I was driving too quickly, wanting to get home in case Julia realized I had left Isabelle with Val and didn't approve, and turned the corner too sharply, tipping over the bag of groceries. I took my eyes off the road while craning my neck over the seat, trying to see if I crushed the eggs. It was only a second, but when I looked back, I was careening toward the parked car. I jerked my wheel, barely avoiding disaster.

Just one thing after another.

At least Isabelle was easy. She was still sleeping when I arrived back at the house. Val was cleaning the master bedroom, and Julia's office door was shut tightly. I could feel the tension in my chest start to ease. Everything was fine. I was overreacting.

I was able to put the food away and start dinner before Isabelle woke, which made me breathe even easier. Now, I wouldn't have to race home, and could maybe even relax at the park with the kids. I changed the baby, strapped her in her stroller, and began walking to school. I was going to be a little early, but that was okay. I deserved a few minutes alone, other than Isabelle of course, to center myself after the day I had.

As I passed the old blue Chevy, the same one I had nearly hit earlier, I found myself studying it. It was a lot older and rustier than the other cars in the neighborhood. I figured it must belong to a visitor. Whoever owned it couldn't possibly live in the area.

In fact, hadn't I seen the driver? When I almost hit the car? I could picture it, the dark shadow swooping down, like they were unconsciously ducking as if to avoid me. It was empty now, of course, being over an hour later. Whoever owned the car was likely inside whichever house he or she was visiting. Or maybe it was a worker's car … a gardener or cleaning lady.

Well, it didn't matter. At least I had managed not to hit it. That would have been its own disaster.

The walk was good for me. It helped clear my head, put things in perspective. With Val in the house, it wouldn't have been a good day to dig around in Ashley's belongings anyhow, or to try and break into Julia's office. So, it didn't really matter that it was a bit of a waste. There was always tomorrow.

As I was early, I figured I would be the first at the school, but there was a man already standing there. He looked like he was a few years older than me, with wheat-colored hair covered with a baseball hat with the Brewers' logo on it and dark-green eyes. He smiled in greeting.

"I don't remember seeing you here before," he said. He took a couple of steps toward Isabelle, grinning at her. I noticed he had a slight limp. She responded with a wide smile of her own. "Are you new here?"

I wasn't particularly in the mood to have small talk with strangers, but I didn't necessarily want to be rude, either. "Yes, I just moved."

He tilted his head as he studied me. "You look too young to have kids old enough to go here," he said.

Was he flirting with me? It was hard to tell. Not to mention it'd been a long time since anyone flirted with me. "I'm actually a nanny," I said. I really didn't want to share any details with a stranger, but if he was someone who was here regularly, he might recognize Madison and Levi, and I didn't want him getting suspicious of me.

His eyebrows went up. "Oh, that explains it. I thought I remembered seeing this little one around." He tickled Isabelle's foot, and she laughed. "Who are you a nanny for?"

"The Johnsons," I said. I was wishing the bell would ring, or that I hadn't come early after all. The whole conversation was making me more and more uncomfortable.

"Julia and Max?"

"Yes." I glanced at the door to the school, willing it to open.

"Wow. So, that was fast. Wasn't Heather their nanny earlier this week?"

The sun disappeared behind a cloud, leaving us in shadow. A cold breeze licked at the back of my neck, making the hairs stand on end. "I wouldn't know," I said. "I'm just here to take care of the kids."

"Of course," he said. "I wasn't trying to insinuate anything. I was just surprised. I thought they were happy with Heather."

Despite myself, my curiosity was piqued. "Did you know Heather?" I wondered if I could get some dirt on her. It might come in handy if she decided to push things with Julia.

"Not well. We chatted a few times when she was picking up the kids. Madison and Levi, right?"

For someone who claimed not to know Heather very well, he sure knew a lot of details. "That's incredible. How are you able to remember their names? Are you a friend of the family?"

His smile turned bashful. "No, not really. I'm just good with names, that's all. One of my superpowers."

It was possible. Maybe he really was just good with names. He did seem like a clean-cut guy. His face was open and friendly.

So, why were all my senses on high alert, as if I were facing a monster as opposed to a dad waiting for his kid?

"Do you know what happened to Heather?" His voice was still light, like he was just making conversation to pass the time, but there was a glint in his eyes. Something cold and calculating.

I took a step away, pretending I was just shifting my weight. "I really don't," I said. "It's not my place to ask."

His head bobbed up and down. "Of course, of course. That makes total sense."

I eased another step away. Out of the corner of my eye, I could see more parents lining up. While it didn't seem like they were paying close attention to us, I was reassured by the company. "Are you sure you didn't know Heather very well? You seem very ... concerned about someone you only had a couple of conversations with."

His eyes widened. "Oh! It's nothing like that. Really. It's just ... well, Heather isn't the first nanny to disappear from the Johnsons."

My hands froze on the stroller. I couldn't move, even though every instinct in me said to run away. How did he know? Was he playing a game with me?

Was *he* the stalker?

My eyes raked over his face, searching for a resemblance to *him*.

Oz. The great and terrible.

Kelly's dangerous ex, who was now out of jail.

Could this be him? He didn't look familiar, but prison does change people. Could it have changed him that much?

"What do you mean?" I managed, trying to keep my voice from squeaking.

He held his hands up, palms out, in reassurance. "It's nothing, I'm sure. I don't want to worry you. It's just ... well, you should be careful, that's all. Watch your back."

The second time I'd heard those words in a day.

What did they know that I didn't?

I opened my mouth to ask more questions when the bell rang. I turned to see a teacher prop open the door, and a few kids started streaming out. It suddenly occurred to me that I didn't want the kids to see me with this man. Levi didn't matter so much, but Madison would definitely be a problem. The last thing I wanted was for her to say something to her mother about me speaking to the same man Heather used to "chat" with.

I looked back, ready to tell him the conversation was over, but he was nowhere to be found.

Wait a second. Where did he go?

Didn't he have a child to collect?

And if he didn't, *what was he doing there?*

"Janey, who are you looking for?"

I jerked back to see Madison staring at me. Flustered, I realized she had caught me frantically searching for that man. If I could just see him somewhere, preferably with a school-aged son or daughter, I wouldn't feel nearly as vulnerable. I could convince myself I was totally overreacting, because there was a perfectly logical explanation for his being there in front of the school.

I wouldn't feel like ... a victim in the making.

"I, ah, it's nothing," I said, trying not to let her see how agitated I was.

She gave me a knowing look. "Oh, *him*. Should I go find Levi?" She turned back to the school, craning her neck.

My mouth fell open as I stared at her in shock. "What do you mean, 'him'?"

"The man who's been hanging around," she said.

"You've seen him?" *Janey, you're going to scare the girl, and then where will you be?* Kelly asked in my head. My tone was sharper than I intended, and I forced myself to take a deep breath. "I mean ... do you know who he is?"

"I've never seen him," she said, still looking at the front of the school. "Levi must be talking to Alex again. I should go get him."

"If you've never seen him, then why would you think it's the same person?"

She gazed at me, her eyes unreadable. "You have the same look Heather had after she saw him."

Unconsciously, I reached up and touched my face. Was I that much of an open book? Or was this girl that good?

"Hi, Janey!" Levi yelled, barreling into me. "Can we go to the park? You promised, right?"

"Right," I said. "We're going to the park."

"Yay! Let's go, let's go." Levi started skipping ahead.

"Hold on," I called out, maneuvering the stroller. Madison was already walking with Levi, and I had to hurry to catch up, even though what I really wanted to do was keep searching the school grounds for that man. My mind was racing, trying to put all the pieces together.

Who was he? And what was he doing at the school?

Obviously, he wasn't a parent. That much was clear.

But why did he know so much about the Johnsons? And why was he talking to Heather?

And what did he know about Ashley?

Chapter 19

"Janey. Janey."

The voice floated down the hallway of my parent's house. It was Kelly's.

"Janey. Where are you? Come down here."

I was lying across my childhood bed with my headset on, but I could still hear Kelly calling me.

"Janey. What's taking you so long?"

I squeezed my eyes shut tightly, trying to block out the sound, trying to block out ... her. I didn't want to leave. Maybe if I stayed very quiet and didn't move a muscle, she would get bored and stop, maybe even forget about me altogether, especially when ...

"Janey, you are being very rude. What is wrong with you?"

Something was dragging me off the bed. I couldn't see what it was, but somehow, despite what I wanted, I found myself standing up.

"Come on, Janey. Hurry up."

I was floating out of the room, down the hall, down the stairs, toward the voice. I didn't want to ... I tried to fight it, but it didn't matter. I was trapped—sucked through the house, powerless, unable to stop myself, unable to do anything other than submit.

"There you are! What took you so long?"

They were sitting on the leather couch in the basement, in front of the television. Kelly was her usual polished, beautiful self—her blonde hair perfectly styled, artfully framing her face, and her makeup perfect. She wore a light-blue top that brought out the blue in her eyes. It looked stunning on her.

But next to her ... next to her ...

Was a monster.

He was all black hair and sharp teeth, red eyes, and curving claws. He grinned at me, displaying shiny white fangs that dripped saliva onto his huge barrel chest.

I was paralyzed with fear. I couldn't move. I couldn't breathe.

Kelly scooted over, patting the seat next to her. "Come. Sit down. Join us." The monster next to her opened his mouth, and a red tongue snaked out to lick his lips.

I opened my mouth, tried to force the words out. "Kelly," I squeaked. My voice was so faint, I didn't think she could hear it.

"Well, come on," she said again, still patting the seat, the monster still licking his lips.

I swallowed, tried again. "You're in danger," I said, my voice a little stronger. "Get away from the couch."

Kelly looked surprised. "Danger? What are you talking about?"

I tried to raise my arm, but it felt like I was dragging it through mud. "Right there. On the couch next to you."

Kelly twisted to look all around her. "What? What are you seeing? I'm not seeing anything."

At last, I got my arm to move. "Right there," I said, pointing. "You're sitting next to a monster."

Her expression turned to shock. "Monster? What are you talking about?" The monster next to her lolled, his tongue dangling from his mouth.

"Kelly, he's right there," I said. "He's sitting right next to you."

Kelly's eyes widened. "Him?" She pointed at the monster.

Finally. "Yes!" Maybe now she would move, would get away from him, would help me get away, far away from those teeth that wanted to bite, to devour ...

Kelly burst into laughter. I blinked, confused.

"That's not a monster," she said. "That's Oz. You know Oz. Don't be so silly, Janey. Come here and sit with us."

"No, you don't understand," I tried to say, but Kelly cut me off with a quick shake of her head.

"That's enough. Just stop it, Janey. Don't be so rude. Come here and sit with us." Her voice was firm. There was no room for argument.

I didn't want to. I didn't want to be anywhere near him. But somehow, I found myself floating across the room toward the couch.

And before I knew it, I was sitting there.

Right next to the monster.

I could smell him, his fetid breath and the scent of blood, sweat, and despair on his hair mixed with, strangely enough, what smelled like aftershave, which made no sense. Yet the cloying scent of it seemed to stick in my throat, choking me, suffocating me.

He leaned closer to me, grinning, his teeth growing longer and sharper. I tried to move away, to squeeze myself closer to Kelly. But Kelly was like a brick wall, unbudging. All I could do was sit there, my eyes squeezed shut, as the monster moved closer and closer.

Kelly squeezed my knee. "Relax," she purred. "It doesn't have to be such a big deal. All you have to do is relax."

I awoke with a scream trapped in my throat. I could still smell aftershave in my nostrils. I wanted to be sick. I thought I might be sick.

I rolled out of bed, sweat soaking through the T-shirt and shorts I slept in, and barely made it to the bathroom before throwing it all up. The nightmare, the aftershave, all of it.

Afterward, I lay on the cool floor breathing hard. I didn't want to go back into my room. I was half-convinced the monster would be there, waiting in the dark, still grinning ...

I squeezed my eyes shut. No! It was just a dream. A terrible dream. But still a dream.

The real question was, why was I having such a dream now? What triggered it?

Was it because of that strange man standing outside of the kids' school?

I could see him as clearly as if he were in the bathroom with me. The charming, self-effacing smile. The hint of bashfulness.

Asking about Heather. About the kids.

You have the same look Heather had after she saw him.

I dug my fingers into my temple.

What if he was the stalker?

The words from the letter floated through my head.

I'm being stalked. No one believes me.

First Ashley, then Heather.

And now me.

Was that what my dream was telling me? Was it a warning? That there really was a stalker after all?

And was I next?

I sat up with a jerk, searching the small bathroom, all of the sudden overcome with panic that I wasn't alone. I was being watched by something just waiting for me to let down my guard, to look away, and then, it would pounce ...

Fear buzzed through my head so intensely that for a moment, I couldn't think. All I wanted to do was run downstairs, throw open the front door, escape the house, and never, ever come back ...

There was something tickling me at the back of my head, something important, but I couldn't concentrate on it, as it was drowning in a sea of fear and panic.

Janey, focus! Before I did anything I regretted, I had to get myself under control. I forced myself to breathe slowly and deeply, counting to five as I inhaled and exhaled.

It felt like it took forever, but in reality, it was probably only a few minutes before the fog in my head began to clear, and I could finally start to think again.

It would be silly for me to leave now. If there really was a stalker, and if Ashley/Kelly disappeared because of him or her, I was in the perfect position to investigate. I owed it to Ashley/Kelly to get to the bottom of what was going on.

And the sooner, the better.

I stood up, rinsed my mouth out, brushed my teeth, and headed back to my room. I did pause in the hallway, holding my breath in the dark, straining my ears. I would be mortified if someone were awake, especially if he or she heard me being sick in the bathroom.

But all was silent.

I focused on the kids' rooms, trying to hear if Madison wasn't sleeping. The last thing I wanted was another conversation like I had after the first night. But there was nothing.

I crept to my room, closing the door firmly behind me and turning the light on. I dug my notebook out from where I had hidden it under one of the drawers and flipped it open, intending to review all my notes, but getting stuck on what had happened the day before.

First, Heather. *Watch your back.*

And then, the stranger. *Watch your back.*

Why would they both be telling me to watch my back?

Unless ...

Let's just say that house isn't all that it seems.

Was it possible there was something else going on? Something in the house responsible for Ashley's disappearance?

But what?

Surely it couldn't be anything Julia had done. She seemed genuinely upset about Ashley's disappearance.

What about Max? I thought about his demeanor the first night. He didn't want to talk about Ashley at all.

Was it because he wanted to move on? Or because he was covering something else up ... like maybe a guilty conscience?

No. I dismissed it. It couldn't be either of them. Especially not Julia. I would have sensed something. I could still remember how she hugged me that first day, welcoming me into her family. It just wasn't possible.

Besides, why would they keep Ashley's belongings if one of them were involved?

There had to be another explanation. I just couldn't think of what it might be.

I rubbed my forehead. Maybe what I needed to do was get out of the house for a few hours. Get some space and breathing room.

In fact, maybe I'd try to see Bryn that weekend. I reached for my phone before I realized it was way too late, or too early, depending on how you looked at it, to text.

Yes, that's what I needed to do. Spend some time back in my old apartment, away from the madness, with Bryn. I could tell her what was going on, and she would help me unravel it.

Then, once I got my head back on straight, I could figure out my next steps.

* * *

"That is the craziest story," Bryn said. We were sitting in the living room surrounded by leftover pizza and glasses of cheap red wine. I had offered to take her out to dinner, but it was her idea to stay in. She thought it would be easier to take notes and maybe grab a computer for online research if we stayed in the apartment. As she greeted me wearing no makeup, her wild curls every which way, and dressed in old, grey, baggy sweatpants and an oversized T-shirt, I got the feeling she really just wanted to hang out at home in comfy clothes.

Personally, I didn't care what we did. I was just thankful I didn't have to cook. I was also thankful for the gentle buzz I was feeling from the red wine. I hadn't realized how stressed I had been until right then. Taking care of a household was a lot more complicated than I'd thought. Plus, I still hadn't been able to do any investigating. Friday was a half day for the kids, so there was no time for me to do anything but keep up with my duties. Hopefully, this would all change on Monday.

"So, you're saying there *is* a stalker?"

"I don't know what I'm saying," I said. I had basically told Bryn everything, minus my involvement in getting Heather fired.

I also didn't mention my dreams. That felt too much like going down a rabbit hole that would ultimately do no good.

Bryn tapped her pen on her notebook, in which she had been diligently writing as I spoke. "Okay, let's start at the beginning. Ashley disappeared, yet her stuff is still being stored in the basement. That's actually really weird. Don't you think so?"

"What should they do with it?" I asked doubtfully.

"Give it to the police, for one," Bryn said.

"Maybe the police already looked through it and decided there was nothing there."

"If that's the case, then why don't they just toss it? I mean, Ashley disappeared two months ago. Left them in a lurch, and hasn't reached out. At this point, I would think Ashley isn't all that interested in what she left behind, so if she doesn't want it, why would Julia keep it? She'd be well within her rights to toss it."

"Well, it's difficult throwing someone else's stuff out," I said, feeling my hackles rise. I knew Bryn meant well, but this was Julia we were talking about. She couldn't possibly have had anything to do with it. "And the police did think Ashley disappeared because she had some sort of mental breakdown. So, maybe Julia thinks Ashley will wake up one day and realize what she's done. Maybe she'd need her things back, then."

Bryn made a face. "Maybe. But still. Why would you keep it? It's not like Ashley was family. She wasn't even there for very long. Like it was only a few months, right? So, why would you do that? Would *you* keep it?"

"I ..." I hadn't thought about it. I had just been so thankful they had. Plus, I really didn't like where the conversation was going. "Maybe."

"And look at how they're storing it," Bryn said, warming to the topic and seemingly oblivious to how uncomfortable I was with it. "They're covering it with a sheet? In the middle of a room? If they were planning on keeping it for a while, and they took the time to drag it down into the basement and find a sheet to cover it, why not put it all in boxes? You could label them and stack them in a corner instead of everything being in the way, the way it is now. Anyway, so that's the first strange thing. And, of course, the fact that both Heather and this weird stalker guy said the same thing to you is definitely weird. Are they trying to tell you Julia and Max had something to do with it?"

"I don't know, but don't you think they would be more likely to throw Ashley's stuff away if they did?"

"I would think they would be less likely to throw it away. With it, they can say they're waiting for Ashley to come back."

The pizza I had eaten seemed to turn into a greasy lump in my stomach. I pushed my plate away and reached for my wine. "You seriously think that they ..." I swallowed hard, the word "murder" frozen on my tongue. I wanted to tell Bryn how ridiculous she was being—that there was no way Julia would ever stand for any of that. She was a part of my family now.

But the words just wouldn't come.

Bryn held up her hands. "Hold on. Let's not get ahead of ourselves. I'm not accusing them of anything. I'm certainly not accusing them of ... well, killing Ashley."

"But, you ... just said ..." I stuttered.

"They can be responsible without, well, doing *that*," Bryn said.

"Like how?"

"Well, what if there was an accident?" Bryn asked. "Or a misunderstanding? Maybe Julia and Max fought with her, and Ashley left in a huff. Maybe Max, well, maybe he hit on Ashley, or even worse. It's possible something happened, and Julia or Max, or both, feel guilty about their role in Ashley leaving, so they're keeping her things."

It hadn't occurred to me there might be another reason for Ashley leaving, and that whatever it was, Julia might be feeling guilty about it.

"Maybe it has something to do with this stalker situation," Bryn said. "I know Julia made it seem like Ashley was being unreasonable, and maybe she was, but maybe they fought about it. Or maybe Ashley thought Julia wasn't doing enough to keep her safe, and Julia realized after the fact that Ashley might have been right."

"Or ..." Bryn's voice trailed off and a thoughtful expression came over her face. "What if ... well, this is crazy. But maybe the stalker was never about Ashley."

I blinked. "Wait, what?"

"Well, think about it. If Ashley was being stalked, why is the stalker still hanging around, if that is indeed what is happening? A strange man is talking to Heather. He talks to you. Why is he still even there if Ashley was his target?"

My head was starting to spin. I swallowed the rest of my wine and reached for the bottle to refill. "So, if it wasn't Ashley, then ..."

"Someone in the family," Bryn finished.

Julia. Her name was on the tip of my tongue.

Me, hiding in the garage as she was leaving, frantic because of a phone call.

Was Julia hiding something? Was that at the bottom of all of this? Some secret of hers?

I had to get into her office.

Bryn noticed the expression on my face and leaned closer. "What? You're remembering something."

"I ..." I didn't want to tell her about my breaking and entering, so I didn't mention Julia running out of the house in the middle of the day with no explanation, and instead just focused on how Julia always kept her office locked, even if she was only leaving the house for a short time.

Bryn gasped. "See? That must be what's going on! Julia is hiding something, and whatever that is has resulted in some sort of stalking behavior."

"Which would explain why she's keeping Ashley's stuff," I continued slowly, as the pieces started to come together in my mind. "Because she *is* feeling guilty."

"Exactly," Bryn said, her eyes bright. "She either knows or is pretty convinced this is her fault, so she's trying to make amends by keeping Ashley's stuff. There might even be more things she's doing that you haven't discovered yet."

I could feel myself starting to relax. Of course. This made perfect sense. Julia was such a loving, caring person that she would definitely struggle with guilt, even if it wasn't her fault. "If that's the case, what do you think it might be? What secret could she be hiding?"

Bryn sighed. "I have no idea. But whatever it is, it must be pretty juicy."

I nodded. I definitely needed to get into that office. The sooner I knew what Julia was dealing with, the sooner I could help her.

"Maybe you need to reach out to Ashley's friends," Bryn continued. "They might know something, even if it's something they don't realize could be important. If you talk to them, they might tell you something that, well, clicks."

"I'm not sure who they are," I said doubtfully. "Other than those friends commenting on her Instagram post. And who knows if they're really friends?"

"If I remember correctly, a couple of them seemed pretty upset. They were practically begging Ashley to call or text. I would start with them."

"So, what do I do? Just send them a message on Instagram?"

"Why not?" Bryn said. "It's at least a start."

"And explain ..."

"Just tell them the truth," Bryn said. "You're working as a nanny at the same place Ashley was working, and they still have some of Ashley's stuff, and you were wondering if they know where she is. And hopefully from there, you can start a conversation."

"I don't know," I said. "This sounds a little too easy."

"What do you have to lose? The worst that happens is they refuse to talk to you, but I don't think that's likely. Also, are you able to go through Ashley's things?"

"Yes, I keep meaning to, but it's really a lot taking care of three kids plus cooking and straightening up and just ..." I shook my head helplessly.

Bryn's expression turned sympathetic. "I certainly wasn't trying to give you a hard time. When you can, do it. Again, there might be a clue in there."

"Trust me, I want to go through it more than you."

She tapped her pen and gazed down at her notes. "It would be great to get a pic of the maybe-stalker guy. If you see him again, don't engage. Or don't engage right away. Instead, get a photo of him. Then maybe we can figure out who he is."

I hadn't thought about that. "Good idea."

Bryn grinned. "I'm more than a pretty face," she joked before quickly sobering up. "Seriously, having a picture would do a lot. You could show it to Julia and Max, the police. If he is the stalker, it would be really helpful. Plus ..." she hesitated, and her expression turned a little grimmer. "I don't think you should be talking to him. I don't know how safe it is."

"He was fine at the school."

Bryn's face was troubled. "Yeah, but we still don't know what happened to Ashley. And if he's somehow involved, well, I just think it would make more sense if we find out as much as we can without you engaging with him."

I could see the flop of brown hair, the disarming smile, in my mind's eye. On the surface, he appeared perfectly normal. And he did tell me to watch my back. Was it possible he was a monster inside?

My stomach lurched, and for a moment, I thought I'd be sick. I pressed my hand over my belly and breathed deep.

Bryn looked alarmed. "I'm not trying to scare you. But it would be good to be cautious. There's a lot we don't know."

"I know, and it makes sense."

Bryn pressed her lips together. "You know," she said, pausing as if contemplating her word choices. "No one would blame you if you just didn't go back."

I gave her a sharp look. "What?"

"It's not a normal investigation," she said, her words coming out more quickly. "Think about it. You're in the same house doing the same job as a girl who disappeared. There's a lot of strange things going on. It's okay to put yourself first."

"But, it's my sister," I said. "I owe it to her to find out what happened."

Bryn looked away. "I know that. But ..." she bit her lip, then steeled herself. "What if you don't find her? What if what's going on has nothing to do with her? What if she did just have some sort of breakdown, like the cops think, and in the meantime, you're stumbling into something that could potentially be dangerous for you?"

I stared at her aghast. "You really think it's unrelated? That there might be some awful secret Julia is hiding that has nothing to do with Ashley's disappearance?"

Bryn shrugged. "It's possible. Who knows why people have breakdowns? It could just be a terrible coincidence. Or, like I said earlier, what happened to Ashley was just an unfortunate accident. Maybe she saw something, or heard something, and it was triggered. Maybe she had been stalked before, and whoever is stalking the family triggered her. Or, maybe she was afraid."

"Afraid?"

"Yeah, maybe she stumbled into something and thought she might be in danger, so she just ... ran?"

I was skeptical. "I don't know. Don't you think she'd at least take her stuff?"

"If she was afraid enough, she wouldn't."

Could that be what happened? Ashley was just afraid and running? And I ended up blundering into something potentially dangerous in my zeal to find her? "I still need to know," I said. "I have to at least try. She's my sister. My only family left." Although, that wasn't completely true. At least not anymore.

Now, I had Julia, too.

Bryn reached over to touch my hand. "Of course, I get it." She gave it a gentle squeeze. I wanted to jerk it away, but I forced myself not to. "You know, there's one other possibility," she said, her voice brisk. She let go of my hand and drew back.

"What?" I subtly moved my hand further away from her.

"She disappeared because she was in Redemption."

I blinked at her. "Oh, come on. You don't really believe all those old wives' tales?"

"Of course I do. I can't believe you don't."

I shook my head in disgust.

"Look, people disappear from there all the time," she said. "What about those college kids ..."

"Those college kids never disappeared," I said. "They just came out, partied, and left."

She was shaking her head. "No, someone I once met knew someone who was friends with one of those kids ..."

"Oh, everyone knows someone who knows someone," I said. "That doesn't make it true."

"Well, forget the college kids," she said defensively. "There are lots of stories of people disappearing, never to be seen again. What about that sixteen-year-old ... Jessica, I think her name was."

"Wasn't that the girl who ran off to LA to be an actress or something?"

"She never got back in touch with her family," Bryn said. "Ever. Is that normal?"

"Well, maybe something happened to her on the road. Maybe she was hitchhiking, and the wrong person picked her up, which would have nothing to do with Redemption."

She gave me a look. "If you don't want to believe it, fine. All I'm saying is that it's another possibility."

There had always been strange stories around Redemption, ever since its rather strange birth, when all the adults supposedly disappeared. This was back in the late 1800s or early 1900s—I could never remember. I always assumed it was nonsense. How could that even happen? Or, more likely, it was an exaggeration, when what really happened was some disease came through and killed a bunch of adults. Somehow, the reality then morphed into a ridiculous story of disappearance.

Regardless of how it started, since then, there had always been tales of people disappearing. The generally accepted reason? The town *decided* who it kept.

Personally, I found it all a bunch of crap. We had spent plenty of summers there when I was growing up. All of the rumors and gossip were simply that—rumors and gossip.

"Okay, I agree. It's another possibility," I said. "And who knows? Maybe there is something to it. Not that I personally believe it, but if Ashley did, that could have been a trigger."

"Hmm, that's true." Bryn made a note in her notebook. "So, I guess the next steps are to go through Ashley's belongings and contact her friends and see what they have to say. And, if you see that guy again, take a picture."

"Will do," I said. "I'm going to start with her belongings. Maybe there's an address book or something in there. Would make my job easier."

"That would be amazing if you found something like that," she said with a grin. But then she paused, her smile faltering as she glanced at me, her eyes narrowed. "You'll keep me posted, right?"

"Of course. We're a team."

She continued to stare at me, her eyes unwavering. "I mean it," she said. "I'm legit worried about you."

I tried to wave it off. "Don't be. I'm fine."

"Janey, I'm serious. You'll check in with me regularly, right?"

I stared into her wide, blue eyes. Her gaze was so intense. I wanted to tell her not to worry, that Julia would make sure nothing happened to me, but I didn't think she'd understand. "Absolutely," I said. "I promise I will check in regularly with you. Scout's honor."

She smiled briefly, but it didn't quite reach her eyes. "You know I'll worry if you don't."

I picked up my wine glass, trying to lighten the mood. "Bryn, you know I have to talk to someone. I'm a verbal processor. And who else is going to help me make sense of what I'm finding? You have nothing to worry about. I will definitely keep you posted with regular check-ins."

She picked up her glass and clicked it against mine. "I'm going to hold you to that."

Chapter 20

I was debating whether there was enough time to pick the lock on Julia's office before she returned home from the coffee shop when I heard the front door open.

"Oh, you're home early," I said brightly, trying not to reveal my inner panic at how close a call that would have been. Isabelle waved her hands and gurgled as she swung in her swing.

Julia smiled, but it seemed forced. "Can we talk for a moment?" She was holding a cardboard carrier with two coffees and a small bag. "I brought you a coffee and bagel."

"Thanks," I said, even though the last thing I wanted was anything to eat or drink. My stomach churned uncomfortably, and I had a feeling I wasn't going to like this "talk."

We sat down at the kitchen table, where she made a big show of getting plates and setting the food out. All I wanted to do was scream for her to spit it out, whatever she wanted to tell me.

This couldn't be good.

"So, first, I can't tell you how grateful I am for you stepping in the way you did," she began, not meeting my eyes and poking at her bagel. "I don't know what I would have done without you."

I was having trouble breathing. No, this couldn't be happening. She was my family. You don't kick your family out.

Of course they don't want you, Kelly said. *Why would they? Your own family barely tolerated you. Why would Julia want you around?*

"And you've been doing a really great job," Julia was saying, although I could barely hear her over the sound of Kelly's voice and the roaring in my ears. Desperately, I shoved Kelly's voice away. I needed to think, to focus. "But, you do know we really want a nanny who will be with us until Isabelle is old enough for school, and maybe even beyond. So, Max and I decided we would at least put some feelers out, to see what happens."

The edges of my vision were starting to darken. I was trying to catch my breath, but couldn't.

She must have sensed my distress, because she finally looked at me. "Look, nothing is a done deal," she said. "If we can't find anyone suitable, then we'd love to keep you on. Max just thought, well, we thought, it made sense to take advantage of you being here, so we could take our time to find the right person. There's no pressure to find someone immediately, so we can just relax, and if the right person shows up, great. But if not, then you'll be here to keep us going."

I swallowed and licked my dry lips. "Is this because I over-slept that first day?" My voice sounded creaky, cracked, and as dry as my mouth.

Julia's eyes widened. "Oh no. No! It's nothing you did. We'd love to have you stay. You're doing a great job. No, this is really just setting ourselves up for the future, that's all. And we didn't want you to be ... surprised, or shocked, if potential nannies came around for interviews. We're truly so grateful you're here, so we can take our time."

"No problem," I said. "I'm happy to help." I tried to force a smile, but it felt strained and fake. My shock and devastation were slowly transforming to anger, and then kindling to the rage.

How dare they treat me like this? After all I did for them, they were just going to throw me out?

Not if I had anything to say about it.

Julia looked relieved. "I'm so glad to hear that. I know how ... *weird* this is, and we also get how much of a sacrifice you're making by choosing to stay and keep working without knowing how long the job will last. So, if we do end up finding someone, we're prepared to pay you not only through the end of the summer, but to give you a bonus to help you with your housing expenses, too. We'll make sure you don't lose out because you're helping us."

But you're taking away my family, I wanted to scream. *Are you going to let me keep coming back for meals? For holidays? What about all of that?*

But I knew I couldn't say any of it. Not yet, at least.

"I appreciate that," I said instead. "That will help a lot."

"And if you need references or whatever, we're also happy to help," she kept babbling. "Whatever you need. We want you to know how grateful we are." She glanced at her phone and startled. "Oh. I better get to work, but you're good, right?"

"Of course," I said. "I totally understand."

Julia rose to her feet, collecting her coffee cup and plate with the uneaten bagel.

"So, when is this going to start?"

She gave me a quizzical look. "Sorry?"

"When are you going to start advertising for a nanny? Just so I know what to expect."

"Oh. Um ..." Julia dropped her gaze as she focused on fiddling with her food and drink. "I think ... well, it might be as soon as today. Max has someone working on the job description to make it sing."

Today. I tried to keep my mouth from dropping open. That gave me very little time for ... well, for everything. I was going to have to move fast.

"But remember, nothing is a done deal," she said hastily. "And if we do find someone, we will take care of you. Okay?"

"Sure," I said, waving my hand. "Go on. I know you have things to do, and so do I."

Her expression relaxed, and she gave me a big, true smile. "You're one in a million, Janey. I don't know what we'd do without you. I actually hope ... well, never mind. I better get going."

"Oh," I called out as Julia was fumbling with the lock at the door. "I have to run some errands. Is it okay if I take the car?"

"Of course. Whatever you need."

"Thanks."

***

I learned several interesting things after installing the cameras in the family room, living room, and master bedroom.

First, that Julia had lied to me. Max had actually posted the nanny job description on Friday, which was before she had even told me.

So, while I was busy taking care of her children on Friday, thinking all was right in the world, Max was actively looking for my replacement.

It was all I could do to keep from screaming, from stomping out of my room and confronting them as they sat huddled in the family room, sipping wine, confident I was safely tucked up in my room, oblivious that they were discussing how best to get rid of me.

Second, that two applicants were scheduled to interview that Thursday. The plan was for Julia to interview them herself first, and then Max would follow up with a second interview. Julia didn't like that idea; she wanted to weed them out and let Max know who her favorites were, so he could choose from them. But Max wasn't having any of that.

"Are you forgetting that you were in charge of hiring the first two nannies?" he asked. "And here we are, looking for nanny number three, and it's barely been six months."

"We already have nanny number three," Julia said, her expression sour as she swallowed more wine. Her face had that flushed, third-glass look again.

Max flashed her a look that was somehow both patient and condescending. "You know Janey isn't the right long-term fit. Yet again, you jumped the gun and impulsively offered the job to someone unsuitable. All you needed to do was be a little patient and ask a few more questions, and we could have avoided all of this."

"Easy for you to say," Julia shot back. "*You're* not here. *Your* work isn't impacted when there's no nanny. I'm the one who has to pick up the pieces and try and explain to my clients why I'm missing deadlines yet again ..."

"It didn't have to be this way," Max interrupted. "If you hadn't fired Heather, again, impulsively, we could have been looking for someone else while she was still here instead of yet again throwing the entire household into disarray and requiring our kids to get used to yet another person ..."

"You wanted me to ignore her lies?" Julia asked, her voice rising and eyes wide.

"Keep your voice down," Max hissed. "Do you want Janey to hear you?"

Julia gritted her teeth and drained her glass before reaching for the bottle.

Max watched her, his face impassive. "Don't you think you've had enough?"

Julia didn't react, choosing instead to simply focus on filling her glass.

Max opened his mouth like he was going to push the issue before closing it again. "It's your funeral," he said, and then changed the subject back to the prospective nannies.

While the rest of the conversation was, for the most part, civil, the tension was thick enough to cut with a knife, especially when they got to the part about when Max would be interviewing.

"It might make sense to do the second round on Sunday," he said. "Although that might be a little weird asking them to come back on a Sunday. What might make more sense is for them to come the following week late in the afternoon. Maybe we have Janey take the kids somewhere special after school, like to the zoo, and they can eat there."

Julia muttered something into her wine that I couldn't quite make out, but whatever it was made Max's face darken. "We've had this conversation before," he said. "You know I'm trying to get that promotion."

"You were working late before that," she snapped. "There's always an excuse to not spend time with your family. With me."

Max stood up. "I'm not having this conversation with you right now. I'm going to bed."

"You don't want to have this conversation because you know I'm right."

Max stared at her for a moment, a muscle in his jaw working. "You may want to put the wine down and drink some water before coming to bed. Goodnight."

Julia glared at him, but he was already walking away from her. I muted the sound on my computer even though I had earphones in and listened to Max climb the stairs, his steps heavy, and enter the master bedroom.

Thanks to the video feed, I could see Julia had stayed right where she was, finishing her wine as she muttered into her glass. Eventually, I saw her eyes flutter closed, and her chin dropped to her chest. Her empty wine glass slid sideways, leaning against the arm of the couch. Gentle snores floated through the speaker.

Which led me to the third thing I learned: Julia and Max's marriage wasn't as solid as Julia had made it seem … nor was Julia the perfect wife, mother, consultant, and homemaker. On social media, where I monitored Julia's updates, her life was perfect.

Her actual life? Not so much.

I shut the computer and got ready for bed.

After Julia had dropped the bomb about advertising for new nannies, I immediately drove to the store to purchase cameras, which I spent the rest of the afternoon installing. I positioned two out of three in air vents, and one in the living room in the dusty bookcase, which Val clearly never dusted. I was pretty confident it wouldn't be found. It took a little longer than it normally would have, as I had to be careful to check that Julia was on a meeting before I could get to work.

I also installed two outside cameras, one pointing toward the front of the house and the other toward the back. Initially, I planned to get only one camera for outside and hide it up on the roof, in the same area Heather hid her ashtray, which would be perfect for monitoring the backyard. But as I drove out of the neighborhood, Isabelle happily in tow, I saw that same beat-up blue Chevy parked on the side of the road.

What was it doing there? It still looked completely out of place in the neighborhood. Even driving by it caused my hackles to rise, especially when I thought about that strange man at the school.

Could that be his car? Was he parked there to watch us?

I decided I didn't want to take any more chances, and since Julia seemed oblivious, it was up to me to try and save the family.

If that meant installing security cameras inside and outside so I could keep an eye on this nanny-hiring business, so be it.

Overall, I was pleased with my work. The only thing I wasn't pleased about was that I still hadn't gotten a chance to go through Ashley's stuff. *Tomorrow,* I promised myself. *Definitely tomorrow.*

After all, I knew when the potential nannies were going to be interviewed, so I didn't have to worry about them. I could spend the next couple of days focusing on Ashley. And that would leave the end of the week free to figure out how to get rid of the nanny prospects.

Satisfied, I snapped the bedroom light off and curled up in bed. It was all falling into place easier than I'd imagined. Even Kelly had quieted down in my head. I figured I must be on the right path.

It was all working out perfectly.

The Third Nanny

Chapter 21

I awoke with a jerk, sitting straight up in bed and gasping for air, my terror lodged in my throat. The moon spilled across the floor, reflecting off the polished hardwood floor and cozy throw rug.

Wait a minute.

This wasn't my room.

I whipped my head around, trying to take in all the shadowy hulks of furniture at once—strange shapes that were somehow familiar and unfamiliar at the same time.

And then it hit me.

I was in my childhood room.

Why? And what had awoken me with such fear?

I was about to slide out of bed when I heard a noise at the door. I sat frozen, my heart pounding in my chest, so loud I was sure the entire household could hear.

Was someone there?

I strained my ears, trying to listen over my panicked breathing. I tried holding my breath.

Silence.

Maybe I had just been hearing things. Maybe it was just left-over anxiety from my dream—or nightmare, or whatever it was that woke me.

Maybe ...

The doorknob slowly turned back and forth. I gasped, throwing myself as far back in my bed as I could and curling into a ball. I stuffed my fist into my mouth, trying to keep myself quiet, so whoever was on the other side of the door wouldn't hear me ...

The door creaked open. "Hey, Janey. Are you okay?"

It was Kelly. I slumped over, all the tension draining out of my body, leaving me limp and lifeless.

She slipped into the room, closing the door softly behind her. The moon glinted on her blonde hair, turning it silver. Her face was in shadows, morphing her eyes into pools of darkness. The scent of her perfume floated around her like a cloud.

"I guess I had a nightmare," I whispered.

She raised an eyebrow. "Guess?"

"I don't remember," I said. "Not exactly. Something about a monster in the house."

She moved to the bed and curled up at the foot, just like when we were kids. "Well, there's no monster in the house."

"Are you sure? Did you check?"

She laughed, a tinkling laugh that reminded me of glass breaking. "I don't have to."

I was silent for a moment, thinking. I wanted to ask, but was afraid. "What about Oz?" I finally asked, my voice a whisper.

"What about him?" Her voice was much harder, edgier ... as sharp as a broken wine bottle.

"Is he in the house?"

"No! Why would he be in the house?"

"I don't know, that's why I'm asking."

"He's not a monster, you know." Was it my imagination, or was her voice changing? Flatter and hollower, like a hungry predator. Come to think of it, her body seemed to be transforming as well, growing sleeker and more pointed. Her mouth was widening, her nails curling into claws. Even the smell of her perfume was mutating, turning fetid and sour, like it was somehow spoiling.

"I know that," I said, trying to push myself tighter against the headboard, my pulse quickening even as a voice inside admonished me. *She's your sister,* it said. *You have nothing to be afraid of. She loves you.*

The figure that was Kelly licked her lips, her tongue somehow larger than it should be. "Besides," she purred. "I broke up with him."

My eyes widened. "You did?"

"Don't sound so surprised, Janey." She shifted positions, looking more and more like a hunched-over beast waiting to pounce. "You told me you were frightened of him, so I broke up with him."

"Wow, that's great! Why didn't you tell me before?"

"I'm telling you now," she said.

See, the little voice inside me hissed. *She does love you. Told you so.*

Kelly leaned forward, powerful muscles bunching under her shoulder. She licked her lips again. "I broke up with him for you. Haven't you learned yet how much I care? That I'll always take care of you?"

I awoke with a jolt. I was back in my room at the Johnsons', the light a watery grey as the sun prepared to rise. I glanced over at the clock and winced. I didn't need to get up for at least another hour, but I also didn't want to run the risk of oversleeping. Slowly, I sat up, peeling the covers off to get ready for my day, wrinkling my nose in the process. I swore I could smell perfume. Calvin Klein's Eternity. But that was silly. I never used perfume, and Julia's smelled like lemon and mint, which was not even close.

It was lingering from my dream.

I threw on a pair of jeans and a bright-pink T-shirt before heading to the bathroom to wash up and brush my hair into a ponytail. Next, I peeked in on Isabelle, who was still fast asleep on her back, legs and arms splayed out like a starfish. I watched her for a moment, debating whether I had enough time to dig through Ashley's things before she'd wake. Was it worth the risk? Or should I play it safe, maybe start prepping for dinner?

Haven't you learned how much I care?

Guilt twisted inside me. I'd been there a week already and hadn't done much investigating at all. Was I serious about finding my sister or not? I could almost feel her drifting further and further away from me with each passing day.

I glanced at the time on my phone and made a decision. I needed to act. I grabbed the baby monitor, so I would know the minute Isabelle stirred.

I hurried into the kids' bathroom and scooped up an armful of laundry. That would be my excuse if Max was in the kitchen when I came up. I was getting an early start on laundry. As quietly as I could, I hurried down the stairs and into the basement.

It seemed to be colder and mustier than normal, although that didn't make much sense. It also seemed darker, the edges of the room disappearing into shadows that I swore weren't there before. It was almost as if someone had tampered with the lights, so he or she could hide in the darkness, unnoticed by unsuspecting prey until it was too late ...

I gave myself a quick shake. I was being ridiculous. I had a job to do. Ashley was counting on me. I had to find her.

Actually, I reminded myself, it was *Kelly*. My sister was just calling herself "Ashley," probably to hide from Oz.

I shook my head again. I was tired. What I really needed was coffee, but I didn't dare take the time to brew a pot. I needed to focus on the task in front of me.

I tossed the clothes into the washer and started it, barely paying attention to what I was doing, my mind already focused on the investigation at hand before moving toward the storage room and Ashley's things.

It looked exactly the way it had before. Everything was still piled up in the middle of the room and covered by a sheet. I thought about what Bryn had said about how odd it was for the Johnsons to keep all this stuff, and staring at it in that moment, I could see her point. It *was* weird, everything splayed in the middle of a room. It would be nearly impossible to get to anything else in the room without stepping on something.

Why would Julia do that?

I put my phone and the baby monitor down near the corner of the room, took a deep breath, and flipped the sheet off.

The first thing I noticed was clothes—lots and lots of clothes. It appeared Julia had taken whatever Ashley had left in her closet and just piled it all on the floor.

As I started pawing through the jeans, sweatshirts, sweaters, and shirts, I realized they were tossed over a clump of boxes—a half-dozen of them, mostly open.

The first couple were filled with socks, underwear, and bras. Another contained costume jewelry, which I glanced through but didn't see anything that seemed significant. The next had toiletries, shampoo, conditioner, lotion, soap, and meds. I picked up one of the pill containers. The label read, "lithium."

Lithium? That was used to treat bipolar disorder.

Kelly wasn't bipolar. Although as that detective had pointed out, symptoms generally started showing up in the late teens and early twenties.

Was it possible that Kelly was bipolar, and experienced some sort of psychotic break that caused her to run away?

Mental illness did run in our family. My mother had an aunt who had struggled with issues, as well as a cousin.

Could it be that simple?

I thought about all the sleepless nights I'd spent wondering if it was something I did or didn't do that caused her to leave … wondering if I could have somehow prevented it. Wondering why.

It had never occurred to me it might have been a mental breakdown.

I shook the pill bottle. It seemed full. No wonder Julia assumed Ashley hadn't been taking them.

I replaced the bottle and turned to the final boxes.

Both were full of books and papers, and one contained unopened mail. I sifted through it, trying to get a sense of who might be sending mail to a live-in nanny. Much of it was forwarded, apparently from her previous address. It was mostly junk, but there were a couple of envelopes that seemed important. I put them aside.

But at the very bottom of the last box, I found the mother lode: a journal.

I pulled it out and flipped through the pages. It was completely full. I couldn't believe my luck. I wanted to start reading immediately, but I glanced uneasily at the baby monitor. It was getting late, which meant I should probably put everything back and run upstairs before anyone became suspicious.

Right on cue, I heard Isabelle make her little wakeup cry. I froze, staring in horror at the room. The sheet was bunched in a corner, and Ashley's belongings were scattered even further out than they had been before.

I had no time to put it back the way it was. I was going to have to close the door and hope no one came down until I could put things right later.

I snatched up the baby monitor, leaving the journal and the letters off to the side even though it pained me, and quickly left, making sure I shut the door firmly behind me. Isabelle let out another soft cry, and I ran to the stairs, taking two at a time.

Remember, I said to myself. *If Max finds you, you were starting a load of laundry.*

No one was in the kitchen, which was a relief, and I tried to keep my footsteps light and quiet as I ran across the floor and up the stairs to Isabelle's room, praying she wouldn't fully wake up and start screaming before I got there.

I just made it. I burst into her room, just in time to see her tiny red face begin to scrunch up for a truly epic scream.

"Oh, sweetie," I crooned, scooping her up. She was still miffed, but I was able to distract her enough to keep her from the full-blown cry. I snatched up a diaper, clean onesie, and the wet wipes and hurried downstairs with her bouncing against my shoulder, talking to her the entire time as she fussed and held back tears. Getting the bottle ready was key. The quicker I could pop that into her mouth, the quieter she would be. I could change her while it was heating.

I was suddenly conscious of the sweat under my arms and running down my spine. I was panting, and my heart was pounding. Yet as far as I could tell as I strained my ears to hear above Isabelle's frustrated whimpers, the house remained quiet and still. Everyone seemed to still be asleep.

I can do this, I told myself. By the time everyone was up, it would be just like it always was. Isabelle would be clean, happy, and fed. Breakfast would be out. I would be relaxed and calm. No one would have the slightest clue I'd been unearthing secrets before they even opened their eyes.

I can do this.

Chapter 22

It was nearly 9:00 p.m. before I was finally able to escape to my room—to the journal that had been calling me all day.

It had been one frustration after another, starting straight away with breakfast. Even though I had been able to successfully feed and quiet Isabelle before anyone else woke up, I had no time to get back into the basement to right my mess. I knew I could use the laundry as an excuse—surely, that load was done and needed to be switched to the dryer—but I also didn't want to draw attention to the basement. The last thing I needed was for Max or Julia to suddenly remember they had some business down there.

As a result, I was on pins and needles the entire morning. It didn't help that Madison gave me a knowing look when I went into her bedroom.

"Were you in the basement this morning?" she asked, her voice innocent as she stood in front of her closet selecting her outfit.

I had been gently shaking Levi awake when my hand stilled on his chest. I tried to swallow the lump in my throat. "Why do you ask?"

She shrugged. "I dreamed it. You found something in the basement. But ..." she screwed up her face. "It ended up not meaning what you think it does." She turned to face me, but her eyes were on her outfit. "Do you like this?"

I was glad she wasn't looking at me, because I was sure I was doing a terrible job hiding my stunned expression. "I love it," I stammered, even though I was completely unaware of what she was holding in her hands.

How did she know I was in the basement? Had she snuck down and peeked in on me, and I hadn't noticed? I could see it so clearly in my mind—me leafing through one of the boxes, focused on the treasures inside while she stood in the shadows, peering through the doorway, watching me.

I wondered if I should say something. Maybe deny it. Or just casually explain how sure, I *was* in the basement, but only to do a load of laundry. The words stuck in my throat, though, and Madison seemed to have moved on as she warned her brother to get up, or they were going to be late for school.

I went back to focusing on getting Levi ready, who luckily was too bleary-eyed to have understood what his sister had been saying. I probably didn't have to worry about him repeating anything to his parents.

But I had no idea about Madison.

As we walked to school, I debated bringing the topic back up with her, but I didn't get a chance. She prattled on about summer camp—apparently, several of her friends were going, but she wasn't sure if she wanted to or not. She thought she would be more needed at home. Levi bounced back and forth between us, chatting about how he wanted to do baseball camp with dad.

I thought about trying to change the subject. Actually, I was dying to change the subject and ask Madison more questions about her supposed dream, but that would turn it into a bigger deal, which would increase the likelihood of her saying something to her parents. It was also possible Levi might parrot something back to Max or Julia if we discussed it again. I decided I couldn't risk it.

Instead, I focused on getting home as quickly as I could, so I could straighten up the basement before Julia got home.

But even something as simple as that turned into a bigger deal. I had barely unstrapped Isabelle from her stroller before Julia walked in, exhausted and pale. I thought she would go directly to her office for an early start, but she stayed in the kitchen, drinking coffee and apparently wanting to talk to me about Max.

"He's a good-looking guy, don't you think?" she asked as she poured us both a cup of coffee. She was careful not to look directly at me, instead zeroing in on the task at hand, as if pouring our coffee was a life-or-death situation.

I had no idea how to answer her question. Say "yes" and have her think I was interested in her husband? Or say "no" and have her think I was insulting her for marrying an ugly man? And through this whole mental argument, images of the room in the basement with the sheet in a pile in the corner and the evidence of what I had been doing in the early hours of the morning in plain sight remained forefront in my mind.

"Yeah, you two make an adorable couple," I said.

She glanced up at me then, making a slight face. Her eyes were a tad bloodshot, and her makeup didn't really cover the circles under her eyes. Her hair was flatter too, I noticed, lacking its normal bounce. Maybe she needed to book an appointment for a cut and color.

"I know what I look like," she said. "I definitely look my age. Maybe even older. But Max, he still looks pretty hot, don't you think?"

"Julia, you look great," I said. "I don't know what you're talking about. You're a beautiful woman. And Max, sure, he looks great, too. But men always age better than women."

That seemed to be the right thing to say, as she let out a big sigh. "That just sucks, doesn't it?" She handed me my coffee and sat down at the kitchen table. I put Isabelle in her swing and settled next to her, trying hard not to think about the crumbled sheet in the basement.

"It's definitely a sad part of life, that's for sure," I agreed.

She nodded as she took a sip of her coffee. "The thing is ..." she hesitated. "Max is just such a friendly guy. I mean, he really loves people. Loves to talk to them. He always seems really interested in what you're saying. And he's still so good-looking. And I wonder ... do other women misunderstand and think he's flirting with them?"

What was she talking about? Max didn't flirt, at least not with me. And I certainly didn't notice him being all that attentive to anyone, including Julia. I mean, sure, he was with the kids, but that was different, of course.

Then, I realized my puzzlement was probably all over my face, so I picked up my coffee to hide it. "I hadn't noticed anything," I said. "He's certainly never been anything but professional with me."

"That's good," she said, although the tone of her voice didn't make it sound all that good. "I did always wonder about Ashley. Especially with her being off her meds. Did she read into something that wasn't there? It's so hard to know. Heather might have had a little crush on Max, too. Although I'm sure Max didn't do anything to encourage it." She didn't sound like she believed her own words.

"I'm sure that's true," I said. "I mean, I haven't been here that long, but it certainly seems to me that Max adores you. You can see it when he looks at you. His eyes light up."

That was a complete and brazen lie, but Julia blushed. "Oh, after three kids and twelve years of marriage, I hardly think that still happens. Maybe when we were in college." She looked a little wistful, as if remembering a time when what I said was actually true. "I guess, well, I just don't want you to feel uncomfortable or anything. I know Max is really happy with the work you've been doing. We're both so grateful you're here."

Then why are you trying to replace me? I wanted to ask, but I bit my tongue. "That's good to know," I said.

"And I'm glad he's been professional with you," she continued. "I want you to feel comfortable here. Like I said, I know Max's friendliness can get misinterpreted, and I just wondered. I don't want anyone to get hurt, you know? And Max is always working such long hours. I hope no one thinks that means something it doesn't, either."

I wished Julia would just spit out whatever she was getting at so we could have a real conversation. Clearly, she thought he was having an affair, probably with someone at the office.

But what she said about the nannies ... Heather, she'd brushed off.

But Ashley ...

I would not be at all surprised if my sister were having an affair with a married man. Especially her married employer. My hands tightened around my coffee cup, and I wished she was in the room so I could smack her. *She never thinks about anyone but herself,* I reminded myself.

"Oh," Julia said, blinking as she jumped out of her chair. "I have to get to work. I have a meeting in five minutes. And you probably have things to do, too."

"Yes," I said, getting up. "I've got to do some laundry."

But Julia wasn't really listening as she hurried to her office. "That's great. I'll chat with you later."

I got up and moved my cup to the kitchen sink, like I was going to dump it out, but really, I was listening for the click of Julia's office door. The moment I heard it, I ran down the stairs.

The room looked exactly as I had left it. I quickly started picking up, wanting to get it done as quickly as possible, especially since I had left Isabelle upstairs in her swing. She would probably be fine for a few minutes, but the last thing I wanted was for her to get lonely and start to cry, which might make Julia come looking for me.

I had finished cleaning up the boxes and was replacing the sheet when it hit me.

Julia thought Ashley was having an affair with Max.

Was that the reason Ashley had to go?

Was Julia behind her disappearance after all?

I was so stunned by that thought, I stopped moving, the sheet only covering half the boxes.

No. That couldn't be right. Julia couldn't have anything to do with Ashley's disappearance. It wasn't possible. She was a good person. Good people didn't make other people disappear.

Yet ...

Let's just say that house isn't all that it seems.

I gave myself a quick shake. I had things to do. And I especially didn't need anyone finding me standing over Ashley's belongings with sheet in hand.

I finished covering the boxes, collected the journal and letters, and closed the door firmly behind me before transferring the contents of the washer to the dryer.

The rest of the day, I was too on edge to do anything with the journal and letters other than hide them in my room when I took Isabelle upstairs to change her. It seemed like every time I had a moment to myself, even after putting Isabelle down for a nap, Julia would wander out of her office and into the kitchen. She wanted more coffee, a cup of tea, a snack, lunch, a sweet treat. Even though she didn't say much, mostly just standing by the counter scrolling through her phone while she prepared or consumed whatever was striking her fancy at the moment, I still didn't feel like I could safely curl up somewhere and go through the journal. It would be too obvious to her that I wasn't working, so instead, I prepped for dinner, cleaned the kitchen, and did more laundry and other general tidying.

Of course, once I picked up the kids, there was no time for anything else.

It was only at the end of the day, after baths, bedtime, and kitchen cleanup, that I was finally able to lock myself in my room.

I propped myself up in my bed with my computer open and earphones in so I could monitor any conversation between Julia and Max while going through Ashley's writings.

While the journal was calling me big time, I decided to start with the two letters. Carefully, I eased open the flaps, trying hard not to destroy the envelopes, so I would be able to salvage them by taping them up and replacing them with no one the wiser.

The first was junk mail disguised as something else, so I set it aside. The second was more interesting.

It was from a doctor, a psychiatrist, who seemed concerned about Ashley's missed appointments. According to the letter, Ashley hadn't been in since last November. I grabbed my phone and pulled up Instagram to check Ashley's profile. Yes, that was about the time when she moved to Redemption and was hired by the Johnsons.

I thought about the pill bottle I'd found. It was almost full, so she must have gotten a refill at some point. Had she switched to a psychiatrist here in Redemption? I tried to remember when and where the prescription had been refilled, but I had been concentrating more on what it was. I'd have to slip down to the basement again to check it out when I had a moment.

I then read the letter a second time, more carefully. Even though the doctor, Dr. Cynthia Torr, didn't come out and say anything inappropriate, it was clear she was worried. She even went so far as to say she didn't feel that Ashley had resolved her issues, one in particular. I wondered if that was connected to the supposed stalking. Dr. Torr ended the letter by saying she hoped Ashley was still getting help, even if it was from a different doctor.

Hmm. It seemed pretty clear that Ashley really did have some sort of mental issue. I suppose it was possible that this doctor had misdiagnosed her, but even if that were true, there was clearly *something* wrong with her.

Again, I wondered if undiagnosed mental illness was the cause of my sister's disappearance.

Food for thought. I put the letter down and picked up the journal.

I was almost immediately disappointed. The journal stopped at the end of December. The last entry was about how excited she was for the fresh year and start in Redemption at a new job. She also indicated she'd be starting a brand-new journal to make it official.

Ugh. Did I miss another journal in the boxes? Or did she take it with her when she left? I had a sinking suspicion it was the latter, which meant all her thoughts and observations from the two months before she disappeared were missing.

Double ugh.

Still, at least I had something. Maybe there would be a clue as to where she could have gone.

I turned to the beginning and began to read. At first, it was all pretty trivial—mostly complaints about her love life, or lack thereof, and her job. Specifically, one of her coworkers seemed to be intent on sabotaging her, if you were to believe Ashley's account. I skimmed most of it, flipping through the pages, figuring I could always go back and read more carefully if nothing else stood out.

Near the middle, Ashley started mentioning a stalker. She never got a good glimpse of the person, only seeing a figure in the distance when she walked to and from her car at the office, or a car on the street that didn't belong, or someone ducking into a doorframe when she turned around as she walked down the street. Still, she was convinced she could feel eyes on the back of her neck.

And even though she mentioned how no one else ever saw anything—not her neighbors, coworkers, or anyone—she started documenting the sightings, her tone becoming more desperate and paranoid. She said she stopped going out with her friends, convinced whoever was stalking her was following her to the bars and restaurants. Her friends thought she was being irrational. One named Lisa specifically kept telling her she was being silly … that no one was following her. Crystal was more compassionate and seemed more open to believing Ashley, but in the end, even Crystal doubted her.

I scrolled to Ashley's last post on her Instagram account and re-read the comments beneath it. There were some from both names. I checked my notes from my sister's letter, and she specifically mentioned a Lisa having a "big mouth."

Maybe Bryn was right, and it was time to reach out to her friends.

I clicked on Instagram's private message feature and messaged both of them, asking if they were friends with an Ashley Sorrel who had been working as a nanny in Redemption and had disappeared, and if they were, would they be willing to talk to me?

I wasn't sure if I would get anywhere, but it was worth a shot.

I checked in on Max and Julia, who were still watching a show on television. They were sitting on opposite ends of the couch. As I watched, Julia got up with an empty wine glass and disappeared out of the frame. When she returned, the glass was full. Max gave her the side-eye but didn't comment. Julia took several gulps before placing the glass on the small table next to her. After about five more minutes, Max left the room, and Julia's eyes began to flutter closed. Did she always fall asleep on the couch before going up to bed? I would have to keep an eye on that.

I could hear Max's heavy footsteps on the steps and realized I should probably call it a night, as well. I clicked around the other cameras to take a final peek, seeing if there was anything of interest. As far as I could tell, there was nothing going on in the backyard, but the front ...

I looked closely. There was an older-model car parked on the side of the street.

Was it that Chevy? The skin on the back of my neck crawled. I told myself the most likely answer was whoever owned it either lived in the neighborhood or was visiting someone in the neighborhood.

But somehow, I didn't believe my own reasoning.

The Third Nanny

Chapter 23

I was in the kitchen when I heard the front door open and close.

"Hello?" I called out, my hands in a sink full of sudsy water.

There was no answer. I was about to call out again when I heard another door open and close, and footsteps echoing down the steps.

I gritted my teeth. Of course. Val. Julia always called out when she came in, announcing her presence. Only Val would completely ignore me.

I quickly finished washing the couple of dishes left in the sink. I wanted to have a chat with Val before Julia came home.

I was still tired, my eyes gritty from not sleeping well. My mind kept turning back to that car on the side of the road. Was there someone inside? I couldn't tell, no matter how much I squinted at the frame. The camera wasn't nearly that good.

I thought, more than once, that maybe I should go outside and just see whether someone was there or not. I could bring my cell, have it ready to ring 9-1-1 if there was.

But I knew that was foolish, especially since whoever was in the car was likely stalking someone in the Johnsons family. I was expendable.

Instead, I crept down the stairs to make sure all the doors were locked. Julia was sleeping on the couch, the television and lights still on, her nearly empty wine glass on the table by her phone.

I quickly checked all the various doors, finding all locked except for the one that led to the garage, which never was. I twisted the deadbolt, reminding myself to unlock it in the morning. I had no idea if the side door in the garage was still unlocked, and I didn't want to take any chances.

Even that didn't really provide me any comfort. I slept fitfully, sure I was constantly hearing a door open, the creak of a footstep on the stairs.

There was nothing there, of course.

As soon as it was light out, I rolled out of bed to check the camera again.

The car was gone.

Was it a stalker? Or just someone with an early start to the day?

Frustrated, I pushed myself out of bed. The next time I saw that car, I was going to take a closer look at it. Maybe even get the license plate number, to see if I could figure out who it belonged to.

Which led me to Val. I wanted to ask if she knew anything about the car. Or the strange man. Or Heather. Or anything, really.

Not to mention how I still wanted to know why she was so rude to me the week before.

It was possible she was just having a bad day. I wanted to give her the benefit of the doubt. Julia hadn't seemed that concerned when I had mentioned that Val had seemed a little stand-offish to me. She simply brushed it off, saying Val was probably focused on the job at hand and didn't mean anything by it.

But deep down, I didn't think that was the case. Something was off.

And I wanted to know why.

I waited until she was back on the main floor, cleaning supplies in hand. Her back was to me, and she was leaning down, fiddling with the vacuum cleaner.

"Hi Val," I said brightly.

She jumped, her entire body tensing. "Hello," she said. Her voice was muffled, and she didn't turn to look at me.

"Do you have a second? I want to ask you something."

"Julia doesn't pay me to chat," she said. "I have things to do."

Yeah, you're so busy, I thought. *That's why the house always sparkles without a speck of dust anywhere.* "It will only take a second," I said, keeping my voice bright.

She let out a loud huff. "What?"

I bit my tongue, again wanting to ask her why she was being so rude to me, but I forced myself to stick to the plan. I needed answers. "Have you noticed an old car parked on the side of the road?"

"What road?"

"The Johnsons' road. Marigold."

"Why would I be looking at parked cars on the road?"

Patience, Janey. I breathed out through my nose, trying to keep my temper. "I was just wondering if you noticed it, is all."

"I have better things to do than look at parked cars." She glanced up at me, her eyes hard from behind her glasses. "I would think you do, too."

"My *job* is to keep the kids safe," I snapped. "And if I see a car that doesn't belong, I notice. I would think you would, too."

She doesn't like you. Kelly's voice floated through my head. *And I can't say I blame her.*

Val stood up, folding her arms across her chest. "Are you implying I don't care about the Johnsons?"

"What I'm saying is, I think something is going on," I said. "A strange man approached me when I went to pick up the kids at school who seemed to know a lot more about the Johnsons than I was comfortable with."

The moment I said the words "strange man," Val rolled her eyes and leaned over the vacuum. "Don't tell me you think there's a stalker, too," she said, her voice filled with disgust.

"I'm not saying there's a stalker," I said, my voice rising. "What I am saying is a strange man approached me at the kids' school, and I've noticed a strange car parked in the neighborhood. And I'm wondering if you've noticed any of these same things."

"I don't know anything about strange men or cars," she said flatly. "Now, if you'll excuse me, I have to get to work."

"What is your problem with me?" The words were out of my mouth before I knew what I was doing, or could even consider whether asking it was wise. But once I started, I found I couldn't stop. "I've tried to be nice, but all you've been is rude."

She straightened and gave me a cold look. The frames of her glasses caught the light, making them gleam. "You want to know what my problem is with you?"

I squared my shoulders. "Yes, I do."

"Fine." She took a step closer. "I don't understand why you're here. Heather was doing a good job, and the next thing I know, she's gone, and you're here. It makes no sense to me."

"Heather wasn't doing a 'good job,'" I replied. "At least not according to Julia," I quickly amended.

Val's eyebrow raised. "And that is precisely my point. Something isn't right. Not with you and not with this whole situation. Actually, the whole thing stinks to high heaven. I don't know what it is, but I want no part of it. So, leave me alone and out of your talk of foolishness. I have a job to do."

I opened my mouth to respond, but behind me, I heard the turn of the doorknob. "I'm back," Julia's voice sang out.

Both Val and I stepped apart, almost guiltily, like Julia was catching us doing something wrong.

"Oh, good, you're both here," she said. "Val, I wanted to ask you, would you mind taking all the area rugs outside? Give them a good shake and let them hang a bit? They haven't been aired out since last fall."

"Sure," Val said, shooting me one last glare before turning toward Julia. "Right away."

"Great," Julia said briskly before turning to me. "Janey, do you mind going to the store for me? I have a list."

"Of course not," I said, my lips feeling numb as I forced a smile. I was still shaken by what Val had said.

"Perfect. I'll go get it for you," she said while reaching for her office key, clearly oblivious to any tension between Val and me.

"I'll get Isabelle ready," I said, moving stiffly toward the baby, who was still happily swinging.

What was Val thinking? Was she friends with Heather? She must be, although as I flipped through my memories of watching Val and Heather together, I never got the impression they were anything but colleagues.

So, why would she be so suspicious of me? Did she suspect something? Realize there was another reason I was there?

I racked my brain, but recalled nothing I said or did that would make Val think I was anything other than a nanny.

So, what was going on?

Was it possible she knew more about that strange man than she let on? Or the car? Replaying her responses, I realized she never actually answered my questions. Nor did she actually deny seeing either the car or the man.

Was she a part of this somehow? Was that what was going on?

I felt cold all over. I glanced over my shoulder at Val, whose head was down as she gathered up the area rugs.

Could *she* be the stalker? Could she be the one who had driven Ashley away?

Or, maybe Val was the victim? What if the stalker wasn't after the family at all, but it was Val all along?

I quickly dismissed the theory. Val wasn't acting like a victim. It was more likely that she was just somehow mixed up in it all.

Regardless, Val was going to have to go. I didn't trust her to not go complaining to Julia, or heaven forbid, Max, who already didn't like me. I didn't need that headache, especially with new nannies coming to interview the next day.

Especially if Val *was* a part of whatever was going, which became more and more likely in my mind.

It was my duty to encourage Julia to fire her. As her nanny, I needed to keep her and her family safe.

Now, I just needed a plan.

* * *

My initial thought was to frame Val for stealing, but that felt a little risky. How would I make sure Julia knew she stole something? If I slipped it into Val's purse, what reason would I create to then encourage Julia to go through her purse to find it?

And besides, what if Val denied it and said it was me? After all, she had been working for Johnsons longer than me. It was possible that they, or Max, might believe Val over me if she were to point out how nothing had ever been stolen before, yet one week after they hired me, there was a theft problem.

So, then what? While Val vacuumed the living room, I prowled through the master bedroom, seeing if anything inspired me, when my gaze fell on the porcelain figurines. Thoughtfully, I walked over to the dresser to examine them more closely.

Maybe I could do something with them?

I carefully replaced them on the dresser and headed out of the room, an idea percolating in my head. I couldn't do anything until after Val left, which gave me some time to work out the bugs.

By the time I was done, she wouldn't know what hit her.

Chapter 24

"Good morning, Julia," I chirped as I helped Levi pour cereal into his bowl.

Julia grunted as she sunk down in the chair next to Madison. Her hair was a tangled mess, and her eyes were puffy and red-rimmed.

"Would you like some coffee?" I asked.

She nodded as she rubbed her temples. I fetched her a cup and handed it to her.

"Thanks," she muttered as she sipped it. "I woke up with such a splitting headache. Could you also get me some ibuprofen?"

"Of course," I said, and headed for the downstairs medicine cabinet. Julia had never asked for pain reliever before. I wondered if she had more than usual to drink the previous night. She and Max had, well, I wouldn't necessarily call it an argument, but it wasn't a friendly chat, either. Max had been giving Julia strict instructions on how to handle the interviews, while Julia snapped about how she knew how to interview someone—did he think she was an idiot?

"Remember," he kept saying. "You aren't going to offer either of them the job. Just interview them and take notes, and we'll talk about it later."

"Stop repeating yourself. I got it," she retorted.

Once it became clear I wasn't going to learn anything new, I closed the computer and went to bed. I was exhausted, and I had a feeling I was going to need my wits about me over the next few days.

As Julia sipped her coffee, I chatted with the kids, ignoring her as usual while she woke up. She seemed to be moving even more slowly than normal, which made me wonder if she was going to be ready to leave when I was.

Once breakfast was over, I was herding the kids up the stairs to finish getting them ready when she called out to me. "Oh, Janey?"

She sounded like she was forcing herself to sound casual. I braced myself, sure she was about to ask me to be out of the house when the potential nannies showed up. "Yes?"

"I special ordered a piece of art. It's a lovely statue, and it's going to be perfect in my office. I was wondering if you could pick it up for me?"

"No problem," I said. "I'll get it after I drop the kids off."

She shifted in her seat, clearly flustered. "Actually, it won't be ready until early afternoon."

"Okay," I said. "I'll go once I put Isabelle down for a nap."

She was definitely uncomfortable. "The thing is, it's in Riverview. So, I was hoping maybe you could take her with you? I know it's a bit of a drive," she said in a rush, "but I would really appreciate it. I thought you could leave a little early and take yourself out to lunch? Our treat."

She watched me, her dark eyes practically begging me to understand and be excited for the opportunity.

Anger rose up inside me. Did she really think I could be so easily bought? That I would be okay with having some other nanny steal my job, after everything I'd done for them?

But I knew I couldn't say anything. I had to play along with this silly farce, at least until I could watch the recordings and figure out my next plan. I swallowed my anger and forced myself to smile. "Sounds like fun," I said. "I'll leave around eleven." Hopefully, Isabelle would nap in the car, so I wouldn't end up with a fussy baby on top of everything else.

She looked relieved. "Oh, that's fantastic. I'm so glad. You deserve it, you know. You've done such a good job."

I again wanted to shout, "If I've done such a good job, why are you replacing me?" But instead, I nodded and excused myself to get the kids ready for school.

Julia wasn't around when I returned, which didn't surprise me. She was still getting ready when I'd left. I eyed her office door. Was there enough time?

I examined the lock. I would have to be careful, make sure I didn't leave any marks. It would be tricky, and if I screwed up, there was no easy way of fixing it.

I wondered if there was another way. Was it possible there was another key? I had done a cursory search of Julia's bedroom, but hadn't found anything. It was possible she had a hidden spare somewhere.

Or ... I thought about how she would pass out on the couch each night. Did I dare try to make an impression of her key while she slept?

It might be worth a try. While I was out, I would get one of those impression kits and see if the opportunity presented itself.

In the meantime, as much as I wanted to get in there, I was going to have to wait. I twisted the doorknob just in case, but alas, it was locked.

What I probably should do is focus on prepping something for dinner, maybe even use the slow cooker for a healthy soup or stew. I imagined Julia smelling the delicious aromas throughout the interviews and feeling even more guilty about what she was doing. I could just picture her squirming on the couch, trying not to think about how I had been so thoughtful and efficient to plan ahead for dinner before my little "trip" that was actually a guise to get me out of the house.

It was perfect.

I was busy chopping peppers when Julia walked in. "Something smells good," she called out.

"Oh, that's dinner," I said. "I'm just getting it ready."

She came into the kitchen in time to see me stir the onions and garlic sautéing on the stove. "Wow, I didn't expect all of this."

"It's no problem," I said, adding the peppers. "I figured I'd just get it all cooking in the slow cooker. That way it's not so rushed when I get the kids this afternoon."

She nodded, a glazed look in her eyes. Was she already feeling guilty? I was definitely more than a little smug.

"Hey, I wanted to ask you something. Do you mind?"

I felt a little flutter in my stomach. Was this about what Val had "done," or had I been sloppy somewhere along the way? "Shoot."

"Were the kids playing in our bedroom yesterday?"

Ah. Val then. I blinked at her, making sure my expression was puzzled. "No. You said they weren't allowed."

"They aren't. But I just wanted to be sure. What about the day before? Or really any day?"

I shook my head. "No, I never let them play in there. Why?"

She frowned, twisting a piece of hair around her finger. "One of my figurines is broken."

My hand stilled. I cocked my head, trying to keep my breathing in check. "Figurines?"

"Yes, I have a whole collection. You can see them on the mantle in the living room and family room."

"Oh, yes. Those are beautiful. They look like they were made in France?"

She nodded. "Yes, they're antiques. My grandmother passed them down to me."

"They're lovely. You have one in your bedroom? And it's broken?"

"I have two," Julia corrected. "And yes, one is broken. I thought maybe one of the kids did it."

I pressed my lips together, frowning. "No, I don't think that's possible. Unless it happened before I started."

"No, this would have happened probably yesterday. I would have noticed if it had been there for over a week."

"Hmm," I furrowed my brow. "What about Max? Do you think he may have accidentally knocked it over?"

"Max would have said something," she said. "Besides, they're on my dresser, and he never goes near my dresser."

"What about Val?" I kept my voice light and casual. "Do you think she accidentally knocked it over while she was cleaning?"

Julia shook her head. "No, Val knows better."

My heart started beating faster. Did I just hit the jackpot? "What do you mean, she 'knows better'?"

Initially, my plan was simple. After Val left and Julia was still locked in her office, I got the kids set up in the kitchen with a snack before taking Isabelle upstairs to change her. While there, I slipped into Julia's bedroom and knocked over one of the figurines until it chipped. I then stood it back up, positioning it like I was trying to hide the damage. I also only cleaned up some of the porcelain shards, so it would look haphazard—much like Val's dusting skills.

I figured Julia would come to me first, and I'd find a way to slip into the conversation how sloppy a housecleaner Val was. Maybe, I'd offer thoughtfully, now would be a good time to think about replacing her.

But I was starting to wonder if there was a history with Val that I had accidentally stumbled into.

"She knows I need her to tell me the moment anything happens," Julia said. I noticed her hands had tightened into fists.

"I don't understand. What could happen while housecleaning?"

Julia sighed, but her knuckles seemed to be turning white. "Last year, she accidentally broke a vase. It was in the living room, and I guess the cord from the vacuum cleaner got wrapped around it. Anyway, she threw it away and didn't say anything to me about it. I noticed it later that day during a break and asked her about it. She explained the whole thing. I asked her why she didn't tell me right away, and she said she was going to, but she didn't want to bother me while I was working.

"But she had opportunities to talk to me sooner. She had seen me at least twice since she'd vacuumed that room. I always remember when she vacuums, because it's so loud. Plus, she knocked on my office door asking if she could clean my office.

So, she could have brought it up to me then. But she didn't. I was the one who had to mention it."

Julia was getting more and more agitated as she talked, which was starting to make me feel uneasy. She was getting awfully upset over something fairly trivial. I had to make sure she directed all her irritation toward Val and none of it to me.

"So, you're saying you thought Val might be hiding something from you?" I interrupted, hoping to calm her down.

Julia's eyes brightened. "Yes! That's exactly it. She was lying to me. You know how much I hate it when people lie to me. It's just ... it's my biggest pet peeve. And by not telling me, by just cleaning it up and not saying anything, it was like she was lying to me about doing it ... like she was pretending she didn't break the vase at all."

"It wasn't just about a vase," I offered. "It was about breaking your trust."

Julia unclenched her fists and clapped her hands together in front of her. "Yes! Yes! I knew you would understand. Max didn't. He told me I was being silly ... that she was probably going to tell me before she left. She was surely focused on cleaning, not finding the right time to tell me she accidentally broke something. It didn't matter what I said, though. He didn't understand that the way you do one thing is the way you do everything, and this action, as small and insignificant as it might seem on the surface, is actually indicative of how Val does everything."

Her expression grew cloudy. "We fought about it. It ... well, it doesn't matter. The point is, I talked to her. I told her if she ever broke anything again, even something small, she must come and tell me right away. Even if I were in a meeting, she should at least get my attention and tell me she needed to talk to me.

"So, I can't believe she wouldn't tell me if she did this. Not again."

Julia bit her lip, her hands balled into fists again. She wasn't looking at me, instead staring at some spot on the table in front of her.

I took a long, slow, deep breath. "Julia," I said, keeping my voice soft and gentle. "If it wasn't the kids, and it wasn't Max, and it wasn't you, then who else could it be?"

Julia shook her head. "You're right," she sighed. "It's just ... I just can't believe it."

"Well, why don't you talk to her and see?" This was a risky move, as Val could try and blame me. "Let her explain what happened."

"But there's no explanation," she said. "She did exactly what I told her not to."

"That's true," I said. "Or, there's another way you could look at it. I know Val has been working for you for a while, and, well, sometimes when someone has the same job, she can get a little ... complacent."

She gave me a sharp look. "What do you mean?"

"Look, I'm not trying to say bad things about her, but I just think you could probably get someone in here who could do a better job. In my room, for example. I noticed a lot of dust, especially in the corners, and I know you said it was cleaned each week, but ..." I let my voice trail off.

She was silent for a moment, digesting my words. "You may be right," she said. "Maybe it is time to find someone new."

"I think that might be best," I said. "Maybe one who isn't prone to breaking things."

She smiled slightly. "Okay, I'll talk to Max, but I think you're right. It's time for a change." She glanced at her phone and made a face. "Oh. I gotta get to work. And I better leave you to finish up in here before you're off to Riverview."

She seemed flustered at that last sentence, and without meeting my eyes, she hurried away toward her office. "Have fun today. You deserve it," she called.

Hopefully, you'll remember how much I deserve it while you're interviewing the other nannies, I thought. Out loud, I shot her a "Thanks!"

I went back to my chopping, telling myself that evening would come before I knew it.

Chapter 25

The moment I got the kids off to bed, I headed to my room. I already told Max and Julia I was exhausted and was going to have an early night. Neither really responded.

Julia had been subdued most of the afternoon and evening. I wasn't sure what that meant. Was she happy with the prospective nannies or not? I was dying to listen to the interviews, but I knew I had to wait.

Once I got myself situated in bed with my earphones on, I started by listening in to Max and Julia, who were already in the middle of a discussion about the nannies, Celeste and Natalie. Of the two, it appeared Celeste had the edge. Julia liked her the most, and Max preferred her based solely on her resume. Natalie didn't have enough experience for Max's taste. Besides, Celeste could speak French and offered to teach the kids.

"Knowing a second language is really important," Max said. "Even Madison would benefit from lessons. And imagine, Isabelle could be bi-lingual!"

"True," Julia agreed, downing half a glass of wine. Max gave her a sideways look.

"I don't understand you," he said. "You like Celeste. She looks great on paper. She can commit to at least five years. That's exactly what we need. That's what our family needs, and what you need. You won't have to keep interrupting your schedule to look for someone new."

"I know," Julia said, staring into her wine. "It's just ... "

"What?" Max asked impatiently. "Janey? She'll be fine. We already agreed to pay her in full for the summer plus give her a bonus for housing. She'll have two to three months at least to find something else. And who knows? Maybe she'll decide to go back to school after all."

"But I like Janey," Julia said. "I trust her."

Yes! I mouthed, pumping my fist in the air. I knew I could trust Julia. She was my family.

Max breathed hard through his nose. "Julia, we've had this conversation. We need stability. We can't keep going through nannies every few months."

"She said she'd stay ..."

"Maybe a year or two. That's not enough. Do you really want to go through this again in a year?"

Julia didn't answer, or look up from her glass.

Max sighed. "Okay, look. We haven't hired Celeste yet. I want to meet her, anyway. Let's continue with our plan and set up a time for me to interview her, and then we can talk about it more. Maybe she isn't the right person after all, and that's fine. We have Janey. But let's do the second interview and see what happens. Okay?"

"Say 'no,'" I whispered at Julia's bent head. "Tell him you want me. I'm a part of the family now. I'm keeping you safe."

"Okay," Julia said as my heart broke in my chest.

Max smiled. "That's my girl. Can you reach out to her tomorrow and see if she can meet on Monday? Let me know the time, and I'll plan to take part of the day off. And if not Monday, then see about Tuesday."

"Okay, I'll text her in the morning," she said.

I wanted to scream.

I pushed the computer aside and pulled my earphones out of my ears. I needed to get a hold of myself.

Until that moment, I didn't actually believe they were going to go through with it. I was sure Julia would tell Max both of the nannies were unacceptable, and they would have to keep looking. Or maybe stop the search altogether. At some point, I thought there might be a second interview, but I figured that would be weeks, if not months later, and by that time, I would be far more entrenched in their family, and both Julia and Max would be reluctant to replace me.

I honestly couldn't believe Julia had caved so quickly. I truly thought she would have my back when it came down to it and at least stall longer.

How could she betray me like that? Why didn't she stand up for me? Unless ... was it because she was worried about her marriage? Could it be that Max was pressuring her somehow?

Or maybe she was just pretending to go along with it and would find a way to sabotage Celeste later—maybe during that second interview, so it would end up being Max's decision not to hire her.

That made more sense. If Max believed it was his choice, he would be less likely to pressure Julia.

So, what I needed to do was give Julia the ammunition for the sabotage.

But what?

I chewed on my nail while I thought about it. Drawing a blank, I figured I should just watch the interview. Hopefully, it would give me something to go on.

I re-opened my computer and put my earphones back in. Julia and Max were watching television, Julia with a newly full glass of wine. I was about to find the recordings from earlier in the day when my phone buzzed with a text from Bryn, asking for an update. That reminded me about the two messages I had left on Instagram for Ashley's two friends, so I picked up my phone to open Instagram.

One of them had already responded. Crystal. She had been the most worried about Ashley, so it wasn't surprising. She was definitely interested in having a conversation. She also wanted to know if I had any idea where Ashley was or if anyone had heard from her.

I sent her back a message telling her no, no one had heard from her, but it would be great to chat with her about it. Crystal must have been online because she replied a few minutes later. Could we talk Saturday? I told her I would make it work.

Next, I navigated through the controls to find the two inter-views. Luckily, Julia had conducted them in the living room as I had figured she would, as it was the most formal room in the house. So, I had a great view of both the candidates and Julia.

Natalie was first, and I quickly saw why Julia didn't like her. First off, she was young. Even younger than me. Her only experience was with one family with only two school-aged children. She didn't have any experience with infants at all. She was clearly nervous and had difficulty answering questions.

Celeste was next, and the moment I saw her, I hated her. She appeared to be in her early thirties and was polished and professional-looking in a champagne-colored silk jacket and skirt. Her golden hair was styled in a bun, and her brown eyes sparkled. She shook Julia's hand firmly and had a friendly, warm manner about her.

It was easy to like her. Too easy.

She had loads of experience, including a year in France in high school where she worked as a nanny teaching English to the children she was caring for.

She answered every answer perfectly, from her philosophy on child-rearing to how she made a point of showing up at least ten minutes early to every appointment, because to her, "If you are on time, you are late." When Julia asked her about her biggest weakness, her answer was that she was just "too honest." She hated any sort of lying, and sometimes, people found her truth-telling uncomfortable.

She was perfect. Absolutely perfect.

I knew that the moment Max met her, he would offer her the job.

Ugh. What was I going to do? I shoved my laptop away again. No wonder Julia was so down. What parents *wouldn't* want Celeste to be their nanny? Any family would be lucky to have her.

I ran my hands roughly through my hair, pulling it. *Think, Janey.* There had to be a way to get rid of her. There had to be a weakness somewhere. Even Superman had kryptonite.

But the big question was, would I find it in time?

* * *

"Janey, are you doing anything tonight?"

Kelly was sitting at the dresser applying a final coat of red lipstick, but her eyes were locked on me in the mirror. I was on my bed, paging through a *Teen Vogue* magazine.

I shrugged. "I'm not sure. I might go see a movie with Alice. Why?"

"Want to come bowling with us?"

I blinked a couple of times before sitting up in bed, my magazine falling to the floor. "Are you serious?" Kelly almost never invited me out with her and her friends.

Kelly laughed. "Of course I am. Why wouldn't I be?"

"Because you usually don't want me around when you're with your friends."

Kelly waved her hands. "That's nonsense. Of course I like having you around. But there are times it's just not appropriate. You know, someone is having boy problems and needs to bitch for a night. You don't need to hear all that. So, do you want to come?"

"Yes. I would love to. But ..." my face fell. "Don't I need to be sixteen to be there without mom and dad?"

Kelly rolled her eyes. "Don't worry about that. We'll get you in, no problem. So, will you come?"

"Yes! Yes!"

Kelly smiled, her lips stretching across her face, her shiny, white teeth in full view. "Come sit down. Let me do your make-up. You don't want to be a plain Jane."

Obediently, I went to the chair, which Kelly turned around so it was facing her. She hummed as she worked, applying powders and creams to my face. Inhaling her perfume, I asked, "So, who else is going to be there?"

"Oh, you know, the usual. Susan, Cora, Phoebe. The guys. But there's going to be a lot of people. Like a big party, you know? It's almost the end of the season, just a couple of weeks left, so we wanted to start the party now."

She touched my cheek, and I felt a prick. "Ouch," I said, jerking my face back. "What was that? Did you poke me with a needle?"

"Don't be silly," she said. "Hold still." But I could see a drop of blood on the sponge she was holding.

Another prick. "Ouch! You're hurting me. What are you do-ing??"

"Don't be such a baby. I'm not hurting you. Just be still." Her red lips were still smiling, but her eyes had grown hard. Blood dripped from her fingers, as red as her lipstick, and pooled on the floor.

"I'm bleeding." I said more loudly. "Stop!"

"You're fine. Just hold still."

My face was burning with little pinpricks, but I couldn't move away. I could only watch in horror as blood, my blood, splattered across her pink T-shirt with the words "Girl Power" stretched across in gold lettering.

"There." She stood back, tilting her head as she studied me. Blood was smudged across her cheek, and I could even see drops in her hair. "Perfect. Now you can look."

I turned to the mirror expecting to see a bloody mess where my face once was. Instead, I looked flawless. My makeup was natural and delicate, making me look even younger and fresher than my fourteen years.

"Wow," I said, incredulous as to the lack of blood. "But I thought you were going to make me look older, not younger. I need to look sixteen, right?"

Kelly put her hands on the back of my shoulders and leaned closer until her still blood-stained face pressed lightly against mine. "Don't worry about any of it. You look perfect. Absolutely perfect."

Her voice was low, almost a purr. In fact, the more I looked at her, the more she looked like a cat. A large, yellow cat that had just killed and eaten its prey and was now lying sated and satisfied in the sun.

I shifted uneasily. "Maybe I shouldn't go. Alice really wanted to see a movie."

"Don't be silly," Kelly purred. "You can see a movie with Alice anytime. Tomorrow, even. But a party like this only comes once in a while. Come on. Let's pick you out an outfit."

She guided me toward her closet, and I gasped. "You're going to let me wear your clothes?"

"Of course," she said, as she started flipping through outfits. "You want to look good tonight, right? Not like a plain Jane."

I watched her as she searched, muttering under her breath while examining each piece carefully, my emotions an odd mix inside me. On one hand, I was thrilled she was letting me wear one of her outfits. Her clothes were amazing.

But on the other, I couldn't shake the uneasy feeling that something wasn't right. Especially when I watched her leave a bloody handprint on her favorite silk blouse.

"Here it is," she said triumphantly. "The perfect outfit. Don't you agree?"

I looked down at myself. Suddenly, I was decked out in a white silk sheath and white boots. "White?" I questioned doubtfully. "Aren't you worried I'll spill something on it?"

"You won't," she said. "It's perfect. And look how it fits! It's like it was made for you."

I looked down at myself again. "I don't remember this dress. Are you sure it's yours?"

She laughed again. "Don't be silly. It came out of my closet, didn't it? Now, come on. We're going to be late."

She took my arm again, and we were in the hallway leading to the front door. Mom was in the kitchen preparing a rack of lamb while dad relaxed on the couch, holding a glass of red wine. I stared at the liquid, transfixed, the color as red as the blood that had dripped from Kelly's fingers.

"We're going to the bowling alley tonight," Kelly announced.

"Oh, that sounds like fun," Mom said, rubbing sage on the lamb. "But you should have dinner first."

"We don't want to be late," Kelly said.

"You won't be," Mom answered. "The lamb will be ready in a jiffy. It will be the perfect dinner for you before your big night out."

I was mesmerized, watching Mom massage the sage into the lamb. Her fingers moved rhythmically in constant circles. I tried to remember when the last time was that she made lamb. Had she *ever* made it? Had I ever even eaten lamb? I couldn't remember.

"Okay, but we can't be late," Kelly said, turning to look at me. "Remember, when you're late, it's like you're lying. You're not being honest. Especially if it looks like you're lying about the reason."

I blinked at her. "What are you talking about? You're not lying when you're late."

Kelly smiled at me, revealing all her perfect teeth. "Even if we're on time, we're late." She held up a cell phone. "That's why you need to text when you're going to be late. That's the honest thing to do."

"It's polite to text," Mom agreed from the kitchen. "You should always text when you want to change an appointment. It's honest."

Kelly leaned closer to me, her breath fetid against my cheek. Or maybe it was her perfume. Did perfume ever go rotten? "And being honest is the most important thing in the world."

My eyes opened. I was back in the bed at the Johnsons'. I was no longer a child, subject to the manipulations of an older sister who would dress me up in order to satisfy the whims of ...

No! It was only a terrible dream. I wasn't going to think about it anymore. Nothing like that ever happened. My brain was making things up, probably because I was so stressed with everything going on in my life.

Still, I couldn't help but wonder ... could some event have triggered me?

The strange car parked outside, maybe, although I hadn't seen it in a few days. On the other hand, Julia kept sending me away on errands, so really, the car could have been around when I wasn't.

What about the strange man outside the kids' school? I hadn't seen him again, but his presence was always there, lurking behind every shadow.

He didn't look familiar to me, but that didn't mean there wasn't something about him that reminded me of Oz.

Or ... no. I wasn't going there. He wasn't Oz. I would have recognized him, no matter how long he had been in prison.

It was probably just the whole situation, I decided. A strange man and a strange car skulking about while I tried to investigate Ashley's disappearance and do whatever I could to keep the job that allowed me to do so.

When I thought about it like that, it was no wonder I was having such terrible dreams.

The mother in my dream flitted through my memory. *You should always text when you want to change an appointment. It's honest.*

I sat up in bed, suddenly excited. Was that the point of the dream? A message to stop the Celeste nonsense? Could it be that simple?

Julia telling Max she was going to text Celeste to set up a new appointment for next week.

Julia passed out alone on the couch, the dregs of her glass of wine threatening to spill on her shirt, her phone next to her.

Perhaps it really *could* be that simple.

All I had to do was wait.

The Third Nanny

Chapter 26

"Are you going to talk to the man again today?" Madison asked.

My feet suddenly became tangled, and I nearly fell on Isabelle's stroller. "Excuse me?" I managed.

We had almost reached the park. Levi was already running ahead, his little legs pumping madly. Madison was skipping along next to me, her braids bouncing on her shoulders. I had to admit, I had done a pretty good job with them that morning, as they were still intact. Even the pink ribbons that matched her pink shirt and yellow leggings were still attached.

"The man at the park."

My mouth was so dry, it felt like my tongue was sticking to my teeth. "What man?"

"You know. *The* man. The one you were talking to at school." She paused her skipping and turned to me. "I think he wants to talk to you, but you haven't been talking to him. Are you mad at him?"

"Madison," I said, trying hard to keep my voice calm. Inside, it felt like an entire swarm of gnats was crawling around my chest. "Are you saying you saw the man who was talking to me at school here at the park?"

Madison gave me a strange look. "Of course. Don't you see him?"

I licked my dry lips, not sure how to answer her. It felt like no matter what answer I provided, it would be wrong. "Where exactly have you seen him?"

She shrugged. "Just wherever. By the trees. On the sidewalk. It changes."

How could I have not noticed? I had been actively looking for him every day. "Madison, could you do me a favor?"

She had started to skip again, focusing more on the playground in front of her. "Sure."

"The next time you see him, can you point him out to me?"

Her face swiveled back toward me, her eyebrows drawn together and expression confused. "Don't you see him now?"

My head snapped around as I squinted, trying to see what she was seeing. There were four other children already playing on the equipment, including the one Levi's age who Levi was beelining toward. Two mothers were sitting on a park bench, simultaneously checking their phones, chatting, and keeping an eye on their kids.

I didn't see any men around at all.

"Where? I'm not seeing him."

She pointed behind me.

My heart leaped in my throat.

Slowly, I turned around.

There, on the sidewalk on the other side of the street, was the man from the school.

"Madison," I asked, my voice strangled. "Does he always follow us?"

"I don't think he follows us," she answered, her voice so light and innocent, so child-like, and so at odds with the conversation we were having. "He just appears sometimes. Like he's watching us."

My eyes never left the man. He had paused on the sidewalk, his head cocked, observing us. Was there a faint smile on his face?

"Does he follow us home?"

"I don't think so," she said. "It's like I said. He just appears and disappears. Can I go play now?"

Yes, the man was definitely grinning at me.

"Sure," I said, risking a quick glance behind us to check on Levi. He was still playing with his friend. "Can you keep an eye on your brother?"

Madison huffed a sigh, the long-suffering sigh of an exasperated ten-year-old. "I suppose. Are you going to go over there to talk to him?"

That was exactly what I had been intending to do, but hearing the words from her mouth shifted something inside of me. I straightened my shoulders and deliberately turned my back on him. "No," I said. "But he might come talk to me."

Madison studied me, her expression unreadable. Her eyes, the color of the rich earth, were so much older and wiser than her age. On one hand, she looked like the spitting image of her mother. On the other, she seemed more like the mother and Julia her daughter. Her eyes narrowed slightly before she gave me a tiny nod, as if she were saying, "You got this, and don't worry about Levi."

She turned without another word and ran across the grass, braids flying behind her in the wind, as graceful as a gazelle.

I pushed Isabelle's stroller to a nearby tree on the other side of the park bench where I usually sat. I was painfully aware of the bench's angle, which kept my back to the route from school. How long had he been studying me, learning to "appear" only in my blind spots?

The words from Ashley's journal appeared in my mind. She had actively looked for her stalker, but still couldn't catch him in the act.

I hadn't completely understood how that was possible, but here I was, in the exact same situation.

How could I have been so stupid? So oblivious?

I leaned against the tree, watching Madison and Levi on the playground and rocking Isabelle in the stroller with one hand while feeling for my phone with the other. Next to me, a couple of bright-yellow dandelions poked out of the lush carpet of green grass, while a few feet away a discarded brown paper bag—perhaps someone's leftover lunch—crinkled in the wind.

"I was wondering when you would finally notice me."

I recognized the voice immediately, but refused to look at him, instead keeping my eyes on the kids. "Why are you following us?"

"You say it like it's a bad thing."

"You think it's a *good* thing to follow perfect strangers?" Oddly enough, I wasn't afraid. Simply curious. I had never talked to a stalker before.

"If it's to help."

I eyed him. He had a friendly, open face. Like a boy scout. He wore a blue T-shirt, a pair of jeans, and the same baseball cap with the Brewers' logo on it as before. Exactly what a normal, all-American guy would wear. A small smile teased his full lips. I wondered if he would have that same disarming smile even while stabbing someone. "What's your definition of 'help'?"

He burst out laughing. Such a warm, affectionate laugh. Who would ever suspect him of anything?

"Are you always this suspicious?" he asked once he got himself under control.

"I think I would be foolish not to be," I said. "I don't know who you are or why you're following me. Wouldn't you be suspicious?"

"When you put it that way, I suppose," he said. "But things are not always as they seem."

I was starting to get impatient. Why wouldn't he give me a straight answer? "Then enlighten me," I said. "Or go away. I don't care either way, but I'm getting bored with this game."

He cocked his head, widening his green eyes. "I doubt that," he said. "Unfortunately, I'm not in a position to tell you everything."

I rolled my eyes. "Oh please. If you wanted to, you could tell me. That's crap."

"All right, I'll admit it. I can't tell you yet because I don't want you to spoil my fun."

A cold trickle of sweat dripped down my spine. "What kind of 'fun'?"

He smiled again, but this time it was flat, empty. "Do you believe in karma?"

Alarm bells were starting to go off in my head. "What does that have to do with anything?"

"I do," he said, his voice causal, as if we were talking about the weather. His cold eyes told a different story. "I like to make sure people get what's coming to them."

My throat had gotten so tight, I wasn't sure if I could answer. "If you hurt them ..."

"Relax. No one said anything about hurting anyone."

"You just said ..."

"I said I wanted to make sure people get what's coming to them. That doesn't mean anyone is getting hurt. At least physically."

I forced myself to swallow. "Then what does it mean?"

He leaned closer. I could smell his aftershave, something trendy, I thought. "It means, Janey, you're living in a snake pit. Be careful you don't get bit."

My eyes widened. "How do you know my name?"

"I know a lot of things," he said. "Including how, if you make the wrong person in that house mad, you could end up just like Ashley. Disappeared."

My mouth was like sandpaper. Somewhere, far in the distance, I could hear the kids' shrieks as they played. A raven landed on the ground a few feet away from us, studying us for a moment with its dark, beady eyes before poking at the bag.

"Who are you?"

"I'm just a guy trying to do the right thing," he said.

"Do you have a name?"

He grinned, some of the warmth sliding back in. "Let's just call me your guardian angel," he said.

I snorted. "I somehow doubt that."

He grinned again and took a step backward, his limp pronounced. "Watch your back. Keep your eyes open. And be careful who you trust."

I wanted to chase after him, demand he tell me his name, but then I remembered the kids, especially Madison, watching from the playground. The mothers could be watching as well, and I couldn't be sure who Julia's friends were. I took a quick peek around. The one was still on the phone, but seemed to be looking in my direction. The two on the park bench were still dividing their attention between their phones and their kids, but that didn't mean they didn't notice me.

I suddenly realized I was squeezing both hands into tight balls, so I forced myself to loosen my grip. One hand was clutching the stroller handle, but the other was gripping my phone.

My phone!

I slid it out of the pocket as I turned toward the strange man. He was a few feet away, his back toward me, his limp more pronounced on the uneven grass.

I pushed the stroller toward him, not wanting him to get too far away as I punched my code into my phone and clicked on the camera icon. From the corner of my eye, I saw the raven flying away, big black wings flapping, cawing angrily at me for interrupting his snack. I held the phone close to the stroller, trying to hide it as much as I could.

"Hey," I called out, my voice loud. "Hold on a second."

He paused, turning toward me, his expression back to affable boy scout. He raised an eyebrow as I squeezed the red capture button.

"Don't follow us anymore," I said. "Don't come near me or the kids. And if I catch you, I will call the cops. Got it?"

He studied me, his expression unreadable, before giving me a tiny nod—of approval, it seemed. Then, he turned and continued his slow, limping journey over the grass.

I turned away so I could check the pictures and was immediately disappointed. They were terrible. Not only was he barely in the frame, but they were all out of focus.

So much for the having some sort of record of him.

I sighed and tucked my phone back into my pocket before suddenly realizing how exhausted I was. My knees seemed to collapse in on themselves. I sagged against the stroller, unable to hold myself up on my own accord.

I just need a moment to catch my breath, I thought. *Just one moment to get myself together, and then we can go home.*

Home.

Otherwise known as "the snake pit," according to the man with the limp.

The man who knew my name, even though I still didn't know his.

I wondered how he could have figured out who I was. Did he know Max or Julia? Or maybe Val?

Ugh. Briefly, I closed my eyes. She never did answer my questions.

Well, I couldn't think about that. I had a lot to do, starting with getting the kids home safely.

I called them over. Levi grumbled, but eventually climbed off the structure. I suspected he was getting hungry and wanted his snack.

Madison didn't need a second request. She jumped off the swing and skipped toward me, her braids beginning to come undone.

"He's not very nice, is he?" she said, her voice low, as if we were sharing a secret.

I wanted to pretend I didn't know what she was talking about, in the hopes of keeping her from saying anything to her mother, but I was suddenly sick of pretending. Besides, would that even work with this child who seemed to see and know all?

"He's not very nice at all," I said. "You should definitely stay away from him."

She nodded, her face solemn. "Heather didn't like him, either," she said in a confiding voice.

Well, apparently there was one thing Heather and I could agree on. "Heather was right," I said. "I told him to leave us alone, so if you see him again, anywhere near us, will you tell me right away?"

She nodded.

"And don't go anywhere near him," I said. "And don't let Levi near him, either."

"I won't," she promised as Levi ran up to us.

"I'm hungry. What's for dinner?" he asked.

"Something delicious," I said, making my voice sound cheery and normal. "But we better get home so I can finish it up."

"Okay," he said as he started to run ahead.

I asked Madison questions about school and listened with half an ear as she told me about an incident in math class where she knew the answers, but the teacher kept calling on the other students instead of her. At least I think that was what she was saying. It was hard to follow, because the weird conversation I'd had with the man at the park kept swirling through my head like a flock of ravens circling madly, waiting for an opening to dive-bomb its prey.

What was going on? Was this man a threat? Should I call the police? Although the police hadn't believed Ashley, so would they even take me seriously? Or maybe I should tell Julia? Or Max?

You're living in a snake pit. Be careful you don't get bit.

What if this was the man Ashley thought was stalking her? What if she told Max and Julia about conversations she had with him? What if she even got a picture, just as I had, and showed it to Julia and Max?

If you make the wrong person in that house mad, you could end up just like Ashley. Disappeared.

I felt sick to my stomach. What should I do? Who could I trust?

While I obviously shouldn't trust the man with a limp who appeared to be stalking me, I couldn't rule out something strange going on in the Johnsons' house, either.

Who knows what I might unleash if I said something?

Especially since it appeared they were ready to replace me, anyway. What if I tipped my hand, and they decided it might be easier to have me disappear than to fire me?

I was both sweaty and freezing. Sweat beaded up under my arms and between my breasts and shoulder blades. I could feel it drip down my spine, leaving a trail of cold fire in its wake.

What was I going to do?

Bryn. I had to talk to Bryn. She would help me sort it out. I decided to text her as soon as I got to the house to see if we could meet the next day.

We turned down our block, Madison still prattling away, oblivious to my rising panic. A part of me couldn't help but wonder how it was that she could understand so much most of the time, yet be completely unaware of the puddle of sweat and stink I was melting into.

At the end of the day, she is still ten, I reminded myself.

I was so fixated on my worry that I almost missed the car.

Parked on the side of the street, just like before.

I wanted to stop. I almost stopped. I even jerked the stroller, but something told me to keep going. I had all the kids with me, after all. Was I really going to run up to an unfamiliar car and pound on the window in front of them?

What if the car wasn't empty after all?

Instead, I glanced down at the license plate. Maybe I could memorize it and try and trace it that way, although I wasn't entirely sure how to access the technology for something like that. It also occurred to me that I could give the license plate number to the cops and let them handle it. If they would take me seriously, that is, which seemed like a big "if."

I studied the plate—889ABX.

It seemed familiar. Where I had seen it before? On the video?

No, the video was too far away. I wasn't able to make out the license plate.

Had I noticed it when I had passed the car in the street earlier? I wasn't sure, but I didn't think I had looked at it until now.

"What are you looking at?" Madison asked.

Her voice startled me, yanking me back to the present. I had nearly forgotten about her and Levi. Speaking of Levi, I quickly looked around for him and saw him running up the driveway of the house.

Oh good. He was safe. One less thing for me to worry about.

"That car," I said. "I've seen it parked here a lot."

Madison peered behind her, squinting her eyes. "Oh. Yeah. It is."

My heart began beating faster. "Do you know who it belongs to? Is it someone in the neighborhood?"

She screwed up her face. "No, I don't think so. But maybe. Mom doesn't like it."

My senses started tingling. "Your mom doesn't like what? The car? Who owns it?"

"I'm not sure. But she always makes a face when she sees it, like she's smelling something bad. She says it's an eyesore."

An eyesore. Well, I had to agree with her on that.

I wanted to ask her more questions, but we were almost at the house and Levi had left the front door open. Julia was probably in her office, but what if she wasn't? And besides, Madison had changed the subject to what she wanted for a snack, and she might find it suspicious to keep talking about the car. Especially after the episode at the park.

As I pushed the stroller up the driveway, I focused on taking deep, cleansing breaths. It was time to be Janey, Supernanny. I had snacks to prepare, a meal to cook, baths and bedtime to attend to. I had to pretend everything was fine and dandy.

Even if every part of me was screaming inside.

Chapter 27

The rest of day was nearly unbearable.

My cheeks hurt from forcing the fake smile to stretch across my lips. My throat was sore from pushing out the phony, cheery voice whenever I had to speak. I tried not to reveal how I was analyzing every word and gesture of both Julia and Max's. Did they sense something? Were they signaling each other that I was a problem and needed to be taken care of?

Watch your back. Keep your eyes open. And be careful who you trust.

It was exhausting, pretending everything was normal.

Even though I knew I couldn't drop my guard for even a moment, I was still having difficulty seeing Julia as a threat. Watching her at dinner as she sipped her wine, barely speaking and hardly touching her food, she just seemed like a grey, tired version of herself. Like someone had made a copy of the real Julia, or maybe even a copy of a copy, and what was left was faded and worn.

Whatever demons she was struggling with internally seemed to be taking their toll.

Max, on the other hand, seemed perfectly fine. He teased Levi, asked Madison about her day, complimented me on my cooking. He was the center of attention. The more I thought about it, the more I realized he was always sucking up all the air in the room.

He certainly wasn't acting like a man with a guilty conscience. Or one who was actively trying to break up his family.

Could he really be a monster?

Finally, I was able to escape to my room. I turned on the computer, clicked over to the cameras, plugged in my earphones, and picked up my notebook. Julia and Max were in the family room with the television on, just like normal. I listened to Julia reassure Max that they were set to interview Celeste on Monday

("Do you want me to show you my phone? I told you, it's all set up ...") before discussing the errand they would send me off on just to get me out of the way.

Julia was clearly in a foul mood, not happy at all about having to send me away again. They eventually decided I'd go gift shopping for two of Max's office workers who were retiring the following week.

"We can tell her my secretary forgot to order anything online," Max said. "See if she doesn't mind doing a bit of shopping. It should take her at least an hour or so."

"Glad you don't mind throwing your secretary under the bus," I said to the screen.

Julia stared bleary-eyed at Max. "*Did* your secretary forget?"

"What does that matter?" Max said impatiently. "We'll be able to use what Janey picks up eventually."

"So, she didn't forget."

"She ordered them late," Max said. "So, it's not entirely a lie. But it doesn't matter. We can either return them or save them for the next time we need a gift."

"Why is she still your secretary if she keeps messing up?"

Max pressed his lips together into a thin line. "You're drunk," he said, his voice filled with disgust. "I'm done with this conversation."

"Why don't you answer?" Julia persisted. "It shouldn't be that hard to answer."

"The answer is, she *doesn't* mess up very often," he said. "And, in this particular case, I forgot to tell her."

"You shouldn't have to tell her. She knows just as well as you when people retire."

"It's not that simple," he said. "It's not always appropriate to buy gifts. This is a ridiculous conversation. You're drunk, and I'm going to bed."

"It's not the first time she messed up though, is it?" Julia called out at Max's retreating back. "Yet you still keep her."

"Goodnight, Julia," Max's voice floated through the speaker.

I watched, fascinated, as Julia muttered darkly to herself, gulping down most of her wine. She disappeared for a moment, and then returned with another full glass. She picked up her phone, almost spilling her wine, before figuring out she needed to put her glass down to maneuver the phone.

I left the camera on, keeping an eye half on it while flipping through my notebook. I wasn't really looking for anything, more just passing the time until Julia passed out on the couch.

But then, a piece of paper fluttered out from the pages and landed on the floor.

I bent over to pick it up. It was the scrap of paper I found the day I moved into the room, presumably left by Heather, although it was also possible it had been left by Ashley.

I flipped it over, and my heart stopped.

889ABX.

Oh no. It couldn't be the same. It couldn't be.

But I knew it was. Even as I anxiously fumbled through my notebook, nearly tearing the pages in my haste, in my heart, I already knew it.

It was the license plate number.

I stared at the slip of paper and my own scrawl from earlier. Identical.

I wasn't the only nanny to capture that license plate number on a piece of paper.

The question was, why?

Had Ashley and Heather seen what I had? A car that didn't belong, yet nevertheless continued to show up?

Or was it something else?

I glanced at the computer screen and saw that Julia had fallen asleep, her glass half-empty. Her phone was resting on the couch next to her. When I checked on Max, I found him propped up in bed watching something on his tablet.

It was the perfect time to go down. I knew I should before it got much later, but I found I couldn't move.

What was going on? What secrets were buried in this house?

It's not like you'd ever be able to figure it out, Kelly said. *Maybe you should just let them replace you. Celeste probably would be better. She certainly couldn't be much worse.*

No. I wasn't going to let myself be replaced. Julia needed me, even if she didn't completely realize it. Max certainly wasn't on her side, and the kids were too young. She needed someone to help protect her. And who knew what side Celeste would take?

I closed my computer, removed my earphones, and slid out of bed. I slid the key impression kit into my shorts' pocket, and then quietly moved to the door to open it a crack.

The door to the master bedroom was closed, but a faint light radiated out. Max would be focused on whatever he was watching. He likely wouldn't notice anything at all.

I closed my bedroom door softly behind me and crept down the stairs. The family room light was on, and faint noise still emanated from the television. Julia was sprawled out on the couch, her mouth open. There was a wet stain across her plain black shirt. Wine, I assumed. I could see the thin gold chain around her neck from which I knew the office key hung.

I had to concentrate on my phone plan, though. I didn't have much time to move the Monday appointment, whereas if I had to, I could try to get the key impression another day.

Still. I gazed longingly at the chain. If this didn't work (and there were so many ways it could go wrong!), I wouldn't have much time left in the house. And I had to know what Julia kept hidden in her office.

I had to know if that parked car and the strange man with the limp were somehow connected to her.

But I also knew I had to be smart. I needed more time to figure out what was going on and to track down Ashley. I couldn't let my desires control me.

Someone had to be the grownup, and it certainly wasn't going to be Julia.

Slowly and carefully, I reached out and plucked her phone from the couch. She didn't stir.

I backed away from her and headed to the kitchen. I could pretend to be making a cup of tea, just in case Max decided to come downstairs or Julia woke up.

I had watched her enough to know her passcode, and after unlocking her phone and turning off the sound, I opened her texts.

I scrolled down until I found the exchange with Celeste. After taking a quick peek behind me to make sure I was still alone, I started to type.

Hi Celeste. It's Julia. So sorry to bother you, especially on a Friday night, but something has come up, and Monday won't work. Can you do Tuesday at 11:00 instead?

I hit send, then drummed my fingers as I watched for her reply. I hadn't quite figured out what I would do if she didn't. I figured I could take the phone up to my room with me for the rest of the night, as Julia likely wouldn't miss it. When she woke up, she would just stumble off to bed. I could replace it in the morning, and no one would be the wiser.

But, if Celeste didn't respond before I had to replace the phone, what then? Should I just send another text saying, "Oh, never mind ... Monday actually works—see you then"? Then delete everything?

I had no idea. I just had to hope that she would respond soon.

Just then, I saw the three little bubbles appear, indicating that Celeste was typing. I could feel my heart in my throat.

Sure. No problem at all. Still at your house?

I closed my eyes, a wave of relief washing over me.

Yes, same place. Thanks for being so flexible. We'll see you Tuesday at 11.

See you then, came the response.

I quickly deleted the entire exchange, turned the sound back on, and returned it to lock screen. Just as long as either Celeste or Julia didn't text to confirm again, all should be well.

I was about to put the phone back when it buzzed in my hand, accompanied by a friendly little text alert. I jumped, nearly dropping the phone in my panic.

The screen lit up. It was Celeste.

Oh, I meant to ask you. Is there anything more I need to bring, or do you have everything you need?

My eyes darted to Julia, who seemed undisturbed. I had no way of knowing if Max heard anything, although it was unlikely, as he was upstairs with the door closed and watching whatever on his tablet.

I quickly backed away into the dark kitchen and ended up running into the chair, which made a shuddering, grinding noise as the legs dragged against the floor. I froze, straining my eyes to see if Julia awoke and my ears to hear if Max was coming down to investigate.

Nothing.

My fingers shook as I tried to unlock the phone. It took me two tries before I finally got in and muted the sound again.

I took a moment to catch my breath. I was still trembling, and my palms were sweaty. When I finally felt like I had myself under control, I clicked on the text to answer.

No, we don't need anything more. Just bring yourself.

Great. I'll see you Tuesday.

I deleted the texts and closed the phone screen again, but stayed where I was in the dark, my back against the chair. I pressed the phone to my chest, feeling my heart pound, waiting to make sure there wouldn't be any other texts. I could feel the sweat trickle down my back and dot my forehead.

Five minutes. Ten minutes.

I heard a soft sound in the living room, and for a moment, I was sure my heart was going to stop. Julia was awake. What was I going to do?

My T-shirt was drenched in sweat, and I was sure I stunk to high heaven. If anyone came near me, they would know something was wrong immediately. I strained my ears to discern what Julia was doing, but I couldn't hear anything over my harsh breathing.

Finally, I forced myself to take a step forward, so at the very least, I could peer down the hallway.

Julia was still on the couch. At least, it appeared she was. There was definitely a Julia-sized lump, although I couldn't see her clearly anymore. I wondered if she had just slumped over.

I backed up again and continued waiting. Just a few minutes more to make sure Celeste wasn't going to text or Julia wake up.

Another five minutes. Then ten minutes crawled by, and I finally decided I had waited long enough. Even though I felt safer in the dark kitchen, where I was able to monitor both the upstairs inhabitants and the one downstairs, I knew I couldn't very well just stand there all night. As I clutched Julia's phone like a drowning man clings to a life preserver, I gathered my courage to move. Julia wouldn't stay on the couch all night, nor could I trust that Max wouldn't decide he needed a glass of water or midnight snack. Plus, a kid could wake up. No, it was time to finish my plan.

The only problem was getting my body on the same page. After a few more minutes of standing there, I finally got my legs to move. Stiffly, I crept into the living room and replaced the phone on the couch. The moment I set it down, I remembered I had turned the sound off.

Argh.

I glanced at Julia. She was still sleeping, but she had toppled over onto her side with her neck twisted one way and her body contorted in another, in what looked like a very uncomfortable position. She was going to wake up with one incredibly stiff neck. I wondered if there was a way I could straighten her out without waking her, but almost immediately realized it was a terrible idea. I needed to stay focused. Did I really want to risk waking her now?

My eyes never leaving her, I picked up her phone on more time, turned the sound back on, and replaced it on the couch. Julia slept on, completely unaware.

It was done. I could almost picture the scene. Celeste wouldn't show up on Monday. Max would be annoyed and assume Julia had forgotten to text her. Julia would then show Max the text exchange to prove herself.

They would then text or phone Celeste to make sure nothing happened to her.

Celeste would respond that Julia had rescheduled.

But there would be no record of that exchange.

I suspected what would happen next is that Julia and Max would argue. Max would assume Julia rescheduled while she was drunk, especially since he knew how reluctant she had been to set up the interview in the first place. Julia would likely think Celeste was lying to her, probably because she was hiding something, and would start to obsess over what that was.

Perhaps Julia would begin suspecting Max and Celeste were somehow involved.

Either way, Julia would want nothing to do with Celeste. And even if Max wanted to give Celeste another chance, he would find the missing texts suspicious, as well.

With all the fighting around Celeste, the chances of them continuing the interview process would drop. Julia would be even less interested, and Max would likely just give up pushing it.

Regardless of what happened, I would surely buy myself enough time for them to lose all interest in replacing me. After all, I was part of their family. Julia already knew it. She just needed a little more time to convince Max.

Now that Celeste was taken care of, there was still the matter of the key.

All I had to do was make that impression, and my work would be done. No more skulking around, that night or any other.

However ... I was exhausted.

All I wanted to do was get back in my room as quickly as possible. Was I really up to this? Especially since this was by far the more difficult of the two tasks. I was going to have to touch a key that was lying on Julia's skin, while feeling tired and shaken from the close calls that already occurred. I wasn't even sure if accomplishing this feat was possible under the best of times, which this certainly wasn't.

But, when I took a closer look at Julia, I realized it would be easier than I thought.

When she had fallen over, her shirt bunched up, and the key was no longer lying on her chest. It was actually on the side of the couch. All I had to do was ease the impression kit under it, press down, and boom. Impression made.

Simple.

Wouldn't I feel better just getting this over with already?

I took a wary glance at the kitchen, but it looked exactly as it did before. Dark and still.

I peeked at Julia. She was snoring.

If I was going to do it, I needed to do it now. I couldn't just stand there like a crazy person staring at her. How would I explain it if anyone found me?

You're an idiot, Kelly said. *You really think this is going to work? You're so clumsy. You're going to wake her. You took care of Celeste—take the win and go to bed.*

No. I straightened my shoulders. I wasn't going to listen to Kelly. I could do this. I wasn't her awkward kid sister anymore.

I removed the impression kit from my pocket and opened it. I took one last look around, then sucked in a deep breath, and leaned over.

Gently, I picked up the key, trying hard to not put any pressure on the chain, and slid the impression kit around it. I pressed down.

Julia shuddered, and I nearly dropped everything in panic. Her eyelids fluttered but didn't open. Her breathing became shallower as she shifted positions, jerking the chain of her necklace. She snorted.

The sound of her snort was what jolted me out of my frozen trance. I dropped the key as if it had burned me and immediately started backing up, without even checking to see if I had gotten a decent impression. I didn't care. I just wanted to get back upstairs as quickly as possible.

Behind me, I thought I could hear her moving, but I wasn't sure, and I certainly wasn't going to chance turning around to look. So I kept going, trying to move both quickly and quietly as I hurried up the steps and into my bedroom. I shut the door behind me and barely made it to the bed before collapsing, my knees as weak and wobbly as Jell-O.

Had Julia seen me? I didn't think so. Her eyelids had fluttered, but I was pretty sure she stayed asleep. Even if she had woken up a minute later, I would have already been gone.

But wait. I could check. All I had to do was open my computer and look.

My hands were shaking so much, I could barely open my laptop. It seemed to take forever to click over to the camera.

Julia was still lying on the couch. I sagged against my pillows, all the adrenaline rushing out of my body in a whoosh. I could only stare at the screen, watching her chest rise up and down.

She was still asleep. I was safe.

I needed to sleep, as well. Morning would come before I knew it, and after the night I had, I needed to get some rest.

I was too exhausted to move, though. I continued to lay there, watching the screen, trying to bring my breathing under control.

Eventually, I became aware of something digging into my side. I reached over to give it a tug. It was the impression kit.

I flipped it open. As far as I could tell, it looked good. I was so panicked there at the end, I wasn't sure if I had smudged it or not.

Despite the harrowing conclusion of events, maybe everything had worked out after all.

A movement on the screen caught my attention. Julia shook herself a couple of times, which caused her phone to slide to the floor, before stumbling to her feet and slowly dragging herself out of the living room.

Watching her made me feel slightly queasy. Had she been awake the whole time? Just lying on the couch trying to gather herself to get to bed?

No, she would have moved sooner. I was sure of it.

Right?

I was suddenly aware that any minute, Julia would be coming up the stairs and see my lights on. Roughly, I shoved my computer away and stumbled out of bed to flip them off.

I'm just being safe, I told myself over my harsh breathing. *Just in case Julia suspects anything. I don't want her to realize I'm still awake.*

I stood in the dark, ear pressed against the door, trying to hear where she was. What if she saw me click my light off? Ugh. That might be worse than her just seeing it on.

As I stood there trying to calm myself, I was sure I could hear the familiar creaking of the stairs before the padding of her footsteps on her way to the master bedroom.

I closed my eyes and leaned against the door. If she had been on the stairs, and I was pretty sure she had been based on the sounds I'd heard, there was no way she would have seen my light on.

There was nothing for me to worry about.

I was safe.

Chapter 28

"You can take off early today," Max said as Levi tried to hand him a miniature Thomas the Train. He smiled at me, warm and inviting.

I didn't like that smile. Nor did I trust it. Not one bit.

It hadn't been a good day. For starters, I was still so wound up after my night adventures that I wasn't able to fall asleep until it was nearly time to wake up. I managed to make it down the stairs before anyone else, which allowed me to take a quick peek at Julia's phone.

No texts from Celeste. At least that was good news.

Max hadn't said much to me, but then he rarely did in the mornings. Most of the time, it didn't bother me, but for some reason, I kept thinking about how he was with Heather. Why didn't he treat me the same way? Did he not like me? Why not? I was the one who saved his family, after all. He should be grateful, instead of treating me like a second-class citizen.

Julia was up later than normal as well, so by the time she made it downstairs, the kids were almost done with breakfast.

"Morning," I said, trying to force myself to sound more chipper than I felt. I wanted to ask her how she slept, but I didn't dare until she had her coffee.

She grunted as she poured herself a cup. She looked like I felt, her hair every which way and deep lines across her cheeks and under her eyes. She sat down heavily at the table, burying her head in her hand as she sucked down coffee. I pretended to focus on the kids, when really, I was watching her carefully. Was she treating me differently, as well? Or was she just really hung over?

Levi and Madison finished their cereal and ran into the family room to watch some early morning television while I cleaned up the table. Julia was still staring into her coffee cup, so I wasn't sure if I should say anything to her or not. Was it my imagination, or did she seem even more withdrawn than normal?

"Janey, do you mind getting me some ibuprofen?" she asked. "I have a splitting headache."

"Of course," I said, heading into the downstairs bathroom. Maybe that was all this was. Nothing else to worry about.

"Thanks," she said when I handed her the bottle. "I didn't sleep well last night," she added.

"I didn't, either." It slipped out before I could decide if it was a smart thing to say. I clamped my lips together, not wanting anything else to come out before I could think it through.

Yet another reason why I should always make sure I got enough sleep. Definitely wasn't on my game.

She gave me a sharp look. "You either? Were you downstairs at all?"

I ducked my head, pretending to sweep some imaginary crumbs off the table, when really, I was trying to keep her from seeing the horror in my eyes. I had no idea how to answer. Would it be better to say "yes" in case she did see me last night, or "no," and let her think it was all a dream?

"Downstairs? Why do you ask?" I forced myself to close my mouth. I had to get myself under control, especially since I wasn't sure that was the right way to respond, either. I was simply buying time.

"Just that ..." she let out a self-conscious laugh. "It was just strange. I'm not sure if it was a dream or not."

I titled my head to give her a questioning look. "What? What did you see?" I started walking back to the coffee maker to get the pot, thinking it would give me something to do with my hands.

"I was asleep on the couch," she swallowed hard. "Max and I were watching a movie, and I must have fallen asleep. I had such a stressful week. A really big project due."

I nodded, arranging my face in an understanding expression.

"Anyway, at some point while I was sleeping, I thought you were leaning over me. Like you were, I don't know, tucking me in or something." She huffed that self-conscious laugh again. "But, when I woke up, I was alone. So, I assumed it was a dream, but maybe I saw you downstairs or something, and that's what happened."

My expression felt like it had frozen on my face. The back of my neck was like ice, even though I could feel my armpits sweating. I concentrated on topping off her coffee "What a weird dream," I said lightly. "I did get a glass of water at one point, but I didn't look to see if you were in the family room or not."

Her face relaxed. "Oh, maybe that was it, then. I was probably on the couch and woke up enough to incorporate you into my dream."

"That makes sense," I said, taking the coffee back to the kitchen. I used the time while my back was turned to get control of myself. My hands were shaking so badly, I was sure I would spill the coffee. I clumsily replaced the pot, knowing if she saw me, even as hung over as she was, she would immediately sense something was wrong. What was I going to do?

Luckily, Isabelle saved me. She started to fuss.

"Oh, I better get her changed," I said, hurrying over to Isabelle while giving Julia a wide berth. Julia wasn't paying attention to me anymore anyhow, as she focused on opening the ibuprofen bottle, which was not cooperating.

I scooped up Isabelle and fled upstairs.

It's okay, I kept repeating to myself, even as another part of my brain screamed, *she DID see me!*

She doesn't suspect anything, I reassured myself. *It's fine.*

I told you that you'd screw it up, Kelly said. *When will you finally listen to me?*

I shoved all the voices down and pushed a lid over them. Everything was fine. Julia was fine. Celeste would be out of the picture soon, and I would have a key to Julia's office. There was nothing to worry about.

Julia eventually made it into her office, and I took the kids to the park. They were just finishing lunch when Max came home.

Max was never home that early on a Saturday.

And he had just told me to take off early.

Heather never got to leave early. It always seemed to me they wanted her to stay all the time, as if they were reluctant to have her leave.

So, why was I being pushed out?

Could Celeste be coming that afternoon?

No, the kids were home. And Max and Julia had been clear that they didn't want anyone meeting the kids until they'd made their decision. Even though they knew it was risky to not have Celeste meet them first in case the kids really didn't like her, they also didn't want to confuse Madison or Levi, especially Levi, with any more nannies until a permanent decision was made. Max was already a little worried they had introduced too many new adults into their lives in too short a time. Julia had argued that was a good reason to keep me, but Max countered about how my going back to school in a year would only make things worse.

Maybe I should keep an eye on things. Just to be sure. After all, Bryn was working and wasn't expecting me until later in the afternoon. My only plan for the day was to call Ashley's friend Crystal. I realized I should probably drive somewhere with Wi-Fi access, so I could talk to Crystal while accessing and monitoring the cameras.

Julia was still in her office when I came back down, so I gave the kids a goodbye hug and waved to Max before heading out the door.

I drove off, trying to figure out the best place to go. It took a bit of trial and error, but I was finally able to make it work in a MacDonald's parking lot. I bought a large cup of coffee and got myself set up with my computer balanced on my lap between me and the steering wheel, freeing up one hand for my coffee and the other for my phone.

I started by messaging Crystal to see if she was able to talk. She immediately responded "Yes," so I dialed her number.

"I can't tell you how glad I am to have gotten your message," she said right out of the gate. Her voice was breathy and high-pitched, like Marilyn Monroe's. "I've been out of mind worried about Ashley. Do you have any news?"

The desperation in her voice twisted like a knife in my gut, and I was suddenly ashamed of what I was doing. I wasn't trying to give Crystal false hope, nor was I really lying to her—I was just withholding the whole truth. Still, I felt bad, like I was picking at a wound that hadn't quite healed yet, bringing a fresh wave of pain and blood to this woman whose only crime was being friends with Ashley.

"Unfortunately not," I said sadly. On the screen, Max was shepherding the kids down to the basement while the rest of the house remained empty and still.

She sighed, a deep, hollow, empty sigh. "I was afraid that would be your answer. That's been everyone's answer. No one knows anything. Everyone feels bad but, oh well! Life goes on. She'll turn up when she's ready, right? No one seems to care even a tiny bit that a grown woman just vanished overnight. How does that even happen?"

"Does she have any family?"

"No one I know of. I think she said once her parents are dead, and there was a sibling, but she was estranged from him or her. I can't remember if she said it was a brother or a sister." I could feel my heart quicken. Ashley talked about me! Even if she did say we were estranged, at least she hadn't forgotten about me. "The whole thing was very sad," Crystal continued. "But she didn't want to talk about it. She said it all happened a long time ago, and she was over it."

"What about a partner or significant other?"

"Nope. She had neither."

"Other friends?"

Crystal laughed, but there was no humor in it, just pain. "You mean, other than me? There's a group of us, but Ashley hasn't been in touch with any of us. And, because I'm just a friend, I haven't been able to get any information out of anyone, nor does anyone believe me that there is something very wrong. I know something happened to her. I can feel it."

I could hear the anxiety in her voice and again felt a stab of guilt. "So, you don't think she had some sort of mental breakdown that caused her to leave?"

"No! Not at all. The last time I talked with her, she was perfectly fine. She was taking her meds. And even if she had stopped, there wasn't enough time for her to have this so-called breakdown."

"How do you know she was taking her meds? Did you ask her?"

"You sound just like them," a note of bitterness creeping into Crystal's voice. "You don't think I can recognize when a good friend is in the middle of a crisis? Trust me, you can tell."

"I'm sorry," I said, feeling another rush of shame flood through me. "I wasn't trying to question you. I was actually just curious. That's all."

"Hmph." Crystal didn't sound convinced "So, why did you call me?" Her voice turned suspicious. "And how did you even know who I was?"

"Julia, Ashley's boss, has kept Ashley's things."

"She did?" Crystal sounded shocked. "I didn't think she cared enough to do that."

The shame swirling inside me turned to anger. I instantly wanted to defend Julia, but I forced myself to keep going. I had already alienated Crystal once, and I knew I might not get another chance. "There was some mail to Ashley. One letter was from a psychiatrist in Riverview."

"Oh, that was probably Dr. Torr," she said. "Yeah, Ashley quit seeing her a few months before she left for Redemption."

"Oh, was there a problem?"

"Just that Dr. Torr didn't believe her about the stalker, and she told me she couldn't go to treatment with a doctor who believed it was all a delusion."

"Did you believe her?"

Crystal was silent for so long, I thought she had hung up on me. "I wanted to," she said softly. "But there was never any proof. You know? And then when she said she thought she was being stalked in Redemption, too, I just ... I didn't know what to think."

I cleared my throat. "Well, there is definitely something weird going on here. She wasn't wrong about that."

Crystal gasped. "Is it a stalker? Don't tell me that's it. I'll never be able to forgive myself."

I blinked as my brain whirled, trying to keep track of the conversation. "What are you talking about? Forgive yourself for what?"

"Just ... our last call. I ... well, I didn't believe her about the stalker, either. She got mad at me and hung up. If that ends up being the last time I spoke with her, and I didn't believe her, I just ... I don't know what I'll do."

On the screen, I watched Julia emerge from her office, lock the door behind her, and shuffle her way to the kitchen. "Well, while there might be a stalker, I don't think he was after Ashley," I said.

Another long pause. "Say again?"

When I first reached out to Crystal, I had every intention of telling her as little as possible. I wanted information from her, not necessarily to share what I had learned. But hearing the pain in her voice, and knowing I was somewhat to blame for bringing it all back, made me rethink my strategy. "So there *is* a strange guy who does seem to be hanging around a lot," I said. "But I'm pretty sure he's not connected to Ashley. I think it has to do with the family."

Crystal swore under her breath. "Are you serious? Are you seriously telling me that of all the nanny jobs available, Ashley managed to find the one that actually has a stalker? I can't even. This is too nuts. Ashley always had terrible luck with everything—jobs, relationships—but this is a new record even for her. Although when you quit your job and pack up your apartment without any other offers or a backup plan, this is what happens. I know she was super excited to land a job and a place to stay as fast as she did, and I don't think she checked it out much before she accepted."

"I know," I said. "It's hard to believe. So, that's why I reached out. Something is going on. I'm not sure what, but I wanted to see what, if anything, you knew."

Crystal didn't appear to be listening. "But Julia didn't listen to her," she said. "She pooh-poohed her. Told her it was all in her head. And all along, there really was a stalker who might be after *Julia?*"

I shifted uncomfortably in my seat. On my screen, I watched Julia brew a fresh pot of coffee before fishing a bottle of brandy out of the liquor cabinet. "It may not be Julia," I said. "I don't know who it is. It could be Max, her husband. Julia really might not know."

Crystal snorted. "Of course she knows. You don't think a mother knows if her family is being stalked? I don't care who it is, she knows. And she made Ashley feel like she was losing her mind. That woman is evil."

I bit my lip, trying to control the hot rush of words that threatened to pour out of my mouth. *Julia is NOT evil. She's my family. She may be misguided and drink a little too much and not stand up to Max like she should, but inside, she's a good person. She just needs someone to protect her. Like me.*

Yet I couldn't say any of it. I still had questions that needed answering.

"Julia really isn't like that," I said as I watched Julia top off her coffee with more brandy, her body swaying slightly against the kitchen counter. "She seemed to care for Ashley. She saved all her stuff."

"Probably more like she has a guilty conscience."

Julia stumbled slightly as she wove her way to the family room, a small amount of liquid sloshing out of her cup. Could that be why she drank so much? A guilty conscience? "So, what do you think happened, then?"

"If I had to guess, I think something happened to her."

My body jerked like an electric shock jolted through me. No! There was no way I was going to accept that. She didn't disappear years ago only to have something happen to her now before I could find her. "You think someone ..."

"Killed her," Crystal said, her voice cold as she finished the words I couldn't push past my tongue. "That's exactly what I think."

"But why?"

"That's the million-dollar question," she said. "At first, I thought it might have been an accident. Ashley loves being out in nature, hiking or cross-country skiing or whatever. When she took that nanny job, she took one look at that lake and decided to throw herself into ice skating. She used to rollerblade a lot here in Riverview, and did some ice skating as well, but not weekly like she was doing in Redemption. I asked her once about it, and she said she felt more like herself on that lake than anywhere else. She said it was peaceful. Anyway, I wondered if maybe something happened, like the ice cracked and she fell in. Maybe she couldn't get out and drowned. But the cops searched the lake for any signs of that and didn't find anything. And, of course, the accident theory doesn't explain why her car is missing. So, then I started to think maybe someone killed her."

"You think someone killed her at the lake while she was ice skating? Why would they do that?"

"I didn't say they killed her at the lake," Crystal said impatiently. "I don't even know if she made it to the lake that Sunday. I never did get a straight answer from the cops on that. She could have been killed anywhere, really. For all we know, she never left the Johnsons' house."

I gasped. "You think the Johnsons did this? Why?"

"If I knew that, don't you think I would have done something by now? Told the cops? The media?" Crystal sighed. "Look, I don't have any proof. I don't know of a motive. I don't have anything other than a gut feeling that something bad happened to her, and no one is doing anything about it. I don't buy that she would have left and not reached out to me at some point. We were friends. *Best* friends. She would have at least told me she was okay and not to worry. So, the fact that she hasn't is an issue."

Crystal was hiding something from me. I could hear it in her voice. But what? I thought about what the detective had told me about Ashley and her friends. And then it hit me.

"But the detective told me Ashley has done this before," I said. "Disappeared, I mean. Has she?"

Crystal sucked in her breath. "Who are you talking about? That Officer Hicks? He's a liar."

The venom in her voice was so sharp, it felt like she had slapped me in the face. "Why do you say that? What is he lying about?"

"Because that's NOT what she did," Crystal cried out. "I mean, yes, she was troubled. Ashley has mental issues. And there was a time, a couple years ago, when she did disappear for a while. She had stopped therapy and was having a lot of problems. She just had to get away for a while. That was all. But the difference is, her phone was still on, so we could leave her texts and voicemails. And she did eventually reach out to me. She also came back."

My head was whirling at this new information. "So how is Officer Hicks lying?"

"Because he's twisting the truth! Yes, I did tell him she took off a couple years ago, because she mentally just ... couldn't handle it anymore. And yes, she is on medication, and she was seeing a psychiatrist and had stopped. And yes, she thought she had a stalker in Riverview, and that stalker followed her to Redemption, even though no one else ever saw any evidence of it. And she was under a lot of stress with her nanny job. Julia never did anything, according to Ashley. Ashley was practically raising those kids by herself. But ..." there was a long pause, as if what she was saying sunk in right then.

"You think she just took off, too," she said, her voice defeated.

"I don't know what to think," I said honestly. "I will say, there is something going on at the house. I don't think Julia is behind it or knows about it, but there is something going on. And you're right about Ashley not reaching out to you. That does sound strange, especially since the last time she did this, you had heard from her."

"Yes!" I could practically hear the fist bump. "That's it. That's what Officer Hicks kept ignoring. She wouldn't have just fallen off the face of the earth. She would have reached out. Or she would have showed up at my door or something. How is she living? What is she using for money? The cops told me her bank account hasn't been touched, or her credit cards. And what was she wearing? She didn't have many clothes with her. She would have needed someone to help her, and it would have made sense for her to reach out to her friends. We were like her family. But she didn't."

"I get it," I said. "I do."

Crystal breathed out a long stream of air. "Thank you."

There was a lull in the conversation. On the computer, I watched Julia wander back into her kitchen holding her mug. Was this what she did every Saturday? She never seemed this bad when Heather was the nanny.

Was something else going on?

"If you find anything, will you tell me?" Crystal asked, her voice tentative.

"Of course," I said heartily, even though I wasn't entirely sure I would. *It depends on what I find,* I added in my head.

"And ..." she paused again. "You said Julia kept her things. I know I'm not family or anything, but is there any way you could tell Julia I would take them?"

"I could try," I said doubtfully. "I don't know how she'll react, though."

"I know," she said, her voice quiet and devoid of emotion. "I'm not family. I get it. But, if she ever plans to throw them away or give them away, let her know I'll take them. Okay?"

"Okay," I said.

We signed off, and I stayed where I was, watching Julia sit in the family room, television on, sipping from her coffee mug.

I felt like I was sitting in front of a huge jumble of puzzle pieces, and it was my job to sort it out. Yet I wasn't even sure if all the pieces came from the same puzzle. Crystal had just dumped a few more on top of all the others, and I had no idea what to do with them.

What I probably needed to do was sort it out with Bryn.

Chapter 29

"This is the craziest thing I've ever heard," Bryn said, a plastic glass of regular, cheap red wine dangling from her fingers. She had been so engrossed in my story, she had forgotten to drink any. "What in the world did you get yourself into?"

We were back in my old apartment living room, although this time, instead of the coffee table being covered with leftover pizza, Chinese take-out boxes were strewn about. The smell of garlic, ginger, and soy sauce still permeated the room.

"What did *Ashley* get herself into?" I corrected. "She's the one who's still missing."

Bryn cocked her head and gave me a strange look. "You mean Kelly, right?"

"Well, yeah. Of course."

"You just keep calling her Ashley, is all," Bryn said.

I was feeling flustered and wasn't sure why. Kelly and Ashley were the same person—what did it matter which name I used? "Well, she did change her name. Plus, everyone around me knows her as Ashley, so that's the name I need to use."

"Fair enough," Bryn said. "And yes, I would love for you to find her, as well. But, Janey, you're the nanny right now. You're the one poking around. Are you sure you're safe?"

"I'm keeping my eyes open," I said. "But remember, Julia told me they're looking for another nanny. So, how much danger can I really be in?" I was careful not to add any details that I shouldn't know, nor did I mention anything about cameras or my late-night texting adventure.

"That would probably be the biggest blessing, if they did find a replacement for you," Bryn said.

I looked at Bryn in horror. "What? No! I can't leave yet."

Bryn held up a hand. "I get it. I know you're still trying to figure out where your sister went. But, Janey, what else do you think you're going to find out? You talked to Crystal. You searched her room. You went through what was left behind. What else are you going to do?"

Go through Julia's office was on the tip of my tongue, but I swallowed it. I also hadn't told Bryn about making the key impression. I had a feeling she wouldn't approve. "But I still don't even know where to look."

Bryn's gaze softened, and she leaned forward to put her hand on mine. "Janey, I know how difficult this must be. But you have to face the possibility of maybe never knowing what happened to your sister."

I snatched my hand away. "No. I refuse to accept that. There has to be a clue somewhere, something I've overlooked. There has to be."

Bryn sighed and leaned back to flip through her notebook. "Okay, let's start from the beginning and see if there's anything we missed. You've checked her social media, right? There are no new posts."

I shook my head. "Nothing."

"And none of her friends have heard anything."

"No."

Bryn sighed again as she flipped through her pages. "Unfortunately, pursuing the doctors she was seeing is a dead end. They won't talk to you. The police appear to have closed the case." She shut her notebook and rubbed her forehead. "Honestly, the only thing I can think of is to do your own investigation."

"That's what I'm doing."

"No, that's not what I mean. I mean to actually try and track down what she was doing that last Sunday. Go to where she went ice skating and see if anyone saw her. Go to the coffee shop she always hung out at. At this point, it's a long shot, but maybe you can find something, some clue or, well, something, and maybe you can bring that to the police. Maybe then, they'd reopen the case."

Something inside me twisted, like a giant serpent had just woken up and slithered over to my stomach, wrapping itself around it and squeezing. "How can I do that? It's been too long."

"I know, that's why ..." Bryn paused as the thready note of panic in my voice finally sunk in. " You knew if there was nothing you could trace back to your sister in the house, the chances of you locating her would drop significantly. At this point, you need a break. Someone remembering something is your best bet."

My mouth was dry, and I reached for my glass of wine. "I get that," I said. "And, I don't mind asking around, especially in town, but going to the lake ..." my voice trailed off as the serpent tightened its coils. The Chinese food had turned into a greasy, uncomfortable lump inside my stomach.

Bryn shifted closer to me, her expression concerned. "What about the lake?"

In my mind, I was fourteen again, in the boat with my sister, the scent of suntan lotion and her perfume in the air, cold droplets of water occasionally landing on my hands and arms.

"It's just, I don't do lakes," I said.

Her forehead wrinkled. "I don't understand."

I wasn't sure if I could fully explain the dread I felt every time I thought of visiting a lake. Any lake. It brought back horrible memories ... memories that were better left deeply buried.

"The last time I saw my sister, we were on a boat," I said. "On a lake."

Bryn's face shifted, her expression filled with compassion. "Of course," she said. "I should have remembered. I'm sorry for my insensitivity."

"There's nothing to be sorry about," I said. "Of course you wouldn't remember."

"Well, quite honestly, now that I think about it, it would probably be a waste of time for you to visit the lake anyway," she said. "Ice skating season is long gone, so whoever is there now would likely not have been there this winter. So, I don't know what you'd really get out of it anyhow. It would probably be better to focus on where she went before and after, see if you can track down someone she talked to. Hopefully, that would give you a direction to go."

"That's a good idea," I said. Maybe I could do some asking around the next time I had to run errands.

"Of course it's a good idea," she sniffed. "I have lots of good ideas. If only you would listen."

I chuckled at her put-upon expression. It felt good to laugh, even if it was just a little one. It made me wonder how long it had been since I had laughed at anything.

"The best part of that plan is you don't have to be a nanny to follow it."

My expression felt like it froze on my face. "I don't understand."

Her face grew serious. "Look, I'm really worried about you. Something is going on in that house, and we have no idea what it is. Not to mention that weird guy who keeps showing up and that car that seems to always be parked on the street. I don't think it's safe for you. I think you should seriously consider quitting, even if they haven't found a nanny to replace you yet."

My eyes widened. "I can't quit and leave them in a lurch. I can't do that to Julia. She needs me."

"I'm sure she needs someone in your position, but it doesn't have to be you," Bryn said firmly. "Janey, it's okay to put yourself first. Besides, wouldn't it be so much easier to hunt for your sister if you weren't working full-time?"

She had a point. It would be a lot easier to dig in and investigate if I didn't have to work it in around my job.

But I couldn't leave Julia. That was non-negotiable. She was family, and you don't leave your family in a lurch. And besides, Julia needed me to protect her. Not just any nanny, but me. I was the only one who understood her. A new nanny wouldn't.

"I'll be fine," I said. "I can handle both. And I'll be careful. Promise."

"Are you sure?"

"Yes. Really. It will be fine."

Bryn didn't look convinced. "Promise me you'll be extra careful then."

"I promise."

Bryn still didn't look happy. "Well, hopefully they will hire a new nanny, and then the problem will take care of itself."

My throat seemed to close up. I tried to smile, even though it felt like I was breathing through a tight straw. How could she want that for me? Why did she want to tear my family apart?

"Whatever happens, I'm sure it will all work out," I said through gritted teeth.

Bryn smiled at me, a real smile. Hopefully, she didn't sense how much I hated her in that moment.

***

"Wanna drink?" A tall glass filled with ice and Coke appeared in front of me. I twirled the red straw before taking a sip.

And nearly choked.

"That's not soda," I gasped, looking up to see Kelly standing next to me, laughing.

"Au contraire," she said. "There's soda in there. And a little something else besides." She winked at me.

"But you're not old enough to buy alcohol," I said. "How did you get it?"

She just smiled a secret, knowing smile while reaching over to clink my glass with hers. "Cheers," she said. "Now, drink up. It's a party, you know. It's supposed to be fun."

I took another cautious sip. Now that I knew there was alcohol in it, it went down a lot easier.

"See," Kelly said. "It's pretty good, right?"

"Yeah, actually it is good," I said, taking another sip.

Kelly's grin widened, and she leaned closer to me. "Just don't drink it too fast. You don't want it to go to your head."

Then she was gone, melting into the crowd, leaving me sitting alone at a high table in the corner.

I kept sipping my drink as I scanned the faces, looking for anyone I recognized, but all were unfamiliar. There was no sign of Kelly at all, nor did I even see any of her friends. I was lost in a sea of strangers.

I wondered what I should do. Look for Kelly? Go up to someone and start talking? Or maybe just leave? It's not like I was having a good time, anyway.

I slid off the stool, thinking maybe I'd at least try and find Kelly. She brought me, so I figured she should talk to me at least a little. Right?

The entire room seemed to tilt to one side. I staggered forward, trying to walk in a straight line while everything pitched and swayed. A group of women frowned at me, their faces huge, like giant, bobbing balloons.

"Watch where you walk," a voice shrieked at me.

"Sorry," I said, trying to discern where the voice came from, but all the faces surrounding me were glaring at me, their eyes like slits, their mouths scowling.

"You don't belong," another voice hissed.

"I'm just trying to find my sister," I said. "Kelly. Have you seen her?" But the words didn't seem to come out right, and the faces looked even more displeased.

"Hey," a voice whispered at my side, and I felt a strong hand grip my elbow. "I got you. You're safe."

Suddenly, the world stopped spinning, and I found I could stand up straight. The balloon faces seemed to recede, growing fainter and smaller. "Thanks," I said, turning to see my savior. "I really appreciate ..."

My voice dissipated as my mouth dropped open.

It was Oz.

He was wearing a tight, black T-shirt that stretched across the muscles in his chest. His dark hair was too long, hanging in one eye. He smiled at me, revealing very white and pointed teeth.

"What are you doing here?" I asked, my voice slurred. I could smell his aftershave and something else, something underneath the clean scent. Something rotten. Like maybe he had a decayed tooth hiding among the ultra-bright ones.

Like a wolf in sheep's clothing.

His smile widened. "Now, is that anyway to talk to someone who just saved you?"

"I thought Kelly broke up with you. Why are you here?"

"We're still friends," he said. "Do you want to find Kelly?"

"Yes."

"Okay, let's go find her." His tone was friendly as he started walking forward again, still hanging on to my elbow. I wanted to tell him to loosen his grip. It was too tight, and he was hurting me. But somehow, I couldn't form the words.

The world started swaying again, spinning around me. I couldn't recognize anyone. And even though I kept trying to focus on their faces, they continuously shifted and disappeared.

We were moving faster and faster. I wanted to tell Oz to slow down. How could we find Kelly if we were walking so fast? I wanted him to let go of my arm. I wanted to tell him I could find her myself.

But I couldn't form words.

Then, we were in the parking lot. The cool, humid air slapped at my cheeks as my shoes clicked on the cement. I looked down to see I was wearing a white dress and thigh-high white boots with a very tall heel. No wonder I couldn't walk. I never wore heels that high. And why was I wearing white in a bar?

"Why are we out here?" I finally asked. "I thought we were looking for Kelly?"

"We are," he said, tugging at my arm. "She's out here waiting for us."

"She's waiting in a parking lot?"

"Just over here," he said. "We were going to talk out here where it's quiet."

It made no sense to me. Kelly wouldn't be hanging around a parking lot waiting for anyone, much less someone she broke up with. Kelly would insist he come to her. She would demand to be courted and seduced. She didn't do the chasing.

I wanted to say that to Oz, but his hand was still gripping my elbow like a vice, and he was moving so quickly, it was all I could do to stumble after him in my too-high boots.

"Here we are," he said, jerking me toward a shiny black pickup truck gleaming almost unnaturally under the light of the moon. I was starting to get a very bad feeling.

"I don't see Kelly," I said.

Oz continued to smile at me, his teeth so white, they appeared to be gleaming as unnaturally as the truck. "She'll be here. Why don't we wait inside for her?"

"I think I should go find her," I said, trying to wrench my arm away, but he was holding it too tightly. He seemed oblivious to my flailing and managed to pull me closer to him.

"You look very beautiful tonight," he said. His breath was sour and rancid, like something had died in his mouth. "Kelly did an awesome job with you."

My stomach turned to ice. "What are you talking about?"

"She got you ready, right? Dressed you, did your hair and makeup?"

My chest froze as much as my stomach. "How do you know that?"

He laughed softly. "Well, it's obvious. Normally, you don't wear makeup. The only time you do is when Kelly doesn't want you to be a plain Jane. She likes transforming you."

Transforming you. The phrase seemed to echo around me, jolting through my body like an electric current.

Was that what Kelly was doing? *Transforming* me?

Into what?

Oz leaned closer, and suddenly, he was kissing me, his mouth pressed painfully against mine, my teeth cutting into my lips. He shoved his tongue roughly into my mouth.

I pushed against him, twisting my head away. "Stop," I said, but my voice was so quiet, I could barely hear it myself. "Stop."

But he didn't stop. He kept forcing himself against me, despite my struggles.

"Just relax, Janey," he said against my mouth. "It's better if you relax."

"No," I said, straining to get away from him. But he wasn't Oz anymore. He had turned into a monster, all black hair and sharp teeth, red eyes and curving claws.

I screamed as loud as I could, trying to get someone's, anyone's, attention. But the noise that came out of my mouth was barely a whisper on the balmy night breeze.

"You want this," the monster said, saliva dripping from his fangs so white, they glittered in the pale moonlight. "Admit it. You're a slut, and you want this."

I tried to scream again, but then I was inside the car, shoved in the corner as he towered over me, his red eyes glowing with excitement. A forked, red tongue slid out of his mouth, licking his lips.

"You're a virgin, aren't you?" the monster hissed. "Just the way I like them. Young and untouched. You're perfect."

He was hurting me, and the pain was so intense, I tried to scream again, but I still couldn't. No sound emerged from my mouth, and there was nothing I could do but suffer in silence while inside, I couldn't stop screaming ...

I woke with a jerk, shoving myself out of the bed and onto the floor with a loud thump.

I needed to get out of that truck.

I tried to crawl, only dimly aware of the braided rug beneath me, the material rough under my sweaty palms. I was gasping and choking for air, but all I could think about was escape. I had to get away. I couldn't let it happen again ...

My head bumped against something. A wall, no it was a door. A bedroom door.

Slowly, I sat up and looked around. I was on the floor of my bedroom at the Johnsons'.

There was no monster. I was safe.

I pulled myself to a standing position, my limbs still shaking, and cracked open the door. The house was quiet and still. Despite my throwing myself out of bed and scrambling across the floor, it seemed I hadn't awakened anyone.

I slipped out of the room to creep down the hallway just to be sure. Everyone was asleep. I paid special attention to Madison, trying to see if she was actually asleep or just faking it. But her chest rose and fell in a slow, steady rhythm.

I continued my creeping to the bathroom, where I splashed cold water on my face and neck before heading downstairs for a glass of water. I almost had another heart attack as I walked into the kitchen, sure that the refrigerator was a hulking monster, just waiting to pounce.

It was just a dream. Just a terrible dream.

I thought about making tea, but it felt like too much work. Instead, I pressed a cold glass against my chest and neck, trying to calm my nerves.

Why would I have such a dreadful nightmare? I searched my day, but it was a normal Sunday. After a late-night chat with Bryn, I slept in, had a late breakfast, and logged onto my computer to watch what was going on at the Johnsons', where all seemed pretty normal. I left my apartment late in the afternoon, stopping for dinner on my way to the house and still making it back in time to greet the kids before they went to bed.

There was nothing out of sorts. Max was a little standoffish, but he was always that way. And Julia had at least seemed happy to see me.

It didn't make sense. Why would I have such a dream, unless ...

Of course. I felt like slapping myself on the forehead, it was so obvious.

It was all Bryn's fault.

She was the one who kept saying I was in danger.

Ever since Kelly disappeared, I had always associated danger with Oz, as I was sure he was the one who had done something to her.

No wonder I dreamed about him. My subconscious was processing all the fear Bryn tried to fill me with.

I was going to need to stop talking to her. That was the only solution. I couldn't afford to keep having my sleep disturbed. Even though it helped to talk things through, I had to stop.

I had bigger things to focus on.

Feeling better now that I knew the source of my nightmare, I refilled my water glass and headed back to my room. Hopefully, I could still get a little more sleep before I had to start my day.

I had nothing to be afraid of. Everything was fine.

I was safe.

Chapter 30

Once I pushed my nightmare aside, I told myself I was going to relax and enjoy the day. After all, by nightfall, Celeste would no longer be a threat, and with any luck, Julia would get a much-needed wake-up call about how lucky she was to have me. Then, she could start defending me to Max.

But even if that didn't happen, the whole "new nanny" nonsense would be well on its way to an early grave.

At first, it appeared like all was going just as I had planned. Julia sent me away for errands around lunch, which is what I figured would happen. I took my time shopping with Isabelle, enjoying my afternoon and feeling confident that everything would work out perfectly.

I knew all was not well the moment I arrived home. I had assumed I would find Julia in the kitchen, or that she would appear shortly after to talk to me. While I knew she likely wouldn't tell me about Celeste directly, I figured she would at least want to connect with me.

Except she never appeared. She stayed in her office until long after I fetched the kids from school, got them their snack, and started helping Madison with her homework.

Max actually came home before Julia left her office. I watched Levi run up to meet him, screaming, "Daddy's home, daddy's home." Julia had to have heard him. Still, she didn't come out.

It made no sense. She was always done with her day before Max arrived home, and on the few occasions she worked a little later, she always, *always* appeared when he walked in the door.

What was going on?

Maybe she and Max had a huge fight when Celeste didn't show. I was dying to run upstairs and check the video footage, but I knew I had to wait.

After Max greeted the kids, he told them to go watch a little television while he fixed himself a "grown-up drink." I puttered around the kitchen, pretending to be putting the finishing touches on dinner, as he located a bottle of wine.

"Where's Julia?" he asked me, hunting for the corkscrew.

"Still in her office," I said. "She must be finishing up a project."

He nodded as he reached for two wine glasses. "I know things have been pretty stressful for her lately. She's in the middle of a couple of big projects, and then on top of that, she had to deal with firing Heather and getting you on board. Don't get me wrong—we're both very appreciative of how you've stepped in the way you have. But I know she ... hasn't been herself."

I nodded, keeping my face composed despite my spinning mind, trying to figure out where he was going with the conversation and if it was going to be as bad as it was feeling. "You know I'm happy to help," I said. "You can count on me."

Max uncorked the wine bottle with a gentle pop. "And we appreciate that," he said again, but he was also careful not to look at me. "So, you know, Julia's way of dealing with the stress and unwinding is to have a few glasses of wine at night, and I know sometimes she's fallen asleep on the couch."

I grew very still. This was really not heading in a good direction. Had Julia told Max about seeing me? How was I going to handle it now?

"I was wondering if you ever went to help her at any point? Maybe just to check on her or pick up a wine glass that had fallen on the floor?"

I swallowed and arranged my face into an expression of confusion. "I'm not sure I understand. Whenever I've seen her asleep on the couch, I just figured she was exhausted. Lots of people fall asleep on the couch. My dad always did while watching TV. Is there a reason you're asking?"

"No reason," he said quickly. Too quickly. "I was just curious if you ever went in and helped her up the stairs. Sometimes, people can be pretty groggy when they wake up."

"I just assumed she needed her sleep," I said. "Is there a problem?"

"No, no problem. I'm just a little worried about her, that's all." He forced himself to smile at me, but it didn't reach his eyes. "I guess I'm just a little protective. I don't want you to think badly of her."

"I love Julia. I don't think badly of her at all," I said forcefully. Maybe a little too forcefully.

Max went back to focusing on pouring the wine. "That's good. I'm glad to hear that. I just wanted to be sure." He put the bottle down and picked up the glasses, giving me another awkward, forced smile. "I'll go check on her, see how long she's going to be. Dinner smells great, by the way."

"Thank you," I said as I watched him walk out of the kitchen holding the two glasses. For someone who appeared to be concerned about Julia's drinking habits, it was surprising to see him bringing her wine.

But that was the least of my worries.

What was he getting at? Did they suspect I had something to do with Celeste being a no-show?

Or was there something else going on?

The nightmare from the night before slithered through my mind, and I shivered. Could Max have triggered it? He had been cordial when I arrived. Although, thinking back, had he been more standoffish than usual? Was he already planning ahead to when Celeste would replace me?

And why was he so interested in replacing me, anyway? Was it because he found Celeste more attractive? Or was there something else going on?

Bryn's warnings echoed in my ears, despite my trying to push them away.

I was desperate to watch the video from earlier in the day, but I knew I had to wait until the kids went to bed.

When Julia eventually emerged from the office, she seemed remote. Distant. She gave me a weak smile when she first saw me, but otherwise, her focus was on her wine.

I was making myself so sick with anxiety, I nearly begged off of bedtime duties so I could watch the video, but I knew that would be too suspicious.

Finally, the kids were tucked away, and I was able to escape to my room. I quickly plugged in my earphones and started the video.

Initially, it was exactly how I thought it would be. Max arrived home, and he and Julia sat in the living room waiting for Celeste. Well, Julia sat. Max paced. And talked. It was clear he was quite excited to meet Celeste, which wasn't lost on Julia, whose face grew more and more sour with every passing minute.

It wasn't until she was about ten minutes late that they started to wonder what was going on. Max kept asking Julia if she was sure she told her the right time, and Julia kept saying "yes." After about the fifth time, Julia pulled up her texts and showed her phone to Max.

At that point, the discussion turned to concern—maybe something had happened to her. So, Julia texted her.

Celeste responded almost immediately. Based on the conversation that followed, it was safe to assume that Celeste was confused … Julia had texted her on Friday that the meeting was changed to Tuesday instead of Monday.

"Did you do this?" Max demanded. "Change the meeting?"

"What? No!" Julia said. "I showed you my phone. Why are you believing her instead me?"

"Because I know you'd rather not hire her," Max said through gritted teeth. "You want to keep Janey."

"Of course I want to keep Janey," Julia said. "She's been great. She's loyal and honest. Why would I want to throw that away?"

"Because she isn't right for us, for our family," Max nearly shouted. "We've had this discussion. I'm not comfortable with her in my house."

My head reared back like he had reached through the camera and punched me in the face. He wasn't *comfortable* with me in *his* house? This was my family he was talking about! How dare he?

He was the one who was never home. I was the one taking care of the kids, making sure there was food in the house and dinner on the table, not to mention keeping a watchful eye over everyone.

How dare he?

Julia was speaking, but I had missed part of it being so wrapped up in my inner fuming. "… everything is always about you. Why can't we ever do what I need?"

"We always do what you need," Max said. "You made the decision with every single nanny so far, and look where we are—about to hire our fourth one in six months."

"We don't have to hire a fourth one," Julia insisted. "We can keep the one we have."

"I don't trust her," Max said, his voice firm. "We need to replace her."

"*Why* don't you trust her?"

"Because she's hiding something from us. She's not telling us the truth."

"What is she hiding?"

"If I knew that, she wouldn't still be hiding it from us," he snapped.

"Then how do you know she's hiding anything?"

"It's a gut feeling."

Julia rolled her eyes. "Oh please."

"You can scoff all you want, but you do the same thing."

"Well, MY gut isn't saying any such thing."

Max ran his hands through his hair. "This just isn't making any sense," he said. "When I spoke to Celeste last week …"

"You *spoke* to Celeste?" Julia squeaked.

"I was setting up the appointment for you," he said.

"Isn't that what your secretary is for? What exactly does she do all day?"

Max glared at Julia, his eyes narrowed. "She *is* doing work. Company work. She's not paid to handle my personal affairs."

Julia muttered something under her breath I couldn't catch, but Max ignored it. "She was so excited about this opportunity. And when I spoke to her references, they made a point of saying she was always punctual and very detail-oriented."

"So?"

"So, it makes no sense why she would lie about this."

"So you think I'm the one lying?" Julia demanded. "I showed you my phone. There's nothing there."

"No, I don't think you're lying, but ..." His voice trailed off.

"But what?"

Max turned away and walked toward the window, pushing the curtain back and staring outside. "You have been drinking a lot." His voice was quieter.

"No, I haven't," Julia was indignant. "No more than usual. And what does that have to do with anything?"

"Just that ..." Max swallowed. I could see his Adam's apple bobbing in his neck. "Maybe you weren't ... yourself, when you did it. Maybe it was an impulsive move, and afterward, you deleted your texts."

Julia was shaking her head. "No. I swear, I wouldn't do such a thing. I ..." her voice stopped, but her mouth hung open, and her eyes grew very wide. I could almost see the memory flash across her face.

Were you downstairs at all?

I gasped, my heart in my throat. Oh no, oh no, oh no. This couldn't be happening. She was going to tell Max about seeing me downstairs. Of course he would then assume the worst.

I knew you were going to screw it up, Kelly whispered in my ear. *It would have been fine if you had just left the phone on the couch and walked away, but no, you had to push and push. And now look what's happened.*

"Shut up," I muttered out loud to Kelly, trying not to let her hear the panic in my voice. "Just shut up."

On the computer, Max spun around. "You what?"

Julia swallowed. I stared at her, my eyes feeling like they were bulging out. *Don't tell him. Please don't tell him. We're family. I'm on your side. I'm taking care of you. Don't let him take that away.*

"Nothing," she muttered.

"No, what were you going to say?"

"I wasn't going to say anything," she insisted. "And I'm tired of defending myself. I didn't do anything. If you don't think Celeste is lying to us, maybe she just made a mistake. It happens. Even to perfect people." Her voice grew bitter.

Max gave her a long look. "We can talk about this later. I'm going back to work." He strode over to the side table where he scooped up his keys before heading out of the camera's range.

Julia stayed where she was on the couch, her head propped up on her hands. I couldn't read her expression. The longer I watched her, the more uneasy I felt.

Maybe she didn't remember, I told myself. *Maybe she was thinking about something else. Like how pretty Celeste is. And how her husband was calling her when he was supposed to be working.*

Maybe it had nothing to do with me.

Maybe.

The more I watched her, the more uneasy I felt.

Finally, I flipped over to the live camera to see if I could glean any other details, but unfortunately, I was too late. Max was already in the bedroom watching his tablet while Julia sat drinking in the family room with the television on.

I thought about how Max had taken Julia a glass of wine in her office that afternoon, and how they had stayed in there for nearly fifteen minutes, their voices too low to make out.

My uneasy feeling was turning into alarm. The problem was, what was I going to do about it?

I switched back and forth between Max and Julia for a while, hoping against hope I would see one of them go to the other and finish their conversation. But neither did.

This would be a non-issue if you had only listened to me, Kelly spoke again. *You are such an idiot.*

Leave me alone, I shouted back in my head. *Nobody asked you.*

She laughed, a harsh, cold sound. *Maybe you should have. Maybe things would be better if you had. Have you ever considered that? The reason you keep screwing up is because you don't listen to me.*

I squashed her voice down, refusing to listen to her anymore. She didn't know everything.

What I needed was a way to find out what Julia was really thinking, so I could figure out a plan.

I thought again about them talking in Julia's office, a room that had no camera.

I chewed on my thumbnail and fretted.

Chapter 31

I sat up in bed with a jerk. Something had woken me.

Not that I had actually been sleeping. More like a fitful doze as my mind replayed the conversation between Julia and Max over and over again.

Why had Julia paused like that? What were they talking about in her office?

But something had pulled me out of my half-conscious musings. Something I couldn't immediately identify.

What was it?

I looked around the room to see if anything was different. The moon splashed across the floor, turning it into a silvery-grey and the pieces of furniture into unrecognizable shapes, but nothing appeared out of order. My laptop was on the desk where I had left it, and my phone was charging next to my nightstand, the screen dark. I reached over to wake it up, on the off chance I had received some sort of notification. Nothing.

I leaned back and was in the middle of telling myself I was imagining things when I heard it again.

A soft sound, like a footstep outside my door.

I froze, hardly daring to move. Who was outside my door in the middle of the night?

Was it one of the kids? I knew I ought to get out of bed and see, in case one of them needed something.

But the kids would knock and call out to me, asking if I was awake. They wouldn't be skulking around outside the door.

So, if not the kids, then who?

I don't think it's safe for you.

There's something in that house.

Watch your back.

Bryn, Heather, even the strange man with the limp—their voices filled my head.

Were they on to something after all?

The floor creaked again, and I pressed my hand against my mouth, feeling my upper teeth cut into my lip, trying to keep myself from screaming. Maybe, on second thought, I *should* scream. Wake up the kids, the baby. That would likely give whoever was outside pause.

Or ... would it? Would whoever was on the other side of the door find a way to explain it all away?

I stared at the doorknob, wishing I had locked it. Not that there was much of a lock in a "privacy" lock—it's really just a little twist in the doorknob, but still. It would have been something to at least stop whoever was on the other side from just sneaking in.

The idea of someone creeping into my room in the middle of the night made my heart skitter in my chest. I couldn't breathe, couldn't think.

Who was on the other side of the door?

It couldn't be Julia. She was my family. She wouldn't hurt me. Besides, she had enough wine at dinner that she wasn't capable of moving that stealthily.

It had to be Max.

But ... what if it wasn't?

My breath seemed to both freeze and burn in my chest at the same time. I shoved my fists into my mouth, biting down to keep myself from screaming or passing out.

What if the strange man with the limp had broken in?

Or worse?

I could hear myself starting to whimper, so I removed my fist and shoved a pillow into my mouth instead. I couldn't let whoever it was hear me. I couldn't.

I don't know how long I sat there, staring at the door, barely able to breathe with the pillow in my mouth, the taste of oil and sweat on my tongue, before I heard another creak.

Except rather than coming toward my door, it seemed to be moving away.

I still didn't move. I couldn't, actually. But there were no more creaks or footsteps. All was silent.

Finally, I forced myself out of my bed and crept over to the door. I pressed my ear against the wood. Still silence.

Did I dare open it? All I wanted to do was turn the lock and dive back into my bed, burying myself in the covers. But I knew I would spend the rest of the night staring at the door, waiting for a twist of the doorknob or a creak on the floor, unless I looked.

I had to.

Slowly, carefully, I opened the door a crack and peered out. I was prepared to see a person there, maybe even an eye staring into mine.

But the hallway was empty. The house was silent.

I shut the door, locked it, and got back into bed. Was it possible there was no one there at all? That all I heard were sounds of the house settling, and my imagination distorted it into something it wasn't?

That must be the answer. Because the alternative was unthinkable.

I tried to relax, to doze off in the final few hours before I had to get up for the day, but sleep was even further away than it had been before.

***

I had just pulled my head out of the refrigerator, my arms full of almond milk and yogurt, when I noticed Max right behind me.

I shrieked, nearly dropping the milk. "Max, you scared me."

Max's face was lost in the shadows, but his eyes had a curious, flat sheen to them. "Sorry," he said, but he didn't sound sorry at all. "I was getting coffee."

"Of course," I answered, trying not to look at his empty hands or at the coffeemaker stationed on the other side of the

279

kitchen. It would have been far easier for him to go the other way.

In my mind's eye, I heard the creak on the other side of the bedroom door, and it suddenly hit me how alone Max and I were. Other than Isabelle, who was gently cooing in her swing, it was just us. Everyone else was asleep upstairs.

I swallowed hard, the coppery taste of fear on my tongue, and forced my legs to move to the kitchen table. "I'll get out of your way then," I said, my voice squeaking.

I turned, desperate to place the kitchen table between us, but my feet didn't cooperate, and I stumbled, nearly falling.

"Careful," he said.

"I'm okay," I said, managing to keep my balance without dropping the food. I moved closer to Isabelle, successful in keeping the table between us.

Max hadn't moved. He was still standing in the same place, watching me with his flinty eyes. "How did you sleep?"

"Okay." *Other than when I heard you skulking around outside my door.* "How about you?"

"Mostly fine," he said. He finally moved, walking over to the coffeepot to fetch his coffee. "I thought I heard someone walking around the house last night. I was wondering if it was you."

My hands jerked, knocking over one of the yogurts. "No, it wasn't me."

He leaned against the counter, cupping his coffee in both hands. "It was probably just the house settling then. I checked everything, including the doors and windows, but all seemed normal."

Why was he telling me all of this? Was this his way of letting me know he knew I was awake?

Was he warning me somehow?

Again, I registered how alone we were. My eyes darted around the kitchen table, trying to find anything I might use as a weapon, but there were only spoons and plastic bowls and cups. The heaviest item would be the half-filled container of almond milk. I didn't even have my coffee nearby, as I had left it on the counter.

My only chance was the kids. Hopefully, they would be up soon. And, if nothing else, Isabelle was wide awake and looking around. I could only pray he wouldn't want to do anything in front of her, even if she was too young to understand.

I was contemplating whether I should pick her up or not when some of his words sunk in. He had checked the doors and windows. Was that just an excuse, or did he think someone actually could have come in the house?

"You checked the doors and windows?" I asked. "I thought this was a safe neighborhood. Did you really think someone tried to break in?"

"Oh no," he quickly assured me. "It's very safe. But that doesn't mean it's not smart to check or be prepared. Wouldn't you agree?"

He was staring at me so intently, it felt like some sort of test—one I was sure I was about to fail. "Well, yes," I said cautiously. "It's always good to be prepared."

"It's especially important when you have a family to protect," he continued. "You need to be even more vigilant when it comes to your family, especially if they aren't able to sense the danger."

Prickles of fear rose like goosebumps over my arms. Next to me, Isabelle made a laughing sound as she kicked her feet. I wanted to snatch her up, hold her in front of me like a shield. I wanted to demand he tell me what he did to Ashley, because now, it was clear to me it must have been him. He did something to her. Somehow, she had done something or said something that Max perceived as a threat, and he did what he "had" to do. Alone. Because he was protecting his family from something they didn't know was dangerous.

Max stared at me, his eyes hard and flat, waiting for my answer. I squared my shoulders and lifted my chin. I couldn't let him see my fear. I had to be strong. For Julia. For Madison. For Levi. For Isabelle.

It was up to me to protect them.

"Yes," I said, my voice clear and unwavering. "I most definitely agree. You must protect the innocent and the ones who don't know or can't sense the danger."

We stared at each other. I made my expression as unyielding as his. I wouldn't back down. I couldn't. There was too much at stake. Not only my safety, but the safety of the rest of the family members.

And justice for Ashley.

I would prevail.

I don't know how it would have ended if Levi hadn't run into the kitchen right then, greeting us both. "I'm hungry," he announced, pulling the chair out. "Can I have breakfast first and then get dressed?"

"Of course," I answered, keeping my eyes on Max. "Let me help you with your cereal."

"Dad, will you eat breakfast with me?"

Max smiled, a cold, flat smile that matched his eyes. "Sorry, champ. I'm running late. But your sister should be down soon."

"She's still getting ready," he said, reaching for the cereal box. I put a discreet hand on it to help guide the flakes into the bowl. "She sent me down."

"Oh?" I asked as Max stalked out of the kitchen.

He nodded vigorously as he watched me fill his bowl. "Yeah, she told me I should get out of bed and start eating without her."

I reached for the almond milk as I gazed at Levi thoughtfully. Was it possible Madison heard us from upstairs? "Did she say why?"

He shrugged. "Just that if I hurried, I might be able to eat with Daddy, but ..." he sighed heavily. "I guess I didn't hurry enough."

I added almond milk to his bowl, wondering why she would have said that to him.

***

The door slammed, startling me so, I spilled the orange juice I was pouring for Levi's snack.

"I have to go," Julia shouted. Almost immediately, the door to the garage slammed shut.

I looked around the table. Madison and Levi stared back at me, their eyes round. I could feel their worry coming off of them in waves, an echo of the low-grade anxiety that had followed me around all day.

Anger flared up inside me, hot and sudden. Although really, it wasn't sudden. All day had been a struggle—a mix of exhaustion, anxiety, and fear. Ever since Max threatened me that morning, I hadn't felt safe. I could still feel the pressure of the knife I had slipped into my pocket. Never again would Max catch me unaware or unarmed. If he tried anything, he would get a nasty surprise.

So, it wasn't like I didn't have enough to deal with already, yet there went Julia, doing something completely out of character and leaving me to deal with the aftermath.

I pasted a fake smile on my face. "I guess Mommy had to go," I said, trying to make a joke out of it.

Levi smiled back and reached for a cracker. Madison furrowed her forehead, making her look much older than her age.

"I don't like it when Mommy leaves like that," she said to her empty plate.

I slid crackers and tofu cheese onto a plate for Levi. "She's done it before?" I asked, trying to sound nonchalant, but even as I said it, I remembered the day I snuck in to toss Heather's ashtray from the roof. She had run out exactly the same way.

Madison nodded, still staring at her plate. I pushed the platter of crackers and tofu cheese closer to her. "When she gets upset with Dad."

Levi stopped chewing. "Is Mommy and Daddy getting divorced?" Except he didn't pronounce "divorce" quite right, and with his mouth full of crackers, it sounded completely muddled. Not that it mattered. I knew what he meant.

So did Madison, apparently. "I don't think so," she said. "Mommy likes that Daddy has a good job and makes enough money to take care of us."

Surprised, I glanced over at Madison, but she was concentrating on filling her own plate. Quite a cynical take for a ten-year-old.

But, for a five-year-old, it apparently made perfect sense, as Levi went back to eating. "I like Daddy being around," he said. "My friend Tommy at school, his parents are divorced, and his daddy doesn't live at home. He gets sad."

"That is sad," I agreed before turning back to Madison. "So, how do you know that Mommy is upset with Daddy?"

"Because they fight. She thinks Daddy is doing something, and he says he isn't. I don't know why she doesn't believe him."

Could this be about the cheating? Was that what this was all about? Julia thought he was with another woman and went barreling out to catch him?

But then the memory of Max that morning shoved its way in again, and I grew cold. Could that be it? Had Julia discovered a different secret?

Or, despite Madison's uncanny knack for always knowing what was going on, it was possible that Julia's rushing out had nothing to do with Max at all. What about that strange man with the limp? Or the car outside? Or what if it was about something completely different?

I wished again I had a camera in her office. I was going to have to see if I could put one in. In the meantime, I had a job to do, making sure the kids were safe and protected.

"Well, sometimes things are complicated with grownups," I said.

Madison shot me a look. "Now you sound like Mommy. She says I'll understand when I get older." She shook her head, her exasperation all over her face.

I hid a smile before leaning forward. "You know, sometimes even when you're an adult, adults can be hard to understand," I said in a mock whisper.

Her eyes widened. "Really?"

"Yep. Adults can do some very strange things."

She screwed up her face for a moment, as if she were thinking something through, before nodding. "That makes a lot of sense."

"I won't do anything strange when I'm grown up," Levi announced.

I ruffled his hair. "I'm sure you won't."

But inside, I wondered. Where was Julia going? And why?

Chapter 32

The moment I saw Val walk into the house, I scooped up Isabelle and headed upstairs.

Julia had asked me that morning to make myself scarce when Val arrived, so she could talk to her. I had completely forgotten about the broken figurine a week ago, so I took it as a good sign Julia had remembered and was going to talk to Val.

And I needed some good signs.

Julia continued to remain standoffish with me. Well, with everyone. She was barely talking to Max either, which is what I kept reminding myself. It might have nothing to do with me. It probably didn't have anything to do with me. She was most likely depressed because of the state of her marriage.

Max basically ignored me, which was good, although I was very careful to not go anywhere in the house alone when he was home. I also made sure I always had the kitchen knife I was borrowing with me.

I carried Isabelle into her room, pretending to change her. I wondered if I had enough time to slip into my room and watch the conversation, but it felt like I might be pushing it. If Julia abruptly ran upstairs to find me and give me an update, I would run the risk of her catching me in my bedroom, and I didn't want to do anything to arouse her suspicion. It would be better to just hang around upstairs and find out later what happened.

I waited until I heard the vacuum start before venturing back downstairs. Julia was in the kitchen, busy writing as she stood by the kitchen counter. A cup of coffee was at her elbow.

I moved closer to her. "How did it go?" I asked, keeping my voice low.

"Fine," she said, not looking at me. "I've got a couple other things for you to do today along with grocery shopping. Do you mind?"

"Not at all," I said, trying to hide how stung I felt. I was so sure she was going to open up to me. Maybe she was waiting until Val left, even though Val clearly couldn't hear us with the vacuum running. I was a little disappointed she was still there, as I had hoped Julia would fire her on the spot. But maybe she worked something out where Val would clean for a few more weeks until Julia found her replacement. I could offer to help with that.

I straightened the kids' bedroom and bathroom, started a load of laundry, and got ready to leave. Hopefully, I'd have some answers by the time I returned.

* * *

"Janey, can I talk to you for a second?" Julia called out from her office as I walked in, balancing a sleeping Isabelle in her carrier with one arm and a grocery bag in the other. Her office door was open a crack—not enough to let me see in, but enough for me to hear her. "Sure," I said, my heart pounding. Finally, some answers. "Do you want me to bring in the rest of the groceries first?"

"Yes, that's fine. You can put everything away, as well."

I dragged everything into the kitchen. Val was putting away the cleaning supplies. She caught my eye as I walked by and smiled at me.

A snake before it struck its prey. Cruel. Triumphant.

My heart skipped a beat. I didn't like that smile one bit.

I was desperate to run into the office and demand Julia tell me what was going on, but I restrained myself. The last thing I wanted was for Val to see me freaking out. So, I forced myself to go back out to the car and drag the rest of the bags in. By the time I had everything in the kitchen, Val was quietly letting herself out.

I stood for a moment in the stillness, debating whether or not I should go into Julia's office, but she had asked me to put the food away. If I truly had no idea what was going on, that's what I would be doing. I started to unload the bags.

I was about halfway finished when Julia appeared. She didn't say anything, and it was only when I turned to put a box of cereal away that I noticed her. "Oh," I said, pressing my hand against my heart. "I didn't see you there."

Julia didn't respond. She looked terrible. Her face was pale, her eyes rimmed in red, and there were puffy, black circles under her eyes. Had she been crying? Or not sleeping well? Had she found something out about Max? Her hands were clasped behind her back.

I cocked my head and looked at her, trying to keep my expression neutral as my heart continued to beat erratically. "Did you want to sit here and talk? I could make us both a cup of tea. Or brew a pot of coffee or ..."

"How could you?"

Her voice was low and hoarse, like she had been crying. She wasn't looking at me, but at my side. My heart, which had been beating violently in my chest, nearly stopped dead. All the blood in my body seemed to fall at once to my feet, leaving me dizzy and lightheaded. I put one hand on the fridge to steady myself.

"I'm sorry?"

"How could you?" Her voice was stronger now, and she lifted her face. "How could you? How could you?" She was practically screaming at the end, spittle flying from her mouth.

My fingers gripped the fridge, turning white. "How could I what? What are you talking about?"

"This." She thrust her hands that had been hiding behind her back forward, and my eyes widened. In them, she was clutching one of my cameras.

"What is that?"

"You know what it is." She shook her hand. "Are there more? Where are they?"

"I don't know what you're talking about."

"You were recording us! How dare you?"

"That's not mine," I said, raising my voice. "Where did you find it, anyway?"

Her eyes glittered. "Val found it in the living room while she was dusting."

I gritted my teeth. Of course it would be Val. She was probably trying to prove a point after Julia talked to her about being sloppy. I should have hidden the camera somewhere else, or even just removed it once I knew Julia would talk to her. Stupid, stupid, stupid.

"Why are you so sure it's mine?" I asked. "You had other nannies. What if one of them installed it?"

"Val would have found it, that's how. It had to be you."

I wanted to tell her how dusty that bookcase was, and that there was no way Val would have found anything if she hadn't been trying to spite me. How could I have been so sloppy? "Maybe Val pretended to find it and gave it to you even if it wasn't there," I said. "Have you considered that? Val never liked me. She was always rude to me. Maybe she's trying to get me fired."

"Val wouldn't do that," Julia said, but was there doubt in her voice? Maybe I could use it to my advantage.

"Well, someone did, because I don't know anything about it. What if it was Max? He has it in for me, as well. Maybe he installed a nanny cam and didn't tell you."

She dropped her hand and started to pace. "I don't know what's going on," she said. "Something isn't right. I can't sleep. I can't think. I don't know what to do."

I tentatively took a couple steps forward. "Let's sit down and talk about it," I invited. "I know you've been under a lot of stress. Let's see if we can figure it out together."

"Max is talking to Celeste. Did you know that?"

My face paled, but Julia wasn't paying any attention to me. "How do you know?"

"Because she showed Max texts that were sent from my phone on Friday night changing our second interview. What else are they talking about? What else is she doing with him?"

I thought fast. "Maybe she's lying. Or maybe she's doctored it somehow. Did she send Max a screenshot? She could have Photoshopped it."

"I don't know. I just know that Max believes her and thinks I did it. I can't believe he believes someone he just met over his own wife. What exactly is the nature of their relationship?"

"You can't trust her," I said softly, taking another couple of steps forward. "She doesn't have your back. Not like I do."

"I always thought you did," Julia said, still pacing. "But now I don't know. I don't know what to think."

"Sit down," I invited. "Let me make you a cup of tea. Let's talk. I can help you sort this out. We'll figure it out together."

She paused, and for a moment, I was sure I had her ... she was going to sit at the table, and I would make tea while she told me everything. We'd have a huge breakthrough, and our relationship would be even better. Maybe I could even share with her how her husband was skulking around the house in the middle of the night threatening me, and I ...

Her head shot up, and she gave me a hard look. "You didn't ask me who Celeste is."

I quickly ducked my head, trying to hide the shock I was sure had passed across my face. "I ... you told me," I said. "She's one of your nanny candidates, right?"

Julia was shaking her head. "No, I didn't."

"You told me the same day you said you were going to interview candidates."

"No, I'm sure I didn't. I was careful not to tell you. I didn't want to hurt your feelings."

"You must have. Otherwise, how would I have known?"

The minute the words were out of my mouth, I knew I had made a colossal blunder. Julia's eyes widened, and she raised her hand with the camera. "You *know* because you were watching us! You heard us talk about her! Or maybe you even watched the interview yourself! I bet it was you who texted Celeste, wasn't it? While I was sleeping on the couch? I know I saw you standing over me. That was what you were doing, wasn't it?"

"I would never hurt you, Julia," I said, desperation filling my chest. Everything was sliding away from me so quickly, it felt like I was trying to hang onto water. "You're my family. Everything I do, I do to protect you. To keep you and your family safe. I would never ..."

"You're fired."

Stunned, I snapped my head back, as if she had slapped me. "You don't mean that," I gasped. "I'm the only one here on your side."

"I mean it," she said, her voice sharp. "You betrayed me. You betrayed all of us. You didn't tell me the truth. How could you? I trusted you." Her voice broke. "I thought you were my friend."

"I AM your friend," I said. "I'm on your side here. I'm the only one on your side. Let me help you ..."

"No," she shrieked so loudly, I wondered if she would wake the baby. "You are NOT my friend. Friends don't secretly record their friends! You're fired. Get out! Now."

Suddenly, I was angry. How dare *she?* I had done everything for her, and this was the thanks I got? "You can't fire me," I howled. "I'm part of your family. You can't fire family."

"You're not my family," she said. "You're not my friend, either. You work for me. Correction, you USED to work for me. Now get out. Before I call the cops and tell them you're trespassing."

She wouldn't do that. Not to me. She couldn't.

She stood straight and tall, her eyes narrow, her face unyielding.

I tried one last time. "This is all Max's fault. He filled your head with poison about me, probably because he wants to sleep with Celeste, and it would be easier if she was working here rather than me ..."

Julia's face went white, and for a moment, I thought she was going to faint. "I was on your side," she said, her voice strangled. "I defended you. I wanted you to stay. You should have trusted me. But instead, you went behind my back and filled my house with cameras. Now, get your things and get out."

I opened my mouth, not believing this was it. It couldn't be it. But then, she turned her back on me.

Told you, Kelly said smugly. *No one wants you to be a part of their family. And why would they? You're a pathetic loser.*

I wanted to deny it. I wanted to tell Kelly she was wrong.

But I couldn't.

I waited another minute, trying to will Julia to turn around, to say this had all been a huge mistake.

But she didn't.

Seething with rage, I went upstairs to pack.

Chapter 33

I sat in my car, watching as Julia and Celeste went their separate ways. As soon as they disappeared around the corner, I was out of my car and heading for the house.

I didn't have much time, but it was my best shot at finally getting into Julia's office.

I was still furious at Julia, but I had to keep cool, so I kept my wits about me. I couldn't go half-cocked. I was determined to get to the bottom of whatever secret Julia was hiding about Ashley.

And that meant getting into that office.

I headed up the driveway, my hair tucked inside a baseball cap and my face covered with giant sunglasses, walking with purpose and determination. Even though I had given back the original spare key to the house, I of course had made a copy.

At that time of morning, most of the neighbors were either gone or focused on getting their own day started, so I wasn't too worried about anyone noticing me. Quite honestly, Julia had pretty much ignored her neighbors, so it probably wouldn't have mattered what I did—no one would be paying attention.

I let myself in, then locked the door behind me. I briefly checked the alarm system but, like always, it wasn't set. I wasn't sure why they even bothered having one when they never seemed to use it. Maybe it wasn't even hooked up and was just for show.

I moved to the office. This was the part that concerned me the most. I had never used a key made from an impression, and if it didn't work, I was going to waste valuable time trying to break in.

As it turned out, there was nothing to worry about. The key slid in just as easily as any other, and the door unlocked with a gentle click.

I slipped inside, locking it again after me.

My first impression was absolute shock. Julia's office was a mess—a complete disaster.

Stacks of paper, books, file folders, etc. were everywhere ... on the floor, the bookshelves, a chair in front of the desk. My heart sank as I stared. I would need at least a solid week to go through it all.

And I didn't have a week. I had less than an hour.

Gingerly, I picked my way to the huge desk near the window. There was a closed laptop on it along with more piles of paper, Sticky Notes, and a planner covered in Julia's spidery handwriting.

I sat at the chair, flipped open the laptop, and started opening drawers. I had no idea what I was looking for, but I hoped something would present itself.

Of course, the laptop required a password, so I focused on the drawers. The first one contained a bunch of office supplies—pens, Sticky Notes, paperclips, even an old-fashioned letter opener. The second drawer held packages of blank paper.

The third drawer was locked.

A locked drawer in a locked room. Very interesting.

Going back to the first drawer, I didn't see any keys, so I picked up the letter opener and jammed it into the lock. I knew if I did so, there would be no going back—no way of sneaking out of the office and pretending nothing happened.

I no longer cared.

It took a bit of effort, but I finally broke the lock and wrenched the drawer open.

It was full of notebooks and old newspaper clippings.

I sat down on the floor next to it, picked up a notebook, and started flipping through it. It appeared to be some sort of documentation. There were lists of dates with notes under them.

Max was twenty minutes late. He said he was finishing up work, but I'm sure I could smell perfume on his shirt.

Max took over an hour to respond to my text. He said he was in a meeting. But when I called the office, the receptionist didn't say anything about him being in a meeting.

Max mentioned a new hire. He was managing her. Laughed about how young the new hires were getting and how old he was getting, but said she seemed to be doing a good job. Who is this new hire????

Max talked about how well the new hire is working out. How? What are her new job duties? Max was evasive. Why?

Pages and pages went on like this. Glancing down at the cover of another, I realized why it looked so familiar. It was similar to the notebook she was writing in each morning at the coffee shop.

Was that what she was doing? Documenting Max's actions and words? For what purpose? Was she trying to build a case showing he was cheating on her just in case she ever had to divorce him?

I thought back to what she said when I first asked her about the notebook. "It's just something I need," she had answered.

Something she "needs"? Keeping a list of Max's "proof" of supposed indiscretions?

My lips curled with disgust and dropped the notebook back in the drawer. Not my problem anymore.

Next, I scooped up the newspaper clippings and started leafing through them. They appeared to be about a six-year-old boy named Hunter Taggard who was killed in a hit-and-run accident outside his home.

I skimmed the article, wondering if there was some link to Julia. But as far as I could tell, there was no connection. The boy had two brothers—one older and one younger. An infant, actually. That was part of what made the whole thing so devastating. Mom was focused on the baby and didn't realize her six-year-old was running around the front of the house.

Tragic, yes. But what did it have to do with Julia? And why were the clippings in a locked drawer?

I dug deeper. More newspaper clippings, as it seemed the entire community was outraged at this hit-and-run driver. I was nearly at the bottom when one of the articles caught my eye, and my entire body went cold.

It was a picture of the family before the baby was born. Father, pregnant mother, six-year-old, and his older, teenage brother named Porter.

Who was the spitting image of the strange man with a limp.

My hands started shaking uncontrollably.

Why did Julia have a picture of the strange man who had been following her family locked in a drawer?

I glanced in the bottom of the drawer and felt a second shock jolt through my system. Near the bottom was an old color photograph of another family. Mother, father, and daughter, maybe ten years old.

The daughter could have been Madison's twin, except she had a wide, happy grin on her face, whereas I had only ever seen Madison wear solemn expressions and tiny, tentative smiles.

Clearly, it was Julia as a child.

But that wasn't what made my heart start to pound erratically.

It was the father.

He was the same man in the newspaper photo.

I gasped, dropping everything, and scooted away.

Was that the connection?

Were Porter—and the little boy who died—Julia's stepbrothers?

What was going on?

There was a file folder underneath the color photo. I stretched out my hand to reach for it when I heard the sounds of the front door opening and closing.

Celeste. Back from dropping the kids off at school.

I heard Celeste's footsteps as she moved to the kitchen. Hopefully, she would take Isabelle upstairs to change her in a few minutes, which would give me the opportunity to slip out of the house undetected.

Except, of course, the locked drawer was broken.

My hand hovered above the file folder. I should leave. It would be smart to leave.

But chances were high that this would be my only shot. Julia would know someone had broken in and would likely take steps that would make it more difficult for me to finish the job. And who knew if I would even be able to find the folder again.

I reached in, slid it out, and opened it.

It was full of identification papers for someone named Jewel Necker.

I had no idea who that was.

I studied the picture of the sixteen-year-old on the driver's license, but she didn't look familiar—jet-black hair that hung in her face, gothic makeup, black clothing.

Who was this girl, and why did Julia have her identification in a locked drawer?

I was still sitting on the floor, staring at all the files and trying to make sense of it all, when I heard the key in the lock.

A moment later, the door opened, and Julia was there.

For a second, she just stared at me, as if she couldn't believe her eyes. "What ...? How ...? What are you doing here? I fired you!"

I ignored her questions. "Who is Jewel?" I asked, waving the file folder.

"Jewel is none of your business," she snapped, striding into the room and nearly tripping on one of her paper files. "You're not supposed to be here. I'm calling the police."

"You *should* call the police," I said. "I think they would be interested in seeing proof of your stealing someone's identity."

"I'm not stealing anyone's identity," she began. At the same time, Celeste appeared at the doorway. "Julia? I heard voices ... wait, who are you?"

"Celeste, call the cops," Julia said. "Janey is trespassing."

"Julia is stealing identities," I countered. "Not to mention she has a stepbrother named Porter who is stalking her family."

All the blood drained out of Julia's face at the mention of Porter. "No, it can't be," she gasped.

Celeste's eyes darted between me and Julia. "Are you okay?" I noticed, bitterly, how perfect Celeste looked with her expertly applied makeup, blonde hair pulled back in a smooth ponytail, and sparkling, pink tank top. How on earth did she manage to look so pulled together and still get the kids to school on time?

"Porter can't be here," Julia said, her voice almost pleading. "He doesn't know where I am."

"Oh yes, he does," I said. "He's been at the park and at the kids' school."

"No!" Julia yelped, sinking to the floor like her legs couldn't hold her. "No, he can't know where my kids are. He'll kill them."

"What?" Both Celeste and I reacted together. Celeste looked as horrified as I felt. "Who is Porter?" Celeste demanded as I asked "What do you mean, he's going to kill the kids? Why?!"

"Revenge," Julia said, pressing her hands against her face.

"For what?" I asked.

"Who is Porter?" Celeste asked again.

Julia started shaking her head. "No. You're wrong. It can't be Porter. I've been watching for him. That's why I go to the coffee shop every day. I check to make sure he's not following me."

I thought about the notebooks and grimaced. That wasn't the only thing she was doing. But that was beside the point. I waved the newspaper articles. "You are doing a piss-poor job," I yelled. "He's been parking right on the street ..."

"No!"

"He's following the kids to the park, to school ..."

"No. It's not possible. I have a private eye watching him. I check every day. He's nowhere near here. He has a new family now. He doesn't care about me."

"You might want to investigate your private eye, too. I've had a couple conversations with Porter, so he's definitely here. Even Madison has seen him hanging around."

Julia gasped, pressing a hand to her heart. "Madison has seen him?"

"Who is Porter?" Celeste nearly shouted.

"Her stepbrother," I said.

Julia looked like she wanted to deny it, but I waved the newspaper articles at her again, and she fell silent.

"Your stepbrother?" Celeste stared at Julia, her face a strange mixture of disbelief and shock. She took a tiny step backward. "Why would your stepbrother want to kill your family?"

"That's a great question," I said. "I'd like to hear the answer to that, as well. Does it have something to do with Hunter's death?"

It was Celeste's turn to gasp. "What?" She took another step backward.

Julie buried her face in her hands. "You don't understand," she whispered.

"Then explain it," I snapped.

She started shaking her head back and forth, but kept her face buried. "It's his fault. He promised us, but he lied."

Celeste and I exchanged glances. "Who lied?" I asked. Celeste continued edging out the door. I found myself perversely enjoying her discomfort as she tried to weasel away. Julia was likely going to have to try and find yet another nanny after all this.

Julia muttered an answer, but I couldn't make it out. "Speak up," I said. "Who?"

"My father."

My mouth dropped open. I hadn't seen that coming. "Your father? How is he involved?"

Julia lifted her face from her hands. Her skin was ashen, which made the black circles under her eyes even more pronounced. "He promised he loved me. That he would always be my father. That we would always be a family. But he left us. He found another family. He lied to us. To me. He's a liar."

I glanced down at the newspaper article, trying to make sense of what Julia was saying. "I still don't understand. Your father divorced your mother and married Porter and Hunter's mom, right? I get why you're upset with your father, but what does Porter have to do with all this? And why would he want to kill your family?"

"Because he blames me for Hunter's death," she burst out. "He's always blamed me. And I know he wants revenge."

I studied the newspaper article and Hunter's smiling face. "But Hunter was killed by a hit-and-run driver. How does that have anything to do with you? Unless ..." I lifted my gaze and stared at her in horror. "It was you?"

"It's not my fault," Julia said.

Celeste covered her open mouth with her hand. She was nearly all the way through the door, but she continued hovering like a bystander watching a train wreck, unable to tear her eyes away as much as she wanted to.

"It's not your fault that you hit a little boy?"

"It's not like that," Julia said. "When I found out my father had another child with that ... that *woman*, I had to talk to him. I wanted to drive over to their house so I could talk to him, but I didn't. And even if I had, I could never kill anyone! But Porter wouldn't stop blaming me. He was convinced it was my fault. So, finally, my mother and I had to move. We even had to change our name."

My head was spinning, trying to follow her disjointed statements. "You're Jewel."

It was a statement.

She nodded. Tears streaked her face, leaving her skin red and puffy, almost like an open wound. "He threatened to go to the cops, to the media, if I didn't confess. I kept telling him it wasn't me. I hadn't driven to their place in months, but he wouldn't believe me."

"Then why did he think it was you?"

She wrapped her arms around her knees, curling up into a little ball. She started rocking. "I don't know," she said, but she didn't look at me.

It was clear she was lying.

I opened my mouth to yell at her to tell me, but at the last moment, decided to try a different tactic. "I know how Porter is," I said. "He can be a real jerk."

Her head snapped toward me. "You do?"

"I told you, he's been following me around and talking to me," I said. "So, I can see how he didn't believe you. Once he gets something into his head, you can't talk him out of it."

She nodded vigorously. "Yes, yes. That's Porter."

"But there must have been something that set him off. What was it?"

She paused, looked away again. "There's just ... this big, black hole," she said. "I can't remember what I did that afternoon, but I *know* I could never hit anyone. I know that. And I know I needed to talk to my father. I couldn't believe he'd betrayed us so badly—that he actually *replaced* me. He replaced me! With another child. But I know I didn't drive over there. It's true that I cut school that day. I needed to think. I was just so upset. And I knew I wanted to talk to my father. But Porter ... he knew I wasn't at school that day. So he decided I must have been the one to do it. No one believed him, but it didn't matter. He kept saying I did it, and he was going to ruin my life unless I confessed. So, we had to leave."

"So, you've been hiding from Porter ever since?"

"Yes! He can be so irrational. I didn't want him anywhere near me or my family. For years, I kept a low profile. Changed my hair, my name. I thought I was safe. It's been so long, and the private eye was keeping an eye on him. At least, I thought he was. I didn't think I had anything to worry about. But if he's found me, I don't have any idea what to do."

"Oh. My. God." Celeste's face was as white as Julia's. She looked like she might be sick. "I can't believe this."

I couldn't believe what I was hearing, either, but unlike Celeste, I knew I hadn't heard the worst. "Is that why you had to get rid of Ashley?"

Celeste let out a noise that sounded like a little scream. "Ashley? Who is Ashley?"

"The first nanny," I said.

Julia gave me a puzzled look. "Ashley? What does she have to do with it?"

"Isn't that why you had to make her disappear? Because she found out about Porter?"

"You had a nanny who disappeared?" From the look on Celeste's face, it was clear she was done. I wished I could feel sorry for Julia, but all I felt was a tired sense of triumph. Julia had gotten what she deserved. And now, she had to reap what she sowed.

Julia was shaking her head again. "No. Ashley just left. We had nothing to do with that. Unless ..." her expression changed to horror. "Do you think Porter did something to her?"

I thought back to my exchanges with Porter. It was possible, I suppose. Anything was possible. But the way Porter talked, it didn't seem like he had anything to do with it.

It was far more likely it was Julia or Max. Still, observing Julia's confusion, I was starting to have my doubts.

"Does Max know about any of this?"

Julia's eyes were round. "No! Nothing. That's why I go to the coffee shop every morning and use that tablet. Max doesn't even know I own a tablet. It's all separate."

I wondered if she also used the tablet to keep tabs on Max's extracurricular activities, but decided not to mention it.

While I was glad that I finally knew the secret Julia was hiding, I was disappointed. None of it led me any closer to finding Ashley.

I was back at square one.

Either Max had gotten rid of her for some reason I hadn't uncovered yet, or I was still missing a giant piece.

Chapter 34

I got out of the car and leaned against it, staring at the forest as I forced myself to breathe deeply. My stomach was squirming like a giant slug.

There was no cover anymore. Nothing to do except face my fear.

After I had left the Johnsons' for the last time, with Julia on the floor still rocking herself like a child and Celeste looking pale and shell-shocked, muttering about how she needed to talk to Max, I spent a few days doing exactly what Bryn had suggested—talking to people around town to see if any of them could shed any light on Ashley's disappearance.

Unfortunately, no one knew anything. While a few remembered something happening a few months before, nothing really stood out to anyone. As one person, a petite waitress at the little diner called "Aunt May's" said, "People disappear from here all the time. That's just what happens here." No one had been all that surprised.

Even as I walked through town, I had known. Known I would end up at the edge of the huge, wooded area that overlooked the lake. The place where hundreds of people spent summers camping and hiking and swimming, and winters cross-country skiing and ice skating.

The place of my worst nightmares.

But I had no choice. If I wanted to get to the bottom of what happened to Ashley, I knew I had to do it.

I took another deep breath, squared my shoulders, and started down the path.

It smelled green and fresh, of mulch and moss. Birds twittered as they flew past, and sunlight dappled the ground. So very different than it was during the winter months, when it was all brown and white, mounds of muddy snow and barren sticks and trunks of trees that would later flourish.

I plodded along the path, my feet automatically guiding me to where I needed to go.

The edge of the lake. I pushed my way through the leafy, green branches and stood in the warm sun. I could smell the lake, the dampness, the algae. The waves lapped against the shore, and a couple fishing boats bobbed on the calm, mirror-like surface.

A beautiful day to spend by the water.

I could see it in the winter, frozen and grey. Little ice fishing encampments would dot the landscape, the tiny huts ensuring no would see anything by the shore.

An old, rotten log was perched near the shoreline. It would likely be full of insects and grubs, so not an ideal place to sit and enjoy the view.

But in the winter, it was a different story. It would be frozen and cold, and the perfect spot to put ice skates on or take them off.

And it's exactly where I'd found Ashley.

She started when she saw me, one boot half off. She wore a bright-blue, puffy jacket with a red scarf and matching mittens. Red and blue were always such good colors for her, bringing out her golden skin tone, blue eyes, and bright-blonde hair.

For a moment, we stared at each other. Her face was a mix of confusion and fear.

We were alone. This was my chance.

"Kelly," I said, taking a step forward. "It's me. Your sister."

Her confusion deepened. "My name isn't Kelly. And I don't have a sister. I don't know what you're talking about."

"Kelly, stop it," I said. "Stop teasing me. I know you know it's me."

She jammed her boot back on. "I don't know what you're talking about. You have me mistaken with someone else."

"It doesn't matter that you left," I said, feeling desperate, taking another step forward. I could feel I was losing her already, and I couldn't bear it. "I forgive you. I even forgive you for not reaching out after our parents died."

Another look passed her face—shame? Guilt? Or maybe grief. "I'm sorry about your parents," she said.

"*Our* parents," I said. "And it's okay. You're here now. We can be sisters again. We can be a family again."

Ashley stood up. "I really am sorry about your parents, but honestly, I'm not your sister. I don't know what you're talking about. And I'm really sorry I'm not. I'm sure it's been rough for you."

"No, but you are," I said. "I saw you back in Riverview, so I know you came back."

The look of fear was back on her face. "You saw me in Riverview? How did you know I lived there?"

"Because I saw you. And I knew. You're Kelly. It's okay if you have to go by a different name." The words started tumbling out of me. "Oz is in jail. Did you know that? You don't have to keep pretending to be Ashley. You're safe with me."

Ashley had scooped up her bag and started backing up. "Have you been following me? Are you the one?? I knew it! I knew I had a stalker. Get away from me!"

"No, you don't understand." I began quickening my steps as I moved toward her. She was starting to run, darting back through the trees. "I was just watching you! Keeping an eye on you. I wanted to keep you safe. That's all. I would never hurt you, Kelly."

"Stop calling me that!" she burst out. "Stop following me, you hear? I'm going to call the cops. They'll throw you in jail if you don't leave me alone."

This was not going the way I had imagined.

For months, I had pictured our first meeting. I was sure once she realized it was me, she would stop pretending to be Ashley. I just had to make sure we were alone. I was positive if there was a witness, she would never admit it. It would be too embarrassing for her.

Even so, I still had to work up the courage. Even though there had been other days she had been alone at the lake, I couldn't bring myself to approach her.

But today ... today was the day.

Which was why I didn't understand how it was all going so horribly wrong. She was my sister. She was supposed to love me. We were supposed to be a family.

And she was rejecting me. Again. Just like she did when I was a teenager.

Suddenly, I was filled with rage. How dare she do that *again?* How dare she ignore and mock me?

I raced along the path to catch up with her.

I could see the horror in her eyes as I came closer, but she was too slow to react. Her feet tangled up on themselves, and she fell on the path.

It took only a few minutes.

She tried to raise her arms, to swing her bag holding her ice skates at me, but I brushed it off. I grabbed the edges of her scarf and tightened it around her neck.

Her face turned red, then purple, then blue. Her hands, in her cheerful red mittens, patted ineffectually against my black-gloved fingers.

I watched as the light died in her eyes and her body slumped over. I let go of her.

"Was it so difficult to be my sister?" I asked her, tears filling my eyes. "Why couldn't you just love me like sisters are supposed to?"

She didn't answer. Her face had gone slack.

I sat back on my heels, shaking my head. Why couldn't she have cooperated? Would it have been that difficult? Was I so unlovable?

I wasn't sure how long I sat there before Kelly's voice interrupted me.

You idiot, she hissed. *You're going to get caught if you stay here like this. Is that what you want? You want to go to jail?*

"No," I said.

Then move! Clean up this mess!

So, I did.

I dragged Ashley's body to her car and stuffed it in the trunk. There, I found her journal, and paged through it until I found what would pass for a letter. I signed her name and stuffed it in an envelope that I then placed in the "We Care" bag from the post office, which I pocketed the summer before when I worked there, sure it would one day come in handy.

I hid my car about a half-mile up the road, on a small service road past the trees and a few mounds of snow. After destroying the battery in Ashley's phone, (but not before I opened her Instagram and made her profile public again; I still remember the day she had made it private so I couldn't monitor it anymore— even thinking about it made me gnash my teeth … after all, I was only trying to protect her!) I drove Ashley's car with Ashley still in the trunk to my parents' old house and stowed it in the garage, where it remains to this day.

I took a cab to the airport, and then a different one from the airport back to Redemption to fetch my car and drive it home. I wanted to make sure no cab driver would remember driving me from my house to Redemption. Cabs between the airport and Redemption were common, but from residences to Redemption, not so much.

As for Ashley's body, I removed it from the trunk of her car and dumped it into a freezer chest, leaving her there until the lake thawed.

Because Ashley was going into the lake.

Where Kelly was.

***

"What is your problem?" Kelly demanded.

She had just finished removing her top and tucking it in her bag so she could stretch out across the boat, allowing the sun to continue tanning her perfect body. Her tiny blue bikini hugged her curves, and her oversized sunglasses covered her face. She didn't look at me, instead stretching out her neck toward the sun. "You've been a total bitch these past few days. Either spit it out or get over yourself."

I pressed my lips together tightly. Actually, my whole body felt tight and hot, like a coiled spring. I knew I had to talk—to do something to relieve the pressure that was growing, growing, growing inside me, but at the same time, I couldn't. The words still wouldn't come, and those that did sat on my tongue. It was impossible to push them out of my mouth.

Kelly lowered her sunglasses to glare at me. "Well?"

I swallowed, licking my dry lips. The air smelled of lake, suntan lotion, and Kelly's perfume. Her awful, cloying, perfume.

"You told me you broke up with Oz," I said, my voice low.

Kelly blinked. "What? Speak up, I can't hear you."

"Oz," I said, my voice louder. "You told me you broke up with him."

"I did break up with him."

"Then why was he at the bowling alley?"

"How should I know? We broke up. I'm not his keeper."

Her face was turned away from me, looking toward the shore, but there was stiffness in her limbs that was unlike her, and the truth crashed over me like a wave, drowning me.

"You knew."

"I just said we broke up."

My entire body was vibrating, like I was about to explode into a million pieces. "You knew! Has he been hanging around all this time? Was he the one stalking you?"

"I don't know. Maybe."

"Maybe? Do you also know what he did to me?"

"Janey, calm down."

"Calm down?" I shrieked. "Are you kidding me?"

Finally, she turned her head to look at me. "Yes, calm down. It's not a big deal."

For a moment, I could only sputter, so great was my indignation, when a second, even more horrible truth came crashing down upon me.

"You set me up."

"Don't be absurd. I'm your sister ..."

I screamed, the oars clattering to the bottom of the boat. "You set me up! It was your idea that I go to the party. You dressed me up. You gave me the drink. What was in it? Was it just alcohol, or something else?"

"Janey, stop it," Kelly snapped, sitting up and quickly looking around to see if anyone was listening. But the lake was empty, the boat bobbing alone and gently. "Keep your voice down."

"Keep my voice ..."

"Yes," she said. "Yes, I knew. *You* were the one Oz wanted." Her voice was bitter. "Don't you know? He was only hanging around me to get to you."

I was gasping, unable to get my head around the enormity of what she was saying. "So, so, you *gave* me to him?"

"It's not like that." She leaned closer to me. "Janey, don't you understand? Oz is *useful*. There's a lot of things he can do for us. He has connections. He can take care of us."

"So, so, so, you *pimped* me out?"

"It's not just me. It's for you, too. Both of us. Look, it's not such a big deal. It's just sex. And if he was a little too rough, I can talk to him. And who knows, eventually you may even learn to enjoy it. And the best part is, if you play your cards right, you won't have a thing to worry about. Think about it—you won't have to worry about school or a job or any of that crap. You'll be free. Isn't that worth a little sex?"

There was a roaring in my ears, so loud I could barely hear what she was saying. I was fixated on her mouth, those juicy, red-lipsticked lips, the way they moved as every word dripped out and entered my veins like poison. My vision seemed to narrow to only those lips, a tiny oasis surrounded by a black, pulsating fog.

"You're my sister," I said, although the words sounded far away, like I was in a bubble, and my voice was somewhere outside of it. "You're supposed to protect me. To love me. Not *sell* me."

"I didn't 'sell' you," she said. "Stop being such a drama queen. I told you, this is a good thing. For both of us. You'll see. One day, you'll thank me."

Her lips, so red and shiny. Like blood. Wet blood from a fresh kill. Dripping from a hungry mouth that had just devoured its prey but was searching for more, because the hunger was never satisfied, never sated. There was always a need for more and more. Eating and sucking and draining until there was nothing left but a hollow, empty husk, withering away on the vine.

And in that moment, I knew. I had to stop those juicy, bloody, red lips from devouring anyone else.

It was too late for me. But I could still save some other poor, innocent soul.

I wasn't even aware of my actions when I picked up the oar and smashed those red lips. They split and fell backward, cracked and bleeding, parting in surprise, as Kelly's body crumpled onto the bottom of the boat.

I brought the oar down again and again.

And finally, there was stillness.

I dropped the oar and stared at the ruined face of my sister, broken and bloody.

"You were supposed to protect me," I whispered, my voice hoarse.

I don't know how long I sat there, allowing the boat to gently carry us across the lake, staring at the face of my dead sister. I had lost all track of time, but more than that, any awareness of self.

Until her voice cut through my fog.

Now you did it, Kelly said.

Startled, I glanced around, half expecting to see Kelly sit up, brush herself off, and reach for her bag to find her compact so she could fix her makeup. But she remained where she was, motionless on the floor of the boat.

All you've ever done is mess things up, but this, dear sister, really takes the cake.

"But you're dead," I whispered.

You don't think I know that? she snapped. *If you don't start moving, you're going to go to jail for killing me. Not that you don't deserve it.*

"I don't understand."

Oh my God, you truly are stupider than I thought. Get rid of my body. Now. Before someone sees you out here.

Still moving as if in a fog, I reached for the anchor, wrapping it around her neck, her body.

Tighter!

I tied several knots, making sure it was secure, before rolling her body and the anchor over the side of the boat.

She slid under the waves with barely a splash, as if the lake was welcoming her home. Kelly always had loved it there. Maybe she knew, deep down inside, she was where she needed to be.

There was a roaring in my head. I couldn't concentrate. My vision seemed to dim, go black. What was happening to me?

Why was I just drifting in the middle of the lake by myself?

I rowed the boat back to my house, trying to figure out where all the blood had come from. Had I gone fishing after dropping Kelly off? I must have. There was no other explanation for it. I must have caught a bunch of fish and then butchered them on the boat. Did a terrible job of it, too, by the looks of it. There was even some on the oar.

What was I thinking? I wouldn't do that ever again.

Dad would be terribly upset with me. He raised me to be able to take care of myself. I knew how to filet a fish and butcher a deer. But if he saw the mess I had made of those fish ... I'd better clean the boat. It would be better if he didn't know. I'd just get it all clean, and no one would ever have to know.

Man, I must have been in a fog. I even lost the anchor. How did I do that? I wondered if I had caught a Northern. Or ... a Muskie? Oh, that must have been what happened. I had never heard of anyone catching a Muskie in this lake, but just because I hadn't heard about it doesn't mean it didn't happen. Muskies have razor-sharp mouths. I bet that Muskie must have gotten tangled in the anchor rope and probably cut it, which is why I lost the anchor. Probably where all the blood came from, too. I must have cut myself while fighting with it. That was what happened. Dad would no doubt yell at me for not handling myself better. After I clean the boat, I'll take a shower and wash my clothes. What he doesn't know won't hurt him.

But, before I take a shower, I have to do what Kelly asked. Bury her belongings. When I dropped her off, she said she was planning on running away, and wanted to make it clear to my parents she wasn't coming home. I had to bury her computer, some clothes, and her makeup. Plus, I had to destroy her cell phone.

Hadn't she also asked me to talk her friends into driving me to Chicago, so I could mail a postcard from her to our family? Yes, I was sure that was what she said. She didn't want Mom and Dad to worry, after all. I told her I would take care of it for her, and give them some peace.

Kelly of course should have packed her own stuff and mailed her own postcard, but that was Kelly for you. Always expecting other people to pick up after her.

And, as a good sister, I always came through for her.

Always.

Epilogue

It's not uncommon to lose your memory when something traumatic happens to you. Sometimes, if it's really severe, it even has a different name: a "fugue state." I'm not sure if I had suffered an actual fugue state or just amnesia, as clearly, I never received a professional diagnosis. Instead, I had to diagnose myself based on my paltry psychology training.

The trauma of what happened to me and what my sister told me in the boat that day caused me to snap and lash out. Afterward, my brain buried it all, allowing me to forget the horror of that dreadful afternoon.

And it stayed buried. For years. It was only with the sudden, tragic death of both my parents that something shifted.

Even then, I knew I needed help. I could sense that something dark and scary was trying to emerge from the depths of my subconscious.

And I knew I couldn't do it alone.

My therapy had barely started when I ran into Ashley. I was arriving as she was departing. Ashley, whose only crime was looking enough like Kelly to be her twin. It was simply misfortune, her selecting the same therapy office I had. A mistake.

Kelly, clearly, had deserved everything she had coming to her. She was a psychopath. I did the world a favor by getting rid of her before she could hurt anyone else.

But what happened to Ashley was unfortunate.

The moment I saw her, my obsession started. See, my secret didn't want to be revealed. It was simply easier to decide Ashley was my long-lost sister who ran away when I was a teenager.

Yes, I was Ashley's stalker. Just like I had 'stalked' Kelly that summer, keeping an eye on her. I hadn't trusted her even then. I knew something was off, but I wasn't sure what.

Unfortunately, I discovered too late just how right I had been about my sister.

Ashley was different, which I see now. At the time, however, I only saw her resemblance to Kelly, so naturally, I treated her just as I had Kelly. I dropped out of school and quit my job to spend my days following her. I had money from my parents' inheritance, so I could continue to pay rent and pretend I was a student. Bryn never had a clue.

I even put Ashley to rest in the same lake as Kelly. So much was the same. Even the amnesia state that overcame me again after I killed Ashley.

All I knew was I needed to find my sister. And the obvious place to start was with Ashley's last-known employment.

Where she worked as a nanny.

Looking back now, I was amazed that, of all the nanny jobs Ashley could have gotten, she managed to choose to work for someone who was, for all practical purposes, my soul sister. Another lost teenager haunted by her past because of one terrible mistake.

Or, *was* it a mistake? Maybe Julia's father, with his new wife and baby, drove Julia to it as much as Kelly drove me to my actions. Maybe Julia was as much as a victim as I was.

I'll never know.

What I do know is that Julia ended up running away. Again. She left her kids and husband and disappeared, but not before Max filed for divorce.

Porter was the one who told me. He approached me one day as I was asking about Ashley around town.

"You found out, didn't you?"

His mouth was flat—the big smile that was there during our prior meeting was gone.

I shrugged. "What does it matter?"

"I told you, she has to pay for what she did. And now, she's gone."

"I'm sure she'll turn up. Eventually."

He pressed his lips together so tightly, they turned white. "What were you doing there anyway? Why the cameras?"

I narrowed my eyes. "How do you know about the cameras?"

"It doesn't matter."

"It does if you want me to answer your question. Was it Val?"

"What if it was?"

I clenched my fists. I knew it. Julia should have listened to me about her. "How did you meet Val, anyway? And how did you convince her to help you in whatever crazy scheme you cooked up?"

"It's not like that."

"I should tell Max about this."

Porter scoffed. "Like Max would listen to you.

I raised my eyebrow. "You want to test that theory?"

Porter was silent for a moment. "Val's my godmother."

My eyes widened. "What? Your godmother? I don't believe you. How would Julia not recognize her?"

"Because Julia never met her. You have no idea. Losing Hunter destroyed my mother. She's never been the same. We had to do something."

"And what was that exactly? Val was to work as her housekeeper while you skulk around and scare the nannies?"

Porter looked away. "It's complicated. After it happened, my family just fell apart. My mom had a breakdown, and my parents got divorced. It was a mess. Jewel, I mean *Julia*, disappeared in the middle of it. At the time, there wasn't much I could do to find her. I was still a kid myself, and my life was in turmoil. I was into drinking, drugs. It all came to a head when I was in a drunk-driving accident. I wasn't the one driving, but ..." he was silent for a minute. "We hit a mother and daughter, killing them both. She had a husband and another child at home. It was ... awful. It was like I had done to that family what was done to me. It was where I got this limp, too. A daily reminder of how I helped destroy a family.

"It took years to rebuild. To get my life back. Julia destroyed so much. It's all her fault. I never would have been in the car, never would have done the things I did if it wasn't for her. I had always intended to come after her ... to make her pay for all the destruction she caused for multiple families, not just mine. But then, a year ago, that useless private eye she hired to watch us approached me." Porter huffed out a cold, hard laugh. "He told me he had been hired to watch me and my family for years, and for a bunch of money, he'd tell me who had hired him and where to find her. Clearly, he wanted a big pay day. But I didn't have the money he was asking for, so I struck a deal for less, and in return, I'd wait a while to make my presence known, so he could double dip. He agreed.

"We started monitoring Julia and discovered she was looking for a housekeeper. It took a bit, but Val eventually got herself hired. And then, we simply watched and waited."

"For what?" I asked, interested despite myself. "What were you waiting for? What was the plan?"

"Initially, it was just knowing that Julia was still paying that private investigator for not doing his job." Porter flashed a small smile, a cruel echo of his all-American grin. "But the longer Val worked for Julia, the more we realized how unstable Julia is. So, what if we simply drove her crazy? Made her so mad, she destroyed her own life?

"We targeted the nannies, so they would quit. Although we didn't expect Ashley to simply vanish. That car I was parking on the street? That was the same make and model as the one Julia was driving when she killed Hunter. It took me a while to find it.

"We had other things planned as well, but then you suddenly appeared." He grimaced. "Val knew you were trouble, and she was sure you got Heather fired and yourself hired for some reason, which we never could figure out." He narrowed his eyes. "So, now that you know my story, what's yours? Why were you there? Did Julia ruin your life, too?"

I thought about it. In a way, Julia *had* ruined my life. If she had simply stood up to Max and refused to hire a replacement nanny, none of this would have happened. I would still be there, keeping an eye on her and making sure my family was safe and sound.

But, instead, I now remembered *everything*.

Bitch.

"You could say that," I said.

His expression was impatient. "So, what happened?"

I gave him a thin smile over my shoulder as I turned to leave. "Good luck finding her. I'm sure she'll turn up eventually. I'll be rooting for you."

His eyes went wide. "Wait. You aren't going to tell me? How dare you! I trusted you."

I shrugged and gave him a cheery wave as I walked away, leaving him seething in the middle of the sidewalk.

I never saw him again.

As for myself, I've moved as far away from Redemption, Wisconsin, as I could get. Even though I'm fine now (no more amnesia/fugue state), considering I remember everything, it's probably better to keep as much distance as possible between me and that town.

After all, both of my "states" happened while I was there, and I don't even live there. How weird is that? Maybe Bryn was right all along, and there WAS something to all those rumors and myths swirling around about Redemption being haunted.

Wouldn't that be something?

In fact, the more I thought about it, the more I wondered whether Redemption was the reason Julia and Ashley even found each other. After all, the townspeople thought Redemption decided who stayed and who left ... would it be that much of a stretch to think it brought those two together? That the rumors of it being haunted might be true?

Kind of crazy to think about. But it also kind of makes a lot of sense.

I live in Mexico now, on the beach, working as a waitress in a dive bar under a different name.

The old Janey is long gone.

I have a new life now.

More than that, a new family.

They don't know my history, and that's exactly the way I like it. After all, what would be the point? All they need to know is that I'm here to protect and take care of them. I would do anything to keep them safe.

Because that's what families do.

Author's Note

Hi there,

I hope you enjoyed reading *The Third Nanny* as much as I enjoyed writing it. If you did and would be willing to leave a review, I would very much appreciate it.

Redemption is pretty creepy, wouldn't you say? If you'd like to dive in a little deeper and discover more secrets around this haunted town with a disturbing and violent past, I encourage you to check out my Secrets of Redemption series, starting with Book 1: *It Began With a Lie.*

I've included an excerpt on the following pages to whet your appetite.

And for more of my books (plus a free novella, *The Secret Diary of Helen Blackstone*, which is also in the Redemption universe), check out my website MPWNovels.com.

But first, turn the page for more Redemption …

Chapter 1- It Began With a Lie

"You're right. It's perfect for us. I'm so glad we're here," I said, lying through my carefully pasted-on smile.

I tried to make my voice bright and cheery, but it sounded brittle and forced, even to me. I sucked in my breath and widened my smile, though my teeth were so clenched, my jaw hurt.

Stefan smiled back—actually, his mouth smiled but his dark-brown eyes, framed with those long, thick lashes any woman would envy, looked flat ... distracted. He hugged me with one arm. "I told you everything would be okay," he whispered into my hair. His scent was even more musky than usual, probably from two straight days of driving and lack of shower.

I hugged him back, reminding myself to relax. *Yes, everything is going to be okay. Remember, this move represents a fresh start for us—time for us to reconnect and get our marriage back on track. It's not going to happen overnight.*

His iPhone buzzed. He didn't look at me as he dropped his arm and pulled it out of his pocket, his attention already elsewhere. "Sorry babe, gotta take this." He turned his back to me as he answered the call, walking away quickly. His dark hair, streaked with silver that added a quiet, distinguished air to his All-American good looks was longer than normal, curling around his collar. He definitely needed a haircut, but of course, we couldn't afford his normal stylist, and not just anyone was qualified to touch his hair.

I wrapped my arms around myself, goosebumps forming on my skin as a sudden breeze, especially cool for mid-May, brushed past me—the cold all the more shocking in the absence of Stefan's warm body.

He has to work, I reminded myself. *Remember why we're here.*

I remembered, all right. How could I forget?

I rubbed my hands up and down my arms as I took a deep breath, and finally focused on the house.

It was just as I remembered from my childhood—white with black shutters, outlined by bushy green shrubs, framed by tall, gently-swaying pine trees and the red porch with the swinging chair. It sat all by its lonesome in the middle of a never-developed cul-de-sac, the only "neighbors" being an overgrown forest on one side, and a marshy field on the other.

Okay, maybe it wasn't *exactly* the way I remembered it. The bushes actually looked pretty straggly. The lawn was overgrown, full of dandelions going to seed, and the porch could definitely use a new paint job.

I sighed. If the outside looked like this, what on earth waited for me on the inside?

Inside.

I swallowed back the bile that rose in the back of my throat. It slid to my stomach, turning into a cold, slimy lump.

The house of my childhood.

The house of my nightmares.

Oh God, I so didn't want to be here.

Stefan was still on the phone, facing away from me. I stared longingly at his back. *Turn around*, I silently begged. *Turn around and smile at me. A real smile. Like how you used to before we were married. Tell me it's going to be okay. You don't have to leave tonight like you thought. You realize how cruel it would be to leave me alone in this house the first night we're here, and you don't want to do that to me. Please, tell me. Or, better yet, tell me we're packing up and going back to New York. Say this was all a mistake; the firm is doing fine. Or, if you can't say that, say we'll figure it out. We'll make it work. We don't need to live here after all. Please, Stefan. Please don't leave me alone here.*

He half-turned, caught my eye, and made a gesture that indicated he was going to be awhile.

And I should start unpacking.

I closed my eyes. Depression settled around me like an old, familiar shawl. I could feel the beginning of a headache stab my temples.

Great. Just what I needed to complete this nightmare—a monster headache.

I turned to the car and saw Chrissy still in the backseat—headset on, bobbing to music only she could hear. Her long, dark hair—so dark it often looked black—spread out like a shiny cloak, the ends on one side dyed an electric blue.

Oh, yeah. That's right. I wouldn't be alone in the house after all.

Chrissy closed her eyes and turned her head away from me.

It just kept getting better and better.

I knocked on the window. She ignored me. I knocked again. She continued to ignore me.

For a moment, I imagined yanking the door open, snatching the headset off and telling her to—no, *insisting* that—she get her butt out of the car and help me unpack. I pictured her dark brown eyes, so much like Stefan's, widening, her pink lip-glossed mouth forming a perfect O, so shocked that she doesn't talk back, but instead meekly does what she's told.

More pain stabbed my temples. I closed my eyes and kept knocking on the window.

It's not her fault, I told myself for maybe the 200th time. *How would you act if you were sixteen years old and your mother abandoned you, dumped you at your father's, so she'd be free to travel across Europe with her boy toy?*

I squelched the little voice that reminded me I wasn't a whole heck of a lot older than said boy toy, and started pounding on the window. Stefan kept telling me she was warming up to me—I personally hadn't seen much evidence of that.

Chrissy finally turned her head and looked at me. "What?" she mouthed, disgust radiating off her, her eyes narrowing like an angry cat.

I motioned to the trunk. "I need your help."

Her lip curled as her head fell back on to the seat. She closed her eyes.

I had just been dismissed.

Great. Just great.

I looked around for Stefan—if he were standing with me, she would be out of the car and helping—a fake, sweet smile on her face, but he had moved to the corner of the street, still on the phone. I popped the trunk and headed over to him. Maybe I could finally get him to see reason—that it really was a dreadful idea to leave the two of us alone in Redemption, Wisconsin, while he commuted back and forth to New York to rescue his failing law firm. "See," I could say, "She doesn't listen to me. She doesn't respect me. She needs her father. I need you, too. She's going to run wild with you gone and I won't be able to deal with her."

Stefan hung up as I approached. "The movers should be here soon. You probably should start unpacking." Although his tone was mild, I could still hear the underlying faint chords of reproach—what's going on with you? Why haven't you started yet? Do I need to do everything around here?

"Yes, I was going to," I said, hating my defensive tone, but unable to stop it. "But there's a problem I think you need to deal with."

His eyes narrowed—clearly, he was losing his patience with me. "What?"

I opened my mouth to tell him about Chrissy, just as her voice floated toward us, "Can I get some help over here?"

I slowly turned around, gritting my teeth, trying not to show it. Chrissy stood by the trunk, arms loaded with boxes, an expectant look on her face. The pain darting through my head intensified.

"Rebecca, are you coming?" Stefan asked as he headed over to his charming daughter, waiting for him with a smug expression on her face, like a cat who ate the canary. I took a deep breath and trudged over, the sick knot in the pit of my stomach growing and tightening.

What on earth was I going to do with her while Stefan was gone?

Chrissy threw me a triumphant smile as she followed her father to the house. I resisted the urge to stick my tongue out at her, as I heaved a couple of boxes out of the trunk.

Really, all the crap with Chrissy was the least of my worries. It was more of a distraction, than anything.

The real problem was the house.

The house.

Oh God.

I turned to stare at it. It didn't look menacing or evil. It looked like a normal, everyday house.

Well, a normal, everyday house with peeling paint, a broken gutter and a few missing roof shingles.

Great. That probably meant we needed a new roof. New roofs were expensive. People who had to rescue failing law firms tended to not have money for things like new roofs. Even new roofs for houses that were going to be fixed up and eventually sold, ideally for a big, fat profit.

Would there be *any* good news today?

Again, I realized I was distracting myself. New roofs and paint jobs—those were trivial.

The real problem was *inside* the house.

Where all my nightmares took place.

Where my breakdown happened.

Where I almost died.

I swallowed hard. The sun went behind a cloud and, all of a sudden, the house was plunged into darkness. It loomed in front me, huge and monstrous, the windows dark, bottomless eyes staring at me ... the door a mouth with sharp teeth ...

"Rebecca! Are you coming?"

Stefan broke the spell. I blinked my eyes and tried to get myself together.

I was being silly. It was just a house, not a monster. How could a house even BE a monster? Only people could be monsters, which would mean my aunt, who had owned the house, was the monster.

And my aunt was dead now. Ding, dong, the witch is dead. Or, in this case, the monster.

Which meant there was nothing to fear in the house anymore. Which was exactly what Stefan kept telling me back in New York, over and over.

"Don't you think it's time you put all this childhood nonsense behind you?" he asked. "Look, I get it. Your aunt must have done something so dreadful that you've blocked it out, but she's dead. She can't hurt you anymore. And it couldn't have worked out any more perfectly for us—we have both a place to live rent-free right now, while I get things turned around. And, once we sell it, we can use the money to move back here and get a fresh start."

He was right, of course. But, still, I couldn't drop it.

"Why did she even will the house to me in the first place?" I persisted. "Why didn't she will it to CB? He was there a lot more than I was."

Stefan shrugged. "Maybe it was her way of apologizing to you all these years later. She was trying to make it up to you. Or maybe she changed—people said she was sick at the end. But, why does it matter why she willed it to you? The point is she did, and we really need it. Not to mention this could be a great way for you to finally get over whatever happened to you years ago."

Maybe. Back in New York, it had seemed so reasonable. So logical. Maybe the move wouldn't be a problem after all.

But, standing in the front yard with my arms filled with boxes, every cell in my body screamed that it was a really awful idea.

"Hey," Stefan whispered in my ear, his five o'clock shadow scratching my cheek. I jumped, so transfixed by the house that I hadn't even realized he had returned to me. "Look, I'm sorry. I should have known this would be rough for you. Come on, I'll walk in with you."

He rubbed my arm and smiled at me—a real smile. I could feel my insides start to thaw as all those old, exciting, passionate feelings reminiscent of when we first started dating swarmed over me. I remembered how he would shower me with red roses and whisk me off to romantic dinners that led to steaming, hot sex. He made me feel like a princess in a fairy tale. I still couldn't fathom how he ended up with me.

I met his eyes, and for the first time in what seemed like a long time, I felt the beginnings of a real smile on my lips. *See, he does care, even if he doesn't always show it. This is why the move was the perfect thing for our marriage; all we needed was to get away from the stress of New York, so we could rekindle things.* I nodded and started walking with him toward the house. Over her shoulder, Chrissy shot me a dirty look.

The closer we got to the house, the more I focused on my breathing. *It's going to be okay,* I repeated to myself. *It's just a house. A house can't hurt anyone. It's all going to be okay.*

An owl hooted, and I jumped. Why was an owl hooting in the daytime? Didn't that mean someone was going to die? Isn't that what the old stories and folklore taught? My entire body stiffened—all I wanted to do was run the other way. Stefan hugged me closer, gently massaging my arm, and urged me forward.

"It's going to be okay," he murmured into my hair. I closed my eyes for a moment, willing myself to believe it.

We stepped onto the porch, Chrissy impatiently waiting for Stefan to unlock the door. He put the boxes on the ground to fumble for his keys as I tried hard not to hyperventilate.

It's just a house. A house can't hurt anyone.

After an eternity that simultaneously wasn't nearly long enough, he located the keys and wrenched the door open, swearing under his breath.

His words barely registered. I found myself compelled forward, drawn in like those pathetic moths to the killing flame.

I could almost hear my aunt excitedly calling, "Becca? Is that you? Wait until you see this," as I stepped across the threshold into the house.

It was exactly like I remembered.

Well, maybe not exactly—it was filthy and dusty, full of cobwebs and brittle, dead bugs lying upside down on the floor with their legs sticking up. But I remembered it all—from the overstuffed floral sofa where I spent hours reading, to the end table covered with knick-knacks and frilly doilies, to the paintings lining the walls. I found myself wanting to hurry into the kitchen, where surely Aunt Charlie would have a cup of tea waiting for me. It didn't feel scary at all. It felt warm and comforting.

Like coming home.

How could this be?

Stefan was still muttering under his breath. "I can't believe all this crap. We're going to have put our stuff in storage for months while we go through it all. Christ, like we need another bill to worry about." He sighed, pulled his cell phone out, and started punching numbers.

"Dad, what do you mean our stuff is going into storage?" Chrissy said, clearly alarmed.

Stefan waved his arms. "Honey, look around you. Where are we going to put it? We have to put our things into storage until we get all this out of here."

"But Dad," Chrissy protested. I stopped listening. I walked slowly around, watching my aunt dashing down the stairs, her smock stained, arms filled with herbs and flowers, some even sticking out of her frizzy brown hair, muttering about the latest concoction she was crafting for one of the neighbors whose back was acting up again …

"Earth to Rebecca. Rebecca. Are you okay?" I suddenly realized Stefan was talking to me, and I pulled myself out of my memories.

"Sorry, it just …" my voice trailed off.

He came closer. "Are you okay? Are you remembering?"

There she was again, the ghost of Aunt Charlie, explaining yet again to the odd, overly-made-up, hair-over-teased, forty-something woman from the next town that no, she didn't do love potions. It was dangerous magic to mess around with either love or money, but if she wanted help with her thyroid that was clearly not working the way it should be, that was definitely in my aunt's wheelhouse.

I shook my head. "No, not really. It's just ... weird."

I wanted him to dig deeper, ask me questions, invite me to talk about the memories flooding through me. I wanted him to look at me while I spoke, *really* look at me, the way he did before we were married.

Where had it all gone wrong? And how could he leave me alone in a lonely, isolated and desolate house a thousand miles away from New York? Sure, Chrissy would be there, but the jury was still out as to whether she made it better or worse. The memories pushed up against me, smothering me. I *needed* to talk about them, before they completely overwhelmed and suffocated me. And he knew it—he knew how much I needed to talk things through to keep the anxiety and panic at bay. He wouldn't let me down, not now, when I really needed him.

Would he?

Chapter 2 - It Began With a Lie

The empty coffee pot mocked me.

It sat on the table, all smug and shiny, its cord wrapped tightly around it.

I had been so excited after unearthing it that morning—yes! Coffee! God knew I needed it.

The night before had been horrible, starting with the fights. I ended up in the living room, where I spent the night on the couch, a cold washcloth draped over my face in a feeble attempt to relieve the mother of all headaches.

Several times, I'd have just dozed off when the sound of Chrissy's footsteps would jerk me awake, as she paced up and down the upstairs hallway. I couldn't fathom what was keeping her up, so finally, after the fourth or fifth time of being woken up, I went upstairs to check on her. She must have heard me on the stairs, because all I saw was of the trail of her white nightgown as she disappeared into her room. I stood there for a moment, wondering if I should go talk to her, but the stabbing pain in my head drove me back downstairs to the safety of the couch and washcloth. I just couldn't face another argument then, in the middle of the night.

She must have decided to stay in her room after that, because I finally drifted off, only waking when the sun shone through the dirty living room window, illuminating all the dust motes floating in the air.

Coffee was exactly what I needed. Except … I had no beans to put in the coffeemaker. Not that it mattered, I realized after digging through the third box in frustration. I didn't have any cream or sugar either.

Well, at least my headache was gone, although what was left was a weird, hollow, slightly-drugged feeling. Still, I'd take that over the headache any day.

I sighed and rubbed my face. The whole move wasn't starting off very well. In fact, everything seemed to be going from bad to worse, including the fight with Stefan.

"Do you really need to leave?" I asked him again as I followed him to the door. He had just said goodbye to Chrissy, who had immediately disappeared upstairs, leaving us alone. I could see the taxi he had called sitting in the driveway and my heart sank. A part of me had hoped to talk him out of going, but with the taxi already there the possibility seemed even more remote.

He sighed. I could tell he was losing patience. "We've been through this. You know I have to."

"But you just got here! Surely you can take a few days—a week maybe—off to help us unpack and get settled."

He picked up his briefcase. "You know I can't. Not now."

"But when? You promised you would set it up so that you could work from here most of the time. Why can't you start that now?" I could tell his patience was just about gone, but I couldn't stop myself.

He opened the door. A fresh, cool breeze rushed in, a sharp contrast to the musty, stale house. "And I will. But it's too soon. There are still a few things I need to get cleaned up before I can do that. You know that. We talked about this."

He stepped outside and went to kiss me, but I turned my face away. "Are you going to see *her*?"

That stopped him. I could see his eyes narrow and his mouth tighten. I hadn't meant to say it; it just slipped out.

He paused and took a breath. "I know this whole situation has been tough on you, so I'm going to forget you said that. I'll call you."

Except he didn't. Not a single peep in the more than twelve hours since he had walked out the door. And every time I thought of it, I felt sick with shame.

I didn't *really* think he was cheating on me. I mean, there was something about Sabrina and her brittle, cool, blonde, perfect elegance that I didn't trust, but that wasn't on Stefan. I had no reason not to trust him. Just because my first husband cheated on me didn't mean Stefan would. And just because Sabrina looked at Stefan like he was a steak dinner, and she was starving, didn't mean it was reciprocated.

Worse, I knew I was making a bigger mess out of it every time I brought it up. The more I accused him, the more likely he would finally say, "Screw it, if I'm constantly accused of being a cheater, I might as well at least get something out of it." Even knowing all of that, I somehow couldn't stop myself.

Deep down, I knew I was driving him away. And I hated that part of myself. But still nothing changed.

To make matters worse, it didn't take long after Stefan left before things blew up with Chrissy. I asked her to help me start organizing the kitchen, and she responded with an outburst about how much she hated the move. She hated me, too—her life was ruined, and it was all my fault. She stormed off, slammed the door to her room, and that's how I ended up on the couch, my head pounding, wishing I was just about anywhere else.

Standing in the kitchen with the weak sunlight peeking through the dirty windows, the empty coffee maker taunting me, I gave in to my feelings of overwhelm. How on earth was I ever going to get the house organized? And the yard? And my aunt's massive garden? All the while researching what it would take to sell the house for top dollar, and dealing with Chrissy? My heart sank at that thought, although I wasn't completely sure which thought triggered it. Maybe it was all of them.

And if that wasn't difficult enough, I also had to deal with being in my aunt's home. Her presence *was everywhere*. I felt like an intruder. How could I do all of this, feeling her around me? How could I be in her home, when she wasn't? It wasn't my house. It was Aunt Charlie's. And I wasn't even sure I WANTED it to feel like my home.

Because if it did, then I would probably remember everything.

Including what happened that night.

The night I almost died.

God, I felt sick.

I needed coffee. And food.

Maybe I should take Chrissy out for breakfast as a peace of-fering. We could get out of the house, which would be good for me at least, and then go grocery shopping before coming home to tackle the cleaning and organizing.

I wanted to start in the kitchen. It was Aunt Charlie's favorite room in the house, and I knew it would have broken her heart to see how neglected and dingy it had become. When my aunt was alive, it was the center of the home—a light, cheery place with a bright-red tea kettle constantly simmering away on low heat on the stove. Oh, how Aunt Charlie loved her tea—that's why the kettle always had hot water in it—she'd say you just never knew when a cup would be needed. She was a strong believer that tea cured just about everything, just so long as you had the right blend. And, surprise, surprise, you could pretty much always find the right blend outside in her massive garden, which I had no doubt was completely overgrown now. I didn't have the heart to go look.

I could almost see her, standing in that very kitchen, prepar-ing me a cup. "Headache again, Becca?" she would murmur as she measured and poured and steeped. The warm fragrance would fill the homey kitchen as she pushed the hot cup in front of me, the taste strong, flavorful, and sweet, with just a hint of bitterness. And, lo and behold, not too long after drinking it, I would find my headache draining away.

I wondered if I would still find her tea blends in the kitchen. Maybe I could find that headache tea. And maybe, if I was even luckier, I would find a blend that would cure everything that ailed me that morning.

With some surprise, I realized just how much love encom-passed that memory. Nothing scary. Nothing that could possibly foretell the horror of what happened that dreadful night.

Could my aunt actually be the monster?

My mother certainly thought so. She forbade any contact, any mentioning of my aunt even, refusing to allow her to see me once I woke up in intensive care following the stomach pump.

She refused her again when I was transferred to a psych unit, after becoming hysterical when I was asked what had happened that night.

My mother blamed my aunt.

And, I, in my weakened, anxious, panicked state, was relieved to follow her lead. Actually, I was more than relieved; I was happy, too.

But sitting in that kitchen right then, I felt only love and comfort, and I began to question my choices.

My mother had been completely against us moving back here, even temporarily. At the time, listening to her arguments, I had chalked it up to her being overly protective. Now, I wondered. Was that it? Or was something deeper going on?

Chrissy chose that moment to stroll into the kitchen, her hair sticking up on one side. She was wearing her blue and red plaid sleep shorts and red tee shirt—the blue plaid almost an exact match to the blue highlight in her hair. Staring at her, something stirred deep inside me—a distinct feeling of wrongness ... of something being off—but when I reached for it, I came up empty.

She leaned against the counter and started checking her iPhone. "How sweet, you're being domestic."

I shook my head—that off feeling still nagged at me, but I just couldn't place it. I really needed coffee. Coffee would make everything better.

She tapped at her iPhone, not looking up. "Anything to eat in this God-awful place?"

I sighed. Maybe I should be looking for a tea that would cure Chrissy.

Chapter 3 - It Began With a Lie

Chrissy wrinkled her nose. "What a dump."

She said it under her breath, so neither the bustling waitresses nor the other customers could hear. But I could. I gave her a sharp look, which she ignored.

We were in what *I* thought was a cute little diner called Aunt May's. It felt friendly and familiar and had a respectable number of customers in it for a Monday morning. In fact, on the drive over, I had been amazed at how bright and cheery the town was—it was almost like I had expected to see dark, grimy, stains tainting the buildings, the streets, even the deep green grass. Instead, the sun shone down on clean, well-kept houses and cute stores complete with maintained lawns and pots of colorful flowers.

Chrissy clearly wasn't impressed by any of it.

She poked at her menu. "Do you think anything here is gluten-free?"

I sighed, flipping over my coffee cup. "You'll have to ask."

Chrissy made a face and stared darkly out the window.

Despite the inauspicious start, she seemed to be in a better mood. Well, maybe "better" wasn't quite the right word—"subdued" was probably more accurate. It was almost like our fight had drained vital energy from her, leaving a shell of her former self.

The waitress appeared, coffee pot in hand. "Are you two visiting for the summer?" she asked as she filled my cup. I shot her a grateful look. She looked familiar with her dark, straight hair cut in a chin-length bob and Asian features. Japanese maybe. But I couldn't really place her. Maybe I had run into her years ago, while visiting my aunt.

"No, we just moved here," I said, pulling my coffee toward me, doctoring it with cream and sugar.

The waitress raised her eyebrow at me. "Really? Where?"

"Charlie, I mean Charlotte Kingsley's house."

The waitress set the coffee pot down. "Becca? Is that you?"

Something inside me seemed to twist in on itself, hearing that name out loud. *I'm not Becca*, I wanted to say. *Becca's gone. It's Rebecca now.*

At the same time, I found my brain frantically searching for a wisp of something, anything, to give me a hint as to who this waitress was. "Uh ..."

"It's Mia—Mia Moto. We used to hang out, remember?"

I blinked at her and suddenly, it was like the dam opened— memories crashed down into me. I sucked in my breath, feeling physically jolted by the impact. "Mia! Oh my God, I hardly recognized you!"

She laughed in delight and held out her arms. Somehow, I found myself on my feet, swept up in a giant bear hug—impressive, considering how tiny she was. She smelled spicy, like cinnamon and coffee.

"It's so great to see you," Mia said, when we finally separated. "I mean, after that night, we were all so worried, but the hospital wouldn't let any of us visit you."

"Yeah, well, my mom ..." I fumbled around, not really sure what to say. The truth was, I hadn't wanted to see them. I had become hysterical again, when one of the nurses said I had visitors. And, until that very moment, I had never even considered how it must have looked from their point of view. They were my friends; they cared about me, and I had almost died. Of course they would want to see me. I felt sick with shame.

"I can't believe it's you," I said, changing the subject. "Who else is still here? Is ..."

"Daphne's still here," Mia interjected. "In fact, she's still living in the same house, right by you. She moved in after her mom got sick to help her out. I know she'd love to see you."

"And I'd love to see her too," I said, jolted again by how much I really did miss hanging out with Mia and Daphne.

"And Daniel is still here, too." Mia continued. "He's engaged now."

A rush of conflicting feelings started swirling through me at the sound of his name, anger being the most prevalent. "I'm married," I said shortly, smiling at the last second to soften my tone.

Daniel. God, I had totally forgotten him, too. For good reason, considering he had not only stood me up, all those years ago, but he also had then ignored me completely .... like I didn't even exist. Talk about painful. Snapping back to reality, I turned my attention back to Mia. "In fact, this is my stepdaughter, Chrissy."

Mia turned her 40-thousand-watt, infectious smile on Chrissy. "Great to meet you, Chrissy. Make sure you ask your stepmom where all the hot places are to hang out." Chrissy's lips twitched upward in a semblance of a smile, and her "nicetomeetyoutoo" almost sounded friendly.

I elbowed Mia. "I don't know if that's such a good idea."

Someone near the kitchen yelled Mia's name, but she waved him off. "We definitely need to catch up."

"Yes," I agreed, sliding back into my seat. "I'm really surprised you're here. I thought you would be long gone—California, right? Stanford? Law school?" I had vague memories of Mia going on and on about being the next Erin Brockovich. She had nearly memorized that movie, she had seen it so often.

Mia's smile slipped. "Well, yeah. It's complicated. After that night ... you ... Jessica ..." her voice trailed off and she pulled out her order pad. "I better get your order."

Jessica.

It felt like all the air had been sucked out of the room. I could hear Chrissy asking about gluten-free options, and not getting the answer she wanted, but it seemed like the conversation was taking place outside of the bubble I was trapped in, as I could barely hear anything but a warbling echo.

Jessica. How could I have forgotten about Jessica?

Mia, Daphne, Jessica, and me. We were the four amigos that summer. The four Musketeers. Hanging out at the beach, the mall, at my aunt's house (because she was by far the coolest of all the adults we had to choose from).

Until that night, when Jessica disappeared ... and I ended up in the hospital, broken, mentally and physically.

I rubbed my eyes, the faint wisp of a headache brushing my temples like a soft kiss. I realized that while my memories from that summer were finally returning, that night was still a total blank. Actually, the entire day was a black hole. I didn't even remember taking the first drink, one of many that would put me in the hospital, having to get my stomach pumped, followed by a complete and utter nervous breakdown.

"Becca?" Mia asked, pen poised on her pad. "You okay?"

I reached for my coffee cup, glad to see my hands weren't shaking, and tried on a smile that felt way too small. "Yeah, I'm fine. Just still recovering from moving."

Mia didn't look like she completely believed me, but I could tell she needed to get back to work. I ordered the American breakfast—eggs, bacon, fried potatoes with onions and peppers, and rye toast—even though I was no longer hungry. I knew I had to eat. I had barely eaten anything the day before, and if I didn't start eating, I would probably trigger another headache. I figured chances were decent I'd get one anyway, but at least eating something would give me a fighting chance.

Along with the lack of gluten-free options, Chrissy also voiced her displeasure around the coffee choices, wanting a mocha, or latte, or something, made with some other type of milk than, well, milk from a cow, so she ended up with a Coke. I restrained myself from pointing out that soda was probably a lot less healthy choice than something with gluten or dairy in it. Ah, kids.

She blew the paper off the straw and plopped the straw in her soda, then pulled out her iPhone. "Who's Daniel?"

I didn't look at her as I added a little more sugar to my cup, and carefully stirred. "Just a guy I knew from back when I would visit during the summer."

"Hmmm," Chrissy said, lifting her head from her iPhone to narrow her eyes at me. "Sounded like more than that."

"Well, it wasn't," I snapped. Chrissy looked up at me in surprise, one eyebrow raised. I took a deep breath and reminded myself that I was the grown-up.

"Sorry, I didn't sleep well last night. All your pacing kept me awake." *Oh, great, Rebecca. Fabulous apology right there. Maybe I just should have just cut to the chase and said "Sorry, not sorry."* I tried smiling to soften my words and turn it into a joke.

But, Chrissy was frowning at me. "Pacing? What are you talking about? I slept like the dead."

I stared at her, that sense of "wrongness" I felt in the kitchen that morning rushing through me again. "But, I mean, I saw you ..." my voice trailed off as images flashed through my mind.

The white nightgown disappearing into Chrissy's room.

Chrissy standing in the kitchen wearing her red and blue sleep outfit.

I rubbed my temples, the coffee turning into a sick, greasy lump in my stomach. Oh God, I hoped I wasn't going to throw up.

Chrissy was looking at me with something that resembled concern. Or maybe it was alarm. After all, I was the only adult she knew within 1,000 miles. "Are you okay, Rebecca?"

I reached for my water glass. "Yeah, I'm fine. It's an old house. Old houses make all sorts of noises. I'm sure that's what kept me awake."

Chrissy didn't look terribly convinced, but she went back to her iPhone. She was probably texting her friends about how I was losing it. Or worse ... texting her father.

I drank some water to try and settle my stomach. I was being ridiculous. Old houses make all sorts of creaks and groans and can sound exactly like footsteps, which is what kept waking me up last night. And as for what I saw … well, clearly, I hadn't seen anything. Just a trick of the light, or the moon, or something. And with the pounding of my head, I really wasn't paying that close attention.

I just needed to get some food in my stomach. And hopefully, some decent sleep that night. Then I could forget about all the house nonsense. Stefan and I could laugh about it … assuming he finally got around to calling me back, that is.

Okay, I so didn't want to go down *that* road. Instead, I sat back in my seat, sipped my coffee, and watched Mia top off the cup of a cute guy who looked like a contractor, laughing at something he said. I still had trouble believing Mia was waiting tables at the diner. Of all of us, she was bound and determined to get out and never come back. I remembered how driven, how passionate she had been about all the injustices in the world, and how determined she had been to right them. She was going to be a lawyer and fight for everyone who couldn't help themselves. What had happened?

A couple of older, neatly-dressed women sitting at a table next to us were staring at me. They wore nearly identical pantsuits, except one was baby blue and the other canary yellow. Their half-eaten food sat in front of them. Taken aback at the open aggression in their eyes, I looked back at them, wondering if I should know them.

Were their stares really directed at me? Did I do something in my youth my traitorous memory had yet to reveal? Maybe they were actually looking at someone sitting behind me. I turned around to look, but no one was there. When I swiveled back, their identical gaze looked even more antagonistic.

I dropped my eyes, only half-seeing the paper placemat covered with local advertising, feeling a growing sense of unease in my belly. They didn't look familiar at all. Who were they? And why me?

"Why did the waitress call you Becca?" Chrissy asked, startling me. For once, I was glad she was there to distract me, even though part of me instantly wanted to scream at her to stop calling me that.

"It was my nickname," I said, willing those older women to get up and leave. Out of the corner of my eye, I saw them lean toward each other, whispering, hostile eyes still watching me. I adjusted my head until I couldn't see them anymore.

Chrissy went back to her iPhone "It's cute. Better than Rebecca."

I ignored the twist of pain inside me and put my hand on my heart. "Wait. Did I just hear an almost compliment there?"

Chrissy rolled her eyes. "I'm just saying. I think I'll call you Becca."

"Don't," I said, before I could stop myself.

Chrissy looked surprised. And, if I didn't know her any better, a little hurt. "What, only people you *like* can call you Becca?"

Cripes. I could have smacked myself. Why on earth wasn't there a manual out there on how to be a stepmom to a daughter who is only fifteen years younger than you?

"That's not it," I said, stalling for time as I tried to put the feelings that had swamped over me into words. "It just … it just triggers bad memories. That's all." I cringed—I sounded so lame, even to myself.

Chrissy gave me a withering look as she furiously pounded on her iPhone. I opened my mouth to say something—I had no idea what … something to bridge the gap that yawned between us—but Mia's voice interrupted me. "Daniel! Look who's here! It's Becca!"

I closed my mouth and turned to look. A police officer was standing at the counter watching Mia fill up a to-go container with coffee. Could that be Daniel? I searched the room, but only saw only a handful of people finishing up their breakfast. It had to be him.

I looked back at the cop. Broad shoulders and dark blonde hair—Daniel. Mia glanced at me and winked. I made a face back at her.

He turned. He was older of course, but yes, it was most definitely Daniel. He wouldn't be considered traditionally handsome—not like Stefan with his almost pretty-boy looks. Daniel's face was too rugged, with sharp cheekbones and a crooked nose. But his lips were still full and soft, and his eyes were still the same dark blue. I found myself suddenly conscious of my appearance. I hadn't taken a shower in two days, and I was wearing an old, faded New York Giants tee shirt. I had scraped my unruly mass of reddish, blondish, brownish hair back into a messy ponytail in preparation for a full day of cleaning and organizing. But I quickly reminded myself that I was being silly. I was a married woman, sitting with my stepdaughter, and he was engaged.

Besides, he had made it more than clear years ago he wasn't the slightest bit interested in me.

"Becca," he said coming over, his face friendly, but not exactly smiling. "Welcome back to Redemption." It didn't sound much like a welcome.

"Thanks," I said, mostly because I couldn't think of anything better to say. Instinctively, I reached up to smooth out my hair, since as usual, a few curly tendrils had escaped and hung in my face. "Not much has changed."

He studied me, making me really wish I had taken an extra five minutes to jump in the shower and dig out a clean shirt. "Oh, plenty has changed."

"Like you being a cop?"

He shrugged slightly. "Pays the bills."

I half-smiled. "There's lots of ways to pay the bills. If I remember right, you always seemed more interested in breaking the law than upholding it."

"Like I said, things change." He lifted his to-go coffee cup and took a swallow, his dark-blue eyes never leaving mine. "I take it you're still painting then."

I dropped my gaze to his chest, feeling a dull ache overwhelm me—the same pain I felt when I heard the name Becca. "As you said, things change."

"Ah." I waited for him to ask more questions, but instead, he changed the subject. "So, how long are you staying?"

I shrugged. "Not sure. We've actually moved here."

His eyebrows raised slightly. "To Charlie's house? You aren't selling it?"

"Well, yes. Eventually. That's the plan. But, at least for the foreseeable future, we'll be living in it." I sounded like an idiot. With some effort, I forced myself to stop talking. Why on earth did I share so much detail? How was this any of his business?

He looked like he was going to say something more but was interrupted by a loud snort. The two pant-suited women both scraped their chairs back as they stood up, glaring disgustedly at all of us before heading to the cash register.

"What's with them?" Chrissy asked. I had forgotten she was there.

I shrugged, before remembering my manners and introducing Chrissy to Daniel. I made a point of gesturing with my left hand to flash my wedding ring.

His head tipped in a slight nod before looking back at me. "Will you be around later today? I'd like to stop by and talk to you."

There was something in his expression that made me uneasy, but I purposefully kept my voice light. "What on earth for? I haven't even unpacked yet. Am I already in trouble?"

The ends of his lips turned up in a slight smile, but no hint of warmth touched the intense look in his eyes. "Should you be in trouble?"

I let out a loud, exaggerated sigh. "Why do cops always answer a question with a question?"

"Occupational hazard. I'll see you later." He dipped his chin in a slight nod before walking away. I noticed he didn't give me the slightest hint as to what he wanted to talk to me about. That sense of unease started to grow into a sense of foreboding.

"Well, for an old friend, he wasn't very friendly," Chrissy said.

I sipped my coffee. "That's for sure."

She smirked. "He was pretty cute, though. For an old guy, I mean."

Man, she did have a knack for making me feel ancient. But, unfortunately, even that didn't distract my mind from scrambling around like a rat in a cage, worrying about what he wanted to talk to me about.

Acknowledgements

It's a team effort to birth a book, and I'd like to take a moment to thank everyone who helped, especially my wonderful editor, Megan Yakovich, who is always so patient with me, Rea Carr for her expert proofing support, and my husband Paul, for his love and support during this sometimes-painful birthing process.

Any mistakes are mine and mine alone.

About Michele

When Michele was 3 years old, she taught herself to read because she wanted to write stories so badly.

As you can imagine, writing has been a driving passion throughout her life.

* She's an award-winning, bestselling fiction author, writing psychological thriller/mystery/romantic suspense novels.

* She's a bestselling nonfiction author, creating the popular "Love-Based Business" series of books.

* She's also a professional copywriter, blogger and journalist.

She holds a double major in English and Communications from the University of Wisconsin-Madison. Currently she lives in the mountains of Prescott, Arizona with her husband Paul and southern squirrel hunter Cassie.